300

ROMANTIC TIMES RAVES ABOUT *NEW YORK TIMES* BESTSELLING AUTHOR CON...

THE BL...
"Ms. Mason has ...
romance filled with tourn...

THE OUTLAWS: SAM
"Ms. Mason always provides the reader
with a hot romance, filled with plot twists and
wonderful characters. She's a marvelous storyteller."

THE OUTLAWS: JESS
"*Jess* . . . is a delight. Typical of Ms. Mason's style,
Jess is filled with adventure and passion. Ms. Mason delivers."

THE OUTLAWS: RAFE
"Ms. Mason begins this new trilogy with
wonderful characters . . . steamy romance . . .
excellent dialogue . . . [and an] exciting plot!"

GUNSLINGER
"Ms. Mason has created memorable characters
and a plot that made this reader rush to turn the
pages. . . . *Gunslinger* is an enduring story."

PIRATE
"Ms. Mason has written interesting characters
into a twisting plot filled with humor and pathos."

Independence Public Library

MORE *ROMANTIC TIMES* PRAISE FOR CONNIE MASON!

BEYOND THE HORIZON
"Connie Mason at her best! She draws readers into this fast-paced, tender and emotional historical romance that proves that love really does conquer all!"

BRAVE LAND, BRAVE LOVE
"*Brave Land, Brave Love* is an utter delight from first page to last—funny, tender, adventurous, and highly romantic!"

WILD LAND, WILD LOVE
"Connie Mason has done it again!"

BOLD LAND, BOLD LOVE
"A lovely romance and a fine historical!"

VIKING!
"This captive/captor romance proves a delicious read."

TEMPT THE DEVIL
"A grand and glorious adventure-romp! Ms. Mason tempts the readers with . . . thrilling action and sizzling sensuality!"

Connie Mason

The Dragon Lord

INDEPENDENCE PUBLIC LIBRARY
175 Monmouth Street
Independence, OR 97351
~~2910 0978~~
4098 4905

LEISURE BOOKS   NEW YORK CITY

A LEISURE BOOK®

November 2001

Published by

Dorchester Publishing Co., Inc.
276 Fifth Avenue
New York, NY 10001

If you purchased this book without a cover you should be aware that this book is stolen property. It was reported as "unsold and destroyed" to the publisher and neither the author nor the publisher has received any payment for this "stripped book."

Copyright © 2001 by Connie Mason

All rights reserved. No part of this book may be reproduced or transmitted in any form or by any electronic or mechanical means, including photocopying, recording or by any information storage and retrieval system, without the written permission of the publisher, except where permitted by law.

ISBN 0-8439-4932-5

The name "Leisure Books" and the stylized "L" with design are trademarks of Dorchester Publishing Co., Inc.

Printed in the United States of America.

Visit us on the web at www.dorchesterpub.com.

THE Dragon Lord

Prologue

London, October 1214

"Harder, Dragon. Oh, God, yes. Don't stop."

Poised atop the dark-haired beauty, Dominic Dragon of Pendragon pumped vigorously between his mistress's plump white thighs. Raising himself up on his elbows, he watched her face as she moaned and tossed her head in wild abandon.

Dominic had taken the young widow as his mistress upon his return from the Crusade two years ago. Lady Veronica was beautiful, cultured and passionate, and Dominic was convinced that she was the woman he wanted to marry.

Dominic had led the Pendragon knights to victory over the Saracens during the Fourth Crusade, earning high praise from king and country. Dubbed the Dragon

11

Lord for his courage and fierce determination to prevail over the enemy, Dominic had become a favorite of King John's court and the king's champion.

Dominic's thoughts scattered as Veronica wrapped her legs around his hips and bowed her back to take him deeper. He pushed himself to the hilt; he was hard and thick, but she took all of him and begged for more.

"You are incredible, my fierce Dragon," Veronica encouraged. "I am nearly there. Just a little more . . . ahhh . . ." She screamed his name, pulled his lips down to hers and thrust her tongue into his mouth.

Dominic flexed his hips and went deep; he could feel his climax building clear down to his toes. Throwing his head back, he opened his mouth and roared as he withdrew from her slippery warmth and spilled his seed onto the pristine sheets. He would have preferred to spill inside Veronica, but there were no bastards in the long, illustrious Dragon history and he had no intention of being the first to tarnish the family's unblemished record.

Breathing heavily, Dominic collapsed beside Veronica, wishing he could remain in her soft bed and even softer arms instead of traveling to Westminster tonight to meet with King John.

"As much as it distresses me, sweeting, I have to go," he said, swinging his legs off the bed.

Veronica placed a slender hand on his chest and pushed him back down. "Must you?" Her lips pursed into a charming pout as she leaned over him so that her generous breasts dangled tantalizingly above his face. "Can you not stay a little longer?" She glanced coyly at his cock, wet her finger and touched the tip.

"The dragon is stirring to life again," she purred.

Unable to resist, Dominic licked her turgid nipples before gently pushing her away.

"The king has summoned me to the royal palace at Westminster and I am already late."

"What does John Lackland want now? How long will his barons stand for his dictatorial ways?"

Dominic uncoiled himself from Veronica's clinging arms and scrambled for his clothing. The puckered scar that ran the length of his leg from hip to knee, the result of a near fatal wound, stood out in pale relief, and he turned slightly away from Veronica, presenting a more pleasing view. He sensed her looking at him and ignored her glittering, almost feral gaze. He wasn't about to let her coax him back to bed.

Veronica stretched luxuriously, smiling with cat-like satisfaction as she regarded Dominic's naked form. She found his scar disgusting, but the rest of him was so perfect she was able to ignore it. His body was extraordinarily fit; his shoulders and upper torso rippled with hard muscles from wielding sword and lance in the lists, and his sculpted belly was flat and taut. Her gaze wandered downward as she watched him pull on his braies and hose, admiring the tight muscles of his thighs and buttocks.

She sighed when he pulled his knee-length tunic over his head and lifted her gaze to his face. His jaw was square and firm, hinting at his stubborn nature. His high cheekbones, the bold slash of his nose and his full sensual lips were compelling attributes. His eyes were midnight dark, so intimidating one felt the need to look away when pinned with his penetrating gaze.

"I cannot speak for Lackland's barons, but my own thought is that the king's cruelty and unjust laws are insupportable," Dominic said. "The barons have been at odds with John since he was routed from France by King Philip's forces and forced to give up most of Normandy. Rumor has it that he killed his nephew, Prince Arthur, who was regarded by many as the true heir to the throne."

Veronica stretched and posed for Dragon's benefit. "I care not what the king does. Will you return to me tonight?"

Dominic fell into a short brooding silence. "I think not. I know not how long he will keep me, or what he wants of me, but he will probably invite me to spend the night at the palace if the hour grows late."

"Pity," Veronica complained. "Tomorrow night then?"

"Perhaps." He assumed a thoughtful look. "Mayhap King John has decided to return to Normandy to reclaim the land he lost and has need of knights to accompany him."

"Bah," Veronica jeered. " 'Tis a wonder Lackland's influential barons have not forced him to abdicate. Why do you continue to serve him?"

"I am his vassal. 'Tis my duty to serve him wherever and whenever I am needed." He buckled on his sword and leaned over the bed. "Kiss me good-bye, sweeting."

Dominic's mood changed abruptly once he left Veronica. His pleasant manner dropped away the moment the door closed behind him, and he became the dark and dangerous knight whose very name made his enemies quake and his friends tread lightly around him.

Dominic was met outside the front door of Veronica's newly constructed stone manor by Raj, a huge Arab who had attached himself to Dominic after Dominic had freed him from Saracen slavery. When Dominic returned from the Crusade, Raj accompanied him to England, serving as squire, faithful friend and protector.

"Where do we go, master?" Raj asked, holding the reins of Dominic's high-prancing destrier as he mounted.

"To Westminster, Raj. I'm late."

Raj mounted his own horse, unfurled the Dragon pennant and rode in silence beside Dominic through the streets of London. They passed St. Paul's Cathedral and crossed the Thames over the new stone bridge, then rode through narrow paved streets crowded with vendors, costermongers and pickpockets. The city, along with its population, had grown, Dominic thought as they passed wharves loaded with goods from as far away as Constantinople. The city was in the process of using shares of its wealth to buy its freedom from royal rule. Soon the city would be able to elect its own mayor and sheriffs.

Dominic and Raj approached Ludgate, the southwest gate of the city, joining the flow of humanity leaving before the gate closed for the night. Suddenly the parade of people slowed, then stopped. Dominic drew rein, his gaze following their pointing fingers, grimacing at the grisly sight he beheld. Another example of King John's cruel justice, Dominic guessed as he gazed at the man's head spitted upon a pike embedded atop the Roman wall. Aware of the king's penchant for torture, Dominic could well imagine the suffering the man had endured before death had claimed him.

"Do you know him?" Raj asked.

"He looks familiar," Dominic reflected, "but I cannot place him. Perhaps the king will enlighten me."

They passed through Ludgate, leaving the city and its teeming hordes behind. The city now spread well beyond its high Roman walls. There was an extending line of rich men's mansions and bishops' palaces along the country road that led from Ludgate to Westminster, where none had existed a few years before. All were imposing, well-constructed manors backed by spacious gardens and trees.

Dominic's distinctive banner was recognized as they approached Westminster's main gate, and they rode past the barbican and gatehouse without being challenged. Dominic drew rein before the studded oak door and dismounted.

"Shall I wait for you here, master?" Raj asked, grasping the reins of Dominic's destrier.

"Nay. See to the horses and find yourself a meal and a bed," Dominic advised. "My meeting with the king is likely to extend past curfew. I will summon you when I am ready to leave."

"As you wish, master," Raj said. "I will not be far away should you have need of me."

Raj led the horses away as Dominic ascended the

stone steps to the palace entrance. A guard opened the door and Dominic stepped inside.

"His Majesty is awaiting you, Lord Dragon," the guard said. "Follow me."

Dominic was ushered into the king's private chambers. At first glance the chamber appeared to be empty. "I do not like to be kept waiting," King John said as he stepped from the shadows of the window embrasure. "You are late, Dragon."

Dominic was more than a little surprised to find the king alone. "I was unavoidably detained, sire," Dominic said, bowing before the monarch.

"Would that we could all be detained by a woman as lovely as Lady Veronica," the king said with sly innuendo. "How fare your sire and his heir?"

Dominic ignored John's reference to Veronica. "Father is well, Your Majesty. So is my brother, the future baron of Pendragon. Frederick's wife is breeding again. Her third, so there is no lack of heirs to Pendragon."

"And your mother?"

Dominic sent him a puzzled look. "Mother is fine, but I hardly think you asked me here to quiz me about the health of my family. As well you know, I have spent scant time at Pendragon after earning my spurs."

"What are your plans for the future, Dragon?"

"Nothing definite. I have been following the tournament circuit and have fared very well in the lists," Dominic said. "And I acquired some wealth during my travels abroad. A landless knight must make his own way, but I have been fortunate and am able to live comfortably. Mayhap I will return to Pendragon in time, to serve my father and brother."

Hands behind his back, John began to pace. Suddenly he stopped and whirled to face Dominic. "You should wed."

A slow grin curved Dominic's sensual mouth. He had been thinking along those same lines. Perhaps the king would reward his loyalty with land and a manor. He had, after all, answered John's call when France threatened to invade England. The invasion never took place, however, because John promised to become the pope's vassal and pledged an annual tribute of 1,000 marks, ending the interdict excommunicating England from the church and the need for war.

"Marriage would suit me," Dominic admitted, thinking of Veronica and the passion they shared.

"Excellent," John said, rubbing his hands together. "You will leave immediately."

Dominic was still thinking fondly of Veronica when the import of the king's words struck him. His head jerked up.

"Leave, sire? Where am I going?"

"To claim your bride. You will be pleased to know your wife comes with a barony, Dragon—rich lands, serfs, villeins and freemen to work your fields and tend your animals. The barony is immense, complete with a thriving village and several fiefs. You will have no problem paying the taxes levied on a great demesne like Ayrdale."

Ayrdale. Where had Dominic heard that name? It mattered not. Dominic had no wish to wed any woman save Veronica.

"You do me great honor, sire," Dominic replied warily. He'd learned through experience that John gave nothing without attaching a price to it.

"I have need of someone I can trust in the North, Dragon," John said. "Ayrdale marches along the border with Scotland, near the Cheviot Hills. The fortress was built by William the Conqueror and given in perpetuity to the Fairchild family. It has played an important role throughout history in maintaining peace along the Scottish border. The former owner, Edwyn of Ayrdale, was one of my trusted barons."

"Former owner?" Dominic interjected.

"Aye. I learned that Edwyn was urging my barons to march on London to force me to sign a document outlining their rights and privileges. The Articles of the Barons, I believe they call it. I ordered his execution to discourage rebellion."

Suddenly Dominic recalled the severed head spitted atop a pike on the Roman wall. "That wouldn't by chance be Lord Fairchild's head I saw as I passed through Ludgate, would it?"

"Aye. He was held in the Tower for several months, but his death was inevitable," John said. "It shall serve as a warning to others who conspire to diminish my power. With Fairchild gone and my barons' loyalty suspect, I need a baron I can trust. Scottish lairds eager to extend their lands into England are particularly worrisome in the North.

"I would not take it amiss if you were to court the friendship of my marcher barons and report their activities to me. I have reason to believe they are plotting against me."

19

"I am grateful for your trust, sire, but why must I wed?"

John frowned. "Lord Fairchild left a widow and daughter, and I do not wish to appear cruel and unfeeling toward them. 'Twould speak well for me if I were to find a husband and protector for Ayrdale instead of giving the barony to a man with a wife. I do not want it said that I turned a grieving widow and daughter out of their home."

Dominic nearly laughed in John's face. Everyone knew the king was bloodthirsty, greedy and treacherous, so why the pretense of kindness? "The barony tempts me," Dominic admitted, "but wedding a woman I have never seen does not."

" 'Tis done all the time," John said dismissively. "And you may choose which you prefer, mother or daughter. I have been told that Lady Nelda, Fairchild's widow, bore her daughter at age thirteen and is still of an age to bear more children. I know naught about the daughter except she is of marriageable age. If Lady Nelda strikes your fancy, she is yours, but I would take the daughter, were I you."

"I want neither mother nor daughter," Dominic proclaimed.

"There is no room for argument, Dragon. You will do as I order. Keep Lady Veronica as your leman if you wish, but you *will* wed one of Ayrdale's ladies. Your marriage is necessary to gain the loyalty of Ayrdale's vassals."

"As you wish, sire," Dominic replied, fuming inwardly. Gaining a barony was a boon he hadn't expected, but marrying a woman other than Veronica, who suited him so well, did not appeal to him. Nor did choosing between a mother and daughter who would certainly be grieving the loss of husband or father.

"How many knights serve under Ayrdale's banner?" Dominic asked.

"A score or more," John said, shrugging. "Eric of Carlyle is captain of the guard. He is a good man, and faithful, if you can win him over after he hears of his lord's execution."

Dominic stared at John in horror. "Have Fairchild's family not been informed of his death?"

John looked momentarily disconcerted but quickly regained his composure. "You are to carry word to Ayrdale of their lord's demise. When you leave London, you will have in your possession my royal seal on a document authorizing your marriage to one of the ladies of Ayrdale. I understand the keep has a resident priest who will perform the ceremony. Can you be ready to leave two days hence?"

Two days, Dominic thought dismally. Hardly enough time to prepare for a journey of a sennight or more, but what choice did he have? "Aye, I will be ready."

"Oh, one more thing, Dragon," John said. "Lady Nelda is Scottish. Her brother is Murdoc MacTavish, a powerful border laird who has had his eye on Ayrdale for many years. 'Tis one of the reasons for haste. Wed and bed your bride the day you arrive. Should MacTavish learn of Fairchild's death before you reach Ayrdale, he will surely try to claim the land for himself."

"If the Ayrdale guardsmen are faithful to their former

lord, they may try to prevent me from entering the fortress," Dominic said. "Should I prepare for a siege?"

"I doubt a siege will be necessary. Once you state that you carry word of their former lord, the gates will open to you. Furthermore, your name and reputation should command the trust and respect of those inside. 'Tis why I chose you for this honor, Lord Dragon. Enjoy Ayrdale and your new bride."

"I intend to rename my barony Dragonwyck," Dominic said with sudden decision. "Lord Dragon of Dragonwyck." He smiled. "Aye, I like the sound of it."

Chapter One

A rose is a rose is a rose is a rose.
—Gertrude Stein

Dominic's destrier danced impatiently beneath him as he drew rein at the moat's edge and stared at the magnificent fortress with its four square crenellated towers honed smooth by decades of wind, rain, snow and sun. Set in a narrow glen between two craggy hills, the stone fortress was surrounded by high walls. Dominic was not pleased to note that the drawbridge securing the keep against invaders was raised, preventing him from entering.

Glancing upward, Dominic saw that the guards on the parapet were looking down at him and his party, but they appeared in no hurry to alert the fortress to his presence or to lower the bridge so he could enter.

A sudden flurry on the battlements alerted Dominic to the fact that his distinctive banner, a rampant black dragon on a red field, had been seen and recognized.

"Think you they will lower the bridge, master?" Raj asked.

Dominic sent Raj a smug smile when he heard the sound of gears and saw that the drawbridge was slowly being lowered.

"You have your answer, Raj."

Once the bridge was in place, Dominic clattered across, followed closely by Raj and the two score knights attached to his service. Dominic's smile turned sour, however, when the grilled portcullis remained firmly in place. He reined in sharply and waited, his famous temper growing shorter by the minute.

"A warrior rides out to meet us, master," Raj said with a hint of amusement.

Dominic saw no reason for levity until his mind registered the fact that the warrior approaching the portcullis was a woman. Tall and shapely, she wielded a sword as if she knew how to use it and wasn't afraid to do so.

Dominic's first thought was that this woman was no vassal. A headdress of semitransparent linen covered her head, held in place by a gold circlet. Her golden hair hung free beneath the headdress, proclaiming her an unmarried woman, and a fringe of bangs across her forehead curled seductively beneath the circlet of gold.

Her deep red under-gown had long, fitted sleeves and appeared to be made of the finest wool. Her over-gown of dark blue was belted at the hips with a gold chain and embroidered at the hem in a green, blue and black motif. She reined in at the closed portcullis and aimed a fierce glare at Dominic. If she hadn't looked so bloodthirsty, Dominic would have laughed at her. She appeared too young to be Fairchild's widow, so he assumed she was his daughter.

If this was the woman he was to wed, Lord help him!

Rose of Ayrdale stared through the iron grillwork at the knight demanding entrance and knew not what to make of his unexpected appearance. No good would come of his visit, she was sure. Clad from head to toe in chain mail shirt, hood and leggings, he sat his destrier as if he were a part of the magnificent animal. His white linen, knee-length surcoat was belted at the waist with leather, and a broadsword hung in its scabbard from a baldric slung over his right shoulder.

Rose studied the dragon emblem emblazoned on the triangular shield he carried, and frowned. Something jogged her memory but was quickly lost when she noted the look of irritation on the knight's ruggedly handsome face and the spark of anger in his dark eyes. He looked so ferocious, so dangerous, that she brought her heavy sword up defensively.

"Who are you? State your business with Ayrdale and be gone."

"Who are you?" Dominic challenged.

"A daughter of Ayrdale. What do you want?"

Suddenly a guardsman came riding up to Rose. He brought his horse close to hers, leaned over and whispered something in her ear. She blanched, took another look at the fierce knight demanding entrance and immediately backed away.

"Why has the Dragon Lord come to Ayrdale?" she asked Dominic.

"Raise the portcullis and I will explain."

"Nay. I am in charge during my father's absence and I deny you entrance."

Sensing his master's waning patience, Dominic's destrier reared but was quickly brought under control with a firm hand. "Open in the name of the king."

Rose glanced past Dragon at the party of armed guardsmen riding with him. She was not at all convinced that letting them inside the keep was a good idea.

"King John is a tyrant," Rose charged. "He has imprisoned my father in the Tower on flimsy charges."

"I bring news of your father," Dominic countered, then added in an aside to Raj. "The woman must be lacking in wits to defy me."

Rose lowered the sword. It had become too heavy a weight for her slender wrists, but she would have wielded it and gladly in defense of Ayrdale. She had trained with her father's knights because she was his firstborn and the closest thing to a son he had. She wasn't as strong as a man, but she could defend herself should the need arise.

"How do I know you speak the truth?"

"Summon someone who can read, and I will show him the king's seal on the official document I carry."

Rose sent him a contemptuous look. "I can read, Lord Dragon."

Dominic stared at her, obviously skeptical, then

shrugged and removed a scroll from a pouch he carried at his waist. He guided his destrier close to the portcullis, unrolled the scroll partway and held it up for Rose's inspection. Rose frowned when she noticed that Dragon had exposed the king's royal seal but left the body of the document concealed. An unsettling sensation twisted her gut. Was he trying to trick her?

"As you can see," Dominic said, "the document bears the royal seal."

"Lord Dragon speaks the truth, my lady," the guardsman said. "He is the king's champion. I have heard tales of his bravery in the Crusade and his skill in the lists. If he says he has news of your father, I am inclined to believe him."

"I trust your judgment, Sir Eric," Rose said. "Order the portcullis raised and inform the guardsmen to keep their wits about them while Lord Dragon and his guardsmen are within the keep."

"Immediately, my lady," Sir Eric said as he wheeled his horse about.

Rose's palfrey inched backward as the portcullis was raised by slow degrees; then she turned and motioned for Dragon to follow as she rode past the barbican and through a passageway leading into the outer bailey. The murder holes in the stone ceiling must have made Lord Dragon nervous, Rose reflected when she looked back and saw him flinch and raise his shield.

"Fear not, my lord," she tossed over her shoulder. "You are not about to be slain."

"The architect was a genius," he replied.

Rose rode through the outer bailey and paused before another portcullis that opened into the inner bailey, waiting for Dragon and his guardsmen to catch up. The portcullis was raised and she rode through.

Dominic followed, admiring the shapely curve of her bottom outlined beneath her clothing. If she wasn't such a sharp-tongued witch he might enjoy being wed to her, but taming the woman was bound to be more chore than pleasure.

Silently he contemplated the young beauty's peaches-and-cream complexion and golden hair, unfavorably comparing her with his mistress's striking dark comeliness and ebony tresses. God's nightgown, why couldn't John have allowed him to wed Veronica, the lady of his choice? He probably loved Veronica as much as he could love any woman. Marriage to either of the Fairchild women would be a disaster.

Dominic passed through the gate into the inner bailey and took stock of his new holding with a critical eye, noting with approval the rectangular towers that topped the curtain wall at regular intervals. Nestled against the wall were various buildings and outbuildings. He identified a brewery, a storage shed, a thatched barn and stables, a smithy, a mews and, next to the keep, a chapel. Stretching his neck, Dominic caught a glimpse of a fenced-in garden, and beyond that an orchard and beehives. Ayrdale appeared to be thriving despite its absent lord.

Fairchild's fair daughter dismounted before the keep's stone stairs and tossed the reins of her palfrey to a squire. Dominic barked out orders to his guardsmen and followed close on her heels as she mounted the long staircase. Another squire sprinted ahead and opened the immense oak doors for them. Trusting no one when it came to his master's life, Raj brought up the rear, his huge hand resting on his sword.

Dominic's appreciative glance swept over the great hall. Trestle tables had already been set up for the evening meal, and villeins hurried about performing their duties. The head table, resting upon a raised dais, was set with fine cloth and plates and cups of wrought silver for the lord, his family and their guests. A huge hearth warmed the large chamber, and the rushes smelled sweet and clean. Comfortable chairs and benches were positioned around the hearth for the lord and his lady to take their ease.

Dominic's sharp gaze focused upon the two women who rose from their chairs and waited for him to approach. He had nearly reached them when he came to an abrupt halt, his gaze riveted on the younger of the two women. She was the exact image of the young woman who had met him at the portcullis. He blinked and looked again. The same hair, the same eyes, the same nose. Identical twins! Had the king known that Lord Fairchild had not one but two daughters?

Smiling, the older woman stepped forward and curtsied. "My lord, welcome to Ayrdale. I am sorry my husband cannot greet you himself but he would want me to bid you welcome. I am Lady Nelda of Ayrdale, and these—"

"Mama," the warrior maiden cautioned. "Lord Dragon brings news of Papa. Perhaps we should hear him out before we offer hospitality."

Lady Nelda's eyes sparkled with excitement and she

clasped her hands over her heart. Though she was older than her daughters, Dominic thought her every bit as lovely.

"You have news of my husband, my lord? Oh, my, 'tis so long since we have heard anything. Please tell me what you know."

Dominic pulled off his hood and bowed over the lady's hand. Telling this kind lady that her husband had been put to death wasn't going to be easy, but being a straightforward man, he got right to the point. No sense in prolonging it.

"Unwelcome news, I fear. I regret to inform you that Edwyn of Ayrdale is dead."

Lady Nelda turned deathly pale, and Dominic feared she would faint. He stood ready to catch her but Sir Eric of Carlyle rushed forward to steady her. The lady did not faint, however, but one of the twins swayed and would have fallen had her sister not placed a bracing arm around her.

The twin who had met him at the portcullis with the bared sword glared at him, her fury palpable. "Did you have a hand in my father's death? I want the truth, Lord Dragon, if you are capable of telling it. The last we heard, my father was residing in the Tower."

This hot-tempered girl was definitely not for him, Dominic decided. He glanced at the more demure sister, his look speculative. She stood with her eyes downcast and her hands folded in front of her; her lips moved in silent prayer. She appeared to be opposite in nature to the spitfire who dared challenge him with blazing eyes and raging temper. If he could not have Veronica, he would take the shy sister and find a husband for the other. A woman with a sharp tongue, bad temper and defiant nature would try his patience.

"I had naught to do with Lord Edwyn's death," Dominic said firmly. "I am but relaying the king's message."

"Our thanks, Lord Dragon," Nelda murmured. "Our steward will direct you to a chamber, where you may rest before returning to London. If you will excuse me, I wish to mourn my lord in private."

"There is more, my lady," Dominic said. He removed the rolled parchment from his pouch and handed it to her. "Perhaps this will explain your situation more clearly."

Lady Nelda read the document, her face turning paler by the minute. "This cannot be true, my lord," she gasped when she'd reached the end.

"What is it, Mama?" the outspoken twin asked.

"The king has given Ayrdale to Lord Dragon. Every hectare of land, the keep and its vassals are his by royal decree."

"The king cannot do that!" the girl exclaimed. "Papa did not deserve to die, and we do not deserve to be turned out of our home." She stomped her foot. "Oh, I wish I had never let Lord Dragon inside the keep. Where is my sword?"

"There's more," Lady Nelda whispered. "One of us must wed Lord Dragon."

The document dropped from her hands, and she groped for the chair behind her. Her daughter picked up the scroll, read it through once and tossed it into the hearth.

"That is what we think of Lackland's orders," she sneered. She turned to the captain of the guard. "Sir

Eric, see that Lord Dragon and his guardsmen are promptly escorted from Ayrdale and sent on their way."

"You will do no such thing, Captain," Dominic said in an authoritative voice. "The castle guards are mine to command. If you have heard of me, you are aware of my reputation as a crusader and warrior. I had naught to do with your lord's death; I am but following the king's orders regarding Ayrdale. If you and Fairchild's personal guardsmen do not wish to serve me, then you may leave immediately. But I sincerely hope you will remain and help protect Dragonwyck."

"Dragonwyck!" the outspoken twin exclaimed.

"Aye. 'Tis the name I've chosen for my demesne," Dominic said, ignoring the girl's gasp of outrage.

Sir Eric looked askance at Lady Nelda. He appeared to be torn between loyalty to his dead lord and the desire to serve the new one. "I am sworn to protect Lady Nelda and her daughters."

"The choice is yours to make," Lady Nelda said faintly. "May I leave now, Lord Dragon?"

"Not yet," Dominic said in a tone that stopped her in her tracks. "You may leave after I choose my bride." He turned to Sir Eric. "Fetch the priest."

Lady Nelda looked deflated, and the meek sister began to weep silent tears.

"I would know your daughters' names, madam," Dominic said. He had already decided not to marry the grieving widow. He wanted passion, not tears, in his marriage bed.

* * *

Rose stared at Dominic in horror. The thought that one of them would be forced to marry the Dragon Lord was incomprehensible—nay, absurd. How could anyone expect her mother to take a new husband so soon after her beloved lord's death? And everyone in the keep knew that her sister was meant for a religious life. Father had promised that Starla could enter the convent as soon as he returned from London. That left . . . Rose, and she knew that no man in his right mind would choose a sharp-tongued bride.

But Rose could not help being the way she was. Though they were identical twins, Rose and Starla were as different as night and day. Sweet, shy Starla had her heart set on entering a convent and becoming a nun. It was all she had ever aspired to. Rose, the firstborn by five minutes, had always known she would be the one to marry and rule Ayrdale once her father was gone, but she hadn't expected the day to arrive so soon.

Rose looked into her sister's stricken eyes and quickly decided she would make whatever sacrifice was necessary to save Starla from the Dragon Lord. Her quick mind had already hit upon a plan. Placing an arm around Starla's quaking shoulders, Rose looked Dragon boldly in the eyes and said in a quiet voice, "I am Starla. Rose is my twin."

Starla started to protest, but Rose gave her such a stern look, she quickly clamped her mouth shut. Lady Nelda merely stared at Rose as if she had lost her mind. None beyond their immediate circle had heard her words.

Dragon seemed not to notice their agitation as he

raised Starla's chin and stared into her frightened eyes. Apparently satisfied with what he saw, he turned toward those gathered around him and said in a loud voice, "I will wed Rose." Every villein, guardsman, squire and freeman in the great hall stared at Dominic with a mixture of fear and disbelief.

"People of Dragonwyck, heed me," Dominic said in a loud voice as the throng of vassals inched closer. "I am Dominic Dragon, your new lord, and Dragonwyck is the name I have chosen for my demesne. You are all invited to witness the marriage of your new lord to Lady Rose."

A tall man of middle years stepped forward. "I am Sir Braden, Ayrdale's steward. May I ask what happened to Lord Edwyn of Ayrdale?"

"I will tell you." It was the warrior maiden, the one named Starla, who answered as she shoved past Dominic. "King John ordered my father killed and gave Ayrdale to Lord Dragon as payment for the deed."

Dominic's temper hung by a single thread. Instinct told him the acid-tongued twin was going to be trouble, and he was glad he had chosen her sister. "Not true. I had no hand in Edwyn of Ayrdale's death," Dominic claimed. "From what I have heard, Edwyn plotted treason. I was given Ayrdale because I am capable of protecting England's border against Scottish invaders."

"So the Dragon says," the girl spat.

Dominic had taken all he could of the viper's jibes. A harsh reprimand was on the tip of his tongue, but he withheld it when he saw a brown-robed man with tonsured hair and a round belly running behind Sir

Eric, holding up his robes to keep from tripping on them.

"Did I hear aright, my lord?" the priest asked when he reached Dominic. "Is Lord Edwyn truly dead? Did you bring his body home for burial?"

Dominic glanced at Lady Nelda and cursed King John beneath his breath when he saw a glimmer of hope in her misty eyes—a hope he couldn't fulfill.

"Nay, Father, I was not charged with that duty. I believe Lord Fairchild was buried in London."

"In unconsecrated ground?" the priest asked in a shocked voice.

" 'Tis all right, Father Nyle," Lady Nelda said. "Our Lord in heaven knows my husband was a good man. We do not need his body to mourn him."

"We must go to the chapel immediately and offer a Mass for his soul," Father Nyle said. He turned to leave.

"Nay, Father," Dominic said, staying the priest. "You will perform a wedding within the hour."

"A wedding?" The priest bristled indignantly. " 'Tis not proper. We are in deep mourning."

"I fear I must insist," Dominic said. "I intend to wed Lady Rose within the hour."

Rose shuddered involuntarily at his words, and her mother stirred herself to object. "I must protest, my lord. 'Tis far too soon to think about a wedding."

"Protest away, my lady, but 'twill do you no good. I am but following the king's orders. Expediency is important for reasons that should be clear to everyone. Dragonwyck has been too long without a master, and dire consequences could result should an enemy of

35

England try to claim the land for himself through marriage to one of you ladies."

Father Nyle sputtered to himself but offered no further protest. "Very well, my lord. If you insist, I will perform the ceremony. The least I can do is see to the legal aspects of the union. Lord Edwyn would have wanted that for his daughter. Furthermore, I feel an obligation to protect our dead lord's widow and other daughter. They deserve the security of a home, my lord."

"I will hie myself to the convent," Lady Nelda said, "and my daughter shall come with me."

" 'Tis your decision, but know that I will not turn you out of your home if you wish to remain," Dominic said.

"Aye, 'tis a perfect solution," Rose said. She turned to her twin and said in an aside, "I will ask permission so Mother can leave for the convent immediately following the ceremony. Just remember to call me Starla and refer to yourself as Rose."

"What are you up to, Rose?" Starla whispered.

"Saving your skin. Unless *you* wish to wed Dragon."

Starla blanched. "Nay, oh, nay. I could not bear it. He is so . . . fierce. Are you sure you know what you are doing?"

"Trust me. Just do as I say before Dragon becomes suspicious."

"What are you two whispering about?" Dominic asked harshly.

"May I ask a boon of you, my lord?" Rose asked.

"A boon?" Dominic asked in a suspicious tone. "Name it, but I can promise naught."

"Allow my mother to leave for the convent with my sister immediately following the ceremony."

"Is that your wish?" Dominic asked Nelda.

Rose sent a warning glance at Nelda, hoping her mother would understand and lend support. Lady Nelda must have suspected Rose had a plan in mind, for she nodded affirmatively.

" 'Tis done, then," Dominic said. "Guardsmen of your own choosing will escort you to the convent immediately following the wedding. You may take your personal belongings, but everything else of value belongs to me and is not to leave the keep. Understood?"

All three women nodded in unison.

"Very well, then. You may repair to the solar to make Lady Rose ready for her wedding."

Grasping Starla's hand, Rose all but pulled her up the stairs to the solar. Lady Nelda hurried after them. Once the door had closed behind them, Rose all but collapsed against it. Then, stiffening her spine, she pushed herself away with the courage and determination that defined her character.

"Come," she said, walking over to the trunk and throwing back the lid. "There is little time to prepare."

"You will explain first," Lady Nelda demanded. "What is your purpose in telling Lord Dragon that you are Starla?"

Rose removed one of her mother's under-gowns from the trunk and placed it on the bed. "Think you Lord Dragon would have a wife with a sharp tongue? Nay. Men want a meek wife they can browbeat into submission. I am not that kind of woman, and he recognized it immediately. I sensed he would choose

Starla, and we all know that wedding her to Dragon would destroy her."

"I will not allow you to sacrifice yourself for me," Starla argued. "You have protected me all my life. 'Tis time I stood up for myself."

Rose sent her saintly sister a tender smile. " 'Tis not in you to be forceful, sister. You have always known you wanted to dedicate yourself to God. Even Papa recognized your piety and gave in to your desire to be cloistered. Now you will get your wish."

"What about Lord Dragon?" Lady Nelda questioned. "Think you he won't know the difference?"

"Not if Starla plays her part," Rose explained. "She knows me as no one else does, not even you, Mama. If Starla puts her mind to it, she will have no trouble pretending to be me until after I wed Dragon. And I will pretend to be the meek sister. He publicly announced his intention to marry Rose and so he shall."

" 'Tis a clever ploy," Lady Nelda said thoughtfully, "but I fear for you, Rose. At some point Lord Dragon will know he has been duped. Then what will become of you? Consider this, daughter," Nelda said earnestly. "Do you know what wedding a virile man like Lord Dragon means?"

Rose had her suspicions but no specific knowledge about what happened in the marriage bed.

"You can tell me later, Mama. Right now we have work to do. Starla, do you remember where Papa hid the cache of gold he kept for emergencies?"

Starla glanced at the hearth, her brow wrinkled in thought. " 'Tis so long since he showed us, but I think I remember."

"Good, get it. Mama, you get your jewelry while I rip out the hems of your gowns."

"Lord Dragon said we are to take naught of value with us to the convent," Nelda reminded her.

Rose sent her an exasperated look. "Devil take Dragon. I will not have you go as paupers to the convent. Mama, fetch your sewing basket."

"The gold is still here!" Starla crowed as she removed a brick from the front of the hearth and lifted out a bulging cloth sack from the cramped space behind it. She carried the sack to the bed and spilled a pile of gold coins onto the counterpane.

They worked quickly, sewing the coins into the hem of Nelda's under-gown, spacing them so they would not jingle together when she walked. They did the same with the jewelry.

"There are sufficient coins here to pay your way," Rose said when they finished. "Starla, go to your room and pack your personal belongings while I help Mama. Dress warmly, mind you."

"What about you, Rose?" Lady Nelda asked as she placed some personal belongings in a small trunk. "Will you be all right? I said naught in front of Starla, but I fear you are placing yourself in danger. Lord Dragon has the look of a man not easily placated. You will bear the brunt of his anger alone when he realizes you tricked him."

"I will survive, Mama," Rose said with more assurance than she felt. "He will not hurt me lest he earn the wrath of our guardsmen. He has need of their loyalty."

"He will indeed need our guardsmen," Nelda agreed

sagely. "If I know my brother Murdoc, and I believe I do, he will try to claim Ayrdale once he learns of your father's death. I would not put it past him to try to force you, your father's heir, to wed one of his kinsmen."

Rose grimaced. Even if Dragon had not arrived, she would not wed a kinsman of Uncle Murdoc's. She had seen them all, and none pleased her.

Starla arrived in the solar a few minutes later carrying a small casket containing her personal belongings. "I packed but a few things, for I intend to become a postulate and wear the robes they provide for me."

"I shall miss you," Rose said, giving her twin a fierce hug. "And you, too, Mama. The convent is but a half-day's journey, and I shall come often to visit."

"Are you sure about this, Rose?" Starla asked in a trembling voice. "I would not ask so great a sacrifice of you."

"You have ever wanted to be a nun, Starla. It would pain me to see you crushed beneath the Dragon Lord's heel."

Starla shuddered, her voice barely above a whisper. "I would prefer death. I do not think I could . . . could submit to a husband—any husband—as a wife should."

Teary-eyed, Rose held Starla close. "Nor will you have to. Go and be happy in your faith. Just remember to pretend to be me until you are well away from the keep, and I shall become meek and biddable until I know you are safely ensconced in the convent."

"Pray God Rose can keep her mouth shut long enough," Lady Nelda said in a prayerful tone.

A loud rapping on the door interrupted their conversation. Rose opened the door to the huge, foreign-looking man who had accompanied Dragon inside the keep. He was dressed strangely in a colorful robe that covered him from neck to toe and a length of white cloth wound about his head. And he carried enough weapons to slay an entire army.

"I am Raj, Lord Dragon's man. My master awaits his bride in the chapel."

"We will be there directly," Rose said.

She tried to close the door, but Raj held it open with one huge palm. "I am to escort Lady Rose to her bride-groom." He looked from Rose to Starla, then back to Rose. "Which lady would that be?"

Rose's demeanor immediately altered to mimic her sister's more reserved nature. She lowered her gaze and forced herself to tremble; though in truth it wasn't all that difficult. "I am Lady Rose."

"Follow me, my lady," Raj said, holding the door open for Rose. "We must not keep our lord waiting."

Rose sucked in a fortifying breath, stiffened her shoulders and walked bravely toward her future.

Chapter Two

What's in a name? That which we call a rose
by any other name would smell as sweet.
—William Shakespeare

Hands clasped behind his back, Dominic paced before the altar, waiting for his bride to appear. Truth to tell, he had little enthusiasm for this marriage. The shy little twin was not his type, but he knew in his heart that his choice had been a wise one. The sharp-tongued sister would make his life miserable, and bedding a grief-stricken widow held scant appeal.

Nor did he expect to derive pleasure from the marriage bed wedded to the meek little twin. She would probably close her eyes, grit her teeth and say a prayer each time he made love to her. Rose was certainly misnamed, he thought with a hint of amusement.

There was nothing thorny about the shy girl he was about to make his wife. He couldn't say the same about her sister, however, who was as prickly as a thistle.

Suddenly Dominic's patience snapped, and he turned on the priest. "Where is she?"

"Patience is a virtue, my lord," Father Nyle intoned. "You stormed into our household and announced our lord's death and your intention to wed one of his daughters, all within the span of one hour. 'Tis unseemly."

Dominic's mouth flattened. " 'Tis the king's will. Think you I want an unwilling wife in my bed? I had plans to wed another when the king gave me his orders. If I must accept this marriage, then so must Lady Rose."

"Lady Rose will obey the king but she does not have to like it," Rose said from the doorway. "I am here, my lord."

Dominic stared at Rose, noting with distaste her downcast eyes and rounded shoulders. Could she not even look at him? How was he to bed a wench who cringed at the very sight of him? His gaze slid past Rose to her sister, who appeared to have a problem meeting his gaze. But suddenly, as if realizing he was staring at her, she raised her chin and looked him directly in the eye.

Dominic flashed her a devilish grin, then turned his attention to his subdued little Rose. At least he would be able to keep Veronica as his mistress with Rose as his wife, he reflected. Should he wed the sister, they would be constantly at each other's throats. But he

suspected that bedding the feisty twin would be anything but dull. To Dominic's surprise, he felt himself
harden beneath his braies.

Dominic brought his wayward thoughts under control and turned to the priest. "Proceed with the ceremony, Father. Forget the Mass. I want this over and
done with as quickly as possible."

Had Dominic the opportunity to glance into Rose's
hooded eyes, he would have seen anger brewing in
their stormy blue depths.

Dominic gestured Rose forward. "Come, lady. Daw-
dling will change naught."

Bolstered by her mother and sister, Rose walked
slowly toward Dominic. When she reached his side,
he placed her hand on his arm and turned toward the
priest.

"You do not have to do this," Starla whispered into
Rose's ear.

Rose pretended not to hear. "I am ready, my lord,"
she said softly.

Dominic repeated his vows in a strong voice but had
to nudge Rose when it was her turn. Moments later
they were pronounced husband and wife, but Dominic could feel no joy. He felt strangely deflated. In fact,
he couldn't bring himself to give his wife the tradi-
tional kiss. He merely brushed his lips against hers in
the lightest of touches.

But something strange happened the moment his
lips met hers. He felt a spark ignite inside him and
warmth flow through his veins. He drew back and
stared at her, his eyes narrowed in puzzlement.

"A wedding feast awaits us in the hall, madam," he

said, more harshly than he intended. Placing Rose's arm on his, he guided her from the chapel. "Will your mother and sister stay to celebrate with us?"

"We will leave immediately as planned," Lady Nelda answered. She took Rose's hands between hers and kissed her cheek. "God protect you, Rose."

Dominic watched through narrowed lids as the sisters embraced and whispered words he could not hear. He saw tears in their eyes and hardened his heart against the regret he felt for parting them. It wasn't as if he were sending Lady Nelda and Starla away; they had chosen to leave of their own free will.

"We are ready, Lord Dragon," Nelda said, drawing Starla away from Rose.

Dominic signaled Raj, who left immediately to alert the guardsmen serving as escorts. "Eric of Carlyle and two of your own guardsmen will see you safely to the convent."

Dominic tried to make eye contact with Starla but failed. He would have liked one more look into those defiant blue eyes before bidding the feisty twin farewell forever, but it was not to be. His sigh held a hint of regret as Lady Nelda and Starla made a hasty exit.

"I ordered a feast prepared to celebrate our wedding and invited our vassals to partake of the meal," Dominic said, returning his attention to Rose. "I hope it pleases you."

Pretending to respond to her new husband as Starla would have, Rose shied away from Dominic. Actually, she wasn't pretending all that much. The brush of Dragon's mouth against hers had left her breathless and confused. For some odd reason, her body tingled clear down to her toes. She peered at Dragon from beneath lowered lashes, then quickly looked away. "If it pleases you, Lord Dragon."

A frown formed between Dominic's dark brows. Before Rose had looked away, he had seen a defiant spark in her eyes that confused him. It was the same fiery response he'd noted in her twin's eyes when she had challenged him at the portcullis. He shook his head to clear it of the provocative image of the warrior woman sitting astride her horse, a sword balanced in one hand and a challenge on her lips. He shook his head again. Something nagged at the edge of his memory but it passed too quickly for him to grasp.

"My name is Dominic," he said as the silence stretched between them. "You have my leave to call me Dominic if you wish."

"I do not wish, my lord."

Dominic felt a headache forming behind his eyes. Consummating his marriage was definitely going to be a chore. He feared he would be making love to one sister while thinking about the other. Damn King John!

Dominic seated Rose at the high table and glanced about the hall with interest. He hadn't taken the opportunity to inspect the great hall earlier, but now he took his time looking his fill.

The walls, he noted, were covered with richly embroidered tapestries and silk hangings, the rushes smelled sweet and clean, and the brass chandelier overhead sparkled. The high table was set with the finest linen, and the silver cups and utensils were polished to a high sheen. Flames danced in the hearth, banishing lurking shadows and the evening chill, creating a welcoming atmosphere that Dominic hadn't experienced since he had left home many years ago to seek his fortune.

The only discordant note was the pale woman at his side. If there was a spark of emotion in her, he had yet to find it. She was a bland imitation of her vibrant sister. Somehow he had to overcome his aversion to the pious maiden long enough to bed her and get an heir from her.

Rose watched Dragon from beneath lowered lids, wondering what he was thinking. His dark, hooded eyes, brooding mouth and harsh jaw were intimidating but not necessarily frightening. She studied him surreptitiously through a curtain of feathery lashes and decided he was a handsome man, in a rugged sort of way. His was a virile face, one of strength and determination.

What would he do to her when he learned he had been duped?

She couldn't suppress the shudder that rippled over her flesh.

"Are you cold, Rose?"

She rubbed her arms. "Nay."

He placed a finger beneath her chin and raised it so he could look into her face. "Are you frightened of me?"

Challenge flared in Rose's eyes but was quickly extinguished before Dragon could question it. It was not safe to reveal too much of herself to her husband. She knew Starla would be frightened of Dragon, so she had to pretend the same emotions her timid sister might feel.

Forcing a tear or two and a quiver in her voice, Rose said, "I would be a fool not to be frightened, my lord. I never wanted a husband. Until the king interfered, I hoped to devote my life to God. I wanted to become a nun and spend my life in prayer and good work."

Her words seemed to anger Dragon, for he spit out a curse and released her chin. "We are wed, madam. There is naught you can do to change that. In time, I expect an heir from you. Did your mother not tell you what to expect in the marriage bed?"

There was no time. "Do with me as you will, my lord Dragon," Rose said in a quavering voice, "but I do not have to like it."

Another curse flew past Dominic's lips. "Think you I wanted to marry you? I intended to wed another, but the king would not allow it. If there is a man you care about, I advise you to forget him, for I will not be cuck-olded."

Rose stifled a gasp. She had never considered that Dragon's affections might lie elsewhere. As for her own affections, they had never been engaged. Though her father had tried to interest her in marriage, she had yet to meet a man who pleased her.

"I told you," Rose whispered in a quavering voice, "I promised myself to Christ."

Dominic opened his mouth to say something but clamped his lips together when servants paraded into the great hall bearing trays laden with food. He had ordered a feast, and a feast was exactly what was served. Platter after platter of roast boar, roe deer, game pies in wine gravy, stewed eels and raw oysters from the sea were placed before them. A second course of capon in lemon and ginger, sea trout in cream, fresh bread and butter and an assortment of vegetables followed in short order.

Dominic was impressed with the bountiful table and variety of food. By the time the wheel of cheese and sweets arrived, Dominic knew without examining the account books that Dragonwyck's wealth surpassed anything he had imagined, anything that even the king had imagined. He glanced sideways at Rose. Should he find no enjoyment in his marriage bed, he would have the pleasure of knowing he was a rich man.

"Your cook is exceptional," he said by way of conversation.

He drank deeply from the goblet they shared and offered it to Rose. Refusing to place her lips where Dominic had sipped, she deliberately turned the goblet and drank from the opposite side. Dominic stared at the drop of wine that clung to her lower lip and had the sudden, inexplicable urge to lick it off with the tip of his tongue.

He was insane. There was no other explanation. Only a madman would feel desire for a woman who cringed at his touch. He would consider himself lucky if he did not suffer frostbite the first time he put his cock inside her. He groaned in dismay when he felt himself harden.

He *was* insane!

"Does the food not please you?" he asked when he noticed that Rose was merely toying with her food. At least her lack of appetite gave him something else to think about besides Rose's lush lips and the hardness of his cock.

"I am not hungry," Rose whispered. "I would like to retire."

"Not yet," Dominic said. "You must wait until the toasts to our happiness have been given."

Rose bit her tongue to keep from spewing out her opinion of those toasts. Happiness? Bah. Not likely. But she had to keep up the pretense of being submissive until her mother and sister were safely sequestered behind convent walls and beyond Dragon's reach. So she blushed with the right amount of modesty when goblets were raised in ribald toasts to their wedding night.

"May I leave now?" Rose asked timidly once the toasts ended and the drinking resumed in earnest.

Dominic rose and offered his arm. "I will escort you to the solar so you may prepare yourself for our wedding night. After a sufficient length of time, I will join you."

Rose stood, and two ladies sitting at a table below the dais rose with her. "There is no need for you to accompany me, my lord," Rose said. "Lady Emily, Sir Eric's wife, and Lady Blythe, Sir Cedric of Waverly's wife, will attend me."

"As you wish," Dominic said. "Perhaps your ladies could enlighten you about what to expect in the marriage bed. You are shy and retiring by nature and in need of instruction. I would prefer not to have my wife faint at the sight of me in her bed."

Her cheeks flaming, Rose was swept away by her two ladies. Lady Emily, a woman past the first bloom of youth but still handsome, led the way, while Lady Blythe, younger and prettier, followed behind.

"What did he mean, Rose?" Lady Emily whispered

as they ascended the stairs and walked along the upper gallery. "Since when have you been shy and retiring? Lord Dragon's description sounds more like Starla."

"Indeed, you seem unusually quiet today," Blythe observed. "But who could blame you? 'Tis a sad day for you, Rose. Being forced to wed Lord Dragon would render anyone speechless."

"One day I will explain to you what actually occurred today," Rose said. "Hurry. I do not want Dragon to come up before I am ready for him."

Rose entered the solar and walked through the sitting room to the bedchamber that had once belonged to her mother and father. Emily and Blythe followed close behind.

"I have been married for many years," Emily began timidly. "I will attempt to answer any questions you might have about . . . the wedding night."

Rose's expression turned fierce. "There will be no wedding night. As soon as you leave, I intend to bolt the door and open it to no one."

"No one?" Blythe squeaked in dismay. "But Dragon is your husband. You cannot deny him your bed."

"Just watch me," Rose bit out. "Run along, both of you. You should not be here when Dragon arrives. I do not want you caught up in the middle of this."

Emily's soft brown eyes narrowed thoughtfully. "What is going on, Rose? Eric has told me a great deal about Lord Dragon. Were I you, I would not defy him."

"Cedric says Lord Dragon has a mistress," Blythe blurted out. "He heard gossip about them when he visited London with your father last year. Rumor had it that Lord Dragon intended to wed the lady before the king interfered."

"Shame on you, Blythe," Emily chided. " 'Tis only gossip."

" 'Tis true," Rose said. "Dragon admitted there was another woman in his life. 'Tis not as if ours is a love match. The king ordered Dragon to wed one of Ayrdale's women, and he had no choice but to obey."

"Lord Dragon chose you instead of Starla, did he not?" Blythe said as if that meant something.

Rose knew better, but she kept that vital piece of information to herself. Unfortunately, the truth was bound to come out soon. Too soon, she feared.

"Go," Rose said, shooing them out the door. "Worry not about me. I will be fine."

Rose closed and bolted the bedchamber door behind Emily and Blythe and sat down on a bench before the fire to soak up the heat. She hugged herself, not really cold but shivering nonetheless. She did not know Dragon well enough to predict how he would react to her deliberate act of defiance, but she suspected he would be furious.

Dominic knew he was drinking too much but he could not seem to stop himself. The longer he sat and brooded, the more reluctant he was to breach his wife's maidenhead. Yet . . . something inside him churned at the thought of the woman awaiting him in her bed. He wanted her, yet he did not want her. Her downcast eyes and bowed head should have pleased him. Submissiveness was a virtue in a wife, was it not?

But was Rose really submissive? He had a feeling

that he was missing a piece of vital information. Once or twice during the evening, when Rose had deigned to look at him, he had noticed a spark of something provocative and challenging in her eyes. But before he could ascertain if he was imagining things, she had either looked away or lowered her gaze.

Raj, who was standing behind Dominic, must have noticed his master's agitation, for he bent from a tremendous height to whisper in his ear. "Your bride awaits you, master. You should not drink too much lest your performance lack luster."

"I am but arming myself for battle, Raj," Dominic answered. "Think you my frightened little bird will welcome me in her bed?" He gave a rueful sigh. "Rose is a timid soul, unlike my passionate Veronica. I fear my cock will not rise to the occasion."

"Perhaps you have not really looked at your bride," Raj ventured.

Dominic gave a harsh laugh. "I wanted a submissive wife and I got one. Rose is frightened of me. Hell, she is afraid of her own shadow."

"Why did you not wed her sister?"

Dominic sent Raj a look of utter astonishment. "Surely you jest. I prefer having my cock frozen in Rose's cold sheath than to risk having it hacked off with the sharp edge of her sister's sword. There is too much fire in the feisty one for my liking."

Now it was Raj's turn to laugh, and he did so with gusto. "Methinks you will live to eat your words, master." He turned away. "I wish you a pleasant night."

Dominic frowned into his empty goblet, wondering whether he should fill it again or join Rose in their marriage bed. He knew he should consummate the marriage as soon as possible, and that delaying the bedding would only prolong the ordeal, but he hated the thought of deflowering a frightened virgin.

Heaving himself out of his chair, Dominic suddenly became the center of attention as his guardsmen offered lewd advice concerning the bedding.

"May your lance find the path to victory!" toasted a tipsy knight.

"You mean the path to ecstasy," another laughed drunkenly.

"Here's to hot blood and a stiff cock," sang out another.

Dominic had heard enough. Turning on his heel, he marched resolutely from the hall. Suddenly his blood was racing through his veins and his heart was pounding. Anticipation goaded him as he took the stairs two at a time. The gallery seemed endless but he finally reached the solar. He strode through the sitting room toward the bedchamber. Mayhap, if he was lucky, he could revive that spark he'd seen earlier in Rose's eyes.

Dominic considered himself a good lover; he knew it to be true, for Veronica and those before her had often praised his prowess. He could not count the times he had left his lovers swooning in their beds. How difficult could it be to arouse a virgin to passion? Dominic had never breached a virgin before, but women were women the world over, no matter their state of virginity. He would give Rose pleasure and leave her swooning despite her shyness and his own reluctance to bed a woman he did not want.

To his surprise, Dominic found that he was nearly

running when he reached the bedchamber. Why was he so eager to bed a woman who did not appeal to him?

Dominic grasped the door handle and pushed inward; the door wouldn't budge. He tried again. The door was latched from the inside. How dare she lock him out of her bedchamber! She was his wife, he was her lord; she could not say him nay.

She could not!

He rattled the latch. "Rose. Unlatch the door."

Her voice was muffled by the thickness of the door. "Find another chamber, my lord. I have no intention of sharing my bed with you tonight. I need time to mourn my father."

"Are you denying me?" Dominic roared through the panel.

"Indeed."

"You cannot. I demand entrance."

"You demanded that I wed you, and so I did."

"I will not beg for what is rightfully mine," Dominic bit out. "Are you going to open the door?"

"Nay, my lord."

Dominic stared at the door in disbelief. The determined woman behind the door did not sound at all like the shy little Rose he had just wed. Had her sister's warrior spirit found its way into Rose's timid soul? A horrifying thought suddenly occurred to him.

Had he been duped into wedding the sharp-tongued twin? If so, he would have the last laugh, for the marriage would not be legal. He had married a submissive maiden named Rose and would accept no other.

His face set in determined lines, Dominic spun on

his heel and returned to the great hall, where merry-making was still in progress. He spied Sir Braden and stalked toward him.

"A word with you, Sir Braden."

Sir Braden gave him a puzzled look. "What is amiss, my lord?"

"A great deal," Dominic said tersely. "You attended the wedding, did you not?"

"Aye, my lord."

"Whom did I marry? Lady Rose or Lady Starla? Do not lie, for I cannot abide liars."

"You wed Lady Rose, Lord Dragon."

"Are you certain? Even I could not tell them apart."

"I have known them all of their lives, my lord. I could not possibly mistake one for the other. You wed Lady Rose."

"Has Sir Eric returned from the convent?" Dominic asked, still not satisfied. Something was definitely wrong, and he was determined to get to the bottom of it.

"Nay, my lord. But Sir Cedric, Sir Eric's lieutenant, is available to attend you."

"Fetch him for me."

Sir Braden hurried off and returned a few minutes later with Sir Cedric. "You wished to speak with me?" Sir Cedric asked.

"Aye. I will ask you the same question I asked Sir Braden. Whom did I wed? Lady Rose or Lady Starla?"

Sir Cedric gave him a startled look. "You wed Lady Rose, my lord. You announced your choice in the great hall, we all heard you. 'Twas indeed Lady Rose you took as your wife. Is there a problem?"

Still unconvinced, Dominic made a dismissive motion with his hand. "Go, both of you. Send Father Nyle to me."

Dominic paced as he waited for the priest. When he arrived, looking like a ship under full sail, Dominic rounded on him. "Quickly, tell me the name of the woman I wed."

Father Nyle looked at Dominic as if he had lost his mind. "Lady Rose, my lord. Have you forgotten her name already?"

"How do you know 'tis Rose I wed and not Starla?"

"Humph, I should know. I baptized them and have watched them grow to womanhood. Starla is the pious twin, the dutiful daughter, always on her knees in the chapel. Rose should have been born a man, for she has none of her mother's or sister's gentle ways. Is there aught else you wish, my lord?"

"Nay, Father, you may go," Dominic said gruffly. He refused to admit that he had been duped, for he still wasn't sure what had happened. Perhaps Rose did need time to mourn her father, and mayhap he was imagining things, but he was sure as hell going to find out.

Rose awakened the next morning refreshed after a good night's sleep. She did not dwell overlong on Dragon's reason for giving up so easily last night, for if she did, she would be too frightened to face him this morning. But now that her mother and sister were safely sequestered, she could be herself.

Rose unlatched the door and walked into the sitting room, where a maidservant was engaged in building a fire in the grate. Rose greeted Tyra pleasantly and asked for food and a bath. Lady Emily arrived with a tray a short time later.

"He is gone," Emily whispered, pulling Rose aside so the servants carrying the tub and bathwater into the chamber would not hear.

"Who is gone?"

"Lord Dragon. He left before Prime. I was on my way to Mass when I saw him ride out."

"Did he go hunting or hawking?"

"I know not. Lord Dragon and that foreign giant who guards his back left together."

"Do you know where Lord Dragon slept last night?"

Rose wanted to bite her tongue after she asked the question. She cared not where or with whom Dragon slept. She had no intention of letting him bed her.

"Did your husband not sleep in your bed?" Emily asked.

Rose's chin angled upward. "I refused to open the door to him."

"God's toenails, Rose, are you mad!"

"Mayhap, but I cannot be with a man I do not know. Dragon does not want me, he never did. He is the king's lackey. I cannot like a man who serves the king who murdered my father.

"Where do you suppose Dragon went?"

"Cedric of Waverly said Lord Dragon was acting strangely last night. He questioned Sir Braden, Father Nyle and Sir Cedric about your identity. Why do you suppose he did that?"

Rose feared she had gone too far last night. Denying Dragon his rights had been something Starla would have been too frightened to attempt. She squared her shoulders. Fortunately, there was naught Dragon could do to remedy his mistake. He had announced his intention to wed Rose, and the priest had blessed their union. Furthermore, Starla was beyond his reach. Rose would be the one to feel the brunt of Dragon's wrath, but she could handle it better than Starla.

"Rose," Emily prodded. "What have you done?"

"There was a bit of trickery involved," Rose admitted. "I guessed Dragon would not wed a shrew when a saint was available, and his choice of bride proved me right. Starla and I changed places. He selected the woman he thought was Rose but who was really Starla. I merely pretended to be submissive during the wedding ceremony so Dragon would not become suspicious. Dragon did indeed wed Rose, the real Rose. Now Starla is in the convent and beyond his reach."

Emily turned deathly pale. "Blessed Virgin save us all," she muttered. "I would not want to be in your shoes when Lord Dragon realizes he wed the wrong sister. Think you he will seek an annulment?"

"It would please me if he did, but 'tis unlikely. The king ordered him to wed one of Ayrdale's women, and so he has. Fear not, Emily—I will survive. Starla is where she belongs. That is what really matters.

"After I eat and bathe, I will join you in the great hall," Rose said. "There is much to be done. I should meet with the steward and go over the list of stores on hand. We are feeding more mouths than we anticipated and will probably need to set aside more supplies to see us through winter. Michaelmas is the time for candlemaking and slaughtering and preserving. I will require everyone's cooperation for those tasks."

Lady Emily hurried off, leaving Rose to her bath, her food and her morbid thoughts.

As usual, the hall was a beehive of activity. Rose glanced about the chamber and noted that Dragon's men were mingling with Ayrdale's personal guardsmen without the animosity one would expect, considering the circumstances of Dragon's appearance at Ayrdale. Nay, her beloved home was no longer Ayrdale. Dragon had renamed it Dragonwyck, lair of the Dragon Lord.

Rose spied Sir Cedric and hurried over to speak with him. "Has Sir Eric returned?" she asked.

"Nay, my lady."

"And Lord Dragon? Did he mention his destination to you when he rode out this morning?"

"He said naught to me, my lady. Lord Dragon and his foreign servant left before prime. Mayhap he went to inspect his demesne."

Rose took her leave and made her way to the chapel. She had missed morning Mass and felt the need to confess her sins. Though she wasn't as pious as Starla, she had a healthy respect for her religion. She feared her lie had offended God and she sought His forgiveness.

She found Father Nyle on his knees before the altar. He heard her approaching and rose to greet her. "You missed Mass," he chided.

"Forgive me, Father. I will try to do better."

"What brings you here, child?"

"I seek forgiveness for a grave sin, Father."

Father Nyle sent her a sympathetic look and indicated that she should kneel beside him. "What is this grave sin, child?"

Rose stared at the crucifix above the altar and said, "I lied, Father, and feel no remorse for having done so."

Father Nyle sent her a thoughtful look. "Did your lie harm anyone?"

"No one but myself," she whispered with a note of defiance. "I lied to save Starla, and I would do it again."

"There can be no absolution without genuine remorse," the priest reminded her. "Do you wish to tell me about it?"

"I am sorry, Father, but I am responsible for what I did and I shall shoulder the blame. I want no one punished on my account. I shall face God's displeasure and the Dragon's wrath with courage, Father."

"May God forgive you, child," Father Nyle said as he lowered his head and offered a blessing.

Chapter Three

The rose has thorns only for those who would
pluck it.

—Chinese Proverb

"There it is, Raj," Dominic said, indicating the large, square structure surrounded by a high wall that loomed before them. The bell in the chapel began tolling the hour of Sext as they approached the gate. They had made good time, Dominic thought as he checked the position of the sun in the sky.

Dominic reined his destrier before a heavy oak gate and dismounted.

"Shall I ring the bell, master?" Raj asked.

Dominic glanced up and saw a large brass bell with a rope attached to its handle mounted atop the gate. "Aye, ring away, Raj," Dominic growled.

Raj grasped the rope and set the bell to clanging. It was so loud Dominic covered his ears with his hands to dull the noise. Then he waited. And waited.

"Try again, Raj," Dominic said, his patience slowly eroding.

Dominic clenched his teeth as Raj set the clapper in motion again. The second time produced results. Dominic watched in grim satisfaction as a woman clad in black and wearing a white wimple on her head approached the gate.

"How may I help you, sir?"

"Open the gate. I wish to speak with your two new arrivals."

Sister Isolda gave her head a negative shake. "Men are not allowed inside. I will relay a message for you."

"Not good enough," Dominic returned impatiently. "My business is with Lady Nelda and her daughter. Either let my man and me inside or send them out."

Raj stepped from behind Dominic, giving Sister Isolda the full benefit of his impressive height and rather ominous scowl.

"I . . . I will summon the abbess," Sister Isolda said, scurrying off.

"Damn!" Dominic cursed. "I do not want to speak to the abbess," he called after the frightened nun. "If you do not send out Lady Nelda and her daughter, my man and I will break down the gate."

Sister Isolda's response was to pick up her skirts and run.

"Think you the little blackbird will send out Lady Nelda and her daughter?" Raj asked.

"We can only hope," Dominic said.

Dominic paced before the gate, his patience wearing thin. If someone did not appear soon, he was fully prepared to break down the gate. It should not be difficult to find a battering ram from among the fallen logs he had seen while passing through the forest.

"Someone comes," Raj said.

Dominic swallowed another curse when he realized the woman approaching was neither Lady Nelda nor Rose's twin. He was in no mood to bandy words with another holy woman, but it looked as if that was precisely what he was going to do.

The nun, stout of body and round of face, planted herself before the sturdy gate and stared at Dominic. Dominic knew the exact moment she saw Raj, for her eyes widened and she took an involuntary step backward.

"I am the abbess. Sister Isolda said you wish to speak with Lady Nelda and Starla. They are newly arrived and resting after their journey. State your name and business."

"I am Lord Dominic Dragon of Dragonwyck. My business is personal," Dominic said in his most intimidating voice.

"The Dragon Lord," the abbess gasped, obviously aware of his name and reputation. It took a few minutes for her to regain her composure. "The gate cannot be opened to you or any man, my lord."

"My temper hangs by a thread, madam," Dominic bit out. "If I cannot come inside, send out Lady Nelda and her daughter so that I may speak with them. I mean them no harm. Lady Nelda is mother to my wife."

The abbess studied Dominic with shrewd brown eyes. After what seemed like an eternity, she nodded, turned and walked away.

"Think you the black crow will send out Lady Nelda and her daughter?" Raj asked.

"Your guess is as good as mine, Raj, but I vow I will not take no for an answer. I refuse to return to Dragonwyck without the truth. I want to know if I was tricked into wedding the wrong daughter . . . and why."

"It appears that your wish will be granted, master," Raj said. "Lady Nelda and Lady Starla are approaching the gate."

"About time," Dominic grumbled. Arms crossed over his chest and a ferocious scowl on his face, Dominic watched them draw near.

Lady Nelda knew why Lord Dragon had come, but she had not expected him so soon. What had Rose done to make him suspicious? she wondered. She could not suppress a chuckle despite the graveness of the situation. Rose was a resourceful lass. Nelda trusted her daughter to find a way to allay Dragon's anger when he learned that he had been duped.

"The Dragon looks angry, Mama," Starla whispered, sidling closer to her mother. "I would never forgive myself if he hurt Rose on my account."

"Remain silent, Starla," Lady Nelda warned. "Let us see how much Lord Dragon knows before we jump to conclusions."

"My lord," Nelda began, "the abbess said you wished to speak to me and Starla. May I inquire about

Rose's health first? I trust my daughter is well."

"I have not harmed her, if that is what you think."

"What brings you to the convent so soon after your wedding?"

"As if you did not know," Dominic snorted. His gaze slid to Starla, who reacted to his glare by cringing behind her mother. "Tell me the name of the twin I wed," he said in a deceptively calm voice. "If you lie, these walls are not high enough to save you from my wrath."

Nelda tried not to flinch beneath Dragon's threat. She had heard that the Dragon Lord was a hard man, and she did not trust him. She had no choice, however, but to answer his question truthfully, whether or not he chose to believe her.

"You wed my daughter Rose, my lord," Nelda said. "I would never lie about something as important as that. Why do you ask?"

Dominic pointed to Starla. "*She* is the one I thought I wed." Starla gave a little squeak and recoiled in fear. "I wanted a submissive wife," Dominic continued, "not a defiant termagant. I was duped."

"How so, my lord?" Nelda asked sweetly. "You chose Rose of your own free will."

"Trickery!" Dominic charged. " 'Tis my belief that your daughters switched places. The bride I chose was *not* the one I wanted."

Starla clung to her mother. "Mama, do not let him take me. I will die if I have to wed him. I am meant for God."

"We all witnessed a wedding, my lord," Nelda said evenly. "You married Rose; the nuptials were blessed by Father Nyle. Go home and try to make the best of

66

your marriage. But if I hear you are mistreating Rose, I will ask my brother Murdoc to rally to her defense."

"Murdoc," Dominic repeated. "Ah, yes, the Scotsman. Fear not, lady, I will attempt to keep my hands from Rose's throat if she will sheath her sharp claws. Nevertheless, you owe me the truth. Explain how I wed an acid-tongued shrew instead of a pious little mouse?"

"Look at Starla, my lord," Nelda said. "Really look at her. She is her sister's image but her opposite in every way. Ever since she was a small child her dream was to become a nun. A man of your vast experience and appetite would gain no joy from her. Is that what you want? A wife who will cower and weep and cringe away from your touch?"

Dominic shrugged. "Perhaps I prefer that to being slashed to pieces by a sharp tongue. 'Tis done now, there is naught I can do to change it. But know this. I will never forgive Rose for duping me, nor will I play the fool for her. She wanted to become my wife, and so she shall be, in every sense of the word."

Seething with fury, Dominic mounted his destrier.

"My lord," Starla called out, finally finding her voice. "Do not hurt my sister. She did naught but make it possible for me to pursue my dream. I will pray for her."

"Mayhap you should pray for me," Dominic replied. "I have to live with that harridan."

Touching his spurs to his destrier's sides, he thundered off.

"What do you suppose Rose did to anger him?" Starla asked as Dominic rode off in a cloud of dust.

Nelda heaved a rueful sigh. "Knowing our Rose, she could have said or done anything." She paused thoughtfully. "Why could she not have held her tongue a little longer? Despite the odds against their happiness, I feel that the match between Lord Dragon and Rose is a good one. I wonder which of them will recognize it first."

"I wonder who will kill the other first," Starla said dryly.

Dominic rode as if chased by the devil. He was angry. Damn angry. He had wanted Starla and through trickery had wed Rose, but truth to tell, seeing Starla again made him glad he had not married her. He thought he had wanted a submissive, unobtrusive wife but felt fortunate that he had not wed the pious twin. That did not mean, however, that he was any the less angry with Rose for making a fool of him.

"You will ride your horse to death if you do not slow down," Raj said as he caught up with Dominic.

Cursing his stupidity as well as his gullibility, Dominic pulled back on the reins. "I do not enjoy being tricked. She will pay, Raj. Aye, Rose will pay for her duplicity."

"The way I see it," Raj mused, "you got the best of the bargain. Piety belongs in the church, not the marriage bed."

"You are a wise man, Raj, but in this you are wrong. Rose must be shown the error of her ways. She knew what she was doing when she duped me into wedding her. She will accept me in her bed or suffer the consequences."

Raj chuckled. "You sound like a man eager to bed his wife, master."

" 'Tis my right. God's nightgown, man! Rose is my wife; she owes me her maidenhead."

"Think you she will surrender it without a fight?"

Dominic's expression turned feral. "She has no choice. Mayhap I will take her maidenhead, then send her to the convent with her mother and sister and fetch Lady Veronica to Dragonwyck. Now, there is a lady who knows how to please a man."

"If you say so, master," Raj said. "Were I you, I would not act precipitously. Pluck your Rose but have a care for her thorns. Mayhap, master," he said, sending Dominic an amused smile, "you will enjoy being pricked."

Dominic could not suppress the smile that lifted the corner of his mouth. "Mayhap you are right, Raj."

Rose was a nervous wreck that night. She had expected Dominic to appear for the evening meal, and when he did not, she was both worried and relieved at the same time. She was worried because she had no idea where Dragon had gone, and relieved because she did not have to sit beside him at the table and wonder if he would force her into his bed.

What would he do if she locked her door against him again tonight? she wondered. Would he break it down and take her roughly? She wouldn't put it past him to hurt her. Men could be beasts when thwarted.

Fortunately, Dragon did not appear and the meal progressed peacefully. Afterward, Rose and her ladies sat before the hearth in the solar, embroidering a new altar cloth for the chapel.

"Listen to the wind," Lady Emily said, looking up from her work. " 'Tis howling something fierce. It would not surprise me to wake up to snow tomorrow morning."

Lady Blythe yawned and stretched. "I am for bed, ladies."

After Lady Blythe left, Lady Emily folded up the cloth and set it aside. "Can I help you undress, Rose? Shall I summon Tyra?"

"Nay, thank you, I can manage on my own."

"Think you your husband will return tonight?"

"Since Lord Dragon did not see fit to tell me where he was going, I know not when he will return. He can stay away forever for all I care. Good night, Emily."

"Good night, Rose. Sleep well."

Rose undressed, washed and slid into bed, pulling the bed coverings up to her nose. The days and nights were growing colder, and the sound of the howling wind sent shivers down her spine. It would soon be Christmastide. She closed her eyes and remembered Christmas last, when her father was still alive. How happy they had been; how blessed and carefree.

Suddenly the joyous memory was shattered by Dragon's image, bringing to mind her father's untimely death and the fact that she had not been allowed to properly mourn him. So much had happened that she had not found the opportunity to shed tears for the exceptional man who had sired her and Starla and had loved them with his whole heart. Rose and Starla had been so fortunate to have Edwyn for a father. He had never complained about the lack of a son and had lavished his love upon his twin daughters equally. Now she would never know that love again.

A terrible grief consumed Rose as tears spilled from her eyes. They fell down her cheeks in a steady stream, soaking her pillow. Her sobs were loud and soul-wrenching, coming from deep within her. She cried until she had nothing left to give, and still she cried.

Tired and chilled to the bone by the raw wind, Dominic entered the keep and strode to the hearth to warm his hands. He was hungry, but saw that no one was awake to fix him a meal.

"Sit and warm yourself, master," Raj said. "I will fetch us something to eat from the kitchen."

"What would I do without you, Raj?" Dominic said as he pulled a chair close to the fire.

"That is something you will never have to worry about, master," Raj replied.

Dominic stared into the dancing flames, his thoughts suddenly consumed with Rose. He wondered if she was sleeping and imagined her tucked cozily into bed, waiting for him. His groin tightened as he imagined her nude body, warm and flushed from sleep. He shifted and adjusted his clothing as his cock began to thicken and harden. He hadn't had a woman since Veronica, and he needed one now.

Raj returned from the kitchen with a tray, shattering Dominic's erotic thoughts. Raj pulled a table over to the hearth, set the tray down and joined Dominic. Together they demolished a small round of cheese, thick hunks of bread, cold capon left over from the evening meal and slices of roast beef, quaffing ale between bites.

"Remind me to compliment the alewife on the excellence of the brew," Dominic said as he emptied the tankard.

"More, master?" Raj asked as he refilled his own tankard.

"Nay, I'm off to bed," Dominic said, rising. "Find your own bed, Raj. We've had a full day."

Dominic glanced toward the solar, wondering if Rose had locked him out again tonight. Anger rose inside him—anger and another, stronger emotion that sent hot blood pounding through his veins. Determination hardened his features as he strode up the stairs and marched resolutely along the gallery. He was in no mood to be thwarted, and woe to his wife if she locked the door against him tonight.

A grim smile curved his lips when the door to the sitting room opened at his touch. He advanced toward the bedchamber, ready to do battle if he found the door locked. His hand froze on the door latch when he heard heart-wrenching sobbing coming from inside the chamber.

Rose was crying! Crying as if her heart were breaking. Had something happened while he was gone?

Testing the door, he found it unlatched and pushed it open.

Rose could not stop crying. She had loved her father dearly and found it difficult to accept his death and all that had happened since. She was alone. Her mother and sister were gone, and her beloved home now belonged to a hard-hearted man who seemed to care naught about her grief or the loss she had suffered.

Rose was still sobbing uncontrollably when she heard the click of the door latch and the sound of footsteps. She suddenly recalled that she hadn't locked the door after Emily and Blythe left.

Rose sensed Dragon's presence, and a moment later a candle flame lit the chamber. He cleared his throat, the sound harsh and obtrusive in the waiting silence. She turned slowly and looked into his eyes. Dark currents swirled within their depths as he held her gaze. She shifted uncomfortably beneath his intense perusal and dashed away the tears dampening her cheeks.

The look in his eyes, his scent, the way he stared at her caused a stirring deep within her. His mouth was moving, but Rose heard naught above the pounding of her heart as treacherous warmth began to spread through her. She hated the feeling and called forth all the hatred she felt for the Dragon Lord.

"Did you not hear me? Why are you crying?" Dominic repeated.

Concentrating on his mouth, Rose finally heard what he was saying.

"What are you doing here?" she choked out.

"I belong here. This is the lord's solar, is it not?"

"Go away. I wish to mourn my father in private."

"Is that the reason for your tears?"

He sounded relieved, and that made Rose wary. "You did not allow me time for grieving."

Unable to stop herself, Rose burst into a fresh round of tears. Dominic muttered a curse. Then he settled beside her on the bed and awkwardly patted her shoulder.

"Wh . . . what are you . . . do . . . doing?" Rose hiccuped between sobs.

"Trying to comfort you," Dominic replied gruffly. "Your tears disturb me."

"Why do you care? You let the king murder my father."

"I did not even know your father."

Rose believed him, but it did not make her father's death any less difficult to bear, nor did it soften the blow of having her home possessed and renamed by the king's champion.

"I am fine now; you can leave," Rose said dismissively. She did not want this hard, overbearing man in her bedchamber. She had no intention of sharing her bed with him, or letting him use her to sate his lust.

Dominic paid scant heed to Rose's words. He had just become aware that she was naked beneath the covers. His hand on her shoulder stilled, his fingers tightening around the fragile bones. She was his wife. He could take her now with or without her consent. She belonged to him; her body was his to do with as he pleased.

He pulled her roughly into his arms, his body hardening with anticipation. Rose must have realized his intention, for she protested vigorously and pushed him away.

Her rejection made Dominic remember where he had been today and what he had learned. His temper flared and his grip tightened. "Do you know where I went today?"

"Nay. You did not see fit to tell me."

"I visited your mother and sister at the convent."

An involuntary cry escaped Rose's throat. "What did you do to them?"

Her words brought a scowl to Dominic's face. "What makes you think I harmed them? I admit I had good reason, but I have never hurt a woman before." His next words held a hint of menace. "Of course, I've never had a wife before."

Dominic would never intentionally hurt a woman, but Rose did not have to know that. His father had never raised a hand to his mother, though 'twas common knowledge that most men beat their wives.

"Why did you visit Mama and Starla?" Rose asked.

"To learn the truth." He glared at her. "*You* are not the sister I intended to wed. I realized I had been tricked when you locked me out of your bedchamber. Your sister would have been too frightened to defy me. My intended bride is wearing the white robes of a postulant, and the woman I rejected is now my wife. How do you explain that?"

He grasped her shoulders and dragged her against him. "Did you want me for yourself? Was that why you changed places with your sister?"

Her shout of denial did naught to allay the anger gnawing at him.

"How dare you suggest such a thing! I wed you to save my sister. She could not survive being wed to a man like you."

"And you could?" Dominic asked.

Her chin rose defiantly. "I think so. Starla is exactly where she wants to be, and I . . ."

His mouth hovered inches above hers. "And you, Rose? Are you where you want to be?"

"Nay, but better me than Starla or Mama."

Dominic's thoughts were drowned out by the frantic beating of his heart. Despite himself, the keen edge of his anger had lost its knife-like sharpness, and all he could think about was thrusting his cock inside Rose. His mouth descended on hers. Her lips were soft and warm and salty from her tears. He traced the shape with his tongue and sucked gently on her lower lip. She tried to pull away, but he would not allow it. He deepened the kiss, plunging his tongue into her mouth when she opened it to protest.

He enjoyed the taste and scent of her so much that he could not bring himself to stop. His kiss turned hard, demanding, but it was not enough. He ripped the cover away from her body, and his hands found her breasts. She fit his hands perfectly; the plump mounds were firm and pert, the nipples taut. If he did not taste one rosy tip now, he would surely perish. Breaking off the kiss, he lowered his head and sucked a puckered bud into his mouth while thrusting one hand between her clenched thighs and parting her pouting nether lips.

The sudden intake of her breath made his pulse beat harder.

"My lord, nay! Do not do this to me."

Dominic heard but did not respond. He could not stop. It seemed that all the blood in his body had collected in his groin and pounded there with burgeoning need. She felt hot and moist against his hand. His fingers moved, parted, eased inside her. He felt her stiffen, heard her sobbing. He groaned, wildly eager to thrust himself into her heated center. Her sobbing grew louder, and he lifted his head and stared into her eyes. He did not like what he saw there.

Tears spilled from their glittering depths and coursed down her cheeks. Her face was pale, and she was shaking. Was she afraid of him? No woman had ever been frightened of him. Men feared him, and rightly so, but women were different. He liked most of them, pleased all he had bedded, and they in turn vied for his attention. Taking a woman too frightened to respond did not appeal to him. He removed his hand from between Rose's legs and held her away from him.

"Why are you frightened? I know you are a virgin and I promise to be gentle. I am not a selfish lover, Rose. I give pleasure as well as receive it."

"Give it to your mistress. I want it not."

"My mistress is in London," Dominic said harshly. "Perhaps I should bring her to Dragonwyck to give me that which you deny me."

Dominic saw a flash of anger in her eyes and decided he could tolerate anger better than tears.

"Bring your mistress into my home, my lord, and I promise to make your life miserable," Rose responded.

Dominic's first inclination was to return her hostility with angry words, but instead he smiled. He did not doubt for one moment that Rose was fully capable of making him miserable in ways he could not even imagine. And for some unexplained reason, he would rather expend his energy taming his wild Rose than wallowing in the arms of his mistress.

"Go away, Lord Dragon," Rose insisted. "I need time to come to terms with the death of my father and our hasty marriage."

"How long, Rose?" Dominic demanded. "Will you ever come to terms with our marriage? I need an heir to assure the succession of Dragonwyck. You used trickery to become my wife; now act like one."

"I did not wed you because I wanted you," Rose retorted.

"Few women have the luxury of choosing their husbands. Most husbands and wives meet for the first time at the altar. Why should you be any different?"

Rose sat up and pulled the bed covering up to her chin. "You do not want me any more than I want you. You said so yourself."

Dominic made a dismissive motion with his hand. "What is done is done. Besides," he said, reaching beneath the covers to caress her breast, " 'tis my duty to consummate this marriage."

"Not tonight," Rose persisted, shoving his hand away. "Mayhap not ever."

Dominic rolled away from her and landed on his feet. "Have it your way, lady. You are right. You are not the woman I want. The woman I want resides in London. I have never had to force a woman and do not intend to start now. But one day, I vow I will have you beneath me, and though it will be an effort to make my cock rise to the occasion, I will do my best to do my duty by you."

Turning on his heel, he stormed from the chamber.

* * *

The relief Rose felt was not nearly as powerful as another emotion raging through her. The merciless Lord. Dragon had torn her pride to shreds. Obviously, he could stand her no more than she could tolerate him. There was only one reason he would condescend to consummate their marriage—to keep Dragonwyck and to get an heir. What really galled her was the knowledge that he would be thinking of another woman while bedding her.

She touched her lips. His kisses had seemed genuine enough, but a man with Dragon's experience could charm a woman into believing anything. Nay, Dragon wanted her not; he had made that abundantly clear.

Dominic's angry steps carried him back to the great hall. How could he let the termagant get under his skin? Why should he desire a woman who wanted naught to do with him? He had been tricked into wedding a woman whose disposition was as sour as bitter wine. Few men would tolerate a sharp-tongued wife. Rose deserved a good beating, but despite his reputation as a fierce warrior, Dominic had little inclination to administer it.

He sprawled in his chair and watched the flames turn to ashes in the hearth. The chamber was growing cold, and Dominic spit out a curse. What was he doing down here when a warm bed awaited him in the solar? He had no intention of spending another night sleeping in a chair before a dying fire. Only a fool or a coward would let his lawful wife ban him from his rightful place in her bed. His anger returned with a vengeance.

Had the servants been present to see the ferocious scowl on Dominic's face when he shoved himself to his feet and strode from the hall, they would have avoided him at all cost.

A muscle flexed in Dominic's jaw as he marched resolutely toward the solar and burst into the sitting room. A half dozen long strides took him to the bed-chamber door. He flung it open and stepped inside. The candle he had lit earlier had burned down to a stub, but he saw the bed and Rose's outline beneath the covers clearly enough. Without breaking stride, he approached the bed.

Rose was sleeping; she did not move despite the fact that he made little effort to be quiet. For one unsettling moment he wondered if she had cried herself to sleep. It should not matter to him, but for some unexplained reason it did. He was not completely lacking in compassion. He would feel just as Rose did if the king had executed his father. Too bad Lord Edwyn had not thought of his family when he committed treason.

Dominic began shedding his clothing, tossing his tunic, hose, braies and boots carelessly aside. Then he raised a corner of the covers and slid into bed beside Rose. The ropes protested the extra weight, but Rose did not stir when he took her into his arms. Warmth surrounded him. An irresistible aura of clean, sweet-smelling innocence enveloped him. His arms tight-ened. He could not remember feeling this possessive of anyone . . . including Veronica.

His eyes narrowed thoughtfully. Veronica had

aroused him to extraordinary passion and satisfied him sexually, but not once had he felt possessive of her.

It had to be his new demesne that gave him the sense of tranquillity and possessiveness, he decided scant moments before sleep claimed him. It most certainly had naught to do with his belligerent wife. Rose had more thorns than the flower for which she was named.

Chapter Four

You can complain because roses have thorns,
or you can rejoice because thorns have roses.
— Ziggy

Rose burrowed her body into the warmth at her back, unwilling to abandon the coziness of the bed yet, or even open her eyes. She sighed and wriggled closer to the solid heat behind her. Nothing was more satisfying than a warm bed on a cold day.

Rose had nearly dozed off again when a thought suddenly occurred to her and her eyes flew open. The heat at her back was too substantial, and something hard and foreign was pressing against her bottom. And suddenly she knew—she KNEW! She turned her head, saw Dragon lying beside her and tried to scramble away, but it was not to be. He grasped her about the waist and pulled her back into the cradle of his body.

"Where are you going, wife?"

Rose swallowed audibly. "What are you doing in my bed?" Her voice was hoarse from crying, and she hardly recognized the croaking sounds that came from her throat.

"This is where I belong." His hand slid upward to cup a firm breast.

"Do not touch me!"

" 'Tis my right to do whatever I please to you."

He trailed a hand over a curvaceous hip and flattened it against her taut stomach. Rose sucked in a startled breath when that same hand inched downward into the thatch of gold fleece crowning the juncture of her thighs.

Rose was not prepared for this. She knew Dragon had a legal right to claim her body, but she was not ready to surrender to the obnoxious blackguard. Unfortunately, her body turned traitor when he rolled her over to face him and forced her against his swollen sex. Heat crept through her veins and pooled in embarrassing places. Her breasts felt swollen and her nipples ached.

Then he kissed her, using his tongue in a way that made Rose feel things utterly foreign to her. He was nude. She was nude. Their bodies were all but glued together, and she felt his man part prodding ruthlessly against the secret place between her thighs. Why was her body reacting so powerfully to a man she did not and never would like? When he thrust his hand between her legs and tried to insert his fingers inside her, she reacted spontaneously. Gathering her strength, she rolled away so abruptly she caught Dominic off guard.

"Dammit! What are you doing?"

"Duty calls. My day begins at dawn."

Dominic's face hardened. "Your duty is to your husband."

Rose sent him a defiant look. "My duty is to Ayrdale and its people."

"You mean Dragonwyck, do you not?"

Rose wrinkled her nose. "Aye, Dragonwyck, if it pleases you. Turn your head, Lord Dragon, so that I may rise and dress."

Dominic's dark brows rose as he linked his hands behind his head and raked his gaze over her. "Go ahead, wife. Watching you dress gives me pleasure. But," he added sternly, "my patience will stretch only so far. I would have already bedded your sister had you not interfered. The least you can do is accept the consequences of your hoax. You are extremely fortunate, Rose, that I did not beat you."

Her shoulders stiffened. "I prefer a beating to what you want to do to me."

"Do not tempt me," Dominic bit out. "Rest assured that what I have in mind will be much more pleasurable than a beating."

He reached for her, but she deftly eluded him. She inched out of bed, trying to drag the linen sheet with her, but Dominic would not release his hold. Her body flushed red from embarrassment and anger, Rose rolled out of bed and reached for her shift.

Dominic watched through lowered lids as Rose fumbled with her clothing. He had awakened before her this morning and watched her sleep. With her golden hair spread out on the pillow and a fetching half-smile on her face, she looked like an angel instead of the prickly harridan he knew her to be. It had taken considerable willpower to keep from pulling her beneath him and taking her virginity before she awakened.

When she'd burrowed her bottom against his loins, his cock had stiffened and he'd sought to arouse her so that she would want him in the same way he wanted her. But Rose was either too stubborn or too frightened to let him pleasure her. How long did she think she could deny him? He did not want to force her, but his patience was wearing thin.

Dominic's dark eyes glittered with renewed desire as he watched Rose struggle into her shift. Her breasts were magnificent, high and firm and just the right size to fit his rather large hands. He had already taken measure of her tiny waist and gently rounded hips, but this was the first time he had glimpsed what his hands had discovered, and he wasn't disappointed.

Dominic groaned aloud when her shift slid into place, hiding her considerable charms from his avid gaze. He had half a notion to leap from bed and pull her beneath him before she finished dressing, and he might have done so had he not been interrupted by a knock at the door.

Rose scrambled into her tunic, adjusted it about her body and looked askance at Dominic. "Go ahead and open it," Dominic said. " 'Tis probably Raj. He is the only one brave enough to invade the Dragon's lair."

Rose opened the door. Raj stepped inside and peered around her at Dominic. "Is the master ready to rise? Petitioners from the villages have gathered in the inner bailey, waiting for you to begin the manor court. Their old lord has been gone a long time, and they want their new lord to rule on their grievances and mete out punishment."

Dominic rose from bed with easy grace, his powerful muscles rippling beneath the skin of his nude body as he reached for his clothing. Rose took one look at him and ran out the door.

"What did you do to frighten your new wife?" Raj asked with a hint of amusement.

"Not what I'd like to do to her, my friend," Dominic retorted. "She's as skittish as a newborn colt."

Raj looked at him in astonishment. "You left her untouched?"

"You ask too many questions," Dominic said with ill-disguised rancor.

A chuckle rumbled from Raj's massive chest. "I have never known a lady you could not charm into your bed."

" 'Tis obvious you have never known a woman of Rose's ilk. She is no Veronica."

"Mayhap one day you will be glad she is not," Raj observed.

"What the hell is that supposed to mean? You know I planned to marry Veronica."

Raj assumed a subservient demeanor that fooled no one, least of all Dominic. "Forgive me for speaking out of turn, master. Shall I inform the petitioners that you will hold court after you have broken your fast?"

Dominic waved Raj away. "Aye, I will hear their petitions. 'Tis my duty as their new lord. Tell the steward to fetch his quill and ink to record my rulings."

Dominic washed and dressed, momentarily forgetting the vassals waiting for him below. His head spun with thoughts of Rose. Her soft breasts, her slim figure, the lush curve of her lips, the tight furrow between her legs he hoped to plow very soon. His cock jerked in response to his erotic imaginings, and he quickly stifled the excitement bubbling up inside him. It would not do for the people of Dragonwyck to see the Dragon Lord lusting after his own wife.

Rose was nowhere about as Dominic broke his fast, so he joined a group of knights at one of the trestle tables and was soon caught up in their conversation. After Dominic had eaten, Braden, the steward, joined him with a fresh supply of parchment, sharpened quills and ink. While Dominic presided over the manor court, Braden was to record the resolution of the cases. Before he began the court, Dominic asked Raj to summon Rose. She appeared a few minutes later, obviously surprised by the summons.

"You sent for me, my lord?" she asked curtly.

"Aye. You are lady of the manor and should sit beside me during the manor court. You know your people better than I and may be of some help in resolving the cases."

Dominic seated Rose, then settled himself in the ornately carved lord's chair beside her. The doors were opened, and a crowd of petitioners and their witnesses flowed into the great hall. One by one the vassals presented their cases. Dominic fined a man who stole his neighbor's pig, ordered another to marry a young woman who was expecting his child and negotiated a peaceful settlement between two freemen feuding over a land boundary. And so the morning went.

Rose listened with growing amazement as Dragon handled the minor and major infractions with a fairness and finesse she could scarcely credit. Not even her father could have done so well. But that did not mean she approved of Dragon. No indeed, there was very little Dragon could do to make her like him or convince her to let him bed her. He was the king's man, and the king had killed her father.

"What think you, my lady?" Dominic said, pulling Rose from her silent musings.

"About what, my lord?"

"Were you not listening? One of our villeins begs permission to wed a freeman's daughter. As you know, such unions are frowned upon."

"Do you love one another?" Rose asked the couple standing before them.

The woman, no more than a girl really, nodded shyly, but the man said loudly, "Aye, my lady."

"What think you, my lady?" Dominic asked Rose. "If I allow them to wed, the freeman's daughter will lose her status."

"Your name is Vella, is it not?" Rose asked the girl.

"Aye, my lady."

"Well, Vella, are you willing to accept the consequences of wedding a villein?"

"Aye, my lady. My station in life matters not to me."

"It matters to me," an older man said, stepping forward. "I did not raise my daughter to wed a villein."

"You are the girl's father?" Dominic asked.

"Aye, my lord. My name is Algar, and I have chosen

another husband for Vella—a freeman who can give her a better life. He can afford to give me the pig I'm asking as a bride's price."

"I do not want to marry David," Vella protested. She clutched the young villein's arm. "I will have no one but Piers."

"I have no pig to give your father," Piers said sadly, "nor a cottage as fine as the one David owns."

Dominic stroked his chin, regarding the couple through narrowed lids. At length he said, "I am inclined to rule in the father's favor."

Vella looked so disheartened that Rose felt obliged to speak up. "You could free Piers, my Lord Dragon."

Dominic looked at her as if she had lost her mind. "That would set a precedent that could have disastrous results. Every villein of marriageable age would begin courting daughters of freemen in order to raise their status."

Rose knew Dragon was being practical, but the couple looked so much in love she could not bear to see them separated. "Master Algar, would you allow your daughter to wed Piers if he had Lord Dragon's permission and offered a pig *and* a cow for her?"

"Careful, Rose," Dominic warned.

"A pig *and* a cow, my lady?" Algar asked, his eyes bulging greedily. "Piers has neither a pig nor a cow."

"Just answer my question, Algar, and let me worry about the rest."

"You are treading on dangerous ground, Rose," Dominic growled. "The decision is mine to make."

"I am mistress here," Rose argued, "and I have a pig and a cow I wish to present to Piers."

"My lady!" Piers gasped, clearly startled. "Truly?"

Dominic's mouth flattened. "My lady wife speaks out of turn."

"Look at them, my lord. They are in love," Rose argued.

"I am surprised you hold love in such high esteem, madam." He searched her face. "Has someone claimed your heart?"

Rose met his penetrating glance with raised eyebrows. "My heart is still unengaged and likely to remain that way as long as I am married to you."

"One day your sharp tongue will be your undoing," Dominic cautioned.

Deliberately ignoring him, Rose returned her attention to the couple anxiously awaiting Dominic's judgment. "Piers and Vella await your answer, my lord. Will you allow them to wed if I provide Vella's bride price?"

A crafty smile curved Dominic's lips. "That depends, my prickly wife," he whispered into her ear, "on whether or not you intend to honor your wedding vows tonight."

Rose went still. The man was ruthless; she should have known he would use underhanded means to get what he wanted. What she could not understand, however, was why he wanted her when he loved another. Was his sexual appetite so voracious that he needed more than one woman to satisfy him? Or did he want her simply to finalize their marriage?

"What say you, madam?" Dominic asked. "Will you force me to consummate our marriage in a way you will not enjoy, or will you give yourself to me like a dutiful wife?"

Rose longed to tell Dragon she wanted naught to do with him, but one look at Piers's and Vella's expectant faces changed her mind. She did not have the heart to disappoint the thwarted lovers; she would give Dragon her body but naught else of herself.

"You win, my lord," Rose murmured. "Give the couple your blessing."

Dominic felt like crowing. His stubborn wife had finally capitulated, and tonight he would have her beneath him. Though he had been tricked into wedding the wrong woman, he was determined to get some enjoyment from this unfortunate marriage.

Reluctantly Dominic turned his salacious thoughts from Rose's voluptuous body to his vassals.

"Think well on this before you answer, Algar. Will you accept Piers as your daughter's husband if he can pay the bride's price?"

Algar's assessing gaze traveled along the length of Piers's muscular young body. "He does have a strong back, my lord, and mayhap can be of some help since I have no sons. David is spindly and frail and would likely be of little help to me. Aye, if Piers can pay the bride's price, I will accept him."

"Then so be it," Dominic said. "You will have your pig and cow before Father Nyle blesses the union."

Vella fell to her knees before Rose and touched the hem of her skirt. "Thank you, my lady. I will never forget your kindness."

"Nor will I," Piers echoed, dropping down beside Vella and touching his head to Dominic's feet.

The next petitioners took their place and the court continued. Rose listened closely to Dominic's rulings but did not interfere again. No man could have done a better job of impartially meting out punishment or dispensing justice. But that still didn't make their marriage any more palatable to her. Rose's father had promised her that she need not wed where she did not love, and she had hoped one day to meet a man she could love and who loved her in return. Never in her wildest dreams had she imagined she would be forced to call a man like Dominic Dragon husband.

Dominic rose stiffly, declaring the court adjourned. Immediately servants appeared to prepare the hall and set up tables for the noon meal. Dominic grasped Rose's elbow and led her toward the solar.

Rose resisted, trying without success to pull away from his grasp. "Where are you taking me?"

"To consummate our marriage."

"Now?" Rose squeaked. "The noon meal will be served soon."

"I will order something sent up to the solar."

They had just reached the staircase when Lady Emily hailed Rose. "Rose, come quickly. Cook and Lord Dragon's man are engaged in an altercation and I fear they will kill one another."

"Raj is arguing with the cook?" Dominic repeated. "I will come with you."

"Nay," Rose demurred. "The kitchen is my domain. I will take care of it."

Rose hurried off, leaving a disgruntled Dominic in her wake. He watched her flounce off, her skirts swirling about a pair of shapely ankles. Charming women into his bed had never been a problem for him, but then, he had never encountered a woman like Rose before.

Rose hurried to the kitchen, grateful for the reprieve. She knew she would not always be so fortunate, that ultimately Dragon would have his way with her, but she wasn't ready to surrender her body to a man she barely knew.

Rose heard the shouting as she burst into the kitchen, fearing she was too late to stop the carnage. She laughed aloud at the scene she had interrupted. The diminutive cook, brandishing an iron skillet, was holding her ground against Dragon's giant. Hands on hips, Raj towered over Cook, a menacing look on his face as he bared his teeth at the woman.

Jumping into the fray, Rose asked, "Is there a problem?"

It took a moment for the combatants to realize they were not alone, but when they did, Cook lowered the skillet, though her expression remained belligerent as Raj stepped away.

"This overgrown lummox is trying to tell me how to prepare His Lordship's food," Cook complained. "I have been cooking for the Lord of Ayrdale many years, my lady, and do not need lessons from a foreign devil."

"My master has a discriminating palate," Raj declared. "I have been overseeing the preparation of his food since the Crusade and do not intend to stop now."

"And I will have no heathen foreigner in my kitchen," Cook declared staunchly.

"Can we not settle this peacefully?" Rose asked. "How about a compromise?"

"No compromise," Cook declared. "Mayhap you should find another cook, my lady. Let the heathen do the cooking if he is so anxious to supervise Lord Dragon's meals."

Raj drew himself up to his full, impressive height. "I do not cook. I merely oversee the preparation of my master's food."

Rose was ready to throw up her hands when Dominic strolled into the kitchen. "I heard the shouting. What seems to be the trouble?"

At this point, Rose was more than happy to let Dominic handle the fracas. With a minimum of words, she explained the situation.

"I appreciate your concern, Raj," Dominic said, "but I am well satisfied with the quality and quantity of food served at Dragonwyck. Should I become dissatisfied, you may intervene, but until then, there are other areas in which I need your expertise."

"If that is your wish, master, then of course I will obey." Turning on his heel, Raj strode off with his dignity intact, but not before aiming an intimidating look at Cook over his massive shoulder.

"Thank ye, Lord Dragon," Cook said adoringly. "With that great buffoon gone, I can get on with the noon meal. I hope ye and the mistress enjoy it."

"I'm sure we will," Dominic said. He ushered Rose back to the hall, seated her at the head table and settled into the chair beside her.

"Your reprieve will be short-lived, Rose," Dominic murmured. "While you were in the kitchen, I learned that Murdoc MacTavish is on his way to Dragonwyck. My border guards report that MacTavish and a large number of his kinsmen have just crossed the border and are heading in this direction. He probably heard about your father's death and is coming to claim Dragonwyck."

"Uncle Murdoc has no claim to Ayrdale, or Dragonwyck, as you prefer to call my home."

"He would if you were to wed one of his kinsmen," Dominic ventured. His intense gaze bored into her. "Even Father Nyle would agree that an unconsummated marriage has no legal status. MacTavish must be given no reason to seize Dragonwyck because of a technicality. You are the eldest daughter, are you not?"

"Aye, I am Father's heir."

"Then you understand why our marriage must be consummated at once. 'Twould be disastrous to England should a Scotsman gain control of Dragonwyck."

Rose winced. She knew Dominic loved another woman, but did he have to be so blatantly truthful? His words made it abundantly clear that bedding her was a duty he must perform for England and his king. Obviously, he found her not in the least desirable.

"Rose, did you not hear me? A Scotsman cannot be allowed to gain a foothold on English soil."

"I heard you," Rose muttered. "I regret that you find your duty so distasteful."

Dominic's dark brows shot upward. "You are putting words in my mouth."

" 'Tis the truth, but I have a solution. Let our marriage remain unconsummated and I will lie to Uncle

Murdoc about it. Only you and I need ever know the truth."

Dominic speared a roasted pigeon from a platter and placed it on his plate. Rose waited with bated breath as he put a succulent morsel in his mouth and chewed with obvious relish.

"Well?" Rose asked with growing impatience. "What say you, my lord?"

"About what?" Dominic answered.

Impossible man! "Did you not hear me? I offered a solution to our dilemma."

"What you suggest is no solution at all, nor do I perceive a dilemma. Your servants have doubtless noticed the lack of virgin's blood on your bedding. By now the entire keep is aware that you are still untouched."

Spots of color appeared on Rose's cheeks. She had not thought of that. "I do not believe you."

Dominic shrugged. "Ask your ladies if you do not believe me."

Rose fell silent as she contemplated Dragon's words.

After the meal, Dominic went to inspect the fortifications, leaving Rose mired in her dark thoughts. Deciding to follow Dragon's advice, she sought out Emily and Blythe and invited them to the solar.

Once they were seated before the hearth, Rose blurted out, "You are the only ones I can confide in. Have either of you heard gossip concerning my . . . my . . . virgin state?"

Blythe blushed and looked away, leaving the older and wiser Emily to provide the answer to Rose's question.

"I cannot lie, Rose," Emily said. "Tyra noted the lack of blood on your bedding when she changed the bed linen, and you know how servants gossip. Besides," she said, shrugging, " 'tis common knowledge that Lord Dragon slept in the hall on his wedding night."

"He was in my bed the following night," Rose maintained.

"Without proof, everyone will assume you were not a virgin when Lord Dragon took you," Blythe dared to suggest.

The conversation was becoming too personal for Rose's liking, so she changed the subject. "Did you know Uncle Murdoc is on his way to Dragonwyck?"

"Aye, Eric told me that Lord Dragon believes your uncle intends to claim your father's holdings."

"I know," Rose said.

"Lord Dragon has naught to worry about if your marriage is legally consummated," Emily asserted. "I know you do not care for Lord Dragon, but women are rarely consulted when it comes to marriage. My own marriage was arranged, but I learned to love Eric. Perhaps it will be the same with you."

"Dragon loves another," Rose contended. "All I will ever be to him is the mother of his legal children."

"Think you he has bastards by his mistress?" Blythe ventured.

"Veronica has borne me no bastards," Dominic said from the doorway. "Excuse me, ladies, my wife and I wish to be alone."

Emily and Blythe made a hasty exit. Dominic closed the door firmly behind them and leaned against it. Rose stared at him, unable to direct her gaze elsewhere. He was Satan incarnate, she thought, with his dark hair, diabolical smile and soul-piercing gaze.

"What do you want?" Rose asked, backing away.

He pushed himself away from the door. "Tell me about your uncle. Is he as greedy as I have heard? How will he react to our marriage?"

"I haven't seen Uncle Murdoc in several years. He and my father were at odds over a piece of borderland both claimed. The land actually belonged to Father, but Uncle Murdoc wanted it. Mother brought it to the marriage with her, but Uncle Murdoc refused to accept that it no longer belonged to him.

"As for his reaction to our marriage, I know not what to tell you except that Uncle Murdoc once tried to talk Father into betrothing me to his stepson. Fortunately, Father rejected the betrothal."

"Ah, that explains a great deal. Obviously Murdoc does not know that I am the new lord and your husband." He gave her a look that sent shivers of apprehension down her spine. He stalked toward her and offered his hand.

Rose stared at his hand but made no move to take it. "Surely you do not expect . . .'tis still daylight. The servants will talk."

"Think you I care? Our marriage *will* be consummated before your uncle arrives. I have been tricked, goaded and denied my rights by a woman who duped me into marrying the wrong sister. This is no longer about what I want or what you want but what is best for England."

"England, bah! I care naught about a country or king that values human life so little. The king executed my father without just cause, leaving a grieving widow and two children behind to fend for themselves."

"You are wrong on both counts, Rose. Your father plotted treason. He tried to rally the barons against King John. And you were not left defenseless. I am your protection."

"The king *should* be removed from the throne," Rose retorted. "He is a menace to England."

Dominic grasped her shoulders and gave her an ungentle shake. "Be careful what you say, wife. One never knows who might be listening. I am well aware that the king's justice tends to be harsh. He is a man who enjoys torturing his enemies. Let my words serve as a warning. No matter how you feel about the king, keep your thoughts to yourself."

Rose went very still. "That sounds like a threat, my lord."

"Take it any way you want. I would not like to see you become a victim of John's cruel nature."

"Like my father," Rose whispered.

"Aye, like your father."

He did not offer his hand again. Instead, he swept her into his arms and strode determinedly toward the bedchamber. The door was ajar and he kicked it open, then banged it shut with his boot heel. He carried her to the bed, pulled back the covering and dropped her onto the pristine sheets. Rose stared up at him and shuddered. His expression was determined, inflexible. Realizing the futility of resisting, she went limp. He could take her without her permission, but she did not have to like it.

Chapter Five

Live now, believe me, wait not for tomorrow;
Gather the roses of life today.
—Pierre de Ronsard

More than a little annoyed, Dominic stared down at
Rose's limp body. He wanted more than she was offering; he wanted a responsive woman capable of passion. The woman lying on the bed with her eyes closed
and her fists clenched held little resemblance to the
warrior woman he'd first encountered.

"Open your eyes, Rose," he demanded harshly.
"Look at me and tell me you find me repulsive. You
don't strike me as a woman who fears a man."

Rose's eyes opened slowly. Surprisingly, they were
not filled with fear as Dominic had expected. Nay, they
glowed with defiance, and for some reason that

pleased Dominic. Better defiance than fear.

"I'm going to make love to you, Rose. If you give yourself over to me, I vow you will enjoy it."

"Why do you care? 'Tis Veronica you want, not me."

He found her hand and dragged it against his groin. "My cock wants you."

She pulled her hand away. "My lord—"

"Dominic. My name is Dominic."

"Dominic, can we not wait until tonight?"

He grasped the hem of her over-tunic and tugged it upward. "I want you now, Rose. Raise your arms."

When she failed to respond, Dominic took matters into his own hands, stripping her over-gown from her and tossing it aside. He started to do the same with her under-gown, but she stayed his hands. "I will do it," she bit out.

"Nay, I *want* to do it," Dominic said, impatiently shoving her hands aside. "Let me."

Rose was wrong to believe he did not want her. He *did* want her, more than he should, more than was prudent. And he certainly did not need to think about Veronica to become aroused. The truth was that he had wanted Rose from the beginning but had chosen to wed her sister because he feared Rose was the kind of woman he could not ignore, while the submissive twin would demand naught from him.

Dominic removed Rose's under-gown, his gaze riveted on her slender form, scantily clad in a thin shift. He gaped at her breasts. They were the finest Dominic had ever seen. There was something arousing about a half-clad woman, but right now he wanted Rose naked.

101

"Your shift," he rasped. "Remove it."

Rose swallowed audibly. "Will you not allow me a shred of dignity?"

His heated gaze raked over her. "Nakedness has its own dignity."

Her eyes downcast, Rose pulled her shift over her head and used it to cover her private parts. With a low-pitched growl, Dominic tugged the shift from her nerveless fingers and flung it away. Then he rocked back and simply stared at her.

"You are magnificent," he said with a hoarseness that betrayed his need. "I am well pleased."

"Think you I care?" Rose shot back. "Go ahead and do what you must. There is naught I can do to stop you."

A pang of guilt shot through Dominic. But he shoved it aside when he recalled that Rose had brought this on herself when she had duped him into wedding her. Still, he did not wish to cause her unnecessary pain. He wondered if she would feel more kindly toward him if he gave her pleasure. It was worth a try, he decided. He hated the thought of spending the rest of his life shackled to a woman who despised him.

Dominic stripped off his tunic, then his shirt. "Why would you want to stop me when I intend to give you pleasure? I am not going to beat you into submission, if that is what you fear." He gave her a cocky grin. "Very soon you will be panting and begging for my attention."

Rose gave an unladylike snort. "Not in this life."

He released the ties on his braies and let them drop, then removed his boots and peeled off his hose. An arrogant grin curving his lips, he posed before her, his rampant cock pulsing hard and thick against his taut belly. He scowled when he realized that Rose was staring at the battle scar that curled along his leg from knee to hipbone, her eyes wide with shock.

"Does the scar repulse you?" he asked sardonically.

She shook her head. "The wound must have given you a great deal of pain."

It took a moment to realize that Rose was not looking at him with revulsion; she was staring at him with a mixture of awe and curiosity.

"It still gives pain when the weather turns bitter, but otherwise bothers me little."

Her gaze drifted downward to his rampant sex, then swept upward, a startled look on her face. "You will kill me with that . . . that thing between your legs."

Dominic laughed aloud. "I think not. Have you never seen an unclothed male before?"

"I am a virgin," Rose said indignantly. "Had I known what awaited me in the marriage bed, I would have joined Mama and Starla in the convent."

Dominic sat on the edge of the bed and eased her over to make room for him. Idly he caressed her breast. "I wonder, will you express those same sentiments after we make love?"

"Like most men, you think too much of yourself. Just get on with it."

"Nay, my thorny Rose. I am proud of my ability to arouse a woman to passion, and I am not going to hurry or let you talk me out of making you want me."

"I am your wife, not your mistress. I do not have to want you."

His gaze traveled the length of her nude body. "Aye, you *are* my wife," he said possessively.

It was true. Rose *was* his. Her body was appealing in every way, even though she was not as voluptuous as Veronica. Dominic had never thought Veronica lacking until he had seen Rose in all her nude glory. He ached to be inside her, to feel her wetness bathe him, but he wasn't going to let his lust get in the way of proving that he could make her hot for him.

He caressed her breasts, paying special attention to her rosy nipples, brushing his palms against them until they beaded into taut little buds. He thought he heard her gasp, but when he looked into her face, she appeared distracted instead of aroused, while he was submerged in lust.

His lips found hers unerringly. They tasted so sweet, his cock swelled harder and thicker. He felt a soft puff of breath escape from between her lips, felt her mouth soften beneath his, and exulted. Rose was not as unresponsive as she would like him to believe. He backed off a little and looked down at her. Her eyes were glazed over and she wore a dazed expression.

"Open your mouth, Rose."

"Why?"

"Don't argue, just do it." He wanted to put his tongue inside her first, then his cock. He wanted to fill her with every part of himself.

Her lips parted, just a bit, but enough for Dominic to thrust his tongue inside the opening and taste her. He kissed her boldly, thoroughly, demanding more of her than she offered. He kissed her until he felt her soft body trembling beneath him. Then he broke off the kiss and whispered into her ear, "Put your arms around me."

Rose had no idea why she obeyed, but her arms slid over the hot, damp skin of his shoulders. She stared up at him, her thoughts tumbling one after another inside her head. The sight of his nude body made her tremble. A tingling sensation lanced through her. Wide of shoulder and broad of chest, he exuded strength and power, like the dark, raging dragon for which he was named. And when he touched her breasts, she had to clench her teeth to keep from moaning.

Curiously, Dragon's scar did not repulse her. She thought about the pain he must have suffered during his recovery and how remarkable it was that he had survived so dreadful a wound.

Even more remarkable were his kisses; they set her blood afire and curled her toes. How could a man she did not like make her tremble like a leaf in the wind simply by touching her and kissing her?

Rose feared she had spoken aloud when Dominic lifted his head and asked, "Do you still hate me, Rose?"

With an emotion almost like despair, Rose acknowledged to herself that it was difficult to hate a man when he was making such sweet love to her. She was so thoroughly mesmerized by his kisses, she could not think clearly. He had touched a passion in her that she never knew existed.

When Rose did not answer, Dragon kissed her again, roughly, his mouth going from gently coaxing to fiercely possessive to demanding. She could not help responding, her mouth moved under his and her lips parted. His tongue thrust into her mouth at the same time as he parted her thighs and slid between them. Rose nearly jumped out of her skin when she felt his hand stroke the soft folds between her legs.

"Let me love you, Rose," Dominic whispered into her ear. "Let yourself feel pleasure."

"Not with you. Never," Rose gasped, though it cost her dearly. Resisting Dragon was not as easy as she had expected. His skin beneath her hands was hot and taut and hair-roughened. Not an unpleasant feeling, but she did not want to like touching him as much as she did.

With a will of their own, her hands moved upward into the dark silk of his hair. He groaned and dropped his head against her chest. Then she felt his mouth on her breasts and could not prevent the soft little sigh that slipped past her lips. The sigh turned into a muted cry when he took one nipple into his mouth and suckled her. Pleasure spiraled through her.

"This . . . has to be . . . a sin," she gasped.

Dominic raised his head. "Why?"

"Because it feels so . . ."

". . . good?" He chuckled. " 'Tis just the beginning."

As if to prove his words, Dominic's mouth trailed a path of fire between her breasts, across her ribs and down her belly. Rose made a mewling sound and arched against him. Never in her wildest dreams had she imagined herself acting the wanton for a man she scarcely knew. What was wrong with her? Women were not supposed to enjoy the marriage bed. Obviously, her inexperience was telling, and Dragon was taking advantage of it. He seemed to know exactly where and how to touch her body to elicit the most response from her.

Suddenly Dragon's mouth began moving downward along her belly, toward the thatch of hair crowning her woman's mound. A startled cry left her lips when he placed a kiss there. She had never thought a man would want to kiss a woman *there*. But obviously Dominic had more than kissing in mind, for he parted her with his fingers and ran his tongue along her cleft.

"Dominic, nay! Cease!"

"Not yet," he moaned as he continued to tease and torment her with his tongue.

Rose tried to shove him away, but he grasped her hands and held them. As desperately as she wanted him gone, there was something she wanted even more, though she could not put a name to it. Her body was thrumming, her head spinning and her flesh burning. Madness, pure madness!

She was panting and writhing beneath him, incapable of thinking. She wanted . . . something, but it slithered out of reach. She thought she had almost found it when suddenly Dragon removed his mouth, leaving her wanting and needy.

"Dominic, don't stop!" He had reduced her to begging, just as he'd predicted.

Slowly he moved up her body. She felt his arousal prodding the opening between her thighs and closed her eyes. After he took her she would never be the same. The thought fled when he began kissing her like one would expect a lover to kiss his beloved. Before she was ready to let him go, he broke off the kiss and raised his head, watching her, his face close to hers. His fingers glided over the tangled mass of her bright hair, drifted downward along her temple to her cheekbone. His fingertip touched her chin, raising it.

"You know what is going to happen now, do you not?" he whispered hoarsely.

"I . . . think so." She suspected how the act was accomplished but knew nothing beyond that.

"I'll try to make it as painless as possible. I never want to hurt you."

Dominic placed his hands beneath Rose's hips and caressed the honeyed warmth between her legs with the tip of his cock, readying her for his entrance. He was so hot, so hard, so ready, he feared he would lose control before giving Rose pleasure. He lowered his head to kiss her breasts, warm and damp with a woman's sweet fragrance, a scent that sent him headlong toward consummation. He felt himself tremble at her cleft, heard her moan, and sank into her velvety folds. He paused a breathless moment at her maidenhead, then breached it with a single stroke.

The soft intake of her breath turned into a moan of pain; he felt her stiffen, felt a tremor run through her, and waited a moment for her to adjust to the feel of him inside her. Then his control shattered. Flexing his hips, he moved deeper. He hoped he had not hurt her too badly, but he did not regret taking her. She was incredibly hot and tight, and if he was not mistaken, she was beginning to enjoy it as much as he.

* * *

Rose released a shuddering sigh. The sense of invasion was beginning to abate as his movements eased something tight and tense within her. With a choked gasp, she strained against him, clutching at his shoulders to anchor her to sanity. She felt his muscles flex and grow taut as he pounded into her, filling her so fully she feared she would burst. The pain had all but disappeared now, replaced by a slowly building pressure that filled her senses. Her body was thrumming; responding, reaching for a culmination that was surrounded in mystery.

"You feel incredible," Dragon whispered against her mouth. "So tight, so hot."

Rose knew how incredible *he* felt, driving into her like a roaring tide, bringing her closer and closer to that elusive peak. He bent his head to taste her mouth, stabbing his tongue into her in perfect rhythm with his thrusting hips.

When the explosion hit her, she was ill prepared for the tumult of white-hot heat and the shattering power that spiraled through her, in her, around her.

She cried out his name as he drove into her one last time, his body convulsing as he spilled his seed inside her. After a long, suspenseful silence, he said, "Had I known a virgin could give me so much pleasure, I would not have waited so long to take one."

Dominic's words were like a splash of cold water in Rose's face. She had given him pleasure, but any virgin would have sufficed. The arrogant bastard! She shoved him away, and he withdrew. The ropes beneath the mattress protested loudly as he collapsed on the bed beside her.

"Leave now," Rose demanded. " 'Tis over. You have done your worst."

Dominic rolled up on his elbow, his brow furrowed. "Did I hurt you? I know I gave you pleasure, too. A man can tell those things."

"I was not looking for pleasure," Rose shot back.

"Stop pretending, my prickly Rose. Once I got past the thorns, I found something rare and inspiring, something I did not expect. There is passion in your body and hot blood running through your veins. I believe we will deal reasonably well with one another. At least in bed," he added.

Rose reached for the bedcover and pulled it up to her neck. "I do not want to deal with you at all, in any way or form."

Dominic grasped the cover and pulled it away. "Hiding yourself from me will do naught but anger me."

"Will you beat me?" Rose challenged pugnaciously.

Dominic's mouth flattened. "Do not tempt me, madam. You do seem in need of a good beating."

"Tempting you is the last thing I want to do," Rose charged. "May I get out of bed now that you have had your way with me?"

"Aye, but from now on we will share a bed. With your uncle on the way to claim Dragonwyck, I want no one, least of all MacTavish, to question the legality of our marriage."

Pulling the cover about her body, Rose scooted to the edge of the bed and sat up before Dragon could change his mind. She did not want him to touch her again. Had she known his touch would trample her will and affect her in ways that made a shambles of her resolve, she would have fled to the convent with her mother and sister. She did not want to like the Dragon Lord, nor did she wish to become a victim of his lust.

Rose left the bed and reached for her discarded clothing. A feeling of stickiness between her thighs caused her to look down. She saw blood staining her thighs and cried out.

"Oh, no!"

Instantly alert, Dominic leaped from bed. "What is it? Are you hurt?"

"Nay! Stay away. I . . . there is blood. It startled me."

Dominic lifted her into his arms and carried her back to the bed. "Did your mother not explain that there would be blood?"

"There was no time. I did not come to the marriage bed totally ignorant but . . ." She turned her face away. "I never suspected . . ."

Dominic poured water into a basin and dipped a cloth into it. Rose stared at him warily when he returned with the cloth and gently spread her legs. When she realized what he intended, her face flamed and she tried to hold her legs together.

"Relax, Rose, I will not hurt you."

Rose was having none of it; her thighs remained locked together. Dominic pried them apart with little effort. Rose hid her face as he ran the wet cloth over her tender flesh, cleansing her. When he finished, he returned the cloth to the basin and stared down at her.

Rose willed herself not to look at Dragon, but her contrary mind refused to obey. Oblivious of his own nudity, Dragon stood over her, hands on hips, legs

111

splayed wide. Her gaze roved freely over broad shoulders, massive chest and powerful arms and legs, noting each and every battle scar that marred his hair-roughened skin. That he had survived countless battles was evident. She gasped in dismay when she saw his male part stir and begin a slow rise upward.

"Keep looking at me like that and 'tis unlikely we will leave this room any time soon."

Rose flushed and looked away. What was wrong with her? Her ruthless husband had just ravished her; she should be looking at him with revulsion instead of admiration.

"I did . . . did not mean . . ." she stammered.

His voice held a bitter edge. "Of course you did not. 'Tis too much to hope that you would welcome me into your bed." He turned away and began pulling on his hose. "We must make the best of this marriage, Rose. Neither of us is wed to a mate of our own choosing, but I suspect it will not be as bad as we expected if we keep out of one another's way during the day." He grinned at her over his shoulder. "The best will come when we retire to our chamber."

Rose said nothing. Dragon thought too much of himself and his ability to beguile women. She knew about his mistress, knew he did not care for her, so why did he pretend? How could her innocence please him when he had known women with considerably more knowledge about sexual matters than she ever wanted to know?

"There is much to do before your uncle arrives," Dominic said once he had finished dressing. "He brings a large fighting force with him."

"Uncle Murdoc always brings a large number of clansmen when he comes to visit," Rose offered. "We had no reason to fear him while my father was alive."

"I do not fear him," Dominic replied. He reached for the door handle. "We will talk later, Rose."

Leaving Rose lying in bed all warm and flushed was not easy for Dominic. His prickly bride had surprised him. She might have been unwilling in the beginning, but her responsive body had melted in his arms. She pleased him so well that he had not once compared her to Veronica.

Raj met Dominic at the foot of the stairs, his face as enigmatic as ever. "Did you find something in your bride to please you, master?"

"More than I expected," Dominic acknowledged. "Any sign of the Scotsmen?"

"Not yet, but the men are watchful. Do you expect trouble?"

"I always expect trouble. If anyone wants me, I will be on the battlements."

As Dominic strode across the hall, he spied Lady Emily speaking with her husband and turned in their direction.

"My lord," Sir Eric said. "Have you instructions for me?"

"Aye. Double the guards. No one is to be allowed inside the gates without my permission."

"I will see to it immediately," Eric said, hurrying off.

"Excuse me, my lord," Emily said timidly. "Is Rose all right?"

Dominic's brow lowered. "Is there some reason why

she should not be?" Did everyone at Dragonwyck expect him to beat Rose?

Emily's cheeks flamed, but she held her ground. "You would know better than I, my lord. Rose can be rather fractious, but she is the sweetest, most caring—"

"Enough! Your lady may be everything you say, but she is also stubborn and contrary. For your information, my lady, I do not beat my women. None have been foolish enough to challenge my authority."

"I am sorry if I offended you, Lord Dragon," Emily said, backing away. "I care for Rose and would be most distressed if she were hurt."

"Go to her and judge for yourself if you do not believe me," he said curtly. "Mayhap she has need of another woman's counsel," he added thoughtfully.

Rose was still lying abed, trying to make sense of her response to Dragon, when she heard someone moving around in the sitting room. Dragon? Her pulse raced. Had he returned for . . . more? Then she heard Lady Emily's voice calling softly through the door.

"Rose? May I come in?"

Rose sat up, pulled the covers around her and gave Emily permission to enter. Emily nudged the door open and slipped inside.

"Are you all right?" she asked, wringing her hands as she hovered over Rose.

Sweet Mary, did everyone know what she and Dragon had been doing inside her chamber? "I am fine, Emily."

Emily gave her a dubious look. "Are you sure? He did not . . . hurt you, did he?"

"I told you he did not."

Emily all but collapsed in relief, but she still appeared skeptical. "When Lord Dragon entered the hall, he looked so fierce, I feared you had foolishly defied him."

"Defy him? Aye, I shall always defy him," Rose said obstinately. She grew thoughtful. "I learned something about Dragon today, Emily. Though his reputation as a ruthless warrior is obviously well deserved, I seriously doubt he would harm a woman. He is a knight, after all."

" 'Tis unlikely he has ever crossed paths with a woman like you," Emily reminded her, "so please watch your tongue. Men have been known to beat women who would defy them."

Rose stood, wincing when certain parts of her body protested Dragon's earlier handling. "I will try to remember, Emily, but it will be difficult."

Emily's attention was suddenly drawn to the bed. "Oh, my," she said, placing a hand over her mouth.

"What is it?" Rose asked, following Emily's gaze.

"Blood. This was the first time for you. We all thought . . . that is . . . it seemed unlikely that Lord Dragon would allow you to remain innocent this long."

A trail of red crept up Rose's neck. "My luck ran out," she muttered.

"Are you sore? Did he misuse you?"

Vivid color spread across Rose's cheeks. Dragon had not misused her; he'd given her pleasure. Her mouth flattened. That particular aspect of her deflowering was something she would admit to no one. Her

115

response to Dragon had shamed her, overwhelmed her and confused her. Did all women feel the same pleasure she did?

"Except for some soreness, I am fine."

Emily brightened. "A soak in a hot tub will do wonders for you. I will see to it immediately."

Rose perked up. "A bath sounds wonderful."

Emily turned to leave.

"Emily, wait," Rose said. Emily halted and looked askance at Rose. "Would you answer a personal question if I asked? I have no one else to turn to."

Emily returned to Rose immediately and placed an arm around her shoulders. "I will try."

Rose took a deep breath and let it out slowly. "I know that things of a . . . sexual nature are rarely discussed, and please feel free to refuse if my question offends, but 'tis important to me."

"What is troubling you?" Emily asked.

Rose glanced down at her tightly clasped hands and asked, "Do you find pleasure in the marriage bed?"

Emily's gasp told Rose that she had crossed the line with her friend. "Forgive me, Emily."

"You do not offend," Emily said. "Your question just startled me. I am older and wiser than you are in these matters, so I will answer truthfully. Aye, I find great pleasure in the marriage bed, but it is not thus with all women. Much depends on a man's expertise, and his willingness to . . . arouse his mate. Some men are too selfish to give pleasure and think only of their own needs. Eric is not that kind of man."

Rose let this all sink in, then asked, "So it is not wrong or sinful for a woman to enjoy the marriage act?"

116

"Indeed not," Emily said with conviction. "Oh, I know that priests contend a woman's enjoyment of the marriage act is sinful, but I for one do not hold with such austere beliefs. Why should men have all the pleasure?"

She gave Rose a frank look. "Did you find pleasure in Lord Dragon's arms? Is that why you are upset?"

Rose nodded, then looked away, embarrassed to admit such a thing.

"Feel fortunate that your lord saw to your pleasure the first time he breached you," Emily counseled. "Many women never experience fulfillment from the marriage act. I suspect 'tis why men take lemans, though more often than not, 'tis the husband's fault his wife is frigid. Now, are you ready for that bath?"

Rose nodded and Emily hurried off. Though Emily had answered her question, Rose did not feel any better. Why could not she be one of those cold women unaffected by a man's touch? Why could not Dragon be the kind of man with little patience or care for his wife's pleasure? Passiveness on her part would have shown her contempt for the king's champion. But, no, she had fallen to pieces in Dragon's arms, enjoying the sensations claiming her innocent body.

How was she to bear it?

Chapter Six

It is by believing in roses that one brings them
to bloom.
—French Proverb

Dominic did not return to Rose's bed that night. He
sat before the hearth in the hall, brooding over the
unexpected pleasure she had given him. Before bedding her, he had feared he might encounter resistance
from his pugnacious wife and lack of desire in himself,
but he'd found the opposite to be true. His innocent
bride had inspired lust in him and turned his brain to
mush. Even more surprising, he wanted her again. As
he breathed in her scent, which still lingered on his
body from their coupling, he had a rather disturbing
thought.

'Twas neither healthy nor acceptable for a man to

want his own wife to the degree he wanted Rose. Wives were for bearing children. They deserved respect but were rarely the object of their husband's lust. Men kept mistresses for that purpose.

Dominic's thoughts drifted back to Rose's deflowering. With a start, he realized he had held nothing of himself back from her. He had been careful not to hurt her and had truly wanted to give her pleasure. Of course, Dominic reflected, 'twas not in his nature to leave a woman wanting, but for some reason, satisfying Rose had been important.

Dominic stared into the dancing flames, recalling the exact moment Rose had placed her body into his care. Whether or not it had been intentional, she had accepted him and let herself feel pleasure, and that gave him a great deal of satisfaction. But he knew intuitively that returning to her bed tonight was not a good idea. Giving in to sexual need displayed weakness in a man and gave women power. Rose was the kind of woman who aspired to power, and he could not give her an edge over him. If Rose thought she could control him sexually, there would be no stopping her. He intended to remain the only warrior in the family.

Dominic puffed out a heavy sigh. No matter how hard he tried to rationalize his reasons for avoiding Rose's bed tonight, he could not deny his body's arousal. He could find a willing woman upon which to ease himself, but curiously, another woman held little appeal.

"Damnation!"

"What troubles you, master?"

Dominic started violently. "I wish you would not do that, Raj."

"Do what, master?"

"Sneak up on me. How long have you been standing there?"

"A long time. You were too absorbed to notice. Has your woman refused you again?"

"Nay."

"Shall I find another woman to serve you? I am sure I can find a wench willing to serve the Dragon Lord in such a manner."

"Do not trouble yourself, Raj. Fetch some furs; I will make my bed before the hearth."

Raj did not immediately obey. "Why are you denying yourself your wife's bed?"

Dominic stared at him. "When did I give you permission to arrange my life? I do not want my wife to think she can control me with her body. Veronica never aspired to that kind of power."

Raj returned his stare. "Perhaps, master, you should count your blessings. Why not control Lady Rose with *your* body. 'Tis a wise man who recognizes his appeal and uses it to his advantage. To my knowledge, none of your women have complained about your sexual prowess."

Suddenly Dominic smiled. " 'Tis a rare man who dares to counsel his master . . . and a foolish one. I will overlook your impertinence, Raj, for you are wiser than I. Forget the furs; a warm bed and a hot woman hold more appeal."

Raj smiled. "I took the liberty of preparing a bath for you in the solar. I had the tub set up before the hearth

120

in the sitting room so as not to awaken your lady."

"What would I do without you?" Dominic said, rising.

"I will assist you," Raj said, falling in step behind Dominic as he mounted the stairs.

Dominic glanced toward the closed bedchamber door when he entered the solar and had to force his thoughts away from his sleeping wife. He was not a man ruled by emotions, and he certainly was not obsessed with Rose of Ayrdale. Plagued, mayhap, but not obsessed.

"Let me help you disrobe, master," Raj said, "before the bathwater grows cold."

Moments later, Dominic lowered himself into the tub, relaxing against the rim as Raj moved behind him to lather and wash his hair.

"Go seek your bed, Raj," Dominic said when Raj took up the cloth to scrub his back. "I can finish my bath myself."

"You will find the drying cloth on the bench beside the tub," Raj said. "I will not be far away, master."

Once he was alone, Dominic leaned back and closed his eyes. His thoughts began to wander. But only as far as the bedchamber where Rose slept. He knew better than to hope that Rose waited for him to join her, her body soft and pliant with anticipation. She was probably sound asleep, dreaming of ways to bedevil him.

Dominic's body reacted spontaneously to his lusty thoughts, and he aimed a speculative glance toward the closed door. Dammit! Rose was his wife, and he wanted her.

Dominic surged from the tub, reached for the drying cloth and dried himself before the fire. His cock was throbbing and already hard when he dropped the drying cloth and strode naked into the bedchamber.

Rose appeared to be sleeping soundly and did not stir as he raised the covers and slid into bed beside her. She lay on her side with her back to him, her breathing deep and steady. Dominic placed an arm around her waist, pulled her into the curve of his body and waited for her to acknowledge him. To Dominic's chagrin, she remained blissfully unaware of his need.

His hand slid upward to cup her breast. Except for a deep sigh, she did not respond to his caress. He cursed beneath his breath and reluctantly gave up trying to awaken her. Anyone who slept as soundly as Rose had to be exhausted and was better left alone. Turning his back to her, he tried to focus his thoughts elsewhere until sleep claimed him.

The night turned bitter cold. The heavy drapery did little to prevent the icy wind from seeping into the chamber. Rose woke up shivering in the darkest part of the night and moved closer to the firm, warm weight planted solidly beside her. Still not fully awake, she curled spoon-like into the beckoning heat and sighed contentedly.

She awoke abruptly to the realization that she was not alone in bed, that the solid mass she was clinging to was hard male flesh.

Dragon.

Embarrassed that she had sought him out in the night, she tried to remove her arm from around his middle and found it trapped in a steely grip. He stirred against her, and she realized he was awake.

"Did I disturb your sleep?" she asked on a shaky breath.

"You did indeed. 'Twas impossible to sleep with your soft body pressed so sweetly against mine."

"I was cold," she explained. "It meant naught."

He turned to face her and pulled her against him, hip to hip, breast to breast. "Let me warm you."

Rose's pulse raced and her breathing became erratic. "I am fine now, thank you."

His hands moved provocatively over her body. "Your flesh is still chilled."

Rose recognized danger when it stared her in the face, even though it was too dark to see Dragon clearly. "What are you doing in my bed?"

"I believe this is my bed."

"Then I shall find another."

"You are being deliberately obtuse, wife. Married couples are expected to share a bed."

His hands were roaming freely over her body, seeking out places that definitely warmed her. "Please, my lord, 'tis the middle of the night."

"Desire recognizes no time. You were sleeping when I came to bed and I did not want to disturb you then. But we are both awake now."

In a surprise move, he pulled her atop him. She felt his tumescence stirring against her, and a biting comment came unbidden to her lips. "Are you thinking of your mistress again, my lord?"

Dragon stiffened beneath her, and she knew she had angered him, but she could not help it. Marrying a stranger was bad enough, but knowing that her husband pined for another woman was a blow to her pride.

"Are you deliberately trying to provoke me?" Dragon asked. " 'Tis your duty to obey me in all things. It is not your place to question my thoughts or logic," he said as he shoved her legs apart and placed them on either side of his hips.

When he found her nipple with his mouth and suckled her, Rose moaned in despair. Not again, she thought. How many times would she have to fight her own desire before she learned to resist Dragon's assault upon her senses? He licked her nipple, and she shuddered. He found the tender cleft between her thighs and teased her with his fingers. She cried out a protest, startled when it came out as a ragged plea.

"I know not why you fight this," Dragon muttered, "when you find it so enjoyable."

"I do not!" Rose denied. Her denial ended in a startled gurgle when he spread her with his fingers and carefully shoved his cock inside her. She was tender still and was surprised that he was careful not to hurt her. She had heard that a man in full rut cared for naught but his own gratification.

"Pull in your thorns, Rose, and let me love you," Dominic whispered against her ear as he slowly filled her until she feared she would burst.

Despair rode Rose. She did not want this, had in fact resolved earlier to remain unresponsive to Dragon's loving, but her body betrayed her. She felt intoxicated, as if her blood had turned thick, flowing hot and burning to her loins. He knew how to touch her and where to touch her in a way that called forth the wildness of her untamed spirit.

Rose bit back a moan when Dragon grasped her buttocks and moved her up, then down the length of his erection, creating a splendid friction that spurred her inexorably toward the ultimate satisfaction. When he grasped a dangling breast in his mouth and flicked her erect nipple with his tongue, she splintered and cried out. She felt Dragon stiffen, heard him call her name and felt his heat explode inside her.

When it was over, Rose was overcome with sadness, surrounded by it, consumed in it. Once again she had responded to Dragon and experienced pleasure. Was there no justice in the world? Why could she not remain limp and impassive while Dragon used her? He filled her mind and body with every part of himself despite her resolve to accept none of him. The shame of it was nearly killing her.

Tears leaked from the corners of Rose's eyes as Dominic held her against him and buried his face in her hair. She lay silent and melancholy in his arms as night air cooled her heated flesh. She wished herself anywhere but in the Dragon Lord's bed.

Dominic held Rose close, listening to her slowing heartbeat while his own still raced out of control. His mouth found hers and he kissed her, surprised when he tasted tears.

"Did I hurt you?"

"Nay."

"Why are you crying?"

After a prolonged silence, she said, "I am crying because I am sad."

Dominic chuckled. "You did not sound sad a few moments ago. You sounded happy." He paused, his curiosity piqued. "Did I give you pleasure, Rose?"

Rose freed herself from his arms and flung herself away from him before he could stop her. "You gave me pleasure I neither wanted nor asked for. Responding to you as I did betrayed my father's memory, and that makes me sad."

"Your father was a traitor; you have naught to feel guilty about. Go to sleep, Rose."

Dominic turned away from Rose but remained awake. He needed a quiet moment to ponder his unaccountable fascination with Rose. What made her different from Veronica or any other woman he had bedded? Naught, he decided. It just so happened that he needed a woman and Rose was handy. Aye, that was it. That simple explanation brought him a measure of satisfaction. He closed his eyes and welcomed sleep.

Dominic was gone when Rose awakened. The noise that had disturbed her was merely Tyra kindling the fire. Rose yawned and stretched and was immediately sorry when the soreness between her thighs reminded her of the unaccustomed activity she and Dragon had engaged in last night.

"Do ye want me to open the drapery, my lady?" Tyra asked when she noticed that Rose was awake.

"Nay, I prefer to keep the cold air outside where it belongs," Rose answered.

"Do ye want me to help ye dress?"

"Not this morning, Tyra, thank you. Have I missed Mass?"

"Aye, the bell just tolled Terce. Lord Dragon said to let ye sleep as late as ye wish this morn."

Rose sighed. She did not want Dragon to be kind to her. She needed to hate him. Rose lingered in bed after Tyra left, not particularly eager to face Dragon after her surrender last night. If he thought he could direct her life, he was sadly mistaken. She could never forget that the Dragon Lord was the king's lackey. Did he not realize how much King John was hated by his people? Her father should not have lost his life because he had tried to help the king's oppressed barons.

Rose pushed aside the covers and rose, still weary despite the lateness of the hour. Had she slept at all last night? She wanted another bath but decided to wait. There was water in a pitcher, however, and she used it to wash Dragon's seed from between her thighs. She had already dressed and was cleaning her teeth with a cloth dipped in salt when she heard a commotion in the inner bailey. Rushing to the window, she pulled aside the drapery and leaned out the window.

Snow had fallen during the night. A gust of wind picked up the flakes and flung them against Rose's face. Impatiently she dashed them away. Her uncle and his kinsmen had arrived. Rose brushed her hair into a semblance of order and hurried down to the hall to greet them.

Rose joined Dragon at the front entrance just as the Scotsmen arrived.

"I decided to let them enter," Dominic said when

Rose joined him. "I doubt your uncle will cause trouble, but we are prepared nevertheless."

"Think you he knows about our marriage?"

"Nay, but it will be interesting to note his reaction once he is told."

Dominic studied the MacTavish clan through narrowed lids. They looked uncivilized, he thought, surprised by their manner of dress. They were clad in fur and leather, from their crude tunics down to their hide boots. They were large men, probably descendants of Vikings, those fiercest of all fighters.

"They look like savages," Dominic said. "How could that tribe have produced your gentle mother? Point out your uncle."

"Uncle Murdoc is the one riding the pure black horse. He is just now dismounting."

Dominic studied the huge Scotsman with curiosity, noting little resemblance between Lady Nelda and her brutish brother.

"Uncle Murdoc is not so bad," Rose allowed. "He always treated us well when we visited him."

The Scotsman looked up at Rose and stretched out his arms. "Rose, lass, come greet yer uncle."

Dominic remained alert and on edge as Rose walked down the stairs and was instantly encompassed within the brawny arms of Murdoc MacTavish. But when another, younger man stepped forward and embraced Rose, it was all Dominic could do to keep from racing down the stairs and tearing her from the young Scotsman's arms. Who was he? Though Dominic noted some reluctance on Rose's part, she appeared to know him well.

Dominic heard Rose say, " 'Tis cold out here, Uncle. Bring Gunn and your kinsmen inside, where you can warm yourselves by the fire."

Dominic stood aside as Rose and her uncle entered the keep, silently counting the men that followed them inside. He counted thirty clansmen, not all of them as young and vigorous as the man that had embraced Rose, but every man carried weapons of one sort or another. Instinct warned Dominic that Murdoc had come to claim the fortress.

Dominic trailed behind the Scotsmen, noting as he strode across the hall that his own knights were alert and watchful. A nod from Eric of Carlyle put his mind at ease as to the loyalty of Lord Edwyn's personal guardsmen. Dominic knew that no Englishman of worth would allow a Scotsman to claim any part of English soil without a fight.

Dominic stood nearby as Rose seated herself before the hearth. Murdoc paid him little heed as he accepted a mug of ale from a servant and plopped down in the chair beside Rose. Murdoc's kinsmen took their ease on benches at the trestle tables, drinking ale and talking among themselves.

"I heard about yer father's death, lass," Murdoc said after drinking down half the mug's contents in one swallow. "I came as soon as I could to help yer dear mother in her time of need. I understand John Lackland ordered Edwyn's death."

"Aye," Rose bit out. "He had no just cause to kill Papa. Papa was no traitor."

"Dinna fret, lass, yer Uncle Murdoc stands ready to take charge. As yer only living male relative, 'tis my duty to see to the care of yer family and yer lands."

He glanced around, spied Gunn and motioned for the young Scotsman to attend him.

Dominic's fists clenched as the brawny young warrior grinned at Rose in an intimate manner Dominic thought inappropriate. But Dominic was not yet ready to identify himself. He wanted to learn what Murdoc was up to first.

"Where are yer mother and sister, lass?" Murdoc asked. "I would offer them words of comfort."

"They both entered the convent after we received word of Papa's death," Rose explained.

Murdoc became immediately alert. "What? And left ye alone? That does not sound at all like my sister. I know yer the heir, and that yer twin's dearest wish was to become a nun, but I canna believe Nelda would leave ye alone to manage a holding as large as Ayrdale."

" 'Tis true. Mama and Starla are both gone."

"Ah, well," Murdoc sighed, " 'tis fortunate I arrived when I did. Ye can rest easy, lass, for I bring an answer to yer problem."

"What problem, Uncle?"

"Surely ye dinna think yerself capable of managing Ayrdale on yer own, do ye? As yer guardian, 'tis within my rights to arrange a marriage for ye. My stepson is the man I have chosen for yer mate. Gunn will protect both ye and Ayrdale from the English king."

Gunn planted himself before Rose, grasped her shoulders in his huge hands and pulled her upright. "I've always wanted ye in my bed, Rose," he said in a voice that set Dominic's teeth on edge. "Now I will have both ye and yer land. We will produce fine heirs for Ayrdale."

Dominic heard Rose gasp and decided it was time to step in and stop this farce.

"Release her!" His voice held a note of menace.

Gunn was so startled, he instantly released Rose. Murdoc, on the other hand, leaped from his chair to confront the knight who dared interfere in such private matters.

"Who is this man, Rose? I dinna recognize him as one of yer father's knights. Apparently he doesna know his place."

"Perhaps you will recognize my name," Dominic said as he went toe to toe with the Scotsmen. "I am called the Dragon Lord."

"Dragon of Pendragon," Gunn muttered beneath his breath.

"The king's lackey," Murdoc spat contemptuously. "What brings ye to Ayrdale?"

"The demesne you refer to as Ayrdale is now called Dragonwyck, and I am the new lord of Dragonwyck."

"John Lackland gave Ayrdale to ye?" Murdoc croaked.

"Aye. Both Ayrdale and Rose are now mine by virtue of holy wedlock."

Murdoc spun around to confront Rose. "Is that true, lass? Did ye wed Dragon?"

"I had no choice, Uncle. Blame the king. He commanded that I wed Lord Dragon."

Gunn turned on his stepfather. "Ye promised me Ayrdale! Ye said Rose would be mine!"

"Silence!" Murdoc roared. He turned back to Rose. "How long have ye been wed, lass?"

"A few days. What does it matter? The marriage was officiated by Father Nyle and is perfectly legal; there is naught I can do about it."

"Mayhap there is," Murdoc said shrewdly. "Has the marriage been consummated, lass? Did the Dragon take yer maidenhead?"

Rose realized her uncle was angry, but she had hoped he would accept her marriage without a confrontation. A shudder passed through her at the thought of being wed to Gunn. She had known him since they were children. He was handsome enough, but he was a bully with a cruel streak she could not condone.

Returning her thoughts to her uncle's question, Rose said, "Aye, Uncle, my marriage to Lord Dragon has been consummated."

"Bastard!" Gunn spat angrily. "Rose's maidenhead belonged to me! Murdoc spoke with her father years ago about a betrothal. Edwyn must have neglected to tell Rose."

"Nay! Not true," Rose denied. "Papa would not do such a thing. He knew I would not agree to marry you."

"Gunn, dinna lose yer head, lad," Murdoc advised.

"You and your kinsmen are welcome in my home as long as you cause no trouble," Dominic warned. "Dragonwyck and Rose are mine; you can do naught but accept it."

Rose watched Murdoc warily. She knew he had a fierce temper and did not like to be thwarted. As soon as she got Dragon alone, she would tell him to exercise caution in his dealings with her uncle.

"How long will you stay, Uncle?" Rose asked.

"I havena decided," Murdoc said, aiming a sidelong glance at Gunn, who was still glaring malevolently at Dominic. "Much depends on the weather."

"I will have chambers prepared for you and Gunn," Rose said. "The others can bed down in the hall or the barracks. If you will excuse me, I should check our stores and confer with the cook."

"I, too, must leave you and your kinsmen to your own devices, unless you care to watch my knights engage in mock battle," Dominic said. "I train with them every day regardless of the weather."

"My kinsmen and I would enjoy watching the great Dragon Lord train his knights," Murdoc said in a mocking tone of voice.

The men left, and Rose hurried off, praying that no further trouble would develop, and that her uncle's visit would be of short duration. She knew, however, that her uncle had come with the intention of seizing Ayrdale and wedding her to his stepson. With a foothold in England, Murdoc would be in a position of power rarely granted to a Scotsman.

Rose shivered when she thought of how close she had come to wedding Gunn. With her father gone, there was no way to prove or disprove Murdoc's claim that a marriage had been arranged between her and Gunn. And since Murdoc was her closest male relative, he would have seized her lands and taken charge of her life to suit his own purposes.

Rose located the steward and together they checked

the stores, which proved to be adequate as long as the hunters continued to bag fresh game. Emily and Blythe joined her as she conferred with the cook and went over the menu for the evening meal. After a day of training in the cold, the men would return hungry.

Satisfied with the adequacy of the stores, Rose left her two ladies to oversee the preparation of the meal while she went to the alehouse to see if there was sufficient ale on hand to satisfy Scotsmen with large capacities for the fermented brew. She retrieved her cloak from a hook beside the kitchen door and headed outside. A yeasty, earthy smell greeted her as she opened the door to the alehouse and stepped inside.

The alewife was not there, but Rose did not need her. She counted the barrels of ale and deemed them satisfactory. When she turned to leave, she found her uncle standing just inside the closed door, blocking her exit.

"Uncle, you frightened me," Rose said. "I thought you were on the training field with the others."

"I was, but slipped away for a private word with ye, lass. I saw ye enter the alehouse and followed."

" 'Tis cold in here," Rose said. "Shall we return to the keep?"

"Nay, 'tis best we speak in private." Hands crossed over his massive chest, legs spread wide apart, he barked, "I dinna accept yer marriage to this English devil."

"You cannot change what is done."

"There is always something one can do, lass."

Rose shook her head. "My marriage has been consummated."

Murdoc made a dismissive motion with his hand. "It matters not. Scottish laws are nay so strict as yer English ones. Ye were wed against yer will, and yer father promised ye to another. Come away with me to Scotland. I have but to grease a few palms to have yer marriage to the Dragon declared invalid, leaving ye free to wed Gunn."

"I cannot leave my home and my people," Rose demurred.

"Ye will not be required to remain long in Scotland," Murdoc promised. "Lowlanders will rally to my cause when they learn I have legal claim to a slice of English borderland. Once we rout the Dragon, you and Gunn can return to the keep as husband and wife. I trust Gunn. He will protect Ayrdale from English aggression. I have long wanted Ayrdale, ye ken."

"Think you it will be easy to rout Dragon?" Rose challenged. Though she had not wanted to wed her husband, she was English and preferred that she and her lands remain that way.

"There isna an Englishman alive or dead who can match a Scot in brains or brawn," Murdoc bragged.

"I cannot leave," Rose reiterated. "Besides, think of the bloodshed and needless deaths. Dragonwyck's knights are all loyal Englishmen and would not surrender easily. Leave be, Uncle. I will try to make the best of my marriage to Dragon."

His face set in harsh lines, Murdoc closed the distance between them and grasped Rose's arms in a bruising grip.

"Ye will do as I say, lass. Ye will pretend that all is well when I announce my intention to return home. When Dragon is occupied elsewhere, ye will disguise yerself as a lad and ride off with us."

"Nay! I will not!"

Murdoc gave her a shake that rattled her teeth. "Ye always were a stubborn lass. Yer father gave ye too much freedom. Too bad yer sister wasna the firstborn. I could manage her. Ye will do as I say, Rose."

"Unhand me, Uncle, you are hurting me," Rose cried, struggling to free herself.

"You heard my wife, unhand her."

Rose looked over Murdoc's shoulder at Dragon. Neither she nor Murdoc had heard him enter, but there he stood, larger than life, his face dark with rage.

Murdoc whirled. He reached for his dirk but thought better of it when Dragon's hand settled on the hilt of his sword.

"I dinna hurt the lass."

Dominic looked past Murdoc at Rose. "Did he hurt you?"

Rose shook her head. "Nay." She slanted Murdoc a speaking glance. "He was but inquiring about my mother."

Dominic gave her a skeptical look. "It looked as if you and Murdoc were arguing. Why did your uncle seek you out here? 'Tis an odd place to talk about family."

"How did you know I was in the alehouse?" Rose asked. "Did you wish to speak to me about something?"

"I grew curious when I saw MacTavish sneak away

and followed. He was not in the keep, and when Lady Emily told me you had gone to the alehouse, I decided to investigate. I see my instincts were right."

"Ye canna keep me from speaking to my niece, Dragon," Murdoc snarled.

"I can keep you from hurting her," Dominic replied. "If you have something to say, tell me instead of intimidating my wife."

" 'Tis all right, Dominic, truly," Rose said, fearing that the animosity between Dominic and her uncle would explode into violence.

"I will leave ye now, lass," Murdoc said, striding past Dominic and out the door. "Think on what I said," he threw over his shoulder.

"What did the Scotsman mean by that?" Dominic asked. "Are you and your uncle conspiring against me?"

"He meant naught," Rose returned. "You are imagining things. I had best return to the keep. There is much to be done with extra men to feed and shelter."

Dominic snagged Rose around the waist and pulled her against him when she tried to slip past him. "Not so fast, wife. Need I remind you that you are an English subject as well as my wife? Your loyalty should be to me and the king."

"I am not dense, my lord," Rose bit out. " 'Tis true I am English, but John Lackland is not a man who commands loyalty."

Rose knew her words tempted fate and invited Dragon's anger, but she could not help it. She was not the only English subject who despised the monarch. She opened her lips to tell Dragon as much when his

137

mouth came down hard on hers. His kiss was not gentle. It was one of fierce possessiveness; a harsh reminder of the absolute authority he wielded over her. Taking exception to his domination, she grasped the eating knife she wore at her waist and brought the small blade against his throat. He released her instantly and backed away, his expression not at all what she expected.

He was smiling!

When he broke out in laughter, she turned and fled.

Chapter Seven

What would the rose with all her pride be
worth,
were there no sun to call her brightness forth?
—Thomas Moore

Dominic laughed until he thought his sides would split. Did Rose think her puny blade would frighten him? He could have disarmed her with a mere flick of his wrist had he wanted to, but her absurd show of bravado amused him. Rose was fierce but misguided. He deemed himself a worthy opponent for his warrior wife; she had not the slightest hope of withholding anything from him, much less winning a battle of wits.

Dominic grinned all the way back to the keep. But the grin faded when he saw the visiting Scotsmen crowded around Murdoc in a dark corner of the hall, speaking together in hushed tones. Dominic supposed they were plotting mischief and realized he must remain extra vigilant and alert until they left.

Dominic couldn't help wondering if Rose had joined with her uncle against him. He knew she did not want him for a husband, but how far would she go to be rid of him? Dominic had dealt with men like MacTavish before and would do whatever was necessary to save his demesne. As for his marriage, Rose had best remember that she was his property, and that challenging him would serve no purpose.

Eric of Carlyle hailed Dominic as he crossed the hall and he went to the captain of the guard. "You wished to speak with me, Sir Eric?"

"The Scots," Eric hissed. "Look at them. I trust them not. They caused no trouble when Lord Edwyn was alive, but with both Edwyn and Lady Nelda gone, they no longer have a reason to respect our borders. Dragonwyck is now fair game. MacTavish would kill for a piece of English soil. They bear watching, my lord."

"I have come to the same conclusion, Eric. I want MacTavish watched every minute of every day they remain at Dragonwyck."

"Aye, my lord," Eric said as he took his leave.

"Do you have orders for me, master?" Raj asked, making his presence known.

Dominic whirled, not at all surprised to find Raj standing behind him. "Aye, Raj, indeed I do. I want you to watch my wife. You are the only one who can do it without attracting notice."

Raj sent him an inscrutable look. "Am I to protect

Lady Rose, my lord? She appears passing fond of her uncle. Think you he would harm her?"

"I am not sure. She might, however, betray me."

Raj was clearly taken aback. "You jest, master. Your lady would not betray you. She is English to the core."

"Rose likes me not," Dominic groused. "She cannot forget that the king executed her father and gave me her demesne. She has good reason to change her allegiance. Her mother *is* a Scot, after all."

"As you wish, master," Raj said, "but who will protect your back while I am watching Lady Rose?"

"Worry not about me, Raj, I am fully capable of protecting myself."

The hall was full to bursting that night as everyone gathered for the evening meal. A bard had shown up at the gate, offering his special skill in return for a meal and a night's lodging. Despite the crowded conditions, Dominic was quick to offer his hospitality. He enjoyed a good tale as much as the next man and looked forward to the evening's entertainment.

Dominic thrummed his fingers on the table as he waited for Rose to arrive so the meal could commence. He noted with a measure of satisfaction that conversation flowed easily, and he hoped that his suspicions about the Scotsmen were wrong. He would not know for sure, though, until MacTavish announced his attention to return home. And even then he would remain watchful.

Dominic glanced impatiently toward the solar, relieved when he saw Rose descending the stairs. His gaze slid over her shapely body, admiring the way her gold-trimmed green tunic flowed over the swell of her hips and the narrowness of her waist beneath a jeweled girdle. She looked almost regal with her blond braids wound around her head like a crown and covered with a sheer linen veil, held in place by a circlet of gold. He noted her eating knife dangling from her waist, and an unbidden smile curved his lips. How could she possibly think she could hurt him with that insignificant weapon?

As Rose glided toward him, Dominic felt himself grow hard in response and wondered how in God's name he was going to get through the meal without embarrassing himself.

"Good evening, my lord," Rose said with cool disdain.

Dominic rose and seated her with admirable aplomb, considering his state of arousal. Thank God for his braies and tunic.

"Your greeting lacks warmth, wife," Dominic said as he signaled the servants to begin serving the meal. "I am your husband, not a stranger."

Rose sent him an acerbic look. " 'Tis no more than you deserve, my lord. I do not enjoy being laughed at. Nor do I like being threatened or falsely accused."

Dominic helped himself from a platter of roasted lamb, chose a tender piece for Rose and placed it on her side of the trencher. "Did I accuse you falsely? Do you deny plotting against me with your uncle?"

Indignation flashed in Rose's eyes. "I do not need to defend myself to you. Think what you want, my lord." She lifted her eating knife and carefully cut her meat into manageable pieces.

"Rose," Dominic warned, "why do you insist on taunting me? Think you that eating knife frightens me? Or that sword you brandished the day you challenged me at the portcullis?"

"Obviously not, but I hardly think it was amusing," Rose huffed.

"I am a warrior. I can't help being amused by women who arm themselves like men and pretend fierceness."

Rose took a dainty bite of lamb, chewed, swallowed, then said, " 'Twas no pretense, my lord." She let that statement sink in, then blithely continued. "Neither of us married mates of our own choosing. We have naught in common. The king you champion is a man I hold in contempt. Yet we must try to make the most of our unfortunate marriage. I have been thinking," she ventured, "that I should like to visit my uncle's demesne. An extended stay in Scotland may be the answer to our dilemma."

A surge of anger nearly toppled Dominic from his chair. So he had not been wrong about Rose. What kind of mischief was she planning with her uncle?

"If you are thinking of dallying with Gunn," he said very slowly, "forget it. No wife of mine will become another man's whore."

Rose knew she was deliberately goading Dragon, but it felt good. She would never forgive him for laughing at her. Though she had no intention of leaving Dragonwyck with her uncle, needling Dragon soothed her hurt pride. It did surprise her, however, that Dragon thought she wanted Gunn. It was even more startling that he sounded jealous of the Scotsman.

Rose suppressed a smile. Dragon cared naught for her, so why would he be jealous? The reason came to her in a burst of insight. Dragon was a possessive man, one who did not relinquish easily that which he considered his. She was his property, like Dragonwyck, and was to be held at all costs. Rose pondered her lowly place in Dragon's life and wondered how long it would be before he sent for his mistress.

"Rose, did you hear me?" Dominic growled. "You will not leave Dragonwyck without my permission, nor are you to seek out Gunn for any reason."

"Once again you accuse me falsely," Rose charged. "I am not interested in Gunn."

"What are you interested in?" Dominic asked.

"My home. My family. Our people."

"Do you want children, Rose?"

"I always thought children would be a blessing and a comfort," Rose said wistfully.

Dragon's expression gave away nothing of his thoughts. Was he thinking about the children he might have had with his mistress? Rose wondered. A daunting thought occurred to her. Did he want that other woman to be the mother of his children?

Rose blurted out the question before she could change her mind. The expression on Dominic's face made her wish she had held her tongue.

"You are the woman who can give me legitimate children, not Veronica."

Veronica. Now she knew the name of the woman he loved. But when Rose considered his answer, she decided he had adeptly evaded her question.

"I know you did not ask," Dominic continued, "but I will tell you anyway. I want children, Rose. There is not a man alive who does not want heirs. One day our son will be Lord of Dragonwyck."

Rose swallowed convulsively. The thought of having Dragon's children brought her no pleasure when she knew that the father of her future children loved another woman.

"Mayhap I am barren," Rose said for lack of a better answer.

"Time will tell," Dominic said. Abruptly he changed the subject. "Did your uncle say when he was leaving?"

Rose was not sorry to see the end of the previous discussion and answered with alacrity. "Nay, but I doubt his visit will be an extended one. He must return soon to protect his demesne from rival clans."

"Good," Dominic said as he placed a portion of stewed root vegetables on the trencher. "I will not be sorry to see the last of him. I have been thinking," he continued, "Christmastide is a perfect time for a celebration. We could invite the marcher barons and their families and announce our marriage at the same time. 'Tis time I met those of King John's barons whom I do not already know."

"You wish to hold a fete?" Rose repeated. " 'Tis a great undertaking, my lord. Rooms must be prepared and the keep cleaned from top to bottom. We need to send out hunters and fishermen immediately, and make sure enough help is available to cook and prepare food for the banqueting tables."

"Can it be done?" Dominic asked.

Actually, the idea of a Christmas celebration excited

Rose. Visiting with friends from other baronies was always a treat. Organizing a grand fete would be difficult in the short time available, but not impossible.

"Aye, it can be done with enough help."

"We can hold the celebration between Christmas Day and Twelfth Night, with activities like hunting and hawking on each of the twelve days," Dominic decided. "My knights will provide fresh game and fish, and I will send out riders with invitations to the marcher barons. Does that meet with your approval?"

"Aye. Mama and Papa always handed out gifts on the first day of January," Rose said wistfully. "Each villein received a length of cloth and food. I hope there is enough cloth in our stores to accommodate our people."

"You must check the stores," Dominic said. "We, too, will make gifts to our people."

Rose nodded silent agreement, keeping her most fervent wish to herself. She wanted her mother and Starla to visit Dragonwyck during the festivities but did not know how Dragon would react to her request.

The meal ended, and a place was cleared in the center of the hall for the bard. Rose had not been on hand when he had arrived earlier in the day and was surprised at his advanced age. Though he was strong in body and limb, his hair was long and white, as was his beard. But his twinkling blue eyes showed no sign of age; they were as bright and inquisitive as a youth's.

"His name is Cynric," Dominic said as the bard sat cross-legged on a bench and signaled for quiet.

Cynric began his story. It was an exciting tale about a brave knight and his daring exploits, and Rose sat on the edge of her seat as the story unfolded. Cynric described a knight of spectacular courage, a veritable dragon, and told of his battles against infidels, of the terrible wound he had incurred, and of the freed slave who had become his shadow and his protector.

It was not long into the tale that Rose realized the story was about Dragon. The flesh on the back of her neck prickled when the bard spoke of Dragon's prowess with women and how he had finally fallen in love with a woman of extraordinary beauty, a fearless warrior woman of exceptional courage. Rose nearly laughed aloud, for nothing could be further from the truth.

Rose glanced at Dragon, surprised to see him watching her. She met his gaze unflinchingly, but warmth heated her cheeks.

"He is talking about you, Rose," Dominic said. "You are the warrior woman in Cynric's story."

"That seems highly unlikely," Rose scoffed, returning her attention to the bard, who was nearing the end of his tale. She knew better than to believe Dragon loved her, for she was no fool. The skilled bard was simply making a story more interesting by embellishing it with untruths.

"Cynric tells a good story," Rose said. "You should invite him to return for the Christmas festivities, or mayhap he will remain for the winter and regale us nightly with his tales."

" 'Tis a thought," Dominic said.

The bard finished his story and began another, this one about a lady imprisoned in a tower and her brave rescuer. Rose was engrossed in the tale when Dominic leaned over and whispered in her ear, "Shall we to bed, wife?"

"Nay. I wish to hear the end of the story."

His eyes glowed hot with desire. "I will tell you the ending in our bedchamber."

Rose hesitated, trying to think of a way to avoid Dragon's attentions. Every time he made love to her, she lost a small part of herself, and that frightened her.

"Since it is still early, I thought I would invite Lady Emily and Lady Blythe to the solar to help plan the feast. There is so little time left and so much to do. You do not mind, do you?"

"Of course I mind, but I will not interfere with your plans. I suppose I can confer with Eric and my knights about tomorrow's hunt, and instruct the scribe to compose invitations to our guests. Very well, Rose. You and your ladies have until Compline, but after that, you are mine."

Rose exhaled a sigh of relief when Dragon rose and joined a group of knights at one of the trestle tables. Now all she had to do was find Emily and Blythe, explain about the celebration and invite them to the solar.

"I thought Dragon would never leave ye alone, lass."

Rose had not seen her uncle approach and was startled to see him. "Was there something you wanted, Uncle?"

"Aye, lass. Come to my chamber. I wish a private word with ye."

"Nay. I cannot forget what happened the last time we were alone."

"Ah, 'tis sorry I am, lass. I dinna mean to hurt ye. I

was always kind to ye and yer family, if ye recollect. Yer mother would want ye to listen to what I have to say."

Rose wanted to refuse but had not the heart to deny her uncle a few minutes of her time. For her mother's sake, she decided to hear him out.

"Very well. I will come to your chamber as soon as I can get away, but I cannot stay long."

"I will be waiting for ye, lass. Dinna delay."

After Murdoc took his leave, Rose sought out Emily and Blythe and asked them to await her in the solar while she had a private word with her uncle in his chamber. When Rose informed them about the festivities Dominic planned for Christmas, they clapped their hands excitedly and agreed with alacrity.

They parted and Rose left the hall, unaware that Raj was trailing behind her.

Rose reached her uncle's room and rapped on the door. A muffled voice invited her to enter. Rose opened the door and stepped inside. The chamber was dark but for the dim light of a single candle resting on a bedside table.

"Uncle? Where are you?"

Suddenly the door behind her slammed shut and she heard the distinct metallic sound of a key turning in the lock. Whirling, she was stunned to see Gunn grinning at her as he dropped the door key into his sporran.

"Gunn! What are you doing here? Where is Uncle Murdoc?"

"Yer uncle isna here."

"I wish to leave. Unlock the door."

"Not yet, lass. I want to talk with ye. Yer uncle planned this meeting between us. We willna be disturbed here."

"We have naught to discuss, Gunn." She held out her hand. "Give me the key."

Gunn moved so quickly, Rose could not escape him. Grasping her arms, he pulled her toward the bed and forced her to sit down on the edge.

"Dinna I just say we needed to talk? Yer uncle has a plan to get ye out of yer marriage."

Rose shivered as a chill crept down her spine. "I already explained to Uncle Murdoc that there is naught anyone can do to make my marriage to Dragon go away. 'Tis legal in every way."

Gunn sent her a sly smile. "Give yer uncle some credit, Rose. 'Tis unlikely yer husband would want ye if ye gave yerself to another man. He might even be relieved to let ye leave with us when we return to Scotland. Murdoc has friends in powerful places. Once ye swear ye were promised to me, yer marriage to Dragon will be declared invalid and no one can challenge my claim to Ayrdale."

He pushed her and she tumbled backward onto the bed. "Do yer part, lass, and all will be well."

"You expect me to give myself to you?" Rose gasped, scooting away from him.

"Aye, that I do."

"You are mad as a loon, and so is my uncle."

"Murdoc is smart as a fox. Lift yerself up so I can remove yer tunic."

"Go to the devil! Touch me and I will scream."

Immediately Gunn clasped a meaty paw over Rose's mouth. " 'Tis too soon for us to be found together."

Rose went wild with panic, struggling beneath the pressure of Gunn's large body. What did Gunn mean? Who was supposed to find them together? This could not be happening to her. She had been a fool to trust Murdoc.

"Hold still, Rose. 'Tis not as if yer a virgin, and I dinna want this to end too soon."

Rose stopped struggling when she realized that her gyrations were arousing Gunn. She felt the hard ridge of his manhood prodding against her stomach and went limp.

"Good lass," Gunn said. "I knew ye'd see things my way."

He removed his hand from her mouth and began raising the hem of her tunic. Finding her mouth suddenly free, Rose let out a piercing scream. Gunn returned his hand to her mouth, abruptly cutting off the sound.

"That wasna smart of ye, lass."

Keeping one hand in place over her mouth, he yanked her tunic up past her hips with his other hand. He spread her legs with his knees and was fitting himself between them when the door splintered and crashed open.

Gunn leaped away from her and reached for his claymore. But it was too late. Raj, charging like an enraged bull, slammed into the Scot. They fell to the floor in a tangle of arms and legs, but Gunn never had a chance. Gunn was big, but Raj was larger and broader.

Rose flung her tunic back into place and rose shakily from the bed, angling around the thrashing bodies toward the door to summon help. Before she reached the ruined panel, Dragon and Murdoc appeared in the opening.

"God's toenails, what is happening here?" Dominic roared. Then he saw Rose and his brow furrowed, as if he could not quite comprehend exactly what her presence in Murdoc's chamber meant.

Rose's gaze flew to her uncle, and she realized that he appeared as stunned as Dragon, though probably for different reasons.

"When you said there was something I should see in your chamber, MacTavish, I had no idea you were referring to a fight between my man and your stepson."

"Och, neither did I," Murdoc sputtered.

"Cease!" Dominic ordered, reaching down to lift Raj off an unmoving Gunn. "What happened, Raj?"

Raj rose to his feet, casting a contemptuous look at Gunn, who was reeling groggily and holding his head.

"I did as you asked, master," Raj explained. "I followed Lady Rose to her uncle's chamber and waited outside the door for her to exit. When I heard her scream, I burst into the chamber and found . . ."

"He found Gunn swiving yer wife," Murdoc said tersely. "Gunn's chamber is not so fine as mine, and he asked if he could bed Rose here. I dinna want to keep the lovers apart, so I agreed. Then I thought better of it and decided to tell ye about yer wife's deception."

Rose felt the walls closing in on her. How could her uncle lie with such ease? Surely Dragon did not believe him, did he? She met Dragon's gaze and felt the heavy weight of his suspicion pressing down on her.

"Nay, he lies! Uncle Murdoc said he wanted a private word with me and asked that I attend him in his chamber. I had no idea Gunn would be here, or that he would . . . would . . ." She turned her face away, unable to look Dragon in the eye.

"Did he rape you?" Dominic asked harshly.

"Rape?" Murdoc repeated. "Ye wrong my stepson, Lord Dragon. Gunn would never rape an unwilling woman. Believe me, my niece was willing, else she would not have agreed to meet alone with Gunn."

"Forgive me, master," Raj interrupted, "but it did not look to me as if your lady was willing."

"What say you, Gunn? Was my wife willing or nay?"

"She wanted me," Gunn lied as he spat out a broken tooth. "Yer man saw what he wanted to see. Ye must not have satisfied Rose, for she was wild beneath me."

"Get out!" Dominic thundered. "Both of you. Take your men and leave now. You have stretched my hospitality to the limit. You and your kinsmen are no longer welcome in my home."

"We will be taking Rose with us," Murdoc said, reaching for her.

Rose skittered out of his reach. "I am not going with you, Uncle."

" 'Tis for yer husband to say," Murdoc said. " 'Tis unlikely he will want ye after another man swived ye. Ye have nowhere to go but with me. We are kin, I willna turn ye away."

Rose opened her mouth to speak but naught came out. She was too stunned by the turn of events to form coherent words.

Dominic turned on Murdoc, his face fierce with rage. "Get out! Now! You are trying my patience."

"Verra well," Murdoc said. "Up with ye, Gunn, we have worn out our welcome." He beckoned to Rose. "Come along, niece. Mayhap Dragon will give ye time to pack a wee bag."

Dominic placed an arm in front of Rose, preventing her from moving. "Rose is going nowhere with you."

Murdoc was visibly shaken. "Ye still want her? Even though Gunn may have put his bairn inside her? What kind of man are ye?"

Dominic felt his control eroding and struggled against his temper. He could not look at Rose. He would deal with her later, after her relatives were gone and his anger cooled. Dominic knew better than to believe Murdoc and Gunn, but he could not help feeling betrayed. Rose *was* in the bedchamber alone with Gunn, after all, and he wanted to know the how and why of it.

"Think you I would accept your word about Rose?" Dominic spat. "Nay, MacTavish. She is my wife. All your machinations cannot change that. Clear your belongings from the chamber and leave. Raj, muster some men and escort the MacTavish clan from the fortress."

"Ye are making a huge mistake, Dragon," Murdoc shouted as he gathered up his meager belongings. When he had everything, Raj manhandled Murdoc and Gunn from the chamber. " 'Tis not right to put a man out on a cold night," Murdoc complained as he stormed past Dominic.

Rose started to sidle past Dominic, but he stopped

her with a shake of his head. "Nay, wife, you have some explaining to do. What were you doing in Murdoc's bedchamber with Gunn?"

"Will you believe me if I tell you?"

Dominic stared at her. "Possibly."

Rose looked into Dragon's eyes and refused to quail beneath his harsh condemnation. "Possibly is not good enough, my lord. I already explained that Uncle Murdoc asked me to meet him here for a private word."

"Did Gunn have you, Rose?"

"Gunn is a strong man, Dominic, and I had no weapon, but I fought him until I realized I was only arousing him. Luckily, Raj arrived before Gunn had his way with me."

"Are you sure Raj arrived in time?" He frowned. "Did Gunn attack you? Tell me you were not a willing participant."

"I was not a willing participant," Rose repeated dully.

He grasped her arms, pulling her against him. "Dammit, Rose! The least you could do is sound like you mean it."

She struggled free. "What do you want from me, Dominic? First my uncle lied to me, then I was attacked, and now you accuse me of betraying you. Did you order Raj to follow me because you did not trust me? What have I done to deserve your suspicion?" She whirled away.

"Where are you going?"

"Emily and Blythe are waiting for me in the solar."

"I sent them away."

Rose glared at him. "When did you do that?"

"After Murdoc told me you were dallying with Gunn in his bedchamber. I did not want to believe him, so I searched for you in the solar. Your ladies were there, waiting for you. I told them you were delayed and sent them away."

"Then I will seek my bed. This night has been a trying one."

Dominic let her go. If what Rose said was true, she had been sorely used. Still, he had not actually accused her of infidelity. He was a fair man, but Rose was his wife, and being humiliated by a woman was a blow to his pride. He was, however, determined to learn the truth. Murdoc and Gunn were not the most reliable sources of information. He had already heard Rose's side, and now he intended to hear what Raj had to say. He left the bedchamber a few minutes after Rose and went in search of Raj.

Dominic did not have far to look. Raj was waiting just beyond the door.

"What do you know about this, Raj?" Dominic asked without preamble. "Tell me exactly what you saw and heard."

"I saw your lady leave the hall, master, and followed as you directed. Since it was her uncle's bedchamber she visited, I was not overly concerned about her safety, but I lingered outside the door nevertheless."

"What convinced you to burst into the chamber? Did you hear something unusual?"

"I heard Lady Rose cry out and did not wait for an invitation to enter. I tried the door and found it locked."

Dominic's breath hitched painfully, but he had to hear the rest no matter how much it hurt. "What did you see, Raj?"

"Your lady trapped beneath Gunn on the bed. She appeared to be struggling, and I liked it not. He had his hand over her mouth and his cock . . . need I say more, master? I arrived before any harm was done. I would have beat the bastard to death if you had let me."

Dominic found he could finally breathe again. "Killing Gunn would have done naught but start a war. The Scotsmen are gone, 'tis all that matters. They will find no welcome at Dragonwyck in the future. I want them nowhere near Rose."

" 'Tis a wise decision," Raj agreed solemnly.

"Now I'd best find Rose and see how much damage has been done. She is not an easy woman to placate, and I fear I have offended her."

As Dominic made his way to the solar, he did not hear Raj chuckle, nor see the sparkle of amusement in his dark eyes.

Chapter Eight

The fragrance always stays in the hand that
gives the rose.

—Hada Bejar

Dominic found Rose in the sitting room. She was standing before the hearth, gazing absently into the dancing flames. She looked upset, and he could not blame her. Her uncle had proved unworthy of her love and respect, and her husband had disappointed her. She turned to look at him when he entered the chamber, and the hurt expression on her face nearly brought him to his knees. He preferred his fierce warrior woman to the crushed rose standing before him.

"I did not really believe your uncle," Dominic said. It was almost an apology, but not quite. "Nor was I convinced that you wanted Gunn."

The crushed rose suddenly bloomed with anger. "Of course I did not want Gunn. Did you not see the look on my uncle's face when his plot to discredit me failed? He was determined to take me with him across the border to Scotland no matter what he had to do or say to accomplish it. He would have let Gunn rape me and felt no guilt as long as it served his purpose."

"Thank God for Raj," Dominic said fervently. He reached for her hand and drew her into his arms. "Did Gunn hurt you?"

Obviously, Rose was in no mood to be placated. "He did not hurt me," she bit out. "If you would be so kind, please explain why Raj was spying on me. Did you think I was going to run off, or betray you?"

"Raj was there to protect you. I trusted neither your uncle nor Gunn, and I was right."

Rose tried to remove herself from Dominic's arms, but he simply held her tighter. He could not let her go; she felt too good in his arms.

"Admit it, 'twas *me* you did not trust," Rose maintained. "I am glad for Raj's intervention, but I cannot forgive you for thinking so little of me that you would have him spy on me."

"I was concerned for your safety," Dominic replied, surprising himself by his admission. He stared into her expressive eyes and could not look away. "You are a beautiful woman, Rose. Anger becomes you. I cannot believe I ever mistook you for Starla. One has but to look into your eyes to see the difference between you."

"Do not try to cozen me, Dominic, for I am not receptive to your false words."

"Shall we see if you are receptive to my kisses?"

159

Rose's murmur of protest ended in a throaty gurgle as Dominic captured her mouth. She tasted of anger and ambrosia, of blazing temper and melting heat. He might never tame his Rose, but he was determined to sweep past the thorns and sample the sweetness beneath her prickly exterior. He had already tasted her passion and wanted, nay, needed to drink deeply of it again.

His dark eyes glowed with desire as he swept her into his arms and carried her to the bedchamber.

Rose knew what Dragon intended and tried to convince herself it was not what she wanted. The flames that warmed the depths of his eyes warned her that he would not be dissuaded from having his way. She could protest till doomsday, but in the end she would lose not only control of her body but a part of herself.

He started to undress her. She stood motionless, neither helping nor protesting, unable to look anywhere but into Dragon's eyes. They were dark, intensely compelling eyes. Eyes that took possession of her, warmed her skin and heated her blood.

Cool air caressed her skin, and Rose realized she had been stripped naked while lost in the hypnotic depths of Dragon's gaze. He brought their bodies together; startled, Rose realized he had shed his own clothing as well as hers. Heat arced between them and filled her.

"We are good together, Rose," Dominic whispered hoarsely. He touched her breasts. "Your body is already swelling with desire." He grasped her right hand, placed it over her left breast and held it there beneath his own hand.

Rose's eyes widened, and she shuddered when he moved his fingers over hers, guiding them over her breasts. A strangled cry rose up in her throat. She had never touched herself like that.

"Can you feel your nipples growing?" Dragon asked. Her fingers grazed over the hardened tips. They felt swollen and were tender to her touch.

Abruptly Dragon flung her hand away and replaced it with his mouth. Erotic sensation overwhelmed her as he licked and sucked her nipples, first one and then the other, his teeth nipping gently at the engorged buds as his hot, throbbing cock probed between her thighs. A sobbing moan slipped past her lips.

"Like that, do you?" Dragon asked, lifting his head from the succulent bounty of Rose's breasts.

Capturing her trembling hand again, he enfolded it around his throbbing shaft. "Touch me," he groaned. "Can you feel how much I want you?"

Her hand tightened around him. The sudden intake of his breath told Rose how much he enjoyed her touch. He was huge and growing larger. Her hand moved down his length, testing the granite-like hardness, then the heavy sacs beneath. If she were honest, she would admit to being tempted by his virile masculinity. The difference in their bodies enthralled and thrilled her. Rose did not want to like this man, but his body spoke to her in ways that broke down her defenses.

She moved closer, brushing her breasts against his

chest, deploring the imp inside her that wanted to taste the passion Dragon could bring her.

Her mouth sought his. A gratified murmur sounded deep in his throat as he returned her kiss, driving his tongue deep inside her mouth. They kissed endlessly, lost in a world of sensual pleasure. Rose scarcely noticed when Dragon lifted her into his arms, settled her on the bed and followed her down.

His dark, sensual gaze was compelling, his hands arousing as they began to stroke her aching, intensely needy body. She strained against him as he rubbed the globes of her breasts, his fingers spreading pure rapture into the stiffened peaks of her nipples.

She wanted him, she realized. Wanted to feel him inside her, filling her, taking her outside herself to a world where stars exploded and pleasure reigned.

Rose's thoughts splintered when she felt the blistering heat of Dragon's mouth and tongue move slowly down her body, creating a trail of fire between her breasts and across her stomach. Her breath hitched when his mouth traveled into forbidden territory.

"Dominic! What are you doing?"

"Making you happy, I hope," Dominic muttered against the musky scent of her arousal. "Relax, Rose. I want you to enjoy what I am doing to you."

He returned to his succulent feast, his tongue rooting amidst the curly blond hair between her thighs and parting the moist petals of her sex until he found the dewy pearl of her femininity.

Shocked by Dragon's bold caress, Rose grasped a handful of dark hair and tugged. "Dragon! Nay! 'Tis wicked. We will surely burn in hell."

Dragon lifted his head, his smile so sinfully unrepentant that Rose feared for both their souls.

"I am already in hell, love. But I am sure hell never tasted this good."

He'd called her his love! Did he know what he had just said?

Before she could respond, he buried his head between her legs and used his mouth and tongue to drive her to the brink of madness. And it *was* madness. Never in her wildest dreams had Rose imagined this kind of intimacy was possible, or even desirable, between a man and a woman. But Dragon was proving her wrong . . . so very wrong.

Rose quivered, then went rigid when his tongue parted the ripe sweetness of her petal-like folds. Turning red with embarrassment, she wanted to die when she heard him inhale deeply of her scent, but when his tongue probed deep inside her, she could do naught but dig her fingers into his shoulders and cling.

With hair tumbling in a golden mass upon the pillow, her head tossed from side to side as Dragon explored her most intimate secrets with slow strokes and bold caresses. She moaned and arched against his clever mouth, certain she would die if he stopped and fearing she would burn in hell if he continued. It was torture. It was rapture. It was heaven and hell. Fire surged through her veins, mixed with her blood, spread through her nerve endings.

Stiff with mounting tension, Rose clung to the pinnacle, then splintered into a thousand pieces as sharp pleasure pierced her body.

She drew a shallow breath and moaned helplessly

as Dragon slid upward, parted her damp cleft and drove inside her while her body was still vibrating. She arched her hips against him, clinging desperately as he began a savage rhythm that carried her still higher. What she felt was primitive, raw, feral. Her body responded to his with renewed passion as Dragon released something wild and tumultuous inside her.

Dominic felt Rose reach for the peak and deliberately slowed his pace. He waited until she steadied, until she was one step away from the edge, then went in deep and held still.

Her hips thrust up against him. "Dominic! Please."

"Do not move."

Another long in-and-out slide sent her into spasms. Hot honey bathed his cock, and the evocative scent of their loving spurred him to the pinnacle as her muscles locked tightly around him. He wanted to prolong her climax, but his own was coming too fast.

She came apart in his arms.

After that, he lost touch with reality. The woman beneath him was his world; he recalled no other. She was everything that was sensual and lush. He sank into her, again and again, driving himself so high he feared the fall back to earth would destroy him.

And in a way it did. Shattered and broken, Dominic returned to reality with the frightening impression that he would never be the same.

Dominic flung himself away from Rose and settled down beside her. He could still feel his heart thudding against his rib cage and he tried to make sense out of what had just happened. He had been certain that the passion he and Veronica shared was unparalleled, but he had been mistaken. Making love to Rose far surpassed his most memorable moments with Veronica. Convincing himself that Rose was no different from any other woman he had bedded was not going to be easy. Lord help him if Rose suspected how he felt. He knew from experience that some women turned shrewish and demanding once they gained sexual power over a man, and Dominic had too much pride to let his passions rule him.

Rose realized that something of tremendous import had just happened. She wanted to deny it, but to deny the significance of what she and Dragon had just shared would be to label herself a wanton. Her heart and mind told her that no man but Dragon could wring the same kind of response from her. The thought of kissing another man and doing the things she and Dragon did together was revolting.

A sob found its way to her throat, and she choked it back. She did not want to like Dragon, fought against it, but her will had betrayed her and her flesh was weak. Dragon created a fire in her blood that made her want him, made her forget that he served the king who had murdered her father.

Turning away from Dragon, Rose forced herself to relax. When he moved close to her, she scooted to the edge of the bed. She did not want him touching her, starting another blaze inside her.

Rose closed her eyes and searched for sleep. She did not find it until she heard the even cadence of

Dragon's breathing and realized he would not attempt another assault upon her senses this night.

Dragon was gone when Rose awoke the following morning. The fire had been kindled in the grate, and cozy warmth filled the chamber. She washed, dressed and hurried to the hall to break her fast. Dragon was already enjoying a hearty breakfast when she joined him. As always, Raj stood behind him, his dark gaze scanning the hall for potential danger.

"I trust you slept well," Dragon said as she slipped into the chair beside him.

He sounded rather distant, as if his mind were occupied elsewhere. Had he already forgotten the passion they had shared last night? She hoped he had, for she intended to do the same. Dragon's ego was inflated enough; he did not need to know that his loving had changed her life.

"I slept just fine, thank you," Rose answered with the same cool reserve.

"I rode out early to make sure your uncle and his kinsmen had returned to Scotland," Dragon said. "I saw the place where they had camped, but they were gone by the time I arrived. Think you they will return?"

Rose helped herself to food before answering. "Uncle Murdoc is a stubborn man. He will not rest until he has what he wants, and he wants Dragonwyck. He could make trouble for you in the future. I do not think ordering him from Dragonwyck was a prudent thing to do. His anger can be formidable."

Dragon's dark eyebrows lifted. "Think you I should have let him stay and abuse you?"

Rose flushed. "I could have handled him."

Dragon snorted. "Just like you handled Gunn? Sorry, my love, I will not offer hospitality to Clan MacTavish anytime in the near or distant future."

Rose was startled by Dragon's endearment, although she knew it meant naught to him. He had called her his "love" last night, but his cool greeting this morning belied his words.

Rose chewed thoughtfully as she considered the rest of Dragon's words. He was right, she decided. Uncle Murdoc wanted her for Gunn, even though she could not abide his stepson. The fact that she was already married bothered Murdoc not at all, for he was determined to claim Dragonwyck as his own.

"I would not be unhappy if you barred Uncle Murdoc from Dragonwyck," Rose admitted.

"Then we are in agreement," Dragon said, rising. "I plan to join the hunters today. Our guests will find no lack of food at our banquet table."

"How long will you be gone?" Rose asked.

He shrugged. "Three or four days."

"Have the invitations been prepared? They should be delivered as soon as possible."

"Messengers carry them to the designated barons even as we speak." In a surprising move, he bent and kissed her lightly on the lips. "Try not to miss me too much," he added in a low growl.

Stunned, Rose touched her lips. She was saved from having to reply when Raj stepped forward and addressed Dragon.

"I will ride with you, master," Raj said.

"I prefer that you remain behind, Raj," Dominic said.

"You and Eric of Carlyle are the two people I trust to protect Dragonwyck in my absence."

Raj frowned. "I like it not."

"Nevertheless, you will follow orders. Stay behind and protect my wife."

Rose sensed that Raj was unhappy with Dragon's decision to leave him behind. Hoping to ease the tension between the two men, she said, "Take Raj with you, my lord. No harm will come to me in my own home."

"I will decide what you need and do not need," Dominic replied. "Raj stays."

Rose bristled angrily. She was perfectly capable of protecting herself. After Gunn's assault, she had decided to carry a weapon. Even now she had a blade much more lethal than her eating knife secreted on her person. But when she opened her mouth to fling a scathing retort at Dragon, he was too far away to hear.

Men, she thought, exasperated. Were they all as arrogant and overbearing as Dragon? Did they all believe women were inferior beings capable of naught but managing a household and bringing children into the world? One day, she vowed, she would make Dragon change his mind about the fairer sex.

Emily and Blythe joined Rose after Dragon's hasty departure. Rose discussed the upcoming festivities with them and asked for suggestions. Both ladies were more than eager to participate.

"I can hardly wait!" Blythe said, clapping her hands. "What can I do to help?"

"Imagine. Twelve days of festivities," Emily said,

eyes shining. "Oh, there is so much to do and so little time."

"Exactly," Rose agreed. She sighed wistfully. "I wish Mama and Starla were here. I have never done this by myself."

"You will do just fine," Emily said encouragingly. "How can we help?"

"If it pleases you, Emily, you can direct the servants in the cleaning of the keep. Every tapestry needs to be taken down and aired. Fresh rushes should be laid down, and whitewash applied to the walls in the hall. I am sure you know better than I what needs to be done."

"Scrubbing, polishing and decorating the hall with holly and pine wreaths," Emily said, nodding eagerly. "Do we have enough help for such a massive undertaking?"

"We will need to summon villeins from the village to lend a hand."

"What about me?" Blythe asked.

"You can be in charge of accommodations. Every bedchamber in the keep will be occupied by guests," Rose said. "Some have not been used for several years. Linens need to be checked, and beds and other furnishings brought up from the storeroom. Ask Sir Braden for a list of guests. That should tell you how many bedchambers are needed."

Rose paused to catch her breath. "I will assume charge of the kitchen and preparation of food. A fortnight is not a lot of time, but I am confident we will be prepared by the time the first guest arrives."

From that moment, the keep became a beehive of

activity. During the four days that Dragon was gone, Rose found Raj's help invaluable. His extraordinary strength was tested more than once as he lifted, hefted and tugged wherever he was needed.

Even though Raj made himself useful, Rose could tell the giant's thoughts were elsewhere. Was he concerned about Dragon? Rose decided to ask him when she found herself alone with him.

"Are you worried about Lord Dragon, Raj? You seem distracted."

"My master thinks he can protect himself, but no man is invincible. He is a strong man with good instincts, but he cannot properly watch his back."

"Is Dragon in danger?" Rose asked sharply. "Who would harm him?"

"I have said too much, my lady. 'Twas not my intention to alarm you."

"Tell me about Dragon," Rose urged. She knew so little about the man she had wed. "Does he have family? I know he has a mistress. How long were they together before the king ordered him to marry me?"

"Lord Dragon's father, mother and brother live at Pendragon in the south of England. I accompanied him after the Crusade, when we first arrived in England. His brother, the heir to Pendragon, married an heiress and sired two sons."

"Did Dragon have a happy childhood?"

"I cannot say, for he rarely speaks of his childhood. His family seemed pleasant enough. I sensed no hostility. But my Lord Dragon is a man who lives by his own rules. He once told me that he broke from his family and sought his independence at an early age.

Since he was not the heir, he saw no reason to live under family restrictions. He joined the Crusade and became the king's champion."

Rose digested all that, then asked, "And what of his mistress? How long has Dragon loved her?"

Raj's face went blank. "I cannot read my master's mind. Love has many guises. Your own influence upon Lord Dragon is not inconsiderable."

Rose sent Raj an amused look. "I know my place in Dragon's life, and it has naught to do with love."

"Those are your words, not mine," Raj contended.

"But you have told me naught about his mistress," Rose complained. "Is she very beautiful? Does she love Dragon?"

"Forgive me, my lady, but I cannot say," Raj replied, withdrawing tactfully. "Ask your questions of Lord Dragon. Only he can tell you what is in his heart."

Rose knew what was in Dragon's heart, and it was not his wife. He seemed to enjoy her body well enough, but Rose wanted more from the man she had married. She wanted her husband, the man who shared her bed, to think only of her, to dream of a future with her, to need her for herself instead of thinking of her as a warm body to serve him while he pined for his mistress. Rose knew she expected too much from an arranged marriage, and that life was rarely fair to women, but she could not help wishing for love. She knew love existed, for her mother and father had loved one another dearly despite their arranged marriage.

Rose sighed and returned to her work. Dragon had

been gone four days, and the anxious expression Raj wore upon his face was not comforting.

Dominic and his party had a successful four days. They had bagged a variety of fresh game, including deer, rabbit, squirrel and wild boar. Another hunting expedition or two should provide the kitchen with enough fresh meat for the twelve days of feasting, supplemented with fish and eels caught in the river and lamb and beef from their own herds. Dominic considered the four days well spent, but he was happy to be returning to Dragonwyck.

Dragon and the hunters were riding at a leisurely pace, laughing and conversing among themselves, when the surprise attack occurred. Without warning, arrows flew out from a stand of thick trees at the base of the Cheviot hills. Dominic and his men immediately took cover behind some nearby boulders, drew their crossbows and aimed into the trees at an enemy no one could see. No one but Cedric, who had been riding beside Dominic at the time, was aware that Dominic had been hit.

Dominic slumped in the saddle, unwilling to succumb to the pain coursing through his body. The arrow had entered his left shoulder and halted when it hit bone.

"What can I do?" Cedric asked, helping Dominic dismount.

"Remove the arrow," Dominic said from between clenched teeth.

Cedric paled. "Are you sure, my lord?"

"Just do it, Cedric. Worry not about hurting me; I can withstand the pain."

Cedric grasped the shaft of the arrow and pulled. The arrow came out, releasing a gush of blood. Dominic uttered a single gasp and turned pale, but remained in full control of his senses.

"We need to stanch the blood," Dominic advised.

Immediately Cedric removed his jacket and peeled off his shirt. He wadded it into a ball, unbuttoned Dominic's jacket and pressed it against the wound. Then he buttoned the jacket over the bulky pad, removed his belt and buckled it around the makeshift bandage to hold it in place.

Dominic rested against a boulder while the hunters loosed a rain of arrows into the trees. The battle was short-lived. Minutes later the assailants turned tail and ran.

"How many dead and wounded?" Dominic asked when James of Bedford reported to him a short time later.

James seemed taken aback when he saw that Dominic was wounded. "Two wounded, none dead," James said. "Are you all right, my lord? Can you make it back to Dragonwyck?"

"Worry not about me, James. Have the men search the area. I want to know the identity of those who dared attack us on Dragonwyck soil."

James left immediately to carry out Dominic's orders. He returned a short time later with a disappointing report. They had found nothing save their own spent arrows.

"All their wounded and dead had been carried

away," James said. "There were bloodstains in the snow, so I know our arrows found some of them."

"We should make haste back to the keep," Dominic said, weaving groggily on his feet. "The wounded need to be treated." He placed a hand on Cedric's shoulder. "Help me to mount."

The skies lowered, and it started to snow before they reached the keep. A cold wind blew fresh snow against the knights' faces, nearly blinding them. Lured by the promise of warm stalls and food, their horses carried them unerringly to Dragonwyck.

Rose heard the call before she saw the men riding into the inner bailey.

"The lord returns! The lord returns!"

Grabbing a cloak, Rose flew out the front door to await Dragon's return. Raj hurried after her. Rose squinted at the riders through a curtain of blowing snow and knew something was wrong. Very wrong. Raj must have read her thoughts, for he lurched forward. "He should not have ordered me to remain behind," Raj said grimly.

Rose searched the face of each knight, seeking Dragon. A cry slipped past her lips when she saw him slumped over his horse's withers. She raced out to meet him, but Raj arrived first.

Raj was already lifting Dragon from his horse when she reached his side. "What happened? How bad is he hurt?"

"An arrow, my lady," Cedric explained as he dismounted beside her. "I do not think the wound is life-threatening. We were attacked on our way back from the hunt. On our own land."

"Carry him up to the solar," Rose ordered crisply.

"I can walk on my own," Dominic insisted. He gave a dismissive gesture with his hand. "I have been wounded before, and this is not a serious injury. Put me down, Raj." Raj looked skeptical but obeyed. Dominic took two steps and collapsed. Fortunately, Raj was there to catch him.

Chapter Nine

Someone said that God gave us memory so that
we might have roses in December.
—Sir J. M. Barrie

"Who did this to you?" Rose asked as she applied a
healing salve to Dominic's wound.

Embarrassed that he had collapsed in front of his
men, Dominic could not look Rose in the eye. Strong
men did not succumb to weakness.

"We did not see them. They hid behind trees and
attacked without warning and left as quickly as they
appeared. Mayhap they were outlaws."

Rose was quiet a long moment as she wound a bandage over Dominic's shoulder. "Could it have been
Uncle Murdoc?"

" 'Tis possible. Your uncle is a vindictive man. My

death would be convenient for him." Dominic winced when Rose pulled the bandage a bit too tight. "You did that quite well. Who taught you healing arts?"

"I learned what little I know from my mother. She knows a great deal about herbs and healing. If you develop a fever, I can brew a tea to cure it."

"Once again you amaze me," Dominic said. He could not imagine Veronica looking at his wound, much less treating it. The sight of blood made her ill. More than once he had caught her eyeing the scar on his hip with revulsion, or averting her face so she would not see it.

"The lady of the keep is expected to treat her vassals' minor wounds and illnesses," Rose explained. "Since I am Papa's heir, Mama taught me the rudimentary skills of healing."

When Dominic started drifting off to sleep, Rose prepared to leave. Suddenly he opened his eyes and grasped her arm. "Thank you. After a short rest, I will join you in the hall for the evening meal."

"You will do no such thing," Rose said sternly. "You've lost a great deal of blood and should rest in bed a day or two before exerting yourself."

Dominic glared at her. "Do not coddle me, Rose."

Rose's chin rose to a determined angle. "You will do as I say. If you try to leave your bed, Raj will stop you."

"Raj is my man. He will do as I say."

"Not in this instance. Really, Dominic, why are you being so stubborn?"

"Because I do not like to be told what to do."

Rose sent him a blinding smile. "I find that I enjoy

it excessively." She turned away. "I will leave you to rest."

"When will you return?" Dominic asked petulantly.

"I will return to check on your wound before I retire."

Dominic's eyes narrowed. "That sounds like you intend to sleep elsewhere."

Rose shrugged. "I thought it best to find another bed while you are recovering."

"Like hell!" Dominic thundered. "This is our bed, and you will sleep in it with me. Have I made myself clear?"

"Perfectly," Rose said sweetly—too sweetly, Dominic thought. She turned to leave. "I will send a tray of food up to you."

Disgruntled, Dominic stared at her departing back. Being told to remain in bed rankled his pride. Being ordered around by Rose made him feel like a weakling. Dominic defiantly swung his legs off the bed and pushed himself to his feet. No puny wound was going to stop him from doing as he pleased, and he would be damned if he would let a woman tell him what he could and could not do.

So far so good, Dominic thought as he pulled on his hose and tunic. Though his head spun dizzily and his shoulder and arm throbbed, he tottered resolutely toward the door. He lifted the latch and shoved the door open. Now all he had to do was negotiate the stairs.

"Where are you going, master?"

Startled, Dominic looked up into Raj's stern features. "Move aside, Raj. I intend to join my wife in the hall."

"Forgive me, master, but the mistress says you are to remain in bed."

Dominic could not believe his ears. This was the first time in his memory that Raj had disobeyed an order. "You forget who is master, Raj."

"Nay, master, but in this instance I must bow to Lady Rose's wisdom. Will you return to bed or must I carry you?"

Dominic knew when he had been outflanked, and this was one of those rare times he could not control the situation. Grumbling with malcontent, he shuffled back to bed. Within minutes he was sleeping. He knew naught until he woke the following morning and found Rose lying in bed beside him. A smile lifted the corner of his mouth. At least she had not defied him in everything.

The fever Dominic developed during the night was of short duration. Rose used her knowledge of herbs to dose him, and from that point on his recovery progressed rapidly.

Within two days Dominic was out of bed and immersed in preparations for the upcoming festivities. Replies to his invitations had begun to arrive, and Dominic fully expected all ten marcher barons to accept. The keep would be crowded, but Rose had assured him that Dragonwyck could accommodate the guests and their entourages.

Dominic sent his hunters out again and was relieved when they encountered no further trouble with outlaws. Dominic wanted to ride with them, but both Raj and Rose had insisted that he would do himself irreparable harm if he tried to ride before he was fully recovered. Dominic allowed them to have their way, but he did not like it.

The days rushed by with uncommon haste. Excitement reigned throughout the keep. The hall sparkled, the rushes were fragrant with basil, and the scent of pine, holly and bay filled the air. Mistletoe and pine-cone decorations were hung, and a Yule log had already been cut and left outside the door. Cook and her helpers worked feverishly, preparing food and delicacies that made Dominic's mouth water.

On December twenty-fourth, the feast of Adam and Eve, a tree was cut, brought into the keep and decorated with apples in remembrance of the first family and their sin. Two barons arrived that evening, John of Sheldon and Blayne of Draymore. Dominic knew of them but had not met them before. Both men were powerful marcher barons who opposed the king. Sheldon brought his wife, Mary, and two young sons, and Draymore brought his bride, Aleta. Large entourages accompanied both families.

Dominic was not surprised to learn that Rose was acquainted with the guests. He learned that nearly all the marcher barons had been guests of her father's at one time or another, and that the last time she had seen them was when they had come to confer with her father about King John's unreasonable laws.

Seven barons and their families arrived on Christmas Day. The last baron, Henry of Ashford, was expected momentarily. The chambers were filled to the rafters with guests, their knights, squires, servants and nursemaids, and the sound of children's laughter drifted through the halls. A caravan of Gypsies on their way south for the winter months had heard about the festivities being held at Dragonwyck and stopped by. They offered to perform in exchange for the right to camp within Dragonwyck's walls. Dominic accepted with alacrity and invited them to set up their camp in the inner bailey.

Rose could not decide what to wear on the first night of the festivities. Officially she was still in mourning, but she did not mention that to Dragon when he had suggested the celebration. She knew her father would rather she celebrated life instead of death.

After considerable thought, Rose chose a dark green under-gown of fine wool with long, close-fitting sleeves. Her long vermilion over-gown trailed on the ground, but she pulled up the excess folds and tucked them beneath the belt circling her hips. The V opening of the upstanding collar was trimmed in gold and green and was large enough to slip over her head. The over-sleeves ended at the elbow and hung down from a moderately wide opening.

Rose wore her long hair plaited into two loose braids, covered with a linen veil and held in place by a gold band studded with green stones. Dragon walked into the bedchamber just as she was adjusting her braids beneath the headpiece.

"I prefer your hair loose," he said, giving her braid a playful tug.

Rose snatched it from his hand. "I prefer it braided. I am a married woman now and should adhere to propriety."

"Propriety be damned. I know what I like, and I like your hair down."

His dark eyes moved appreciatively over her body. "You look beautiful, Rose. You will be the envy of every woman present tonight."

"I do not need your compliments, Dominic," Rose said. She studied him through a lavish fringe of gold lashes. "You look quite handsome yourself, my lord."

It was true, Rose thought. Dominic's belted tunic of purple wool trimmed in silver ended at his knee and was elegant in its simplicity. His short velvet cloak was held together by a jeweled pin and was the same bold purple as his tunic. Rose's gaze slid lower. Never had she seen a finer pair of legs on a man.

He sent her a cocky grin. "Am I magnificent enough to dazzle all the ladies?"

"If that is your intent, you should succeed admirably," Rose mocked. "I am sure all the ladies will swoon over the Dragon Lord."

"Will you swoon, Rose?"

Rose gave an indignant snort. "I have never swooned in my life."

He stepped closer. Heat arced from his skin to hers. The look in his eyes was so intense, so compelling, Rose felt her toes curl inside her shoes.

"Have you not, love? If you recall, I have made you swoon from pleasure on more than one occasion. I know I have been neglecting you of late, what with the preparations for the festivities taking up my time, but I promise to do better in the future." He toyed with the end of her braid. "Tonight, when we are alone, you will wear your hair down for me and I will make you swoon."

"I have not felt neglected at all," Rose retorted. "You have been recovering from a wound, and I have been busy."

Rose wanted to flee someplace where Dragon's compelling gaze could not find her, but his dark desire held her suspended, drawing her to him like a moth to flame.

He laughed and offered his arm. "Shall we greet our guests, my love? The sooner the evening is over, the sooner we can retire to our bedchamber and indulge ourselves."

Rose placed her hand on his arm. "I fear it will be very late, my lord."

"Anticipation is said to be an aphrodisiac."

"Humph! As if you needed one."

"Are you complaining, Rose?"

"This is not a proper conversation, Dominic," Rose chided. "Our guests await us and we are late."

They heard the laughter and hum of voices as they descended the staircase. When they entered the hall, applause greeted them. Dominic guided Rose to the dais and seated her with a flourish. Then he lifted his hand for silence, and though everyone had been welcomed personally upon arrival, Dominic gave a warm welcoming speech and told them about the hunting and hawking he had planned for the next twelve days.

Father Nyle gave the blessing, and then the feasting began. The tables had been set with white cloths, steel knives, silver spoons, dishes for salt, silver cups and *mazers*—silver-trimmed wooden bowls. At each place was a trencher, a thick slice of day-old bread serving as a plate for roasted meats.

Bread and butter were carried in first and distributed among the tables, followed closely by ale and wine imported from English-ruled Bordeaux. The first course was a thick, savory soup. The solid parts were eaten with a spoon and the broth sipped from the bowl. Squires, trained in serving food, stood behind their lords and saw to their needs.

The blast of a horn announced the meat course as servants paraded into the room carrying trays of roasted venison that had been turned all day on a spit, followed in close order by platters of boiled beef, roasted boar and grouse.

Dominic placed tender slices of meat on the trencher he and Rose shared and cut them into manageable pieces. She picked them up and ate with her fingers. Eels and a variety of fish dishes were served next, accompanied by assorted root vegetables swimming in butter and cream sauce. During the meal, Gypsy musicians played softly in the background.

Before the final course of fruits, nuts, cheese and spiced wine, the last baron arrived with his entourage. Henry of Ashford was apologetic as he explained his lateness to Dominic.

"Forgive me, Dragon, for arriving in the middle of your meal. One of our wagons broke down, delaying our arrival. I thank God I did not bring the children along. I am Henry Ashford. We met in London several months ago."

"No need for apology, Ashford," Dominic said. "My wife and I are happy you arrived safely. I do indeed recall meeting you in London and hope your stay at Dragonwyck will be a pleasant one. Did you bring your wife, my lord?"

"Aye, and a houseguest. My wife had invited her cousin for the Christmas holidays before we received your invitation. I mentioned that I was bringing a houseguest in my response to your invitation, did I not?"

"So you did," Dominic acknowledged. "Accommodating one more guest is no problem."

Dominic looked beyond Ashford to the two ladies who had just entered the hall. The hush that followed in their wake should have alerted him, but it was not until Raj leaned over his shoulder and whispered a harsh warning in his ear that he recognized one of the ladies approaching the dais. Dragonwyck was the last place he had expected to see Lady Veronica.

"I was told Lady Veronica is an acquaintance of yours, Dragon," Ashford said. "The other lady is my wife, Lady Cambra."

Dominic stared at Veronica an unseemly length of time. She was as beautiful as he remembered. Memories of the pleasure they had once shared overwhelmed him. It was not until Rose poked him in the ribs that he found his tongue and introduced Rose.

"I already know Lord and Lady Ashford," Rose acknowledged, deliberately ignoring Veronica. "Welcome to Dragonwyck. I hope your stay is a pleasant one."

"I am sure it will be," Veronica purred, looking directly at Dominic. "Your husband and I are old and intimate friends. I am looking forward to renewing our acquaintance."

Independence Public Library

Veronica's little speech earned a frown from Lady Cambra, but the brash beauty seemed not to care. Dominic, however, was flustered. A rare occurrence, and one he liked not. Having his mistress and wife under the same roof for twelve days was going to be awkward. And if Rose's sour expression was any indication, there was going to be hell to pay.

"You and your party must be exhausted, Ashford," Dominic said. "My steward will show you to your chambers and see to your needs. Perhaps you would prefer to sup in your chambers after your arduous journey," Dominic suggested tactfully.

"I am not in the least tired," Veronica said brightly.

"I fear I have not the hearty constitution of my cousin," Lady Cambra said. "Supping in my chamber sounds wonderful." She smiled wanly. "It has been a trying day."

"I will join my wife," Ashford said. "I want to be fresh for the hunt tomorrow. Assuming there will be a hunt."

"Hunting and hawking have been planned for each of the twelve days," Dominic replied. He summoned the steward with a look, and Sir Braden came immediately.

"Show Lord and Lady Ashford to their chamber and provide whatever they require to make them comfortable. They wish to sup in their rooms tonight."

"Of course, my lord, at once. Does Lady Veronica wish to retire to her chamber also?"

"Nay," Veronica said, waving her hand in dismissal. "I believe I will find a seat at one of the tables and join the merriment." She turned a blinding smile on Dominic as Sir Braden ushered the Ashfords from the hall.

"You look wonderful, Dragon. Country air must agree with you."

"And you, my lady, are as lovely as ever," Dominic said graciously.

"Perhaps you and I can reminisce on old times later tonight," Veronica suggested coyly. Her eyes glinted mischievously. "In private, of course."

To Dominic's relief, James of Bedford, one of the knights who knew of his involvement with Veronica, came forward and offered to seat her at an empty place beside him. With a regal toss of her dark head, Veronica allowed James to lead her away, but not before slanting Dominic a look that held the promise of sensual delight.

Rose seethed with outrage as she watched the interchange between Dragon and his mistress. Veronica had made it blatantly clear that she expected to revive her intimate relationship with Dragon. Rose had sensed trouble the moment Veronica had walked into the hall and made note of the uncomfortable hush that followed. She had never seen Dragon's mistress before, but when she heard the lady's name and saw the look on Dragon's face, she came to the painful conclusion that Veronica's appearance was neither accidental nor a coincidence.

Dragon had sent for his mistress. There was no other explanation. Dragon's reason for hosting Christmas festivities at Dragonwyck made perfect sense now. He pined for his mistress and wanted an excuse to bring her to Dragonwyck.

"I did not plan this, Rose," Dominic said, as if reading Rose's mind. "I had no idea Veronica was the houseguest the Ashfords were bringing."

Rose shrugged. "It matters not, my lord. Your mistress seems most eager to renew your acquaintance. It would be rude to ignore her."

"Veronica is my *former* mistress, Rose. I am a married man now."

"Can you deny that you wanted to wed Veronica? That she is the woman you love?"

Dominic opened his mouth to speak, then abruptly closed it.

"What?" Rose taunted. "The Dragon Lord has naught to say in his own defense? How droll."

"Believe what you want, Rose, but I did not invite Veronica to Dragonwyck, nor have I been in touch with her since our marriage."

Rose wanted to spit in his face. Dragon was lying. He had taunted her with his love for Veronica and his reluctance to marry anyone else from the day he arrived to claim her home. Knowing this, Rose should not feel betrayed, but she did.

"I will retire early so you can dally to your heart's content with your mistress," Rose said with a calmness she was far from feeling. "Do not attempt to bring her to the solar, however, for I refuse to allow you to tumble her in my bed."

Dragon remained mute, which to Rose's thinking was prudent of him. She had heard all she cared to hear. She should not have allowed herself to fall prey to Dragon's lust. For a time she'd actually believed he was becoming fond of her. She did not expect love from him, but fondness would have been a big step toward learning to live in harmony with one another.

"I do not intend to rekindle my relationship with Veronica," Dominic insisted. "She knew when I left London there was no turning back."

"If you say so, my lord." Rose scraped back her chair. "Please excuse me if I do not remain for the entertainment. Make my excuses to our guests. Tell them whatever you want, it matters not to me."

Head held high, back stiff, Rose left the hall. She heard the whispers, the speculation, but refused to be brought low by her husband's mistress.

Dominic cursed the fates that had brought Veronica to Dragonwyck. He had finally begun to put his relationship with Veronica behind him and make peace with the life the king had given him. He wondered if he still loved Veronica. He was not sure he knew what love felt like, but what he and Veronica had together was so explosive that he had not wanted to let go.

Now he had Rose, the feisty warrior woman with whom he had found passion and something else, something that went beyond simple lust. Rose and Veronica were two different women, yet there was much to admire about each of them.

Dominic gazed at Veronica through shuttered eyes. She appeared to be having a good time, laughing and flirting outrageously. From time to time she would aim a sensual smile in his direction, and when she did, Dominic could not help wondering if the same magic still existed between them. He glanced toward the solar, his emotions raw and uncertain. He wanted to go after Rose but knew it would be rude to leave his guests in the middle of the entertainment.

Gypsy acrobats were tumbling in a cleared space in the center of the hall, and Cynric the bard had yet to spin his tales of love and adventure. Leaving now would cause too much gossip.

Cynric's stories did not hold Dominic's attention as they usually did, and it was no wonder. Finally the evening ended and the guests started drifting off to their chambers. As Dominic bade each good night, he reminded the men of the hunt planned for the following morning. John of Sheldon was the last to seek his bed, and Dominic soon learned he had a reason for waiting.

"Everyone is aware that you are close to John Lackland," Sheldon said in a hushed voice. "I was chosen by the other barons to speak to you about the injustices and restrictions the king has placed upon us. He shows no respect for his barons. We have prepared a writ we call the Articles of the Barons and want you to join our cause."

Dominic was not surprised to learn that the marcher lords had come with an agenda, for he had planned the celebration with that in mind. King John had warned him about the discontent among his barons and had asked Dominic to pass any information on to him. The king had hoped that Edwyn of Ayrdale's execution would end the plotting, but obviously it had only made the barons more determined to seek justice.

"I will meet with the barons, but I can promise naught," Dominic said. "Tell them I will listen to their grievances after the hunt tomorrow."

"I knew you would be reasonable. Tomorrow, then, Lord Dragon. We look forward to having you as an ally. King John is abusing his power, and we like it not."

Dominic sat before the hearth, brooding, long after Sheldon left.

"You appear troubled, master," Raj said as he joined Dominic.

"The marcher barons want me to join their cause. They believe King John has abused his powers."

"You are one of them now. They expect you to join them in their effort to curtail the king's excesses."

Dominic sighed. "Aye, but we both know I cannot." He gestured expansively. "Look at all the king has given me. He expects me to inform him should I find disloyalty among his barons."

"I am sure your conscience will guide you, master."

"I hope you are right, Raj." Dominic rose and stretched. " 'Tis time for bed."

Dominic wondered if Rose was still angry at him. She had left the hall in a huff, and he could not blame her. There was nothing subtle about Veronica. He knew without being told that these next twelve days were going to be trying in more ways than one.

"You need not stand guard at the door tonight, Raj," Dominic said when Raj started to follow him up the stairs. "Find your own bed. I will see you in the morning."

"Are you certain, master?"

"Very certain. Good night, Raj."

Dominic ascended the stairs, weary after a full day of entertaining his guests. He was eagerly looking forward to climbing into bed with Rose and making love to her. He only wondered if she would welcome him.

A smile stretched his lips. Anticipation made him grow hard beneath his braies, and he hurried along the gallery to the solar. The door opened beneath his hand, and he stepped into the sitting room. The door to the bedchamber was closed, but Dominic thought nothing of it as he turned the handle and pulled. He was disappointed but not shocked to find the door locked.

"Rose, open the door."

No answer was forthcoming.

Anger replaced disappointment. "Rose, I am warning you. Open the door or I will break it down."

"Go to your mistress, my lord. Mayhap she will welcome your attentions."

"You are acting childish, Rose. Had I wanted to be with Veronica tonight, I would not be here now."

"Oh, so now I am childish! Go away, Dominic."

"Do you want our guests to know what a shrew you are?"

"I care not what they think."

"I refuse to stand here and beg for entrance into my own bedchamber," he bit out. "You are right about Veronica. She would indeed welcome my attentions. Thank you for suggesting that I go to her. Good night, wife. Sleep well in your cold bed."

Dominic was in a foul mood by the time he returned to the hall. He had no intention of seeking out Veronica, but Rose did not need to know that. Nay, let her think what she wanted.

Dominic pulled his chair closer to the hearth and

settled down for the night. He had just started to doze off when a whisper of sound behind him jarred him awake. He reached for his sword and recalled that he had not worn one tonight. But he did carry a knife. He had started to unsheathe it when a whiff of perfume he remembered with fondness drifted past his nose.

"I hoped I would find you down here alone," Veronica purred, moving into his view. She caressed his face. " 'Tis good to see you, Dragon. I have missed you dreadfully."

Dominic caught her hand as it began to move down his body in a familiar way. "We cannot be seen like this, Veronica."

Before Dominic knew what she intended, she settled down on his lap. "Why ever not? Our relationship is no secret. Everyone knows we were lovers in London."

"This is not London."

Dominic felt himself stirring and stifled a groan. At one time the woman in his arms had meant everything to him, and apparently she still had the power to move him sexually. He was a man, after all, but did he still want Veronica as much as he had before the king gifted him with Rose and Dragonwyck?

" 'Tis obvious you and your wife are at odds, Dragon, and that the marriage is not to your liking. I will stay at Dragonwyck as long as you like and we can become lovers again. You would not be the first man to bring his mistress to live in his home."

Dominic nearly laughed aloud at Veronica's suggestion. Rose would never accept his mistress in her home. Nor did Dominic welcome the idea of Veronica interfering in his life with Rose. There had been a subtle change in his life since London, and her name was Rose. It was difficult to believe that he had once cared enough about Veronica to marry her. He was still fond of her, but it occurred to him that her appeal was strictly sexual and probably would have waned in time.

A sudden thought occurred, and he grinned. "Rose would skewer you with her sword if I allowed you to remain at Dragonwyck. Go to bed, Veronica."

Veronica's eyes narrowed. "You have changed, Dragon. What has that witch done to you? No lady I know would attack another with a sword. Surely you jest."

"Believe me, I do not jest. There is bite to Rose's bark. I suggest you do naught to trigger her temper during your stay, else you may live to regret it. You may remove yourself from my lap now."

Veronica ground her bottom into Dominic's loins and grinned. "You want me, Dragon. I can feel your cock growing as we speak. Kiss me, Dragon. Let me show you how desperately I missed you."

Dominic knew of no courteous way to discourage Veronica short of dumping her off his lap, and because she had once meant a great deal to him, he could not do that.

Rose began to regret her angry words the moment Dragon left the solar. As she tossed and turned in her bed, she wondered if Dragon had followed her advice and sought solace in Veronica's bed. Driven by curiosity, she donned a dressing gown and left the solar.

Rush lights supported by wall brackets provided light as she crept down the stairs to the hall.

The shadows were dark and deep in the cavernous chamber as Rose paused in the doorway, her wandering gaze stopping abruptly on the couple cozily entwined in the lord's chair.

Dragon and Veronica.

Dragon's arms were wrapped around his mistress, and they were kissing. The sharp intake of Rose's breath pierced the silence. The couple in the chair broke apart and stared at Rose.

"Damn you, Dragon!" Rose shouted, shaking with fury. "If I had my sword I would run you both through."

Dominic leaped from the chair, dumping Veronica on the floor, as Rose turned and fled.

"Dammit, Veronica. Now you have gone and done it. Never say I did not warn you."

Chapter Ten

There is simply the rose: it is perfect in every
moment of its existence.
—Ralph Waldo Emerson

Rose heard Dominic pounding up the staircase after
her. He was but a few steps behind her when she
reached the solar. If he tried to touch her after kissing
Veronica, she would kill him. She opened the door
and rushed inside. He was right behind her. Shaking
with fury, she reached for Dragon's sword, which was
leaning against the wall beside the hearth. She grasped
the hilt in both hands and whirled to confront him.

"Stay back," Rose warned.

Dominic pressed forward until the point rested
against his chest. "Put the sword down, Rose."

Determination and a healthy dose of pride held the

sword steady. "You've humiliated me past bearing," Rose charged.

"I can explain."

Rose glared at him. "What is there to explain? 'Tis no secret you want Veronica. I cannot stop you from taking the woman you want, but I can keep you from making a fool of me in my own home."

"You are not going to hurt me, Rose. Put the sword down."

Rose held her ground. She would not let him touch her.

In a surprising move, Dragon grasped the blade with his left hand. Rose reacted instinctively, drawing the sword back before she had time to ponder the consequences. The blade came away bloody. Color drained from her face as she stared at the blood dripping from the sword. Then she shifted her gaze to Dragon's hand.

"What have you done? Dear Lord, Dominic, what have you done?"

Dominic's brow was furrowed as he stared at his hand.

The sword dropped from Rose's hands with a loud clatter, and she rushed forward, grasping Dominic's wrist. She uncurled his fingers and stanched the blood with the hem of her gown, gaping in horror at the deep gash in his palm and the lesser ones across his fingers.

"I did not mean . . . I am sorry . . ." Her voice ground to a halt as her practical side took over. "Your hand is going to need stitching. Sit down on the bench while I get what I need."

She retrieved her basket of medicinal supplies from

the cupboard and knelt at Dominic's feet. She pressed a clean cloth to his palm and said, "Hold it tight while I thread the needle."

"You cut me," Dominic said woodenly.

" 'Twas an accident, and partly your fault. You should not have grabbed the blade. Had I wanted to hurt you, I would have run you through."

She dabbed at the blood. "It could have been worse. You are lucky you still have your fingers. Hold very still while I stitch the edges together."

Dominic could not believe how stupid he had been to believe Rose would not hurt him. He knew Rose was dangerous when roused to anger, yet he had thrown caution to the wind.

Dominic closed his mind to the pain while Rose stitched his hand. Had jealousy fueled Rose's anger? he wondered. Had she been outraged over Veronica's appearance at Dragonwyck? Probably a little of both, he decided. He had neither encouraged Veronica's visit nor expected to see her at Dragonwyck, but of course Rose did not believe that. She was determined to think the worst of him no matter what he said.

Dominic's thoughts turned to Veronica. Just recently he had asked himself if Veronica still held the same appeal for him as she once had. Now he had his answer. She did not. He had not felt the same about Veronica since Rose burst into his life wielding a sword in her dainty hand.

"There, 'tis done," Rose said, tying off the thread.

She cradled his hand in her palm as she spread salve over the wound. "Hold still while I affix a bandage."

Dominic said naught; he merely stared at his hand, unable to believe what had just happened. When Rose finished, she sent him a wary look and backed away.

"You may have the bed tonight. I will find another," she said.

"You will do no such thing. Do you not understand? I do not want Veronica. 'Tis you I want, Rose."

"Do not lie to me, Dominic. I know what I saw."

"You saw what you wanted to see. I did not invite Veronica into my lap. I told her I was not interested, but like all women she has a mind of her own."

"You were kissing her."

"She was kissing me."

"Do not make feeble excuses, my lord, for they insult my intelligence." She made a wide circle around him.

"Where are you going?"

"To find an empty bed among the servants."

"You will *not* sleep with the servants," Dominic spat from between clenched teeth.

Rose ignored him. Dominic reacted swiftly. Two long strides took him to Rose's side. Her cry of protest did not deter him as he swept her into his arms and carried her to the bedchamber, slamming the door behind him with his foot.

"Put me down!"

"In a minute. First you are going to listen to me."

She hammered his chest with her fists, but he felt naught save the delicious weight of her body. The scent of roses made his head spin and his senses reel.

"Put me down, Dominic."

He set her on her feet, but his hold on her remained firm.

"Let me go."

"Not yet. If you were being honest with yourself, you would admit that you want what I want."

"You flatter yourself, my lord." She tossed her head. "Did you invite your mistress to stay with you at Dragonwyck?"

He yanked her against him, forcing her to hang on to him to keep her balance. He held her, one hand splayed on the back of her head, his fingers tangled in her hair to hold her still as he brought her mouth against his.

"I plan," he muttered against her lips, "to make passionate love to my wife."

"Not if I have anything to say about it," Rose said just before he kissed her.

Why did she bother to fight? Rose wondered. She melted into his arms as if she had no will of her own. She closed her eyes, blotting out the sight of his determined face, those merciless dark eyes and the resolute twist of his mouth. His uninjured hand slid over her breasts in a blatant caress.

Despair rode her. She knew she could not stop him, that her body would respond despite her anger, so she did not resist as his devastating kiss roused her to unwilling passion.

"Damn you. I do not want this," she gasped at last.

He gave her a wistful smile. "I fear we are both damned."

She freed herself and backed away until the wall stopped her. "You are mad!"

He stalked her, pressing her against the wall with his hard body. She felt the stiffened ridge of his sex prodding her between her thighs and she went still.

"Aye, mad for you. I cannot help myself." She shuddered as he skimmed his right hand beneath the hem of her under-gown and upward along her leg. Both under-gown and over-gown slid effortlessly upward, bunching at her waist.

Then he touched her, his uninjured hand moving against her pale skin, caressing the flat of her belly and the golden curls at the juncture of her thighs. She stiffened, the breath catching in her throat and her chest expanding as she dragged in air.

She wanted to protest, to demand that he keep his distance until he sent his mistress away, but she could neither think nor speak with his mouth and hands on her. His tongue plunged deep, destroying her willpower, ravaging her senses and driving out every thought but the rising need to feel him inside her.

As he released ties and rearranged clothing, Rose became vaguely aware that he was touching her with more than just his hand. The velvet tip of his cock pressed wetly between her thighs. His drugging kisses held her captive as he lifted her and arranged her legs around his hips. Rose had had no idea it was possible to make love in this way.

Despite Dragon's injured hand, he exhibited no sign of pain. His face had an arrested look, the shadowed hollows sharp and intense. He touched her again, his fingers delving deep into her secret folds. He smiled, as if what he found there pleased him.

"You are ready, love. Hold on tight."

Resisting was out of the question, for Rose suddenly realized she wanted this as much as Dominic. Her body felt heavy and lethargic as she wound her arms around his neck and held on. He entered her then, with a quick, savage thrust that made her breath stop. She cried out his name as he pounded into her with relentless urgency, creating a blaze inside her, banishing doubts and misgivings, banishing everything but Dragon.

'Tis always like this for me. I am lost when he touches me.

Her hands clutched his shoulders. The muscles were hard and tense. Her eyes drifted shut; she wanted to gaze into his eyes but could not bear to see her passion mirrored in their dark centers. Her heart beat in tempo with his quickening thrusts. Then she was flying, her body soaring with a pulsing ecstasy that came from deep inside her. Her body convulsed. The walls of her sex clutched the hard, thick length of him as he pumped his seed into her.

After a moment of profound silence, Dominic moved them away from the wall. With her legs still spanning his waist, he carried her to the bed and laid her down on the feather mattress. Then he quickly undressed both Rose and himself.

"You will hurt your hand," Rose said when she finally found breath to speak.

Dominic shrugged. " 'Tis of little consequence."

Rose regarded him through a fringe of feathery

lashes. There was so much she did not know about Dragon. She knew his strengths but not his weaknesses, and she wanted to know more about Veronica than Dragon was willing to divulge.

Curious, Rose asked, "Why did you not go to your mistress tonight? Why did you want me when you could have had Veronica? I do not understand you, Dominic."

"I thought I made myself clear. I do not want Veronica."

"Why? I thought—"

"You thought wrong. Veronica is my past. You and I are wed. What is done cannot be undone. 'Twould be stupid of me to pine for a woman that can never be legally mine. Give me some credit, Rose. I would not dally with another woman in your home."

Rose stirred uncomfortably. "Am I to understand that you are content with our marriage? Should I be grateful? Will you take up with Veronica again when you tire of me?"

Dominic sighed. "You sorely try me, Rose. Why do you refuse to believe me when I say I do not want Veronica?"

"A man of your reputation and sexual stamina needs little provocation to make love to a women. Why should I believe I am any different from countless other women you lusted after?"

He touched the tip of her breast with his fingertip, apparently engrossed with the swelling bud. When he lowered his head and flicked his tongue over the taut tip, Rose groaned and arched her back.

"Lust can be a good thing," Dominic observed. "We

should enjoy the one thing we do well together."

He rose abruptly, his body a study of masculine strength and attractiveness as he walked to the low chest and dampened a cloth in a bowl of water. Rose could not help staring at him, admiring the way he moved; the rippling muscles in his arms and torso and the long tendons of his thighs and legs. His battle scars bore silent witness to his courage and detracted nothing from the overall beauty of his body.

Dominic carried the wet cloth back to the bed. "Why are you looking at me like that? Do my scars disgust you?"

Rose blinked, unaware that she had been staring. "I told you before that they did not."

He grinned. "Am I to believe that you find something about me to admire?"

"Your body is . . ." She blushed and looked away. "I mean, you are an attractive man."

He knelt on the bed and spread her legs.

"What are you doing?"

"Washing my seed from between your legs."

Rose gritted her teeth and held very still as Dragon plied the wet cloth between her thighs. She blew out a relieved sigh when he moved away and used the wet cloth on himself. Rose assumed he was ready to go to sleep but learned how very much she was mistaken when Dragon leaned over her and pressed his lips to her nipple.

"I am tired," she demurred.

"I am not," Dominic replied. "This time I intend to love you properly. Making love against a wall leaves much to be desired."

Rose wanted to agree but could not find even a tiny fault with Dragon's skill while making love against a wall. The pleasure could not have been more intense in any other position.

Rose's thoughts splintered when he dragged his mouth down the length of her body, to that place still sensitive and throbbing from his previous loving. His tongue flicked over the hardened bud of her femininity, and she went rigid.

"Do you like that, love?"

She could not find her voice. He must have taken her silence for approval, for he plied his tongue with renewed energy, seeking delicate flesh that burned and pulsed at his intimate touch. Then he inserted his finger into her aching center, and she fell apart. But he was far from finished. She was still hovering on the brink when he rose over her and impaled her, rekindling the flames devouring her as he thrust and withdrew in long, powerful strokes.

The last thing she remembered before losing contact with reality was Dragon's voice, calling out her name.

Dominic shouted Rose's name at the height of his passion and released his seed. Somehow, hearing her name on his lips when he climaxed sounded right. When the storm passed, he pulled out and fell in an exhausted heap beside Rose. He hated to leave the sweet warmth of her body, but he was too tired for another bout of lovemaking. After a short rest perhaps . . .

Dominic did not awaken until daybreak. A morning

of hawking had been planned, so he rose immediately, though he would have liked to linger in bed and awaken his wife with kisses. Sighing regretfully, Dominic dressed quickly and left the solar.

The guests were already gathered in the hall, eager to begin the day's activities. Today they would break their fast with bread and ale, then return to the keep for a substantial midday meal, followed by games and dancing. Hawking was a sport enjoyed by both sexes, and the ladies were as eager to leave as the men.

Since Dominic was late, he grabbed a hunk of bread from the table to take with him and gulped down a mug of ale. Then he led the way to the mews, where the falconer and his helpers awaited them.

"What happened to your hand?" Veronica asked, hurrying to catch up with Dominic.

"A small wound. 'Tis nothing serious," Dominic said with an impatient gesture.

Veronica grasped his hand in both of hers. "*She* did this to you! Do not deny it, Dragon. The woman you wed is dangerous. You should put her away where she cannot hurt anyone. I will bear witness should you need proof of her madness. There are places for women like her."

"I will think on it," Dominic said absently. The suggestion that Rose was unbalanced was ridiculous, but it was easier to agree than to argue with Veronica.

Rose hurried along the path to catch up with Dragon. She had arisen minutes after he left the chamber and was close on his heels. She loved hawking and had no intention of missing the morning's sport. When she saw Veronica join Dragon, she hung back but remained close enough to eavesdrop on their conversation.

What she heard made her want to scream in outrage. How could Dragon think her mad? 'Twas true she had threatened him on more than one occasion, but his injury was as much his fault as hers. It galled her to think she had almost believed he intended to set his mistress aside and honor their wedding vows. He lied as energetically as he loved.

Rose's attention sharpened when she heard Veronica say, "If you convince the king your wife is mad, mayhap he will set aside your marriage so you can wed another. You will still have Dragonwyck without being saddled with a wife you do not want."

Rose winced as Veronica placed a dainty hand on Dragon's chest. "You said you loved me, that I was the woman you wanted to wed. Naught has changed between us, Dragon."

Rose decided she had heard enough. She hastened forward to join the lovers. "Why did you not awaken me, Dominic?" she asked sweetly. "I must have overslept." She rubbed against him and stifled a yawn. "You exhausted me last night."

There, that ought to show her, Rose thought smugly. When she dared a glance at Veronica, Rose noted with satisfaction that the woman had been struck speechless. But the look Dragon gave Rose was one of admiration, and that surprised Rose. Was he not angry with her for taunting his mistress?

They reached the mews before the conversation could be carried forward. The falconer brought Rose's favorite gyrfalcon, and she put on her gauntlet. The falconer placed the hooded bird on Rose's outstretched hand and it settled down, its jesses keeping it from flying away.

"Your father's falcons are among the finest I have ever seen," Dominic commented. "I inspected the mews shortly after I arrived at Dragonwyck and found no fault with either the falcons or the falconer. Our guests will be pleased."

"Our guests have hawked and hunted here before," Rose reminded him. "When my father was alive."

"Rose, I had naught to do with your father's death," Dominic reiterated. "Can we not be friends? We are already lovers."

"You want to be friends?"

"Why not?"

Because I want more than friendship from you. "I will try."

"Our horses are waiting. Come. 'Tis a fine day for hawking. The sky is clear, no snow is on the horizon, and the air is crisp and invigorating."

"The day is indeed fine," Rose allowed. "It would be even finer if Veronica were elsewhere."

"You have naught to fear from Veronica. You are my wife and mistress of Dragonwyck."

"Your unwanted wife," Rose tossed over her shoulder.

Dominic lifted her into the saddle and she rode off, leaving him in her dust. His laughter followed her through the crisp air.

* * *

The day was as enjoyable as Dominic had predicted. Everyone seemed pleased with the falcons and their performance. When they returned to the keep, their catch was turned over to Cook to be made into pies and other delicacies for the next day's banquet. Everyone was in good spirits and rare hunger. The trestle tables had been set and the servants stood waiting to serve the meal. After the guests washed their hands and faces in basins of water, they took their places at the tables and the banquet began. Course after course was carried in from the kitchen, everything from soup and meat pies to roasted meats, fish, vegetables, fresh bread and sweets.

During the long meal, Rose could not help noticing the venomous looks Veronica aimed in her direction. The imp inside her made her lean close to Dragon and lay a hand upon his chest. She might have fooled Veronica but she did not fool Dominic.

"Trying to make Veronica jealous, love?" he asked. Amusement danced in his eyes. "Pray continue."

"Your mistress is too sure of herself, and I simply wish to . . ."

". . . put her in her place," Dominic finished.

"Does that make you angry?"

"Should it?" His expression turned thoughtful. "At one time, mayhap, but as I said before, Veronica is my past. But enough of Veronica; the constant bickering over her upsets my digestion."

Rose lapsed into a sullen silence. The bickering might cease, but Veronica would still be here.

* * *

When the lengthy meal ended, the women joined Rose in the solar while the hall was being cleared for games and dancing. Dominic led the men to a private chamber to listen to their list of demands intended for King John. Though Dominic might agree with the barons, he feared there was naught he could do to help their cause without betraying his king and country.

Once all the barons were comfortably seated or standing according to their preference, Henry of Ashford spoke.

"We need your support for our crusade against the king's unfair laws, Dragon," Ashford began. "Barons throughout England have banded together to draft the articles we wish to present to the king. Some dissidents want to march on London and force the king to put his seal to the articles, but others fear a civil war."

"Until I have read the articles I can commit to naught."

John of Sheldon strode forward and placed several thick pages of parchment in Dominic's hands. Dominic riffled through them, then began to read. The first article had to do with allowing the church to hold free elections. Another dealt with inheritance, wardship, marriage of heirs and financial aid due to the crown.

Dominic read further, discovering a clause that would allow merchants to sell their wares in foreign countries without having to pay unreasonable tolls and taxes, except in times of war. Another clause sought to reform the judicial system, and yet another controlled the behavior of royal officials, particularly those of local government who tried to abuse their authority.

Dominic was stunned by the boldness of the document and doubted that the king would sign it willingly. In Dominic's opinion, the only way the king would accede to the barons' demands would be to avoid civil war. Dominic doubted, however, that a proud man like John Lackland would agree to the last clause, which in effect authorized his subjects to declare war on their king.

"What think you, Dragon?" Ashford asked when Dominic finished reading the charter. "Stephen Langton was one of the drafters. 'Twas his idea to appoint twenty-five barons as guardians of the charter."

Dominic remained thoughtful. He knew that Langton, the powerful Archbishop of Canterbury, preached against absolute monarchy and could see his hand in the wording of the last article.

After a long, suspenseful silence, Ashford repeated his question.

"I agree with most of your demands," Dominic allowed, "but King John will not sign anything that takes so much of his power away."

"You may be right," Blayne of Draymore acknowledged. "But we believe the king is aware of the consequences should he lose his barons' support. Since the church lifted the interdict against King John last year, Stephen Langton has directed and guided us. Our demand for liberties is founded on the coronation charter of John's great-grandfather, King Henry I."

"Will you pledge yourself to our cause?" Ashford asked.

"Let me think about it," Dominic hedged.

"Of course," Ashford acquiesced. "Naught can be

done with winter upon us except to plan a march on London and Westminster should it become necessary. We could use you and your knights, Dragon."

"I will let you know," Dominic said.

The barons went on to discuss various articles of the charter while Dominic's mind wandered. In theory he agreed with all the articles, but loyalty to his king was a strong deterrent. He was a knight, the king's champion, and a man who took his vows seriously. John had gifted him with Dragonwyck, and in return the king demanded his loyalty. He had even suggested that Dominic spy on his barons.

Aye, he would think about it, but something drastic would have to happen before he would betray the king, no matter how unjust his laws.

While the men discussed serious matters, Rose and the ladies chatted amicably in the solar, catching up on each other's families and important events.

"We heard about your marriage to Lord Dragon," Cambra of Ashford said when the conversation lagged. "Are you terribly unhappy, my dear? 'Tis a shame Dragon forced your mother and sister from their home."

Rose went still. She had tried to keep the conversation flowing without touching on her personal life. "Mama and Starla entered the convent of their own accord. Papa promised Starla she could become a nun before he went off to London, and Dragon granted her permission. Mama accompanied Starla because she needed time to mourn Papa in peaceful surroundings."

"Is Lord Dragon truly a demon?" Cambra asked, leaning close. "Is his reputation as a fearless warrior and tireless lover deserved?"

"I would not mind being wed to such a man," Aleta of Draymore sighed. "I could not believe my eyes when I saw Lady Veronica among your guests," Aleta confided. "Are you aware she was your husband's mistress?"

"Dragon did not invite her to Dragonwyck," Rose said in defense of Dragon.

" 'Tis my fault," Cambra explained. "Veronica is my cousin. I invited her to visit during the Christmas holiday, unaware that we would be asked to attend festivities at Dragonwyck. I suggested that we refuse Lord Dragon's invitation, but my husband would not hear of it. The barons intend to ask Lord Dragon to join their struggle against the king."

Rose paled. "Are you referring to the Articles of the Barons, which my father had a hand in drafting?"

"Aye," Cambra said.

"My father was executed because of that charter. I assumed his death had put an end to it."

"Not at all," Mary of Sheldon asserted. "Your father's death made the barons all the more determined to prevail over the king. If they abandon their cause, your father's death will have been for naught."

"Why are the barons asking Dragon to join them? He is the king's champion. Are they not afraid Dragon will betray them?"

"My husband is acquainted with Lord Dragon and trusts that he will not betray a confidence," Cambra explained.

"Your husband should not be so trusting," Rose bit out.

Rose said nothing more, but she was certain King John had given Dragon her father's demesne for a reason. And that reason was to keep track of rebellious activity by the marcher barons.

Fear gripped Rose. She doubted Dragon would join the barons, but what if he did?

She could not bear it if he lost his life like her father.

Chapter Eleven

Roses do comfort the heart.
                              —William Langham

On the first day of January the villeins and freemen from the village were invited to a feast and were presented gifts by the lord and lady of Dragonwyck. In addition to the usual holiday fare served to the guests, there were also suckling pig, plovers, larks and boars' heads, and an abundance of peas, beans and onions in various sauces.

After the meal and before the entertainment, Dominic gave gifts of cloth and food to his vassals, and in return was presented with yearly rents of bread, hens and ale, which the tenants brewed themselves. The castle knights seemed pleased with gifts of tunics, surcoats and mantles that Dominic had found stacked in boxes in a storeroom.

Rose gave Emily and Blythe jeweled hairpins she had purchased from a peddler the previous summer.

"My gift to you has not arrived yet," Dominic said after the last present had been given.

"I have nothing for you," Rose replied. "The material on hand was not grand enough for a lord's tunic or mantle."

"I am sure you will think of something appropriate once we retire to the privacy of our bedchamber," Dominic hinted.

Before Rose could form a reply, she and Dragon were dragged away to lead the dancing and caroling. During the middle of a reel, Rose heard a commotion at the front door and wondered who it could be. Mayhap, she thought, 'twas someone seeking shelter and food on a cold winter night. Rose was struck speechless when two women entered the hall on a blast of cold wind and paused in the doorway.

Then a radiant smile lit Rose's face and she ran toward the new arrivals. "Mama! Starla!"

Happy tears streamed down Rose's face as she hugged her mother and twin, then held them at arm's length so she could look at them. Starla was dressed in the white robes of a novice and a plain woolen mantle, but Lady Nelda wore a colorful gown and fur-lined mantle to fit the occasion.

"How did you get here? I am so happy to see you."

"Lord Dragon sent Sir Eric to fetch us home for the holidays."

"Dragon did that?" Rose asked, stunned.

" 'Tis my gift to you," Dominic said from behind her. "Welcome back to Dragonwyck, Lady Nelda, Starla. I knew Rose's holiday would not be complete without her family around her."

"You did this for me?" Rose asked. Tears flooded her eyes. "Nothing you could have given me would mean more to me. Thank you, my lord."

Rose tugged on her mother's hand. "Come and greet our guests. You know most of them already. Cloistered living must agree with you; you both look wonderful. Are you happy?"

"Very happy," Starla said shyly. "But I think Mama would like to return home."

"That can be arranged easily enough," Dominic said.

"I will consider it," Nelda said. "Right now I enjoy the solitude of the convent. Mayhap I will return one day, when my daughter presents me with a grandchild."

"Mama!" Rose said blushing.

Dominic chuckled. "I will do all in my power to make that happen."

Dominic drifted off as the two new arrivals were surrounded by old acquaintances wanting to greet them. From the corner of her eye Rose saw Dragon walk toward a group of barons deep in conversation. Before he reached them, however, Veronica intercepted him and all but dragged him into a dark alcove. Seething with rage, Rose turned away, unwilling to watch.

"This had better be important, Veronica," Dominic said as he followed his former mistress into a dark alcove. "Make it brief. My time is limited."

"This *is* important," Veronica purred once they were shielded from prying eyes. "I have a gift for you and I wanted to give it to you in private."

"I expected no gift," Dominic said.

"Nevertheless, I have one for you." She delved in her pocket and brought something out in her closed fist. "I hope you like it," she said, opening her hand to reveal her offering.

Disbelief marched across Dominic's face as he stared at the jeweled brooch resting in Veronica's palm. It was wrought in gold and encrusted with diamonds surrounding a larger ruby.

"I cannot accept such a costly gift," Dominic demurred.

"I paid naught for it. 'Twas my brother's, the one who died of fever during the Crusade. I always meant for you to have it."

"Save it for your husband. I am surprised King John has not yet found a man worthy of your hand."

"I am a widow, as you well know. Like other wealthy widows who do not wish to wed at the king's command, I paid a fee that grants me the right to choose my own husband."

She brushed up against him. Dominic felt her soft breasts pressing against his chest, smelled the familiar scent of her arousal and felt trapped. It was not a condition he readily accepted.

Veronica reached up and pinned the brooch to his mantle. "Take it, Dragon. I want you to have it."

"Veronica, I cannot. What will Rose think? 'Tis too valuable a gift for one friend to give another."

"We are more than friends," she reminded him.

"What did your wife give you? Nothing half so fine as this, I wager."

"You sorely try my patience, Veronica."

She ignored him. "Everyone is talking about what you did for your wife. Bringing Rose's mother and sister to Dragonwyck was a kind gesture." She tossed her head. "Kindness does not become you. What has Rose done to my fierce Dragon?"

Had he changed so much, then? Dominic wondered. Was doing something thoughtful for one's wife a sign of weakness? He would have to think on that when he had more time. For now, his main concern was taking his leave of Veronica before Rose decided to raise her sword to him again. He grinned.

Veronica must have seen him smile, for she frowned and asked, "Do I amuse you, Dragon?" She caressed his cheek. "I would rather arouse than amuse you." Her hand slid downward, over his chest and lower. "Shall we see if your cock still wants me?"

Dominic grasped her hand. "Leave off, Veronica. Have you no shame?"

"I need you," Veronica whispered. "Come to me tonight. I will not wound you as your wife has done." Her gaze traveled down his body. "With me, there is only one place you will hurt, and I would take great pleasure in soothing it for you."

Dominic's reaction surprised even himself. He felt nothing. "I must go, Veronica. Please excuse me."

Whirling on his heel, Dominic strode from the alcove, forgetting about the brooch that Veronica had pinned to his mantle. If his guests noticed during the evening, they did not mention it. And Rose, who surely would have noticed, had retired to the solar with her mother and sister, where they could talk in private.

In the solar, Rose and Starla sat on either side of their mother, sharing confidences.

"Are you happy, Rose?" Lady Nelda asked. "Is Lord Dragon kind to you?"

"It was thoughtful of him to bring us to Dragonwyck," Starla added. "He must think highly of you."

"I am not *unhappy*," Rose said after a long pause. "Dragon has done naught to hurt me, though sometimes I deserve his anger."

"What have you done, daughter?" Nelda questioned. "I had hopes that you and your husband would deal well with one another."

"Lord Dragon does not seem as fierce as he did when he first arrived at Dragonwyck," Starla observed.

Rose sighed. She needed to tell someone about her volatile relationship with Dragon, and who better than her mother and twin, who loved and understood her?

"Dragon is kind in many ways," she began, "but he let me know from the beginning that he loved another woman. A woman he hoped to wed."

"Knowing your husband is in love with another woman must be difficult," Starla commiserated. She shuddered. "Thank you for saving me from that fate. Lord Dragon's anger must be frightening."

Nelda laughed. "Mayhap it is, but I do not envy His Lordship Rose's anger, which I know from experience can be quite trying at times."

"We get along well enough," Rose allowed. What would they think if they knew she had wounded

Dragon? Rose wondered. Regret filled her, until she recalled how easy it had been for Veronica to coax Dragon into a dark alcove.

What were they doing in there? Had they been talking? Had Dragon kissed his mistress? Had he caressed her and told her he loved her and wished he were free to marry her?

"Rose? What is wrong, dear? You seem so distant all of a sudden. You *are* unhappy, I can see. Can you tell me what is troubling you?"

"What could be more troubling than knowing your husband loves another woman?" Rose blurted out. "The woman Dragon loves is in the keep right now, Mama, and it is tearing me apart."

"Dragon's mistress is here? At Dragonwyck?" Starla gasped. "Oh, how horrible. Are they . . . have they been . . . together?"

"Dragon denied it, but I am not sure I trust him."

"I cannot believe he would be so cruel as to invite his mistress into your home," Nelda exclaimed. "Since you have no father to reprimand him, I will speak to him."

"He will deny his involvement, Mama," Rose said. "He swore he did not invite her to Dragonwyck. I want to believe him, truly I do, but I constantly find them together."

"For a woman forced to wed, you sound like a jealous wife," Nelda observed. "Have you come to care for your husband?"

Rose's chin went up. "Nay, Mama, you are wrong about that. Dragon is the king's champion. I cannot

221

care for a man who is loyal to the beast who ordered Papa's death."

"Methinks you protest too much, daughter," Nelda said. When Rose started to object, Nelda added, "Stubbornness is not a virtue, Rose, nor does it make for a serene life. If you care for Lord Dragon, tell him."

Rose shrugged. "I . . . cannot. I do not know how I feel. My life with Dragon is anything but tranquil. Nothing has been the same since I was forced to wed him."

"Are you talking about me, ladies?" Dominic asked as he strolled into the solar.

Rose stared at him. "I thought you were entertaining our guests."

"It has been a long day. Everyone retired early so as to be fresh for the hunt tomorrow."

"Then we must seek our own beds, my lord," Nelda said, rising.

"Sir Braden is waiting below to show you to your chamber."

"Thank you, Lord Dragon, for everything. Being with Rose at this time of year means a lot to us."

"This is your home, my lady. I never intended to turn you out. It was your choice to enter the convent."

"So it was. Good night, my lord."

Nelda started to leave, then turned and stared at something on Dragon's mantle. Rose followed her gaze to the magnificent brooch Dragon wore. She was sure she had not seen it before.

"What a lovely brooch, Lord Dragon," Nelda said. "I do not believe I have ever seen a finer ruby."

Dominic glanced down at the brooch, a puzzled expression on his face. Rose held her tongue until Nelda and Starla left, then asked, "I do not recall seeing that brooch before. Is it an heirloom?"

Dominic brushed her question aside. "Forget the brooch. Are you pleased with my gift?"

" 'Twas a wondrous surprise," Rose allowed. "I do so miss Mama and Starla. Starla and I are like two parts of a single entity."

"Is that why you sacrificed yourself for her?"

"I would do it again, if I had to."

"Does that mean you have no regrets about marrying me?"

"Not where Starla is concerned."

"I have another gift for you. I wanted to give it to you in private."

"Another gift? When did you have time to purchase one?"

"I brought it with me to Dragonwyck. I meant to give it to my wife on our wedding day, but the day I arrived did not seem the right time."

Rose frowned. "Why give it to me now?"

"Because it is the perfect time." He walked to his chest, opened it and lifted out a velvet pouch. He placed it in her hands.

"What is it?"

"Open it and see."

Rose pulled open the drawstrings and reached inside. Her eyes widened when she drew out a gold tiara encrusted with diamonds, rubies and emeralds.

"I hope you like it," Dominic said.

"Are you certain you did not buy this for Veronica? She was the woman you intended to wed."

Dragon's expression told Rose she had hit upon the

truth. "I bought it for my wife; that is all you need to know. Do you not like it?"

"It is truly lovely," Rose said, fingering the bright jewels. "But I cannot accept something meant for another woman."

"It was meant for my wife, Rose. Accept it in good faith." He lifted the tiara from her hands, removed her circlet and placed it on her head. "I want to see how you look in it. Do you have a mirror? You can see for yourself how well it becomes you."

Rose walked to her dressing table, picked up a framed metal hand mirror and admired the tiara in the polished surface. " 'Tis truly beautiful."

" 'Tis yours, Rose, but it does not do justice to your beauty."

Rose knew better than to let Dragon's flattery influence her, but he sounded so sincere, her defenses deserted her.

"I have no gift for you."

His gaze slid over her body, slow and sensual, his wide grin giving hint of his lustful thoughts. "I am sure you will think of something, love."

All Dragon had to do was smile at her and Rose felt as if her body were being consumed by fire. His look was darkly sensual, boldly promising. Rose had seen that look before and knew what it meant. Dragon's passion was a lethal combination of intense pleasure and powerful emotions. How could she endure it again?

Taking advantage of her distraction, Dragon caught her lips with his and drew her into his arms. His tongue flicked out, licking across the lush fullness of her lips, then prodding them open. Rose offered no resistance as he carried her to their bed and laid her down.

"Too damn many clothes," Dominic muttered as he unclasped the brooch that Veronica had given him and removed his mantle.

Rose stared at the brooch, an arrested look on her face. Something about the expensive piece of jewelry annoyed her. But her thoughts scattered when Dragon leaned down and kissed her again. She responded boldly, burying her fingers in his hair, shifting her body to bring him closer.

"Wait, love," he whispered against her lips. "Let me undress first."

Reluctantly Rose released him, but scant moments later he was back, gloriously naked, his sex rising full and hard against his flat belly.

"Sit up, love. I want you naked, too."

Unable to resist the lure of his seductive words, Rose was soon as naked as Dragon. She reached for him and pulled him over her, his hard body hot and heavy against hers. She sighed and savored his weight as he teased, taunted and aroused her. When she could tolerate no more of his tormenting caresses, she opened her legs and invited him inside.

One forceful thrust took him deep, so deep she felt him touch her soul. She tightened around him, wanting to hold him and keep him close forever. Every inch of her body tingled with the sensation of having him embedded inside her.

She felt his heart pounding against her chest and heard her own keeping pace. He lifted her, going deep, stretching her and filling her. She held on tightly, losing herself in his passion as he brought her to the peak and released her. A hundred times a hundred shimmering lights shattered around her. Dimly she felt his release and thrust her hips upward, wanting all of him, needing everything he had to give.

Arms and legs intimately entwined, their harsh breathing echoing loudly in the waiting silence, they tumbled together on the bed as passion drained from them.

The following days passed swiftly. The entertainment and feasting continued at a hectic pace. Dragon met twice more with the barons, but Rose had no idea where his loyalty lay.

Dragon arose early the morning before the guests were to depart in order to participate in a final hunting expedition. Though Rose was sad to see her mother and sister leave, she tried to contain her melancholy.

" 'Tis exceptionally cold this morning," Rose said as she watched Dragon dress for the hunt. "Wear your fur-lined mantle."

Dragon sent her a strange look. " 'Tis kind of you to care."

Flustered, Rose said, " 'Twas kind of you to bring Mama and Starla to Dragonwyck. I am but returning the kindness."

"They can both stay if they like," Dominic offered as he pulled his mantle around his shoulders and fastened it with a brooch of wrought silver.

"I know, thank you. Maybe Mama will return one day, but Starla seems happy where she is."

"Do I get a kiss for luck?" Dominic teased as he leaned over her.

"If you like." Rose pursed her lips.

"I like," Dominic said. He pulled her into his arms and gave her a real kiss instead of the peck Rose expected. It was just like Dragon to want more than she offered.

She watched him leave with a bemused look on her face, then washed and dressed. Because she felt chilled, she removed her woolen mantle from a hook and threw it around her shoulders. When she looked for a pin to hold it together, she spied Dragon's jeweled brooch and picked it up to admire it. Dragon had not worn it since the night she had first seen it, and on a whim, she pinned it on her mantle. She did not think he would care, since he was not using it himself. Then she went downstairs to begin her day.

The men had already left for the hunt, and she joined the women in the chapel for morning Mass. After Mass, the women began drifting to the hall to break their fast.

"Everyone seemed to have a good time," Emily allowed as she joined Rose. "But I can truthfully say I will be glad to see the last of them. 'Twas an exhausting twelve days."

"It has been tiring for all of us," Rose agreed. "I am certain Cook will be happy to see the guests on their way. The extra mouths to feed have put a noticeable dent in our stores and taxed the kitchen help."

Rose continued on to the hall to break her fast with bread and ale. A more substantial meal, the main meal of the day, would be served after the men returned.

Rose was soaking a piece of bread in her ale and thinking about Dragon when Veronica sat down beside her.

"Good morrow," Rose said with more geniality than she felt. Dragon's former mistress rubbed her the wrong way. "Do you need help packing? If your maid cannot manage on her own, I would be happy to send someone up to give her a hand."

"I am sure you would," Veronica said snidely.

Rose ignored the remark. "I trust you enjoyed your visit."

"More than you know," Veronica replied cryptically.

Suddenly Rose realized that Veronica was staring at her brooch. Rose ran a fingertip over the large center stone and smiled. " 'Tis lovely, is it not?"

"Indeed," Veronica bit out. " 'Twas my Christmas gift to Dragon. It belonged to my dead brother. Does Dragon know you are wearing it?"

"You gave this to Dragon?"

"Aye, right here in the hall, on the day gifts were exchanged."

"And he accepted it?"

Veronica gave her a smug smile. "He wore it, did he not?"

With shaking hands, Rose unpinned the brooch and threw it at Veronica. "Here! Take your brooch back to London with you. Dragon does not need your gifts."

"Are you sure about that? He kept it, did he not? What did *you* give him?"

"That is none of your concern."

"I have been talking with some of your guests," Veronica asserted, "and most agree with me."

Rose frowned. "About what?"

"About your violent nature. Those who know you claim you were volatile and unpredictable even as a child, and they were shocked when I told them what you did to your husband."

Rose arched her brows. "I did naught."

"Did you not? He said you wounded him. 'Tis a wonder he did not kill you."

"How dare you speak ill of me to my guests! Are you sure Dragon told you I wounded him?"

She ignored the question. "Did you know Dragon is seriously considering locking you away where you cannot hurt anyone?"

Rose stood so abruptly, her chair clattered to the floor. "Please excuse me. Duty calls."

Rose did not want to believe Veronica. Nothing in Dragon's demeanor suggested that he considered her dangerous. She might have threatened him with a sword a time or two, but that did not mean she was insane.

Rose's thoughts kept returning to Veronica and the brooch as she saw to numerous details concerning today's entertainment and games. Why had Dragon kept Veronica's gift? It galled Rose to think that she had given him naught while Veronica had gifted him with a keepsake that meant a great deal to her.

Even more upsetting was the knowledge that Dragon had discussed her mental state with his former mistress. She was so angry, she felt like taking her sword to Dragon again. She grinned. Mayhap she would gain more satisfaction by taking her sword to Veronica.

After the ladies returned to their respective chambers to pack before the men returned, Rose went to the solar and began to pace, and think and fume.

How could Dragon make love to her with such passion if he loved Veronica? He told lies with such ease and loved with such fervor that understanding him was beyond her capabilities.

Rose heard Dragon's footsteps in the gallery and realized that the hunters had returned. She whirled to face the door, her expression pugnacious. Dragon had a lot of explaining to do, and she was not going to let him charm his way out of it this time.

The moment Dragon saw Rose's face, he knew something had upset her, and it did not take a genius to know that Veronica was at the bottom of it. Thank God she was leaving tomorrow.

"What is it now?" he asked, peeling off his gloves.

"Tell me about the brooch," Rose said evenly. "Why did you accept a valuable gift from a woman you swore you no longer wanted?"

"I tried to return it, but she refused to take it back." He glanced toward the table where he had left the brooch and noted its absence. "I intended to return it before she departed tomorrow." He removed his mantle and tossed it on a bench. "Where is it? I could have sworn I'd left it on the table."

"I wore it to the hall this morning because I could not find my own pin. I did not think you would mind."

Dominic stifled a groan. "No, do not tell me. Veronica saw it."

"Aye, she saw it and took great pleasure in telling me she had given it to you. A keepsake, she said. Do not try to lie your way out of it this time, Dragon, for I refuse to believe you. You swore you did not want Veronica, but your lies have caught up with you. Very well, you are welcome to her. Tomorrow I will travel to the convent with my mother and sister."

She began gathering up her things. "Share the solar with her, if you like. Go ahead and declare me mad, it matters not. Your mistress already thinks me insane."

Dominic grasped her arm and swung her around to face him. "You eavesdropped on my conversation with Veronica. You did not hear me agree, did you? You are going nowhere. You are my wife. You belong here with me. And jealousy does not become you."

"I am not jealous. I am furious, and tired of your lies. I know you do not care for me, but please try not to make it look so obvious."

"Where is the damn brooch? I will return it to Veronica immediately."

"Do not bother. I already returned it. Release me. The feasting will begin soon, and I am needed in the hall."

Dominic did not try to stop her. She was in no mood to listen, no matter what he said. Damnation, he hated it that Rose had heard that particular conversation between him and Veronica. It had meant naught. He was just listening to Veronica's inane ramblings until he could take his leave. Rose might be many things but she was not mad. A slow smile curved his lips. She was, however, jealous. Considering everything, Rose's jealousy was not a bad thing.

Dominic washed, changed and hurried down to the hall to celebrate Twelfth Night with his guests. He hoped things would be better between him and Rose after they left. Veronica had been a thorn in his side ever since her unexpected arrival at Dragonwyck. He could not imagine why he had once wanted to wed the woman.

The barons continued to press Dominic to join their rebellion against King John; the urgency of the situation had not diminished. The importance of the charter and Dominic's participation was openly discussed during all their private conversations, but Dominic sat on the horns of his dilemma. He hoped that the king would mend his ways soon, for he truly did not know what he would do should the barons pursue civil war.

The king had given Dragonwyck to Dominic with a definite purpose in mind. He wanted Dominic to report on his barons' covert activities, but Dominic could not in good faith betray men who only wanted what was due them. Nothing in the Articles of the Barons was seditious, and the only rebellious part was the barons' threat to march on London if John did not sign the articles.

"You are deep in thought, Dragon. Dare I hope you are thinking of me?"

Dominic looked into Veronica's glittering gaze and felt a sudden chill. "What kind of tales have you been feeding my wife, Veronica?"

"Naught but the truth. We are lovers—do not pretend otherwise. Rose is no fool."

" 'Tis over, Veronica. We are no longer lovers. Why can you not believe that?"

Veronica gave him a startled look. "Have you developed feelings for the woman you were forced to wed? Never tell me you love her, for I refuse to believe you."

"Love is a strong word, and an even stronger emotion." He grew thoughtful. "Rose is different from any woman I have known. Were she born a man, she would be a fierce warrior. I will not tell you I love her, but one does not have to love a woman to admire her."

"You admired me once."

"Aye, I did, and I still do, but what we had together cannot continue. Our lives have changed."

"Mayhap *your* life has changed, Dragon, but mine has not, nor have my feelings. I will leave tomorrow with my cousin, but you have not heard the last from me."

Dominic cursed beneath his breath as Veronica flounced off. Tomorrow could not come too soon as far as he was concerned.

Chapter Twelve

Roses will always be one of life's great
mysteries.

—Anonymous

The guests left and the castle returned to normal. Rose
missed her mother and sister but respected their wish
to remain at the convent. Her threat to go with them
came to naught, for Dragon refused to let her leave.
Rose acquiesced without a fight; she hoped that living
with Dragon would not be so bad without Veronica
around to make trouble.

Aside from constantly training with his knights in the
tilt yard, Dragon saw to his vassals' welfare, held
manor court and performed countless other duties as
lord of the manor.

Rose assumed the duties that her mother had previously performed. Numerous problems associated with being lady of the keep occupied her days. But her evenings were spent with Dragon in the solar, sitting before the hearth and talking, sometimes alone and sometimes with others. The nights, however, belonged solely to Rose and Dragon.

Dragon was a tireless, experienced lover, and Rose enjoyed every moment of his lovemaking. If he was thinking of Veronica while he loved her, Rose preferred not to know, for her life was going so well that she wanted to keep it that way.

Shortly after Twelfth Night the king's marcher warden paid them a visit. Sir Garth seemed inordinately interested in their recent houseguests and questioned Dragon as to the purpose of their visit. Though Dragon appeared unperturbed, Rose could not help worrying. The intensity and tone of Sir Garth's questioning sounded ominously like an inquisition.

"What was that all about?" Rose asked after Sir Garth's departure.

Dominic shrugged. "The king's lackey was probably miffed because he was not invited to the keep and wanted to let me know he is someone of importance. There is naught to worry about, love."

Rose sincerely hoped not.

January sped by in a flurry of activity. It was a time for repair work. Fences were mended and barns and outbuildings repaired when weather permitted. February arrived, and with it Shrove Tuesday, the day before Lent began. It was celebrated with indoor games and sports. Wheat and rye sown during Michaelmas were already poking up through the ground, and Rose began to anticipate Easter and the arrival of spring. The renewal of all growing things instilled Rose with the hope that her marriage to Dragon would grow and prosper.

Dominic had never been so content. Dragonwyck was prospering, and his marriage to Rose had brought unexpected benefits. Making love to Rose was more pleasure than duty. So much a pleasure that he had completely forgotten he had once wanted to wed Veronica.

Dominic's position as a marcher baron was a precarious one, however, and placed him in an awkward position. He wanted to join the barons' struggle against the king, but his integrity would not let him. Honor demanded that he obey the king's command and betray the barons' plans to march on London, but he could not. Keeping the information from John, however, meant betraying his king. It seemed he could follow neither course with a clear conscience.

April arrived. The Holy Days and Easter were celebrated with great joy. A messenger from the king arrived the Tuesday after Easter. His arrival was unexpected, and Dominic felt a chill of apprehension creep up his spine when the messenger handed him a rolled parchment bearing the king's seal. He sent the messenger off to the kitchen for refreshment, then motioned for Rose to join him as he broke the seal on the parchment and read the contents.

"What is it, Dominic?"

"A message from the king."

"What does he want?"

Dominic spit out a curse. "There is trouble on the Welsh border. The western marcher barons have requested help from the king. John wants me to muster my knights and report to him at Westminster without delay."

"Oh, no! How long do you expect to be gone?"

"I have no idea."

"Must you go?"

"Aye. As the king's vassal, I am bound by sacred oath to defend England."

"I will miss you, but worry not about Dragonwyck. I am perfectly capable of defending the keep should it become necessary."

Her confidence brought a smile to Dominic's lips. "You have the spirit of a warrior, wife. I doubt not your ability to defend Dragonwyck, but you will be leaving when I do. King John asked me to bring you to Westminster."

Dominic tried not to alarm Rose, but something in John's request bothered him. What did the king want with Rose? A terrible thought struck him. Did John want Rose for a hostage? If so, why? He had done naught to earn the king's displeasure.

Unless . . .

Nay, the king could not know that the barons had confided in him, or asked him to join their cause. The meeting with the barons had been private and attended solely by those involved with the articles.

"Surely you jest," Rose said, eyeing the parchment with misgivings. "What could the king want with me? 'Twould serve him better if I remained at Dragonwyck.

Go without me, Dominic. I prefer to remain home." Her voice hardened. "I fear I would spit in his eye should we meet face to face. I cannot forgive the man responsible for my father's death."

Fear rose in Dominic's throat. He was willing to bet that no good would come of Rose's summons to Westminster. Something was amiss, terribly amiss. Furthermore, Rose's enmity toward the king troubled Dominic. After he left for the Welsh marches, Rose would be without protection and vulnerable to the king's whim. The sudden impulse to take his wife where the king's long arm could not reach her rose strong and urgent within him.

"Promise you will show respect for the king," Dominic implored.

Rose sent him a considering look. "It will not be easy."

"Promise me, Rose. Vow that you will do naught to anger the king."

"Very well," Rose said after a long pause.

Her tone of voice did little to reassure Dominic.

"When do we leave?" Rose asked.

"Tomorrow, at Prime. Can you be packed and ready in time? We will travel light, but a cart with your baggage will follow at its own pace."

"I will be ready, though I like it not."

Rose went immediately to the solar, and Dominic left to inform Raj of their plans and confer with the steward and Eric of Carlyle, whom he intended to put in charge of Dragonwyck in his absence. After he had spoken at length to all three men, he followed Rose to the solar. He intended to make love to his wife for the rest of the day and far into the night.

The travelers departed the next morning beneath a lowering sky that promised damp weather. Ten of Dominic's personal guardsmen and their squires accompanied him; the rest were left behind to defend Dragonwyck. Father Nyle was on hand to bless them and see them off. So were Emily and Blythe, who bade them farewell with tears in their eyes.

Dominic saw Rose yawn but could not regret keeping her up most of the night making love to her. During the journey, which he expected to take a sennight, he intended to seek shelter at castles and monasteries along the way, but he doubted that he and Rose would find the privacy they enjoyed at Dragonwyck until they reached Westminster. And even then he could not count on it.

Rose was weary but tried her best to keep pace with the men. She smiled, thinking that she should have refused Dragon when he awoke her for the third time to make love the previous night, but she had wanted him as badly as he'd wanted her. Their lovemaking had been urgent, almost frantic. There was not a place on her body Dragon had neglected as he aroused her to passion with his hands and mouth. Her body still tingled from the aftermath of their last loving.

"Are you all right, Rose?" Dominic asked as he rode up beside her.

Touched by his concern, she gave him a reassuring smile. "I am fine, Dominic."

Rose watched Dominic closely, sensing a wariness about him. It was not what he said but what he did not say about their summons to London that bothered her. Rose was not looking forward to attending John's court. She had promised to do naught to anger the king, but concealing her animosity was going to be difficult.

Dominic set a brisk pace, but Rose kept up with little difficulty during the following days. They were fortunate in finding shelter each night, whether it was with an accommodating baron or at a monastery, and more often than not, Rose shared a chamber with the baron's daughters while Dominic bedded down in the barracks with his men. And of course they were given separate cell-like rooms in the monasteries where they took shelter.

Their party reached the outskirts of London without mishap and headed directly for Westminster. Rose's nerves were on edge at the prospect of meeting the king, and Dominic looked no happier than she did.

Dominic must have noticed her anxiety, for he said, "Worry not, love. The king is naught but a man."

"A man with the power of life and death," Rose shot back. "His summons puzzles me. I cannot help wondering why he ordered me to London."

"Mayhap he just wants to meet you."

"You do not believe that any more than I do. What will I do while you are fighting England's enemies?"

"You will keep to your chamber unless the king summons you. I am leaving Raj behind to protect you."

"Raj will protest."

"He will do as I say."

The gates of Westminster loomed before them, and Rose edged her palfrey closer to Dominic's destrier. She did not feel safe in this frightening place so far from home.

The party rode through the open gate into the courtyard. They left their horses with their squires and were admitted into the palace by a guardsman who recognized Dominic.

"The king is expecting you, Lord Dragon. Follow me." He led them through a maze of hallways to the king's privy chamber.

" 'Tis so grand," Rose whispered, gaping at the display of wealth. There was a soft carpet beneath their feet, paintings on the walls and gilded statues.

"The king does not stint when it comes to his own comfort," Dominic muttered beneath his breath.

"Wait here," the guardsman said. "I will see if the king is ready to receive you."

The wait was not a long one. The guardsman returned a few minutes later and announced that the king would see Lord and Lady Dragon, but his guardsmen must remain without.

"I go where my master goes," Raj said, folding his arms over his massive chest and glaring down his nose at the guardsman.

"No harm can come to me inside the king's chamber," Dominic said. "Remain in the anteroom with the others, Raj."

Raj stepped back reluctantly.

Dominic placed Rose's hand on his forearm and indicated to the guardsman that he was ready. The door swung open, and Dominic ushered Rose toward the ornate throne at the far end of the room, where John sat in pompous glory.

The king sent Dominic a surly look. "You are here at last," he greeted with none of the friendliness Dominic had enjoyed during his last audience with the king.

Dominic bowed low, and Rose executed an acceptable curtsy. "We left Dragonwyck immediately after your summons arrived, Your Majesty."

"Introduce me to your wife."

"Sire, I present to you my wife, Rose of Dragonwyck."

John looked Rose up and down, then smiled. "A comely lass. I did well by you, Dragon."

The chamber was filled with courtiers and ladies. They sidled closer to hear what was being said. When the king became aware of the silent listeners, he waved them all away but for Dominic and Rose.

"Leeches, all of them," John muttered. "Now, Dragon, shall we get to the crux of the matter?"

Dominic gave him an innocent stare. "To what are you referring, sire?"

"I know you invited the marcher barons to Dragonwyck for the Christmas holidays, yet I heard naught from you after they left. Are they or are they not planning civil war? I thought you understood that Dragonwyck came with a price. I can easily take away what I freely gave."

Dominic darted a quick glance at Rose. "They confided naught to me."

"You lie!" John roared, rising from his chair and shaking his fist at Dominic. "I already know about the

Articles of the Barons, and if they think I will set my seal to the document, they are sadly mistaken. I assumed your loyalty to the crown was unshakable, Dragon. 'Tis the reason I gave you Dragonwyck. I expected you to inform me of rebellious activity among my marcher barons."

Dominic shifted uncomfortably. "Aye, sire."

"The truth, Dragon. Exactly what did the barons tell you about their plans?"

"They showed me the articles and wanted me to join their cause."

Dominic felt Rose stir beside him and he moved forward to shield her from the king's scrutiny.

"Ah, now we are getting somewhere. What was your answer?"

"I told them I was loyal to the crown." It was not exactly the truth but close enough.

The king was only slightly mollified. "Are you sure?"

"Very sure, sire." Thank God he had not committed himself to the barons.

"Why did you not inform me of this?"

"To what purpose? You already knew about the articles."

"Did the barons say they intended to march on London? Should I prepare for a civil war?"

"They did not confide in me. They trust me not," Dominic lied. "Why would the king's champion throw in his lot with a group of rebellious barons?"

"Why, indeed?" John replied.

Dominic watched with trepidation as John turned his attention to Rose.

"What think you of the husband and protector I sent you, my lady?"

"I would have needed neither protector nor husband if my father were still alive," Rose retorted.

John's eyes narrowed. "Your wife has spirit, Dragon. I should think, however, that you would have tamed her by now. I like not her tone of voice."

"Forgive Rose, sire. She is not yet reconciled to her father's death."

"Edwyn of Ayrdale was a traitor," King John replied. "His execution was meant to teach the barons a lesson in obedience. Unfortunately, it did naught but make them more determined."

"My father was *not* a traitor!" Rose denied hotly. "He was—"

"Rose, beware," Dominic commanded, stopping her in mid sentence.

"Heed your husband, madam," John admonished. "I have little tolerance for disobedient women."

"There is naught more I can tell you, sire," Dominic said. "It would please me if you let Rose return to Dragonwyck."

"I am hardly the trusting soul you think me, Dragon."

Trusting soul? Dominic nearly laughed aloud at that notion. "Send me to fight your war, but keep Rose out of this. She knows naught about the articles or the alliance of the barons."

"Lady Rose will remain at Westminster as my guest," John declared, "and you will leave immediately for the Welsh marches."

"But, sire—"

"I have spoken, Dragon."

"My men are weary, sire. We have just completed a long journey from Dragonwyck."

Staring at Dominic through narrowed lids, John tapped his chin. After a long pause, he said, "Very well, you and your men may have tonight to rest and refresh yourselves. Do not fail me, Dragon." He waved his hand. "Go now. Find my steward and send him to me."

Dominic grasped Rose's arm and would have taken her with him, but the king stopped him. "Leave your lady here, Dragon. I wish a private word with her."

Dominic gave Rose's arm a squeeze and hurried off.

"Now, Lady Rose, how much do you know about the Articles of the Barons?"

"Very little, sire," Rose answered.

"Are you sure? Did you not hear your father talking about them with the other barons?"

"I am a woman, sire. Men do not discuss matters of import with their wives and daughters."

"Matters of import, bah! I want to know when they intend to march on London so I can prepare. My army is occupied elsewhere, and I cannot afford a civil war."

"If you wish to prevent an uprising, sire, seal the articles," Rose suggested.

"You, madam, are impertinent."

Dominic returned with the steward in time to hear the king's words and sought to make amends. "Do not take offense, sire. She is accustomed to speaking her mind."

"You are too lenient, Dragon. Your wife deserves a good beating." He turned his attention to the steward, a short, balding man who had entered the chamber behind Dominic. "Sir Wayland, find a chamber for Lord Dragon and his lady."

"Immediately, sire. Please follow me, my lord and my lady."

"May I have a private word with you, sire?" Dominic asked.

"A moment is all I can spare," John said impatiently.

"Go with Sir Wayland, Rose," Dominic said. "I will join you shortly."

Rose shook her head. "I prefer to remain with you."

He gave her a gentle shove. "Go, Rose. Please."

Dominic waited until Rose left with Sir Wayland before turning to address the king. "I would know the truth, sire. Is Rose your hostage?"

John shrugged and studied his fingernails. "A king does what he must to secure his vassals' loyalty. Your wife will remain in my protection until you prove yourself worthy of my trust."

"I have ever been your loyal subject, sire. Is my word not enough?"

"I trust no one, Dragon. I sent you to the northern marches to become my eyes and ears and had to learn from my warden that you were entertaining the marcher barons. I wanted you to earn their trust but expected you to report their activities to me. You let me down."

"There was naught to report."

"So you say. I trust no one these days. I am well aware that my barons are angry because of my quarrel with the pope, and because England has lost most its empire in France."

Dominic thought the barons had valid grievances

but wisely held his tongue. For Rose's sake, he feared to ally himself with the barons' cause. He was a warrior, not a politician.

"Consider yourself fortunate that Dragonwyck is still yours," John continued. He stared thoughtfully at Dominic. "You seem quite fond of your wife despite your initial reluctance to wed any woman but Lady Veronica. Prove your loyalty, and Lady Rose will come to no harm."

"Do I have your word on it, sire?"

"Aye. Go fight my battle on the Welsh marches. Give me no reason to believe you have betrayed me, and all will be well."

Dominic did not trust John. The man had no conscience. His cruelty and treachery were legend. The taxes levied on his vassals were unconscionable and his laws favorable only to himself. Dominic had pledged himself to England's defense and sworn fealty to the king, but if John harmed one hair on Rose's head, Dominic would sever whatever relationship he had with the king and become a rabid defender of the Articles of the Barons.

Rose paced the small bedchamber, waiting for Dragon to arrive. The thought of his leaving soon to engage in battle was painful. He could be wounded, or worse. Unfortunately, the king's vassals had little say about where or when they were sent to defend England.

She stopped pacing when the door opened and Dominic entered the chamber. Rose whirled to greet him, but the words died on her lips when she noted his expression. What had the king said to make him so angry?

"What is it, Dominic? What did the king say to you? Were you able to change his mind about letting me return home?"

Rose sensed his desperation and ran into his arms. "The king is adamantly opposed to your leaving, love." He paused, his anger palpable. "He thinks I am lying about my involvement with the Articles of the Barons."

"Are you?"

"Perhaps," he said noncommittally.

"I still do not understand why he insists on keeping me here." Her brow furrowed as a sudden thought occurred to her. "Sweet Virgin, am I his hostage?"

"Rose . . ."

She pulled away from him. "Tell me no lies, Dominic."

He dragged her back into his arms. "Very well, the truth. Aye, you are John's hostage. You are to remain at Westminster until I earn his trust."

"How long?"

"I know not. The king refuses to believe there is naught I can do to stop the barons from marching on London. He thinks that sending me away will stop the momentum, but I am in no way involved in that decision. King John trusts no one, least of all his barons."

Rose shuddered. "I never thought I would admit such a thing, but I am afraid. My animosity toward the king and my father's involvement with the articles have already proclaimed me his enemy."

"I warned you about holding your tongue, but I should have realized that I was asking too much of you. I have long admired your spirit, but I fear it will get you in trouble. Keep to your chamber except when you are summoned to attend the king. I am leaving Raj behind to protect you."

"Has he agreed?"

"I spoke to Raj after I left the king. He tried to change my mind, but it did not work this time. I can protect myself; you cannot."

Rose bristled. "You face an armed enemy; I do not."

"Let me worry about that, love. 'Tis settled. Raj stays. Can we speak of more pleasant things now?"

Rose stirred against him. "Like what?"

"Like making the most of our time together. I leave at dawn."

"I will pray for your safety," Rose whispered. Her arms crept around him. "Let us not waste time talking. Make love to me, Dragon."

"Endlessly, until the moment I must bid you farewell."

He undressed her with speed and expertise, rendering her naked in a matter of minutes. Then he picked her up and carried her to the bed and laid her down. With an emotion bordering on despair, she waited for him to disrobe and join her. Dragon would be facing death, and this might be the last time they would be together.

She reached for him as he stretched out beside her. She lifted her face for his kiss, and his mouth seized hers with heartbreaking anguish. The kiss was more than physical; there was desperation that ignited the love burning in Rose's heart. She gave herself to it completely.

Her hands slid over his hot, damp skin. He kissed her everywhere: her lips, her neck, between her breasts. When he returned to her mouth, her lips opened to the gentle prodding of his tongue, and she cried out at the sweet ecstasy of it.

Dominic was so hard he feared he would explode before he was even inside her. He touched her between the legs; her cleft was weeping sweetly for him. He shifted to enter her, but she pushed him away and squirmed out from beneath him.

He gave her a quizzical look. "I thought you were ready."

Her evocative smile nearly stopped his heart. "I am, but I want to make love to you this time."

He gave her a startled look. Rose was not Veronica; he doubted she knew how to go about it. She had been an innocent before he had taken her virginity.

" 'Tis not necessary, love."

"But it is," Rose insisted. "Just lie back and let me give you pleasure."

Dominic's protest flew out the window along with his doubts as Rose bent over him and ran her tongue down his throat to his chest, pausing to tug and nip at his flat, male nipples. He moaned when her tongue traveled down the furrow of dark hair and delved into his navel. He arched upward as a shock of pleasure shot through him. It was so intense that he clasped her head and buried his fingers in the lush mass of her hair to hold her in place.

To Dominic's dismay, he soon learned that Rose was not finished with him. Her mouth strayed downward.

Through a haze of shock and excitement, he suddenly realized what she intended to do. Brilliant flashes of light appeared before his eyes when she touched her hot mouth to the tip of him, then swirled her tongue over the taut, aching head.

He gave a choked curse and tried to push her away. "You said you wanted to make love to me, not torment me. You are the embodiment of sweet seduction and I am your willing slave. Where did you learn that?"

She smiled coyly. "You tasted me; why can I not taste you?"

Without warning, she clasped his buttocks in both hands and kneaded, then lowered her head to feast upon him. He flung his head back, his eyes squeezing shut, his fists clenching. She was driving him mad! He muttered her name hoarsely when her tongue found a particularly vulnerable spot.

"Enough!" he shouted, lifting her away and rolling her beneath him. "Have done with tormenting me, 'tis my turn."

The heat of her skin scorched him as he used his mouth, tongue and hands to bring her body to a fever pitch of excitement. Her moans and cries were music to his ears as he flicked his tongue over her cleft and delved inside her sweet sheath.

"Now, Dragon, please!" Rose cried, writhing beneath him. "I can wait no longer."

"Neither can I, love," Dominic growled as he moved into position, flexed his hips and thrust inside her until she was fully impaled. He pulled out, then filled her again with a single hard stroke. He heard her inhale sharply and deliberately slowed his movements, making them more seductive, more erotic. Pleasure expanded, swelled, filling his senses completely.

Dominic drove his cock in, then out, each penetrating thrust carrying them higher and higher. He spiraled out of control when she wrapped her legs around him and took him deeper. He felt her body begin to vibrate, felt her sheath tighten around him, felt her heat surround and conquer him as she climaxed. In the moment before he spilled his seed in a violent rush, he had the illogical thought that he and Rose had bonded into one being.

Dominic shifted and rolled to his side. His eyes were closed and he appeared to be sleeping. She stared at him, memorizing his features: the aristocratic line of his jaw, the arrogant slash of his nose, the chiseled perfection of his parted lips. She wanted to remember every flawless detail.

I love you, Dragon.

Chapter Thirteen

There is nothing sweeter than a rose in full
bloom.

—Anonymous

Dragon was gone when Rose awakened. A wail of despair left her lips when she realized she might never see him again. The cry had no sooner left her throat than the chamber door crashed open and Raj rushed inside.

"What is wrong, mistress? Are you ill?" His gaze darted about the room. "Has someone harmed you?"

Rose sat up in bed, hugging the coverlet to her bare breasts. " 'Twas a dream, Raj. Has Lord Dragon left yet?"

"Aye, mistress, hours ago."

"He did not awaken me," Rose lamented, wiping away a tear. "I fear for him, Raj."

"So do I, mistress," Raj admitted.

"Mayhap you should follow him."

Raj appeared to consider her suggestion, then shook his head. "I cannot. I gave my solemn oath to remain at Westminster to protect and serve you. If you are all right, I will return to my post outside your door."

"Were you there all night?"

"Aye, as I will be every night. Shall I summon a maid-servant to help you dress?"

"A bath first, Raj. Do you think you can arrange it?"

"Aye, mistress." He exited the chamber in a more leisurely manner than he had entered.

The maidservant assigned to Rose was a plain-faced, brown-haired young girl named Lillian. She was sweet and compliant but knew little about being a lady's maid. Rose liked her immediately and assumed the inexperienced girl had been assigned to her because the king thought Rose was not important enough to warrant a more experienced maid. Rose was satisfied with Lillian and her willingness to learn, however, and did not complain.

Rose remained quietly in her chamber that day and for several days following Dragon's departure. No one questioned her request to take her meals in her room, and Rose supposed it was due to Raj and his daunting presence. After several days of solitude, Rose was so bored she asked Lillian if there was a private garden in which she could walk and enjoy the fresh air.

"There is a small herb and vegetable garden behind the kitchen," Lillian said after a moment of thought.

"No one but the kitchen staff and gardener goes there. There is even a bench where you can sit and enjoy the sunshine. I sometimes help out in the kitchen and gather herbs and vegetables for the king's table."

"Perfect," Rose said, clapping her hands. "I am bored with naught to do. Mayhap some fresh air will clear my head."

"I will show you the way, for I doubt you can find it on your own."

When Rose told Raj of her intention to walk in the kitchen garden, he protested. "My master said you were to remain inside your chamber unless summoned by the king."

Rose immediately became defensive. "I shall go mad if I cannot leave this chamber. Surely you can understand that, Raj. I need fresh air, and the weather is warm and mild, too nice to remain inside. Besides, Lillian said no one but the kitchen staff ever goes into the herb and vegetable garden. I shall be perfectly safe there."

"Very well, mistress," Raj said in a tone of disapproval. "I will accompany you."

Rose was delighted with the small garden and its peaceful setting. The scent of herbs seemed to soothe her worry about Dragon. She had heard naught from him since he'd left a fortnight ago, and even Raj could learn nothing about the skirmishes along the Welsh marches. All she could do was wait and worry.

Rose's first excursion out of doors went so well that she made a daily habit of strolling about the walled garden. One day Lillian came for her early with a summons from the king.

"The king wishes to see me?" Rose asked.

Lillian nodded vigorously. "The palace guard said you are to attend him immediately, my lady. I came straightaway to get you."

Rose exchanged a worried look with Raj and left the peaceful surroundings of the garden. For all she knew, it might be the last peaceful moment she would enjoy.

"I will accompany you, mistress," Raj said as he fell into step behind Rose.

When they reached the reception chamber, a guardsman stepped between Rose and Raj. "I will escort the lady to His Majesty."

Lillian made a hasty exit, but Raj remained, apparently undaunted by the guardsman's dismissal.

"You," the guardsman said, pointing his lance at Raj. "Return to your duties."

Raj straightened to his full impressive height. "My mistress goes nowhere without me."

The guardsman started to protest but gave way beneath Raj's fierce expression.

Rose entered the king's privy chamber, approached the throne and executed a passable curtsy. "You wished to see me, Your Majesty? Have you heard from Lord Dragon? Is he well?"

"I have heard naught, so I assume the Welsh are still harassing my army. I summoned you for a reason that has naught to do with Dragon."

Rose's heart pounded erratically. "Why *did* you summon me?"

"It has come to my attention that you have not joined us at meals nor attended the games and dancing enjoyed by my court."

"I prefer to sup alone. 'Tis unseemly to enjoy entertainment while my husband fights your war."

King John's eyes narrowed. "Beware, mistress. Choose your words wisely while speaking to me." His gaze shifted to Raj, and his eyebrows lifted. "Why is Dragon's man still here?"

"My master wished me to remain behind to protect his lady," Raj said, not waiting for leave to speak.

"Lady Rose is under my protection; she needs no champion. I give you leave to join your master on the Welsh marches."

"I obey no one but my master," Raj maintained.

John half rose from his chair, and Rose feared for Raj's life.

"Your Majesty, please forgive Raj. He is unfamiliar with our ways. He knows only one master and obeys none but Lord Dragon."

Somewhat appeased, the king sat down. "Consider yourself fortunate, foreigner, that your mistress spoke so prettily in your defense."

"Is there a reason for your summons, sire?" Rose asked, adroitly changing the subject.

"Indeed there is. I wish you to attend me at the feast during Rogation Days. I am certain you will enjoy the three days of feasting and entertainment I have planned. While the meals will not be as sumptuous as those we enjoyed at Christmastide, I am confident you will find something to tempt your palate. Mayhap you will meet some old acquaintances, as well as make new ones."

"Highly unlikely," Rose murmured.

"What did you say? Speak up."

"I know no one in London."

"Nevertheless, your presence is required. Do I make myself clear?"

"Perfectly," Rose answered, making an effort to harness her temper.

The king waved her away. "You are dismissed."

Rose started to back away, then paused. "Are you certain you have heard naught from the Welsh marches?"

"Have I not said so?" John thundered. "You sorely try me, madam. Go, before I forget my promise to Dragon."

Rose fled, grateful for Raj's bulk behind her. She heard laughter following her out the door but cared not what the king's lackeys thought about her, for she thought even less of them.

Lillian helped Rose dress for the feast that night. Rose's baggage had arrived from Dragonwyck, and she was grateful that she had thought to include finery to wear at court.

"You look lovely, my lady," Lillian said, stepping back to admire Rose. "Your scarlet over-gown suits your complexion particularly well. Did you bring any jewelry?"

Rose had little jewelry of her own. Her mother and Starla had taken most of it with them to the convent. She did, however, have the jeweled tiara Dragon had given her. She removed it from her coffer and handed it to Lillian.

" 'Tis all I have."

Lillian took a moment to admire it, then set it atop Rose's head to hold her linen veil in place. "There," she said. " 'Tis perfect. Can you find the banqueting hall on your own?"

"Raj will take me down," Rose said.

Raj was waiting outside Rose's door. Rose smiled when he nodded approval after a brief inspection. Then he turned solemnly and escorted her to the banqueting hall. As she negotiated the staircase, she made a valiant attempt to control her trembling. Mingling with members of John Lackland's licentious court was not Rose's idea of a good time.

A hush fell over the crowd as Rose swept into the hall. Then, as if on cue, conversation resumed. A page ushered Rose to a seat well below the salt, and she sat demurely, relieved to have escaped the king's notice. But when she happened to glance across the table, she was startled to see Veronica of Wynwood, Dragon's former mistress, staring at her.

"Lady Rose, I heard you were the king's guest but did not credit it," Veronica said in a voice laced with mock concern. "Some say you are John's hostage. Is that true? What did Dragon do to earn the king's displeasure? To my knowledge, he has never been disloyal."

"You are correct about Dragon, Lady Veronica," Rose said coolly. "The king's suspicions are groundless."

Veronica's eyes glittered with malice. "If the king distrusts Dragon, the blame lies with you. Whatever happens to Dragon is on your head."

Rose's scathing reply died in her throat when a blast from a trumpet announced the serving of the meal. Immediately servants carried in trays of sumptuous delicacies. Oyster soup, turbot in lobster sauce, veal sweetbreads, roasted swans and peacocks, cakes and pudding made with rose and violet sugar, imported dates, figs, oranges, raisins and pomegranates were but a few of the courses offered. Wine was served instead of ale, and the bread was made of finely milled white flour.

Rose ate sparingly from a trencher shared with Sir Aaron of Trent, the knight who sat next to her. The pompous young man's avid attention annoyed Rose, and she tried to ignore him as those around her ate and drank with gusto. Hours later, when the platters were empty and the guests had stuffed themselves like suckling pigs, the tables were removed so the entertainment could begin. Rose had hoped to melt into the crowd and quietly return to her chamber, but it was not to be.

"Lady Rose, surely you are not leaving before the entertainment," Veronica said as she sidled up to Rose.

"Entertainment does not interest me," Rose claimed. "I suddenly find myself too exhausted to participate."

Veronica's gaze slid insultingly down Rose's figure. "Are you breeding?" she asked sharply.

Her question startled Rose. Long moments passed before she could think clearly.

"Well, are you?" Veronica persisted when Rose failed to reply. " 'Twould be unfortunate if you *were* breeding."

"Why do you say that?" Rose asked when she recovered sufficiently to respond.

"I heard through the gossip mill that the king is considering dissolving your marriage to Dragon. He wants to give Dragonwyck to another as soon as he finds someone powerful enough to influence the marcher barons."

"You lie!" Rose hissed.

Veronica gave her a superior smirk. "I do not lie. I am not saying the gossip is true, mind you, but all too often it is, especially court gossip. Once Dragon is rid of you, he will wed me. Everything will work out as it should; it was always Dragon's intention to make me his wife."

Rose did not dispute Veronica's claim. Dragon had admitted loving Veronica, and Rose knew he would have wed her had the king not interfered.

Tears filled Rose's eyes as pain settled around her heart, but she refused to spill them in public. "Excuse me," she said, turning away from Dragon's mistress.

"Where are you going? The harpist has just begun to play, and a company of mummers is to perform later."

Disdaining an answer, Rose turned and fled. Raj sent Veronica a warning glance and followed.

Lillian was still in the bedchamber when Rose arrived.

"I did not expect you so soon, my lady. You look upset. Is aught amiss?"

"Everything is wrong. Tell me true, Lillian, are the servants gossiping about me? Lady Veronica said that members of the court are openly discussing the state of my marriage. There is speculation that the king will dissolve my marriage to Dragon."

Lillian shrugged. "Gossip is always plentiful at court, but it means naught."

"Have you heard rumors among the servants?"

After a long silence, Lillian said, "Aye, but rumors cannot be trusted. If I were you, I would not let it worry me. Are you ready for bed, mistress? Shall I help you undress?"

"Nay, thank you, Lillian. I wish to be alone. I will see you in the morning."

Rose did not immediately undress after Lillian left. She was too upset. She would enter a convent if King John annulled her marriage. She wanted no man but Dragon. She had unexpectedly found love with Dragon despite his love for another woman. She knew he cared for her in his own way, and she would have happily settled for that tiny part of him she could cherish as her own. Putting herself in Dragon's place, she wondered if an annulment would please him. Would he care enough to feel anything?

Veronica's words weighed so heavily on Rose, she threw caution to the wind and decided to confront the king this very night. Reasonably certain that the entertainment was still in progress, Rose flung open her chamber door and stepped into the corridor before she lost her courage.

"Where do you go, mistress?" Raj asked.

"Do you never sleep, Raj?" Rose asked with asperity.

"I sleep before your door," Raj answered.

"I've decided to return to the hall and enjoy the entertainment," Rose explained. "I was a fool to let Lady Veronica's words upset me." She squared her shoulders. "I am no coward."

A smile crinkled the corners of Raj's eyes. "Indeed not, mistress. Lead the way. I will be right behind you."

Rose did not try to discourage Raj from following; she knew it would do no good. He would leave her at the door and wait for her until she was ready to return to her chamber.

As Rose entered the hall, her gaze found the king seated upon his ornate throne, a goblet of wine in his hand, listening raptly to the harpist's haunting melody. Resolutely, Rose wound her way through the crowd of courtiers, knights and their ladies until she stood just to the right of the throne. She waited until the last strains of music died before stepping before the king and asking permission to speak.

"Now, madam?" John asked irritably. "This is neither the time nor place for serious conversation."

"I ask but a moment of your time, sire," Rose said.

John glanced about at the curious onlookers and sighed. "Not here. We will speak in my privy chamber. Follow me, mistress."

John strode from the hall. When several guardsmen started to follow, he waved them off. "Wait here."

Rose entered the privy chamber behind the king and waited for permission to speak.

"Very well, madam. What is so important that you would take me away from my guests?"

Rose dragged in a sustaining breath and blurted out, "I heard some gossip and want to know if it is true."

The king's expression turned ominous. "You interrupted my evening because of something you heard? How dare you!"

Rose gulped back the lump of fear rising in her throat, refusing to be cowed by a man she despised.

"I beg you, sire, do not turn me away before I pose my question."

King John's frown turned into a lascivious smile as his gaze traveled the length of her body. "You are a comely wench; too bad I wedded you to my champion." He lifted her chin, studying her face with something akin to regret. "I should have made you a ward of the crown and taken you to my bed."

Rose carefully removed his hand and backed away. "Please, sire, kindly remember that I am your champion's wife. May I speak plainly?"

"You always do," John replied sarcastically. "Very well. I am in a good mood tonight, so ask away."

"Do you intend to set aside my marriage to Lord Dragon?"

John's smile did not reach his eyes. "Whatever gave you that idea?"

"Lady Veronica relayed the gossip to me with great relish, but I prefer to hear it from your lips."

"I have no plans to end your marriage, Lady Rose. When last we spoke, Dragon gave me the distinct impression that he is pleased with you. So long as he remains loyal to England and to me, your marriage is not in jeopardy. Does that answer your question?"

Rose breathed a sigh of relief and curtsied prettily. "It does, sire. Thank you for your honesty. Please forgive me for intruding." She turned to leave.

"Wait! I intended to speak with you on the morrow, but since you asked for an audience tonight, I will impart my news to you now."

Rose stopped in her tracks, her blue eyes dark with dread. "You have news, Majesty?"

"A messenger arrived early today from the Welsh marches. He reports that the fighting has been fierce and the Welsh outlaws persistent." He paused. "There is something else you should know."

Rose held her breath. "Is Dragon . . . Is he all right?"

"As far as I know, madam. However, if Dragon should not survive, I shall exercise my rights as your overlord and wed you to another. But as long as Dragon lives and serves me well, I will not tamper with your marriage." He waved her off. "Go now, before I change my mind."

Rose's mind was in turmoil as she fled the privy chamber.

"Lady Rose, I was told you had retired."

Startled, Rose whirled and found herself so close to Aaron of Trent, she nearly tripped on him. "Where did you come from?"

"Forgive me for startling you. May I have a private word with you?"

"Another time, perhaps." She turned to leave.

Aaron grasped her arm, dragging her toward a curtained alcove. "I find it difficult to believe you are as shy as you pretend, my lady. Lady Veronica told me about your many lovers. I aspire to become one of them."

Rose glared at him with outrage. "Lady Veronica is mistaken. I am faithful to my husband."

"Lord Dragon is not here. Besides, everyone knows yours was not a love match, that Dragon preferred another. Take me for a lover, I beg of you, and you will not regret it."

"Release me!" Rose demanded when Aaron's hand clamped tightly around her arm.

He leered at her. "You need not pretend with me, lady."

To Rose's relief, Raj miraculously appeared. "My mistress does not pretend," Raj said as he wrested Rose away from Aaron's grasp.

Aaron looked up into Raj's glowering features and blanched. "Who in the hell are you?"

"Lady Rose's protector." He drew a finger across his throat. "Accost her again, and I will sever your head from your body. Do I make myself clear, sir knight?"

Aaron backed away, his fright palpable. "Aye. I meant no harm to the lady. Forgive me, Lady Rose." He spun away as if the devil were on his tail.

"Thank you, Raj," Rose said. "That man was becoming a nuisance. I would like to return to my chamber now."

"Has the king heard from Lord Dragon?"

"Nay. I am worried about him. Think you he is all right?"

Raj tried to reassure her, but his anxious expression gave her scant comfort. The thought of Dragon dying in battle terrified her. Nay, Dragon would not die. He was too young, too vital, too strong and experienced to fall in battle. He would be home soon; for her own peace of mind she had to believe that.

Rose spent the next two days keeping out of sight. She still ventured out to the garden when weather permitted and took her meals in her chamber unless ordered to sup in the banqueting hall. And still no word came from Dragon.

A sennight passed, then another. One night Rose

awoke screaming in the darkest part of night. The nightmare she had awakened from was so real, she could smell the acrid scent of blood and hear the cries of the dying. Placing her hands over her ears, she began sobbing.

Suddenly the door opened and Raj burst in, a drawn sword in one hand and a candle in the other as his gaze searched the room for an unseen enemy. "I heard you cry out, mistress. Has someone tried to harm you?"

Rose regarded Raj through a veil of tears. " 'Tis Dragon. Something has happened to him."

Immediately alert, Raj approached the bed and set the candle down on the nightstand. "How do you know this, mistress? Did the king tell you?"

"I had a dream, Raj, but it was more than a dream. It was so real I could smell the blood and see the carnage."

"Did you see Lord Dragon in your dream?"

"Aye, as clear as day. I saw him engaged in fierce combat. Men had fallen on the battlefield and were dying. He dispatched his adversary and immediately went to the aid of a knight being attacked by several Welshmen when . . . oh, God, it was horrible."

"Tell me exactly what you saw, mistress," Raj said, clearly distressed.

"I saw a Welshman throw his lance at Dragon. It pierced through a weak place in his mail. I saw Dragon fall, saw blood pouring out of him, and then I awakened."

" 'Twas naught but a dream, mistress."

"Nay, Raj, 'twas no dream. Dragon is in trouble. I feel it in my heart. You must go to him. He needs you."

"You need me here, mistress. I made a promise to Lord Dragon."

"Dragon needs you more than I do, Raj. If you do not go to him, I fear he will die."

The color leeched from Raj's face. "You sound very sure. Where I come from, premonitions are not taken lightly."

Relief washed over Rose. "Then you will go?"

"If I leave you, who will protect you?"

"I can protect myself," Rose said fiercely.

Raj stared at her for the space of a heartbeat, then nodded slowly. "If you command it, mistress, I will find Lord Dragon."

"I command it, Raj. When can you leave?"

"Immediately."

"Thank you, Raj. Do not let Dragon die. You are the only one I can depend upon."

Sleep was impossible after Raj left. Rose paced until daylight, then tried to pretend naught was amiss when Lillian arrived to help her dress.

"What happened to your guard?" Lillian asked conversationally. "He was not outside your door when I arrived."

"I sent him on an errand," Rose lied.

Though nothing more was said about Raj's sudden disappearance, Rose was sure his absence had been noted by others. A man like Raj was not easily overlooked. But luckily King John was not one to heed the comings and goings of underlings.

Rose worried excessively about Dragon during the following days. Would Raj reach him in time? Was Dragon still alive? Was her dream a premonition or merely the concern of a woman in love? All of Rose's worries and questions went unanswered as a fortnight passed and no word arrived from either Raj or Dragon.

Panic surged deep within Rose's heart when she received a summons from the king. She hurried off without bothering to check the condition of her clothing or hair and was immediately ushered into the king's privy chamber.

"Your Majesty," Rose said, executing a clumsy curtsy. "Have you news of my husband?"

King John's solemn expression sent chills racing down Rose's spine. Pursing his lips, he tapped his jaw with his forefinger for long, suspenseful minutes until Rose could no longer stand it.

"Sire, please, has something happened to my husband?"

"Sir Derek of Fenmore just returned from the Welsh marches with welcome news. My army has been victorious. The Welshmen have broken off battle and fled back across the border."

"Thank God," Rose breathed on a sigh of relief. "Will Lord Dragon be returning soon?"

"Brace yourself, madam, for the news I bear is not good."

"Has Dragon been wounded?" Rose asked on a rising note of fear. "I must go to him."

" 'Tis worse, madam, much worse," John said with a solemnity that bespoke his own remorse. "Lord Dragon was sorely wounded and is not expected to live."

Rose blanched and swayed. "Nay, I do not believe it! I would feel it here"—she placed a hand over her heart—"if Dragon were dead. May I speak with Sir Derek, sire?"

"Aye, madam, if it pleases you."

A knight stepped forward. Rose had been so engrossed in the king's message, she had not noted his presence. His chain mail and surcoat were covered with road dust, and his face showed signs of fatigue.

Derek of Fenmore bowed before the king, then turned to Rose. "My lady, 'tis sad news I bring this day. Lord Dragon is truly a legend among men. He will be sorely missed."

Rose began trembling. "Did you see him die? Were you there to witness his last breath?"

"I saw him fall, my lady. He took a lance in the side, and the wound was a mortal one."

"But did you see him die?" Rose persisted. "Please, sir, I must know."

"Nay, my lady, I did not see him breathe his last, but 'twas obvious his death was imminent."

"Where is he now?"

"His knights carried him home to Dragonwyck. He asked to be buried on his own land. His men commandeered a cart and left immediately for Dragonwyck."

"He could have lived," Rose argued. "You did not see him die."

"I saw his wound, my lady, and there was the look of death upon his face. I am truly sorry. Lord Dragon was a great knight and loyal defender of England."

Rose aimed a lethal look at King John. " 'Tis your fault!" she shouted. "You doubted Dragon's loyalty and sent him to his death. I must return home immediately.

I refuse to believe he is dead until I see his body."

"I mourn with you, madam, but I cannot allow you to return to Dragonwyck at this time."

"What! How can you deny me?"

"We must await word from Dragonwyck. Should Dragon survive his wounds, you may return home, but if word of his death reaches me, I will choose a new husband for you. Dragonwyck cannot remain unprotected."

"Dragon is alive, I know it! I must go to him."

"You will *not* leave," John said forcefully.

"If Dragon *is* dead—and I am not saying I believe he is—'twould be cruel of you to wed me to another while I am in mourning."

A suspenseful silence stretched between them; then John said, "Very well, madam. Once word reaches me of Dragon's death, you may have a short time to mourn him before I find you another husband. You are dismissed."

Rose stood her ground. "But, sire—"

"I have heard all I want to hear from you, madam. Shall I have you escorted from my privy chamber?"

Fearing her tongue would betray her hatred for the man who ruled England, Rose stormed off. But she would not obey the king. Somehow she would return to Dragonwyck, for she knew deep within her heart that Dragon needed her.

Chapter Fourteen

When love first came to earth, the Spring
spread rose beds to receive her.
—Thomas Campbell

Never had Rose felt so helpless. Dragon needed her, and the king refused to let her leave. The one thing that kept her going was the knowledge that Raj was with Dragon. She had to believe that Raj had found Dragon alive and would keep him that way. She refused to believe otherwise, for to do so would undermine her belief in God and His goodness.

King John's cruel indifference to her plight appalled and enraged her. He had gone to great lengths to make sure she did not leave the palace, instructing the palace guards to turn her away should she try to leave without his permission. Briefly, Rose had considered climbing the herb garden wall, but decided it was too high and she would probably break her neck.

Once word of Dragon's presumed death swept through the court, John no longer expected Rose to attend his banquets. She was grateful for the reprieve and remained in seclusion while awaiting news from Dragonwyck.

No one, however, could convince Rose that Dragon was dead, and she began exploring ways to escape. She still had a small hidden sack of coins that Dragon had left her. It was enough to see her safely home, even if she had to buy a horse, though she hoped that would not be necessary. Her plan included stealing her mare from the king's stables. The largest hurdle would be getting herself out of the palace, and she had not yet devised a plan to accomplish that.

A fortnight later, Rose awakened in the middle of the night with the distinct feeling that she was not alone. With a sense of dread she opened her eyes and saw someone bending over her. She opened her mouth to scream, but a large, callused hand cut off the sound. A familiar voice whispered "shh!" and she immediately quieted.

" 'Tis Raj, mistress. Nod if you understand, and I will remove my hand."

Rose nodded, and the weight was lifted from her mouth. She leaned on her elbow and saw Raj's stark features illuminated by moonlight. He looked drawn and exhausted, as if he had traveled a long distance without sleep or food.

"Have you seen Dragon?" Rose asked without preamble. "Is my husband alive? Pray do not keep me in suspense. The king said Dragon was dead, but I refused to believe it."

"Much has happened since I left the palace, mistress," Raj began. "I thought about your dream and decided that it was indeed a premonition. Then I asked myself where my master would want to go if he were gravely wounded. The answer came to me as I rode away from the palace."

"Dragon would want to be taken home to Dragonwyck," Rose whispered. "Derek of Fenmore returned from the Welsh marches bearing news of Dragon's death. He claimed he saw Dragon fall during a fierce skirmish, and that Dragon asked his knights to take him to Dragonwyck to die. I feared you would not find Dragon."

"I arrived at Dragonwyck the day after my master was carried into the keep. He was still alive, but barely."

Rose moaned and rocked back and forth, repeating over and over, "Oh God, oh God, oh God. Do not tell me Dragon is dead, for I cannot bear it."

"Lord Dragon was alive when I left Dragonwyck less than a sennight ago. Both Father Nyle and I used our meager knowledge of medicine to help him, but his wound had festered and his body was ravaged by fever."

"Why did you leave him?" Rose asked on a rising note of panic.

"My master calls your name in his delirium. He needs you, mistress. Fear not; I left him in good hands. The holy man said your mother possessed the skill to save Lord Dragon. She is at Dragonwyck now."

"My mother agreed to leave the convent?" Rose asked, astounded.

"Aye. She was most eager to reach Dragonwyck after I explained the situation. She even brought one of the nuns more skilled than she in healing."

"Thank God," Rose whispered in a choked voice.

"I left to fetch you immediately after I escorted them to the keep."

"I cannot leave," Rose lamented. "The king has forbidden it. He has ordered me to remain at the palace until he receives word that Dragon will live. Should Dragon die, John intends to wed me to another." A sob rose from her throat. "I cannot bear it."

"I suspected as much," Raj said, "and discussed your situation with your mother."

"There is naught Mama can do," Rose said sadly.

"You misjudge her cunning," Raj confided. "Look yonder." He pointed toward the door, calling Rose's attention to a cloaked and hooded figure huddled near the closed portal. Raj crooked a finger, and the figure sidled forward.

Consternation furrowed Rose's brow. "I do not understand. Whom have you brought, Raj?"

The figure approached the bed and threw back her hood. Moonlight revealed a head crowned with hair the color of gold. Rose looked into the maiden's face and saw her own image.

"Starla!" Rose squealed. "What in all that is holy are you doing here?"

Starla flew into Rose's open arms. The sisters hugged fiercely, looked at each other, then hugged again.

"I came to help," Starla said. "Raj explained your

predicament when he fetched Mama from the convent. We put our heads together and devised a plan that would allow you to return to Dragonwyck."

"How? This is all so confusing."

" 'Tis simple, really. I shall take your place so you can go home."

Teary-eyed, Rose regarded her twin. "You would do that for me?"

"Why not? You sacrificed yourself for me."

"I would never ask that of you, Starla."

"I am offering, sister. Raj can sneak you out of the palace the same way he got us inside."

"Are you sure? Very sure?"

Though Starla's voice shook, she remained staunchly determined. "Aye."

"I will fetch fresh horses and return for you," Raj said. "Bring only what you need for the journey. Lady Starla can wear what you leave behind, for she brought naught with her but the clothes on her back."

Rose got out of bed and lit a candle. While she dressed and packed a few necessities into a pillowcase, Rose explained everything Starla would need to know. She began with Lillian, her maid, and continued through the list of people in the palace with whom she was likely to come into contact.

"No one will question your desire to remain in seclusion," Rose explained. "The court is aware of my situation, and no one has intruded upon my privacy since word of Dragon's imminent death reached the palace.

"There is a small garden behind the kitchen where I take daily walks," Rose continued. "Ask Lillian to take you there. Should the king summon you to attend him, try to act as I would. Respect his station but do not appear too meek." She paused, then blurted out, "Oh, Starla, I fear this will not work."

"Of course it will. 'Tis not the first time I've pretended to be you. Hurry, Rose. You must be well away from the palace before it grows light."

Rose grabbed up the pillowcase and gave Starla another hug. "Raj will return to you as soon as I reach Dragonwyck. Trust him to protect you. Remember everything I told you, and please pray for Dragon. He must live, for he is my life."

"I will pray very hard for his survival," Starla vowed. "You must love him a great deal, Rose. When he first arrived at Dragonwyck, he looked so fierce, so arrogant and sure of himself, that I feared for your life. If your volatile temper did not land you in trouble, I knew your sharp tongue would. I am glad you and Lord Dragon found common ground."

"Heed me, Starla, there is something we have not discussed," Rose said after a moment of thought. "Lady Veronica. Occasionally she attends court functions and tries her best to upset me. She is ever quick to remind me that she and Dragon were lovers, and that she is the woman he intended to wed. I cannot say if Dragon still has tender feelings for Veronica, but I am heartened that he calls my name in his delirium and not hers."

"I will pray on that, too," Starla confided. "Go now. Do not worry about me. I shall be fine."

Rose moved toward the door. "I will never forget this, Starla."

Connie Mason

"Your generosity of spirit has made my dream come true. Soon I will become a nun. Have we not always helped one another? You are part of me, just as I am part of you."

Fearing she would burst into tears, Rose opened the door and slipped through the opening. Though the corridor was dark, she sensed Raj's presence and felt no fear when he grasped her hand.

"Follow me, mistress. Make no sound lest we alert the guards."

Raj led Rose down the servants' staircase and through a long corridor to the kitchen. They encountered no one, for Raj was careful to avoid the guards. A kitchen lad slept beside the hearth but did not stir as Raj guided Rose through the darkness and out the door into the garden. Rose had been this way so many times that she needed no light to guide her.

What Rose did not understand, however, was how Raj expected to get them out of the palace when the wall was far too high for them to scale. Once out in the moonlit garden, Rose gave voice to her doubts.

"Fear not, mistress," Raj whispered. "On those days you walked and sat in the sun in this very same garden, I explored the perimeter and found a small postern gate grown over with vines and weeds and nearly invisible. One night I returned while the castle was sleeping and cut through the vines. I was pleased to discover that freedom lay beyond that small, forgotten gate and filed the knowledge in my memory for future use."

"No wonder Dragon thinks highly of you," Rose said.

"You are a good man to have around, Raj. Lead the way."

Raj found the gate and fiddled with the latch. It opened with a loud creak. He pulled Rose through and carefully closed the gate. Rose's mare and another horse were tethered within the shadow of the wall, calmly cropping grass. Raj gave Rose a leg up, mounted his own horse and whispered for Rose to wait until the guard on the battlement turned his back.

The delay seemed interminable, but finally Raj gave the signal and they trotted from the deep shadows and rode off into the dark night.

Exhaustion overtook Rose as the towers of Dragonwyck came into view. The pace Raj had set from London had been arduous but necessary. During the journey they had slept in abandoned huts and small village inns, but if the horses had not needed time to rest and recuperate, Rose would have forsaken sleep in her haste to reach Dragon.

"We are almost home, Raj," Rose said anxiously. "What if Mama could not save Dragon? What if—"

"Do not speculate, mistress," Raj admonished. "My master is a stubborn man. His will to live is stronger than the black specter of death."

"I pray you are right."

Rose approached the drawbridge with trepidation. Soon she would see Dragon and everything would be all right. She had to believe that.

The drawbridge was up, sealing the entrance, but was quickly lowered when Raj hailed the guards. He and Rose rattled across the bridge and beneath the raised portcullis. Rose's heart was pounding erratically as she rode through the outer bailey and entered the courtyard by the second gate. She dismounted at the front entrance and ran up the steps. The door opened, and Rose ran into her mother's arms.

"I am home, Mama," Rose sobbed against Nelda's breast.

"A watchman on the battlement recognized you and alerted me. I left what I was doing to come down and meet you."

"Tell me, Mama, pray do not keep me in suspense. Does Dragon still live?"

"Aye, daughter. Sister Agatha and I managed to keep him alive, but his fever still rages. Seeing you will do him more good than any medication I can concoct. Go to him, Rose. He calls for you."

Rose left her mother's arms and ran toward the staircase. "Mind the stairs," Nelda called after her.

Heedless of her mother's warning, Rose took the stairs two at a time, lifting her skirts to her knees so she could negotiate the steps without tripping. She passed Emily and Blythe in the gallery but rushed past with no more than a hasty greeting. When she reached the solar, she flung open the door, ran through the sitting room and charged into the bedchamber.

A nun knelt beside the bed, her hands clasped in prayer and her head bowed. She rose to her feet as Rose stormed into the chamber.

"I am Sister Agatha," she said, "and you must be Rose. 'Tis good you came. I fear we are losing your husband."

"Nay!" Rose cried. "Leave us. I would be alone with my husband."

Sister Agatha pursed her lips and left the chamber with all the dignity of her station. Rose knew she had been rude, but she could not help herself. How dare Sister Agatha tell her Dragon was dying! Putting the nun from her mind, Rose moved closer to the bed. Her first sight of Dragon shocked her. His face was drawn and pale, and his cheeks were unnaturally flushed. She touched his forehead and flinched. The heat radiating from his body frightened her. How hot could a man burn and still survive?

Rose knelt beside the bed and gently whispered his name. His unresponsiveness alarmed her, and she spoke his name again, louder this time. He stirred restlessly, and it gave Rose reason to hope that he had heard her.

Dominic's limbs were heavy and useless, his eyes burned, and his body felt as if it were being consumed by the fires of hell. Through a haze of delirium he heard someone calling to him. Rose? Nay, not Rose. His brow furrowed as he searched his mind for a coherent thought. Dimly he recalled that Rose was the king's hostage, and a cry of despair rose up from his parched throat. He could not . . . would not die until he beheld Rose's face one last time.

"Dominic. Can you hear me?"

Dominic stirred and attempted to open his eyes. He feared he was hallucinating when he sensed her presence nearby. He was tired, so tired, and in so much pain. It was too great an effort to raise his eyelids.

"Dominic, open your eyes and look at me. I am here, right beside you. Do not die, Dominic. Please do not die."

Her urgency finally got through to his sluggish mind, and he made a valiant effort to lift his lids. At first he saw naught but a curtain of red. Then the curtain lifted and Rose's face floated above him. He tried to speak, but his tongue stuck to the roof of his mouth.

"Nay, do not speak," Rose said, touching his lips with the tip of her finger. She held a cup to his mouth, and he sipped cautiously of the cool water. "There, is that better?" He tried to speak again and failed. "Nay, lie still and let me do the talking. You will *not* die, Dominic Dragon. I will not allow it."

Dominic's effort to speak produced a very weak, "How did you get here?"

"Raj fetched me."

"The king . . ."

". . . will never know I left the palace. Starla is there in my stead. John refused to allow me to come to you, so Raj took matters into his own hands and brought Starla to take my place. The king believes you are dead. Everyone at court does, but I knew better. As soon as you are well, my love, I must go back to the palace so Starla can return to the convent."

It was almost too much for Dominic to comprehend. His head was spinning, and the terrible pain he had lived with since he had fallen on the battlefield scrambled his thoughts. He had willed himself to live through sheer stubbornness, but now that he had seen Rose and spoken to her, he was ready to give up.

Dominic sighed and began to fade, but was pulled back to reality by Rose's angry voice.

"Damn you, Dragon! You cannot die! I need you! I want children by you. Dragonwyck cannot prosper without its lord. The king will force me to wed one of his minions if you leave me alone and unprotected."

Rose's words ignited a spark of life in Dominic, and he dragged himself through the darkness into the light. The light was dim, but it was there nevertheless, and so was Rose, calling him back from the brink of death.

Dominic felt something cool brush over his burning flesh and with great difficulty forced his eyes open. He saw Rose hovering over him, pressing a wet cloth to his forehead. Fighting to stay conscious, Dominic savored the coolness against his burning flesh. He closed his eyes, and when he opened them next, Lady Nelda was standing beside Rose.

"How is he, daughter?" Nelda asked.

"Dragon is going to live, Mama," Rose proclaimed. "I refuse to let him die."

Had Dominic not been consumed by pain, he would have smiled. His warrior woman would fight tooth and nail to keep the dark specter of death from claiming him. His mind wandered. Did Rose love him? Her determination to keep him alive was a good indication that she *did* care. She had allowed her beloved sister to take her place so she could come to him in his hour of need, and that revealed a great deal about her feelings.

Dominic started to drift off again.

"Dominic, wake up. Mother has brought you some

broth. She said you must drink every drop. Open your mouth."

Dominic turned his head away. "Nay, I hurt."

"I squeezed out the last of the infection just this morning," Nelda said. "He is in great pain; 'tis why he is unresponsive. Sister Agatha and I both agree, however, that he needs fluids to survive."

"How long has Dragon been like this?" Dominic heard Rose ask.

"He was near death when Raj brought me to Dragonwyck. His wound was badly infected, but we have seen some improvement since we began treating him. I was hoping his fever would break soon. If it does not"—she shrugged—"there is little more we can do for him."

Rose took the broth from Nelda's hands, sat on the edge of the bed and patiently spooned liquid into Dragon's mouth. She had gotten nearly all of it down him when his eyes closed and he fell asleep.

"Is he all right?" Rose asked worriedly.

"He needs all the sleep he can get," Nelda said. "You are exhausted, Rose. Your journey from London could not have been an easy one. You need a bath, food and then rest. Sleep as long as you want. Sister Agatha and I will tend your husband. A tub is waiting in your bedchamber."

"Nay, I could not. What if—"

"I will not let Lord Dragon die," Nelda assured her. "Go, daughter. I will awaken you should he take a turn for the worse."

Rose *was* tired, and a bath *would* be wonderful, but leaving Dragon after she had traveled so far to be with him did not seem right. It took some convincing to get her to agree, and after one last glance at Dragon's sleeping features, she left.

Emily and Blythe were waiting in Rose's bedchamber when she arrived. They must have realized she was too exhausted to answer questions, for they made small talk that required no answers as they helped her undress. Rose could scarcely keep her eyes open. Her head lolled against the rim of the tub while Emily bathed her. Then Blythe helped her out of the cooling water, dried her and slipped a nightgown over her head. She fell asleep the moment her head hit the pillow.

Rose felt someone shaking her and wondered why she was being awakened when she had just fallen asleep. Then she recalled her mother's promise to wake her should Dragon's condition change, and she jerked upright. Panic raced through her when she saw Nelda standing over her.

"Mama! What is it? Is Dragon . . . Is he—"

"Wake up, Rose. Come directly to Lord Dragon's chamber when you are dressed."

"How long have I slept?"

"A night and a day," Nelda threw over her shoulder as she hurried off.

Rose flew into her clothing and out the door. She was panting and out of breath when she arrived at Dragon's bedside. Stunned, she could do naught but stare at him. He had been freshly shaved and was propped up against several pillows. He was still pale, but the unnatural color staining his cheeks was gone.

He gave her a wobbly smile that made her go weak in the knees.

Rose stretched out her hand and touched his forehead. It felt cool to her touch.

"You are real," Dominic said in a whispery voice hardly recognizable as his own. "I thought I dreamed you."

" 'Twas no dream, Dominic. I am here."

"How?"

Rose had explained the day she arrived, but obviously Dragon had been too sick to remember. "The king refused to let me leave the palace, so Raj brought Starla to take my place. I will remain at Dragonwyck for as long as it takes you to recover, but eventually I must return to the palace."

He reached for her. She grasped his hand and carried it to her breast. "I am glad you came," he whispered hoarsely.

"I never expected to see you again. I feared I would die before I arrived home. What happened that day? Were the Welshmen defeated? Did we win the day?"

"The king's forces won more than the day. The battle is over for the time being; the Welsh have retreated. A messenger arrived at Westminster soon afterward. He claimed that you had perished on the battlefield."

He squeezed her hand. "I very nearly did."

"How do you feel?"

"Like I have been dragged from the depths of hell."

"Are you in pain?"

"A little."

Rose knew by his tone of voice that he hurt more

than a little. "You are looking better since your fever broke."

"I have your mother and Sister Agatha to thank for pulling me through."

"And Raj. If not for Raj, Mama and Sister Agatha would not be here now. Raj is a good friend to you, Dominic."

" 'Twas my good fortune the day I encountered him. Where is he? Why has he not come to see me?"

"I sent him back to the palace to look after Starla. I am worried about her. She is such an innocent. I hope she steers clear of Lady Veronica."

Anger flared in Dominic's eyes. "Did Veronica do or say something to upset you?"

"I do not wish to discuss her," Rose said. "I should leave you to your rest."

She leaned down to kiss his cheek, but at the last minute he turned his head and her kiss landed on his mouth. The kiss was short but poignant, and Rose wanted to jump with joy at the sweetness of it. For the first time since her arrival at Dragonwyck, she was sure Dragon would recover.

Dominic's recovery was slow but sure. Each day was a hurdle he had to surmount, but surmount it he did. Knowing that Rose was with him had delivered him from death's door.

A sennight after Rose had arrived, Lady Nelda and Sister Agatha came to his chamber to bid him good-bye. Dominic urged Nelda to remain, but she insisted that she was not ready yet to leave the seclusion of the convent. To show his gratitude, Dominic gave Sister

Agatha a substantial contribution for her religious order.

Dominic's wound was clear of infection now, and he was able to sit up in a chair for short periods. He was impatient to leave his chamber and eager to regain his strength through swordplay and other manly exercise. But more importantly, he wanted to make love to Rose.

Dominic graduated from sitting in a chair to walking about his chamber. The first time he negotiated the winding staircase to join his vassals and Rose at the evening meal, he received a rousing ovation. That was the night he decided he was well enough to make love to Rose.

"You look wonderful, Dominic," Rose said as he settled into the seat beside her. "How do you feel?"

He gave her a cheeky grin. "Ready to tackle just about anything. Ride a horse, engage in swordplay, make love to my wife."

He loved the way her cheeks colored so prettily.

" 'Tis too soon," Rose replied. "Your wound . . ."

". . . is healed. I admit my strength may still be lacking, but I vow I will not disappoint you. I want you in my bed tonight."

"Is that wise, Dominic?"

"Not only wise but desirable. I have been without my wife too long."

"You know what I mean. I have not shared your bed because I did not want to hurt you."

He grasped her hand, pulled it beneath the tablecloth and placed it over his rigid sex. "I am hurting now, love. My cock aches. I need you, Rose."

Rose's color deepened as she removed her hand from his cock and concentrated on the trencher they shared. "Behave."

Dominic sighed and filled the trencher with food. His appetite had returned and he ate with gusto, periodically choosing tender morsels of meat to feed Rose. She looked charmingly flustered, and it took all Dominic's willpower to keep from grabbing her hand and pulling her up the stairs to their bedchamber. He wished he could sweep her up into his arms but feared he lacked the strength. Soon, he thought, very soon.

Dominic rose immediately following the last course and offered Rose his hand.

"Cynric the bard has returned," Rose said. "Should we not stay and hear his wondrous tales?"

"There is something even more wondrous in our bedchamber."

He strode toward the stairs, drawing Rose along with him. When they reached their bedchamber, he slammed the door behind him and regarded her through slumberous eyes.

"You have suffered a great deal," Rose said. "I do not want to hurt you."

He pulled her gently against him. "Aye, I have suffered, but not as much as I will if I cannot make love to you tonight. Kiss me, Rose."

Rose's subtle female scent wrapped around him like a fragrant mist. She pressed her lips to his, but it was not enough. He prodded her lips with the tip of his tongue, and she opened to him. Desire spiraled through him as he savored the sweet taste of her and felt her heat. He broke off the kiss, needing her, wanting to be inside her as he began tearing off his clothing.

"Help me," he panted as he struggled to remove his tunic. His side hurt like the very devil, but a little pain was not going to stop him.

Rose pulled his tunic over his head and tossed it aside. "I told you it was too soon."

" 'Tis not too soon, love. But I need your help undressing."

Rose stared at him as if unable to believe he intended to go through with this. "You want to make love even though it might hurt you?"

"Aye, more than you know."

He sat on the bed and lifted his foot. "My shoes first, sweeting."

His dark eyes glittered like polished obsidian as Rose removed his shoes and hose. When only his braies remained, he stood and untied the string that kept them on. His braies caught on his rigid cock and held. Meeting her gaze, he shoved them down his hips.

An astounding realization suddenly came to him. He was completely, utterly, hopelessly in love with his wife. That startling revelation robbed him of the ability to think or speak.

"Dominic, are you all right? You look so . . . odd. I knew this was a bad idea."

" 'Tis a most wonderful idea. Take off your clothes. I want to see every lovely inch of your body."

He watched through narrowed lids as she undressed. His heart was beating madly in anticipation. Then he lay back on the bed and extended his hand. Rose hesitated no more than a moment before joining him.

Chapter Fifteen

Gather the Rose of love, whilst yet is time.
—Edmund Spenser

Dominic remembered with stark clarity the day the king had ordered him to wed Rose and how displeased he had been. It was Veronica, not Rose, he had wanted. But after making love to Rose that very first time, all thoughts of Veronica had been banished from his mind. Each time he made love to Rose, it was a revelation, opening his eyes to how right they were together.

Now, with Rose's naked body pressed so sweetly against his, everything left Dominic's mind but the need to taste her passion again, to arouse her with his mouth and tongue and hands, to take her in all the ways a man could take a woman. Grasping her face between his hands, he kissed her.

Rose sighed and gave herself up to Dragon's searing kiss. She knew with utter certainty they had explored but the very tip of something immense and glorious. Dragon owned her heart. Their future together was bright with promise, and Rose sealed that promise by putting her heart and soul into the kiss.

His lips were hot and hard and insistent, hardly the kiss of a man who had recently been close to death. It was not a gentle exploration but a demand. She strained upward to meet his kiss, inhaling his breath, savoring his taste and essence.

Placing a finger beneath her chin, he tilted her head up to a better angle, kissing her until she was breathless. Their hearts beat in unison. She wanted more and arched closer. He obliged, his hands moving over her breasts, her hips, between her thighs.

He stroked her nipples. Tremors ran down her spine as his restless hands moved downward, sliding between her thighs again, his fingers exploring her weeping center. A cry left her lips, and he muffled it with his own. She tried to be careful of his wound, but apparently Dominic felt no pain, for he pressed her naked body hard against his. She twisted and writhed, her passion mounting to a feverish pitch as he kissed and touched and stroked.

She bit hard into her lower lip to keep from shrieking aloud when he positioned himself between her legs and penetrated her, going deep, so very deep. Exquisite, thrumming pleasure swept through her. Her hips arched to meet his driving thrusts, and she wound her arms around his neck, matching her movements to his.

How strange, Rose thought in a brief moment of clarity, that not long ago Dragon did not exist for her, nor did she realize such pleasure was possible. Then her thoughts skewered as Dragon whispered soft endearments into her ear, calling her his sweetheart, his only love.

Gasping, moaning, she was possessed by sensations too pleasurable to bear. Her throat ached with love, and she wondered how she had existed without Dragon.

She reached up and touched his lean jaw. "I cannot bear for this moment to end."

"Nor I," Dominic rasped. "You drive me to madness."

But eventually it had to end. Dragon had taken her to the brink, and there was no pulling back. She reached the top, touched the beckoning splendor and clung to it for several breath-defying moments. Then she plummeted, shattering as she fell. The storm in Dominic broke at the same time and he thundered to his own climax, joining her in the swirling void of pleasure.

Much, much later, cozily snuggled against Dragon's uninjured side, Rose was amazed that she had attained that ultimate peak of splendor a second time, but Dragon had made love to her again and she had responded. He would have loved her again the following morning if Rose had not hopped out of bed just as he reached for her. Dull morning light revealed the drawn lines of Dragon's face, and Rose feared he had over-taxed his strength.

Her husband, she thought fondly, recognized no limitations when it came to feeding his lust. Not that she minded. She had enough of her own to match, but it was not she who had barely escaped death but a short time ago. She washed quickly in the pale light and pulled on her clothing.

"Where are you going, wife?"

"The keep does not run itself, husband. 'Tis early yet. Go back to sleep."

"Come back to bed."

She shook her head. "Nay. You are not a temperate man, and I fear you will do yourself harm if we make love again. You are still weak."

A wicked grin stretched his lips. "Did I appear weak to you last night?"

"You know you did not, but you could have a relapse."

He started to rise, then fell back against the pillow with a sigh. "Very well, but do not expect me to remain in bed. I will join you in the hall. I thought to test my strength at sword practice today."

"Men," Rose muttered as she let herself out of the bedchamber. Did they think of naught but war and sex?

Yawning, Dominic lay back on the pillow and recalled every blissful moment of the previous night. He had unleashed a wildness in Rose that filled him with insatiable hunger.

He smiled as he recalled the startling revelation that

had come to him last night. Had he told Rose he loved her? He had whispered so many endearments during lovemaking, he could not recall his exact words. He did know, however, that Rose had not returned his sentiments. Had the oversight been intentional? Could Rose make love to him with such abandon if she did not love him? He did not think so.

Dominic climbed out of bed, stretched and winced. Rose was right about one thing: Though his wound was healing and he was on the road to full recovery, he was still weak. But it was not his nature to coddle himself. He had no intention of limiting his exercise because of a small wound.

Rose was worried about Starla. Now that Dragon was no longer at death's door, she felt it was time to return to Westminster Palace. She confronted Dragon with her fears when he appeared in the hall to break his fast.

"I have been thinking about Starla," Rose ventured. " 'Tis time I returned to Westminster."

Dominic paused with a spoonful of porridge halfway to his mouth. He set the spoon down carefully and said, "You cannot leave until I am well enough to accompany you."

"Dominic, you do not mean that," Rose said reproachfully. "It may be weeks before you are fit for travel, and Starla is out of her element at court. I cannot abandon her."

"Nevertheless, you are not to go to London without me. If something were amiss, Raj would have let us know. You worry for naught, Rose. We will leave Dragonwyck together, when I am able to travel. The king is aware that I live, for a messenger was sent to Westminster with word of my recovery," he reminded her. "Now that John knows I am alive and well, Starla has naught to fear from him."

"I cannot help how I feel. Starla and I are so close, we sometimes feel each other's fear and pain. I must go to her."

"Nay, Rose. I forbid it. Each day I feel myself growing stronger. I will be fit to travel very soon."

Rose's mouth thinned. Soon was not good enough. She needed to return to Westminster now. Getting there without Dragon's permission, however, posed a problem.

Rose knew that her father's vassals were loyal to her and thought she might be able to convince a groom to accompany her. Aye, it was a thought that bore consideration.

"If you are plotting something devious, Rose, forget it," Dominic warned. "You have the look of a woman scheming mischief."

Rose gave him an innocent stare. "I plan no mischief, Dominic."

Though Dragon gave her a suspicious look, he dropped the subject. Rose heaved a sigh of relief and concentrated on her porridge. She hated lying to Dragon, but he was being exceptionally obstinate. She refused to place Starla's life in peril any longer than necessary.

Rose did not mention Starla or her desire to return to London again, but she did not give up. Contrary to Dragon's wishes, she visited the stables soon after that conversation, hoping to convince a groom to accompany her. Unfortunately, the grooms were either too old or two young for her purposes. Rose needed a man capable of defending her should the need arise. Disheartened, she left the stables to rethink her plan.

"My lady, do you remember me?"

Rose glanced up, surprised to see Piers, the man she had championed at the manor court. "Of course I remember you. What are you doing in the stables, Piers?"

" 'Tis my time to serve Lord Dragon. Every vassal owes his overlord a certain length of labor each year, and Sir Braden put me to work in the stables." He shrugged. "I do not mind. I owe you and His Lordship more than I can ever repay."

Rose smiled. "How fares your wife? Are you getting along with your father-in-law?"

Piers's face lit up. "Vella is well. She prays for you daily, my lady. Without your intervention, she would have been forced to wed the man her father chose for her. Algar and I are not friends, but he accepts me."

As Rose stared at Piers, she realized she had before her the man she'd been looking for. Though she expected her journey to London to be without mishap, the need for a protector made an effective argument for asking Piers to provide escort.

But the notion of asking Piers to do something that was likely to anger Dragon made her hesitate.

"You look troubled, Lady Rose. Is aught amiss?"

After a long pause in which Rose wavered between revealing her dilemma and saying nothing, she decided to take Piers into her confidence.

"Can you keep a secret, Piers?"

"For you, anything, my lady."

"I am desperate to return to London and have need of an escort. I had thought to enlist the help of a groom, but I saw no one who met my requirements."

Piers's face wore a stunned look. "Lord Dragon has many knights at his disposal, my lady. Any one of them would serve you better than I."

"Not so, Piers. You see," she confided, "Lord Dragon has forbidden me to go to London until he is able to accompany me. You have seen him. He is still recovering, and it could be weeks before he is able to travel."

"Can you not wait? I do not mean to question your motives for traveling to London before Lord Dragon is ready, but will he not be angry if you leave without his permission?"

Rose heaved a sigh. "You will understand when I explain why I cannot wait." Then she told him about changing places with Starla and why she could not wait for Dragon.

"Will you accompany me to Westminster and escort Starla back to the convent, Piers? I will inform the head groom that I asked you to serve the remaining time you owe Lord Dragon at the castle, so that he will not think you have abandoned your post. I will not order this of you, Piers; it must be your decision. You have naught to fear from Lord Dragon, for I will shoulder the blame. What say you?"

Piers remained silent so long, Rose feared he would refuse. He was her last hope, however, and she would not give up.

"I will not blame you if you refuse, but whatever you

decide will not change my mind about going to London."

"I can refuse you naught, my lady. I will accompany you on your journey."

Relief shot through Rose. "Can you wield a sword, Piers?"

"When your father was lord, he taught all his vassals how to use a sword in case Ayrdale came under attack. Aye. I am not as proficient as a knight, but I can hold my own."

"Do you own a weapon?"

"Alas, my lady, I own no weapon, not even a cudgel."

"I will bring my father's belt and sword. Can you be ready to leave tonight?"

"Tonight, my lady?"

"Aye. Bring my mare around to the postern gate at Matins. I cannot leave until Lord Dragon falls asleep. All I ask is that you wait at the gate until dawn. Should I fail to arrive, return the following night, and the night after that, until I show up."

A troubled frown furrowed Piers's brow. "What troubles you, Piers?"

"You should not travel without a maidservant to attend you. I am naught but a lowly villein, but tongues will wag nonetheless. May I be so bold as to speak my mind, my lady?"

"What is it, Piers? Are you having second thoughts?"

"Nay, but might I suggest that Vella accompany us? If you do not want Vella, mayhap one of your maids will suffice."

Rose considered Piers's suggestion and thought it a good one. "Will Vella agree?"

"Aye, she will agree," Piers said with conviction. "She is in your debt, just as I am. We will be waiting for you at the postern gate tonight at Matins."

Piers took his leave, and Rose spoke to the head groom about the villein before returning to the keep, content that everything was in place for her departure. Dragon would be angry with her, and she regretted that, but she hoped he would understand her reason for defying him. The feeling that Starla needed her was too strong to ignore.

That night Dragon spent more time in the hall with his knights than was his wont. As the hours passed, Rose grew impatient and coyly suggested that they retire. Dragon seemed amused as he excused himself and followed her from the hall.

"It pleases me to see you so eager for my attentions, wife," he teased. "You might have been more subtle, but I am sure my knights envy me your loving regard."

"Your day was a full one," Rose said. " 'Tis your health that concerns me."

His eyes held a mischievous sparkle. "You need not convince me of your good intentions, sweeting. I am most happy to be of service."

He patted her bottom as they ascended the stairs, and Rose felt a pang of guilt for what she was planning to do. Her one consolation for deceiving Dragon was the knowledge that it was for a good cause. But would Dragon forgive her? That question bothered her long after he had undressed her, slowly aroused her to passion and made love to her so sweetly it brought tears to her eyes.

Dragon fell asleep almost immediately after making love. Rose waited until the keep had settled down for the night before easing out of bed and pulling on her clothing. She had already prepared a small bundle of clothing and retrieved it from her chest along with her father's sword and belt before creeping down the servants' staircase. She reached the kitchen without mishap and paused to raid the larder. She placed a small round of cheese, bread, slices of roasted meat left over from the evening meal, apples and a bottle of wine into a basket she found on a shelf, tucked her bundle of clothing on top, and left through the rear door.

Moving stealthily, Rose found her way to the postern gate, stopping abruptly when she saw a knight standing guard. He saw her before she could duck into the shadows and beckoned to her. Her spirits lifted when she recognized one of her father's vassals.

"Lady Rose, 'tis I, Sir Gerard. Piers and Vella await you just beyond the gate."

Rose blanched. "You know about them? About me?"

"Aye. They explained your mission, and I let them pass through the gate. I know you would do naught to harm Dragonwyck so I will tell no one I saw you leave."

"Thank you. Keep my confidence, and I vow no trouble will come to you over this, Sir Gerard."

Sir Gerard opened the gate and Rose slipped through.

"Over here, my lady," a disembodied voice called out.

Rose had chosen the time well, for the night was moonless and as black as pitch. When her eyes adjusted to the darkness, she saw two figures detach themselves from the shadows beneath the wall. Relieved, Rose hurried over to greet Piers and Vella.

"Thank God you waited. Do you have horses?"

"Aye, your mare Ladybird and two others."

"We should hurry, my lady," Vella urged, "before the guards on the walls notice us and alert Lord Dragon."

Piers and Vella led the horses from beneath the shadow of the wall. Rose handed Piers the sword, attached her basket to her mare's saddle and grasped the reins, then mounted with Piers's help. Next, Piers gave Vella a leg up, mounted his own horse and set a brisk pace away from the keep.

Rose kept peering over her shoulder as they rode away. She did not relish the thought of confronting Dragon's rage should they be overtaken and returned to Dragonwyck.

It was slow going in the dark, but Rose was heartened when no one came pounding after them. Dawn was breaking when Rose called a halt to rest their horses and break their fast. She was preparing to dismount when she felt the ground shaking beneath her and heard men shouting. Glancing up toward the hills, she cried out a warning. She saw men charging toward them, and moments later they were surrounded.

Piers leaped from his mount and withdrew his sword, standing ready to defend his mistress. Rose recognized the MacTavish plaid worn by their attackers and realized the men were her uncle's clansmen.

"Lay down your sword, Piers," she ordered. "These men are my mother's kinsmen."

Piers obeyed but remained watchful as Gunn and Murdoc approached them.

"Greetings, niece. Dare I hope ye were looking for me? We heard the Dragon Lord was seriously wounded and near death. Is it too much to hope that he succumbed to his wounds?"

"Uncle Murdoc, greetings. My husband is alive and very well, thank you. My vassals and I are traveling to London," she said. "What are you doing so deep in England?"

"Mayhap ye were looking for me," Gunn said, moving his horse closer to Ladybird. "Has the Dragon Lord tired of ye already?" He looked at Piers and Vella and dismissed them without a second glance. "Could the Dragon Lord not furnish ye with a proper escort? What did ye do to displease him?"

"It matters not," Murdoc cut in. "Rose is my niece, and I will give her succor in her hour of need." He grasped Rose's reins from her hands and started to lead her mare away.

"Nay, wait! I cannot go with you. Starla has need of me in London."

Murdoc scratched his bearded chin. "What is Starla doing in London? And why is yer husband not with ye? That is a story I would enjoy hearing. Ye will be my guest until my curiosity is assuaged."

Dominic awakened with a smile on his face, recalling Rose's passion the night before and wishing she had not left the bed before he could make love to her again. He felt sated and refreshed and eager to resume training again with his men. He knew his refusal to allow Rose to travel to London without him had angered her, but he could not in good conscience place her life in danger. He hoped Rose would forgive him, and he prayed King John had not harmed Rose's twin.

As he washed and shaved, Dominic was surprised the sun was so high. It was at times like this that he missed Raj's steady hand with a blade, but he persevered as he scraped off a day's growth of beard with the sharp edge of his knife. Once his chin was smooth, he pulled on his clothing and left the chamber.

Dominic was not unduly alarmed when he failed to find Rose in the hall. He had slept later than usual, and Rose was doubtless about her many duties. No matter, for he would see her when he returned to the keep for the noon meal. He stuffed bread into his mouth, washed it down with ale and hurried out to the practice field.

The morning went much as Dominic expected. His injured side was weak and would take many more days of practice before he could wield a sword with his former dexterity.

The hour of Sext had already passed and it was nearly None when Dominic returned to the keep. He went straightaway to the solar, hoping to find Rose there since she was not in the hall. He was disappointed but not excessively worried when he saw no sign of her. But when he returned to the hall, Lady Emily hurried over to intercept him.

"Is Rose ill, my lord?"

"Ill? Why would you think that?"

"She has not left her chambers, and she is usually up and about at daybreak."

Dominic felt a sudden chill. "Are you telling me you have not seen Rose this day and it is nearly None? Did she not attend morning Mass?"

"She was not at Mass, and no one has seen her since last evening. Everyone assumed she was ill." Emily began to wring her hands. "Is she not in her chambers?"

"She is not," Dominic said emphatically as he strode away to speak to his captain of the guard. He wanted Rose found, even if it meant searching every nook and cranny inside the keep and every outbuilding.

Three hours later Rose had not been found, and Dominic began to suspect that she had deliberately disobeyed him and gone to London. Anger seared through him when he imagined the danger involved in such a foolish endeavor. Did she care naught about her own safety? Rose had disobeyed him before, but this went beyond anything she had ever done. When he had her back he would either wring her lovely neck or kiss her breathless.

Dominic went to the stables to question the grooms. What he learned sent panic spiraling through him. Rose's mare, Ladybird, was gone, and after the grooms took stock, two other horses were also missing. The mystery deepened. Though Dominic was relieved that Rose was not alone, he had no idea who would have accompanied her without his knowledge or permission. All his men were accounted for.

"Beggin' yer pardon, me lord," the head groom said, "but I think I know who went with her."

"You may speak freely, man. Do you know something about my missing wife?"

"The only reason I am tellin' ye this, me lord, is because I would be blamin' myself if harm came to Lady Rose."

"No blame will be attached to you if you tell the truth."

"I know naught about Lady Rose's plans to leave without yer permission, but I did see her talkin' to Piers yesterday. After they spoke, yer lady told me she had need of Piers at the keep."

"Piers. Is he not the villein who married the freeman's daughter?"

"Aye, right ye are, Yer Lordship."

"There are three horses missing. Have you any idea who might have accompanied Rose and Piers?"

The groom assumed a thoughtful look. "Mayhap Piers took his wife to keep Lady Rose company on the journey."

"Aye, it makes sense," Dominic agreed. "Thank you for telling me. Rest assured Rose will be home before any harm befalls her."

Fear settled deep in Dominic's gut as he walked slowly back to the keep. What if Rose had too great a head start? What if his knights failed to find her before harm came to her? Piers was a villein and could not possibly provide adequate protection should they be accosted by thieves or predators. Rage consumed him. He would have Piers's head on a platter when he returned to Dragonwyck, provided he returned at all.

Dominic questioned each of his knights closely, but no one admitted to having seen Rose leave the keep.

With the mystery unsolved, he dispatched ten knights to bring back his missing wife.

Rose prowled before the hearth in her uncle's hall, her anger palpable. It was despicable of Murdoc, her own kin, to hold her captive. How dare he! What did he hope to gain?

"Sit down, lass," Murdoc invited. "Ye make me nervous."

"I've already explained my reason for traveling to London. Why are you holding me against my will?"

"I told ye when I left Dragonwyck that ye had not seen the end of me. 'Twas a stroke of luck we happened upon ye today."

"You should not have been on English soil."

He shrugged. "We were raiding across the border to steal cattle and mayhap a sheep or two," he admitted without a lick of shame.

Rose knew that stealing livestock from English barons was a way of life for Scottish border lords, and her uncle was no exception.

"But that is neither here nor there, lass. Ye are on Scottish soil now and 'tis all that matters."

"I will not be here for long, Uncle. My vassals and I must be on our way soon."

Murdoc glanced up. "Here comes Gunn. Mayhap he has something to say about that."

"There is naught Gunn can say that will change my mind."

"Rose's vassals are in a safe place," Gunn said as he joined them.

"Good lad. Rose wants to continue her journey to

London, but I told her ye would have something to say about that."

Gunn leered at Rose. "Aye, I do. The Scottish court has declared yer marriage to the Dragon Lord invalid due to a prior arrangement between Murdoc and yer father. Ye will wed me, just as yer father intended."

Rose wanted to burst into laughter, but prudence prevailed. What made them think she would agree to wed Gunn? Even if she were free to wed, she would not choose Gunn.

"You are both mad," Rose charged. "I am English; your laws mean naught to me."

"Ye are Scottish on yer mother's side," Murdoc maintained. "As yer only male relative, 'tis my duty to see ye wed to a man I approve. The court agreed. The wedding will be held as soon as a priest can be summoned. Handfasting might be a better choice, but I want no one, least of all the Dragon Lord, to question the legality of this union."

"I am already wed," Rose asserted. "A Scottish court has no authority over me. Forget it, Uncle. Naught you can do or say will change my mind. Where are my vassals? We will leave immediately."

Murdoc heaved a sigh. "Yer being difficult, lass. Mayhap a day or two alone to consider yer situation will change yer mind."

"Am I your prisoner?"

"Nay, lass, yer my beloved niece and my cherished guest. Ye must be tired. Robina will take ye to yer chamber."

Murdoc shouted for his third wife, the woman he had wed after Gunn's mother died, and a few minutes later Rose saw the thin-faced, anxious-eyed woman hurrying into the hall, wiping her hands on her apron.

"Ye called, husband?"

"Aye, what took ye so long? We have a guest. Ye recall Rose, my sister's bairn, do ye not?"

Robina smiled timidly at Rose. "Welcome, Rose. Had I known ye were coming I would have had yer chamber prepared. How fare yer mother and sister?"

"They are fine, Robina, but do not bother preparing a chamber. I cannot stay. I am leaving as soon as Uncle Murdoc tells me where to find my vassals."

"Gunn," Murdoc said, "our Rose is a mite shy. Mayhap ye should escort her to her chamber."

Rose protested vigorously as Gunn flung her over his shoulder like a sack of potatoes and bounded up the staircase, a flustered Robina following close on his heels.

Chapter Sixteen

A rose is one of life's great mysteries.
—Anonymous

Dominic stared out over the parapet, overwhelmed by his feeling of helplessness. He had heard not a word from the knights he had sent after Rose and he was frantic with worry. He had expected them to return with his obstinate wife long before now. Four days had elapsed, and Dominic imagined any number of disastrous things that could have befallen Rose. His life would not be the same without his feisty Rose. He could not lose her. He needed her to make his life complete.

Dominic was not the only one who was anxious about Rose's welfare. Lady Emily and Lady Blythe went about their duties with long faces and worried looks, and even the castle knights appeared concerned as their gazes scanned the moors and forest beyond the castle walls for their missing lady.

Dominic had reached a decision the previous night while he lay awake thinking about Rose and how desperately he missed her. He was through with waiting for his body to heal. He was going to hie himself to London and bring his wife and her sister home. His strength was nearly back to normal, and his side did not pain him overmuch when he wielded a sword or threw a lance. Aye, he was as ready as he would ever be to confront the king.

"Riders approaching from the south!" a guardsman called out.

Dominic's heart pounded wildly as he peered through the crenel at the riders. His excitement mounted when he recognized the knights he had sent after Rose, then just as quickly subsided when he realized Rose was not with them. Then something caught his eye. A large man wearing colorful garments and a turban.

Raj!

What was Raj doing at Dragonwyck? He was supposed to be with Starla at the palace. Dominic's heart thumped with apprehension as he raced down the spiral staircase to meet Raj and the returning knights.

"Where is my wife?" Dominic asked before the men had time to dismount.

"We did not find her," James of Bedford said. "We were prepared to ride all the way to London, but we encountered Raj on his way to Dragonwyck."

Dominic turned on Raj. "How could you have left

Rose at the palace without protection? Where is Lady Starla? Will someone please explain what is going on? I am frantic with worry."

Raj's somber expression offered Dominic scant comfort. "Lady Rose is not at Westminster, master. We know not where she is. Neither your knights nor I passed her on the road. Sir James explained the situation to me, and I am as mystified as you."

Color leeched from Dominic's face. "Why are you here, Raj? Where is Lady Starla?"

"I came to fetch Lady Rose back to Westminster. Lady Starla is eager to return to the convent. After we received word of your recovery, the king insisted on Starla's presence at his table each night. It has not been easy for Lady Starla to keep up the pretense, master. After learning you would live, I waited each night at the postern gate for Lady Rose to return, and when she did not, Lady Starla feared something had gone awry and suggested that I return to Dragonwyck to find out."

"Rose wanted to return to the palace, but I asked her to wait until I was able to accompany her. I do not trust the king. Apparently Rose decided to disobey me and left without my permission. She traveled alone but for two villeins, Piers and his wife, Vella. No one has seen them since they left Dragonwyck."

There was nothing more Sir James or the others could tell Dominic, so he dismissed them and returned to the hall. Raj followed close on his heels.

"What are you going to do, master?"

"I do not know. Perhaps . . ." The words died in his

throat when Lady Emily and Lady Blythe cornered him.

"Where is Rose, my lord?" Emily asked.

"I wish I knew," Dominic replied. "Raj said she is not at the palace, and my knights did not encounter her on the road to London."

Her face contorted with fear, Emily began to wring her hands, while tears slid down Blythe's cheeks. "What could have happened to her?"

"I cannot say," Dominic answered in a strained voice. "Excuse me, ladies, I need to think this out. Rest assured I will do everything in my power to find my wife."

"I do not like this," Raj muttered after the ladies departed.

Dominic strode to the hearth and stared into the ashes. "What if Rose has left me, Raj? What if she had no intention of going to Westminster?"

"Why would you think that? What did you do to her?"

"I did naught except forbid her to go to London without me."

"Where would she go if not to London? Lady Rose cares for her sister a great deal. I cannot believe she would go anywhere but to the palace."

"Nor can I, Raj. I received no ransom note, but that does little to reassure me." He winced. "Brigands could have kidnapped her for reasons other than ransom." His head shot up, his face alight with sudden comprehension. "God's nightgown! Why did I not think of it sooner?"

"Think of what, master?"

"Is it possible that Rose is with MacTavish? His lands march along the border; he has been known to raid deep into English territory to steal livestock. What if he came upon her and took her against her will?"

"Why would the Scotsman hold your lady against her will? It makes no sense, master."

"It does to me," Dominic said as he headed out the door.

"Where do you go, master?"

"To Scotland. If Rose is there, I will find her. Find the captain of the guard. Tell him to choose two dozen men to accompany me to MacTavish's demesne, then attend me in the armory. We leave within the hour."

Raj found Sir Eric, relayed Dominic's message, and hurried to the armory. He arrived in time to help Dominic don his mail and strap on his weapons.

"I will ride with you, master. You nearly lost your life the last time you left me behind."

"What about Lady Starla? Rose would not like it if we left her twin unprotected. The king is unpredictable; one never knows what goes through his devious mind."

Dominic could tell by Raj's mutinous glare that sending him back to the palace was not an option. Raj's words confirmed Dominic's belief.

"I will not be left behind," he reiterated. "Lady Starla can hold her own despite her aversion to court life. She dislikes Lady Veronica intensely. Your former mistress has the tongue of an asp."

Dominic had no answer to that, for he knew it to be the truth.

Raj appeared thoughtful as he added a knife to his

belt and checked the sharpness of his scimitar.

"Something is on your mind, Raj. What is it?" Dominic asked when he noted Raj's preoccupation.

"Mayhap you should send Lady Nelda to the palace. Who better to protect Lady Starla than her own mother?"

"Raj! You are a genius! Why did I not think of that? Find Sir Cedric. Lady Nelda trusts him. Tell Cedric everything he needs to know and ask him to fetch Lady Nelda from the convent and escort her to the palace. King John would not dare turn Lady Nelda away once she explains that she has come to Westminster to be with her daughter while I am recovering from my wounds. I know the king. He would risk public condemnation should he deny Nelda's request, and he would not like that."

Less than an hour later, Dominic, Raj and two dozen armed knights left the castle, riding north to Scotland. Meanwhile, Sir Cedric rode to the convent to fetch Lady Nelda.

Seething with rage, Rose stared out the window of her chamber. The door was locked, and not even Robina was allowed inside without Uncle Murdoc's permission. A MacTavish kinsman had carried food and water to her on each of the four days of her confinement, but he had refused to answer her questions. She was frantic with worry about Piers and Vella. If her uncle had hurt them, she would never forgive him.

The key rattled in the lock, and Rose spun around to face the door. Her uncle stepped into the chamber, looking far too pleased with himself for Rose's liking.

"How dare you hold me against my will!" Rose blasted before he could speak. "And to think I once was fond of you."

"Och, lass, ye hurt me sorely. I would never harm ye. Ye and yer sister are like the bairns I never had."

"Then prove it. Release me."

"So ye can return to the Dragon Lord? Nay, lass, he isna the man for ye."

"And I suppose Gunn is. I am no fool, Uncle. I know what you and Gunn want. What an achievement it would be to gain a foothold on English soil. You would be the envy of every Scot border lord."

"Ye wrong me, lass. 'Tis yer welfare that concerns me. Have ye forgotten so soon that the English king murdered yer father, that he sent his champion to wed ye and claim yer land? Wedding Gunn makes sense. He can keep your land free from English domination."

"You have forgotten a few things, Uncle. My lands are now and have always been a part of England. I am English, and I am wed to an Englishman. Give it up, Uncle. When Dragon learns what you did, he will be furious."

"Ye left without his permission, and ye said yerself ye were on yer way to London. Dragon willna think to look for ye here. And by the time he realizes ye havena gone to London, ye will already be wed to Gunn. Wedded and bedded all proper like."

"Over my dead body," Rose muttered.

"Och, lass, I see ye need more time to think on this. If I dinna know better, I might think ye have become fond of Dragon."

Squaring her shoulders, Rose shouted, "I *love* Dragon. Naught will ever change that."

"Bah, yer as addlebrained as yer mother. I dinna approve of her wedding an Englishman, but she wheedled our father into agreeing to the union."

"My mother and father were happy together. They loved one another. Tell me, Uncle, did you love any of your three wives?"

"Love is for fools. I wed for heirs, not for love, but none of my wives gave me sons or daughters. Fortunately, my second wife came to me with a son that I adopted as my own when Robina proved as barren as my other two wives."

"Robina is sweet-natured and good. You should appreciate her more."

"My wives are none of yer concern, niece. Wed Gunn and everything I own will belong to ye and yer heirs after I go to my reward."

"I want naught from you, Uncle. Release me and my vassals and all will be forgiven."

Murdoc sighed. "Ye always were a stubborn lass. Yer sharp tongue almost made me forget what I came to tell ye. Father Baen has agreed to come to the keep and perform the marriage ceremony. Ye have a day or two to come to yer senses. The priest willna wed ye to Gunn unless ye are willing."

"That will never happen."

Murdoc gave her an inscrutable look. "Ye are wrong. How fond are ye of those two vassals of yers?"

"Piers and Vella?"

"Aye, if that be their names."

Fear raced down Rose's spine. *"You would not dare hurt them!"*

"Ye donna know me if ye think that, lass. Ah, weel, 'tis yer decision, so I will leave ye alone whilst ye decide."

Her voice rose. "Uncle, wait! Harm Piers and Vella and you will be sorry."

No answer was forthcoming as the door slammed behind Murdoc, leaving Rose to fret over the fate of her vassals. She knew her uncle was a stubborn man, but she had never found him to be unreasonably harsh. Since her father's death, Murdoc had changed. He was no longer the genial man who'd doted on his nieces, but a man driven by greed. He wanted Dragonwyck and would stop at nothing to get it.

Rose returned to the window. Her stomach rumbled, and she wondered if her uncle planned to starve her into compliance. The rattling of the doorknob interrupted her dark thoughts. She stared at the portal, wondering if her uncle had returned to browbeat her into committing bigamy.

The key scraped in the lock and the door opened. Rose tensed, then relaxed when a head crowned with braids poked through the opening.

"Robina. Does Uncle Murdoc know you are here?"

Robina sidled into the chamber and closed the door behind her. "Nay, lass. Murdoc and Gunn have gone hawking. I came to see if I could help."

"You want to help me?"

"Aye, Rose. I dinna agree with everything yer uncle does. He and Gunn are cut from the same cloth, even though they share no blood. I know not why yer here, or what kind of mischief Murdoc plots, for they dinna share their plans with me, but I know yer being held against yer will."

"Oh, Robina, thank you," Rose cried, grasping the other woman's hands in hers. "Uncle Murdoc wants Dragonwyck so badly he would wed me to Gunn to get it."

"Dragonwyck? I know not the name."

"Lord Dragon claimed Ayrdale and became my husband after Papa's death. The demesne is now called Dragonwyck. Uncle Murdoc alleges that Papa promised me to Gunn years ago, and that my marriage to Dragon is invalid."

"So that is why Murdoc traveled to Stirling," Robina said thoughtfully. "He told me he wanted to bring a petition before the court, but I knew not what it was."

"Uncle Murdoc is a devious man. I am an English subject, and Scottish laws hold no sway over me. I cannot wed Gunn, nor would I wed him even if 'twas possible. I love my husband."

Robina's sharp features softened, and Rose realized her uncle's wife was younger than she looked. "Are you happy with Murdoc, Robina?" she probed. "Was your marriage an arranged one?"

"My marriage was arranged, but Papa wouldna have agreed to it if he'd known Murdoc wanted naught but a brood mare. We have been wed ten years." She sighed. "I fear I am barren."

"Are you ill treated?"

Robina looked away. "All was well in the beginning. I was well treated, but as the years went by with no sign of a bairn, Murdoc changed. He made Gunn his heir and began treating me less kindly. He doesna beat me, but if I displease him he shows me the back of his hand."

"You should leave him, Robina. Scottish laws give women more power than English ones. Will your father take you in?"

"Aye, but Murdoc willna let me go. He fears Papa will demand the return of my dowry. But enough about me. How can I help ye?"

"I ask naught of you that would cause you harm, but there is one thing you can do. I am concerned about my vassals. I have no idea what Uncle Murdoc has done with them. I would be grateful if you could find out what has become of them."

"Och, lass, I already know. They are confined in the north tower and they are both well."

Rose nearly collapsed with relief. According to her uncle, however, their safety depended upon her compliance. Dare she ask Robina to set them free?

"I fear for their lives," Rose confided. "Their safety depends upon my willingness to wed Gunn. Oh, Robina, I know not what to do. My husband thinks I went to London. He would never think to look for me here."

Robina looked bewildered. "I donna understand."

Rose explained in a few succinct words why she had been traveling to London and why Dragon had forbidden her to leave without him.

" 'Tis unfortunate Murdoc came upon ye whilst on one of his raids into English territory. May I ask a boon of ye?" Robina asked timidly. "I will free ye and yer vassals if ye take me with ye to Dragonwyck. Think ye yer husband will protect me from Murdoc and help me reach my father's manor? I have six brothers who will protect me from Murdoc, for they like him not."

"Free Piers and Vella and go with them to Dragon-wyck," Rose said. "But forget about me. 'Tis too dangerous. When you reach Dragonwyck, tell Dragon of my plight and ask him to provide escort to your father's home."

"I must go," Robina said, looking nervously toward the door. "I will free them tonight, after Murdoc falls asleep. He doesna know I have spare keys to all the chambers, so I donna wish to be caught where I am not supposed to be."

"Good luck," Rose called softly. Robina let herself out the door and turned the key in the lock.

Elated at being offered help from an unlikely ally, Rose felt a glimmer of hope where none had existed scant hours ago. Dragon had no idea she was in Scotland and had probably sent men south to intercept her. It would take at least a sennight for his men to reach London and learn she was not there, and another sennight to report back to Dragon. By the time he thought to look across the border for her, it would be too late. In order to save Piers and Vella, she would be forced to enter into a bigamous marriage. However, if Piers's and Vella's lives did not depend upon her compliance, Rose would happily defy Murdoc's ultimatum.

Rose's stomach growled hungrily as the dinner hour approached. She had almost decided that Murdoc planned to starve her into submission when the door opened, admitting Gunn.

"What do *you* want?"

"Murdoc sent me to fetch ye. He wants ye to sup with us."

Rose glared at him. "I prefer to eat in my chamber."

Her answer seemed to please rather than anger Gunn. "He thought ye might say that and gave me permission to carry ye down if ye resist. I wouldna mind another feel of yer pert bottom beneath my hand."

He reached her in two long strides, placed his meaty hands around her waist and started to lift her over his shoulder. Rose resisted, to no avail. She pounded her fists against his back as he upended her over his shoulder. When his hand settled heavily on her bottom, Rose's warrior instincts took hold. She grasped the water pitcher by the handle as they passed the washstand, reared up and bashed him on the head.

Gunn shook his head like a bear, staggered, but did not fall. Rose took advantage of his confusion and slid from his shoulder. He was still reeling when she raised her chin to a combative angle and said, "That will teach you to touch me. I can find my own way to the hall without your hands all over me."

That said, she turned and left the chamber with a regal toss of her head.

"Where is Gunn?" Murdoc asked when Rose entered the hall alone.

"He developed a sudden headache," Rose said, trying her best to conceal her smile. "He should be along soon."

"Sit down, lass. Father Baen has arrived. He has come a long way to wed ye to Gunn. Are ye ready to agree to the union?"

Rose shot a look at Robina, noted the slight shake

of her head and decided to hold her tongue.

"My mind wavers," Rose said as she sat down in the empty chair next to Murdoc.

Murdoc sent her a fierce scowl. "Gunn grows impatient, as do I. Father Baen can remain with us but a few days."

"Entering a bigamous relationship is against the law."

"The court in Stirling declared yer marriage to Dragon invalid."

"Dragon will be furious when he learns you kidnapped me."

Murdoc smiled complacently. "As soon as ye and Gunn are wed, my clansmen and allies will rally to me. Dragonwyck isna impregnable, ye ken. If Dragon willna give up Dragonwyck peaceably, we will lay siege and take it from him."

"Your thinking is all wrong, Uncle. You seem to forget that Dragonwyck is on English soil, and even if you force me to commit bigamy, 'twill be for naught. The king will do everything in his power to keep Dragonwyck under English jurisdiction."

"I am not dense, niece. 'Tis common knowledge the king is in trouble with his marcher barons. England is on the brink of civil war, and John canna concern himself with Dragonwyck when discontented vassals threaten his throne. As for Dragon, he is a proud man. Think ye he will want ye once Gunn has rutted betwixt yer legs?"

Grimly determined, Rose vowed, "Gunn will never have me."

Gunn chose that moment to stagger into the hall. "Where is she? Where is the bitch?"

Murdoc scraped his chair back and shot to his feet. "What happened? Ye look done in, lad."

"Ask *her!*" Gunn said, pointing a damning finger at Rose. "The bitch is dangerous. I wouldna be surprised to find ballocks beneath her skirt." He reeled forward. "Let me at her."

"Sit down, lad, whilst I get to the bottom of this."

Gunn sent a menacing glare at Rose as he collapsed into a chair.

"What did ye do to Gunn, niece?" Murdoc asked in a low growl.

"He put his hands on me," Rose retorted, "so I decided to teach him a lesson."

"The bitch bashed me in the head with a pitcher," Gunn shouted. He groaned and clutched his head. "I want her now, Murdoc. I want to teach her how to behave."

Murdoc looked at Rose with renewed respect. "Ye did that to Gunn? Yer a brave lass, but I always knew that." He sighed. "Ye shouldna have hurt Gunn. He isna an easy man to placate."

Rose opened her mouth to tell Murdoc exactly what she thought of him and his stepson but snapped her mouth shut when Robina loudly cleared her throat. Robina was right, Rose reflected. Angering the men would serve no purpose.

"When shall we hold the wedding, lass?" Murdoc said around a mouthful of venison. "It must be soon. As I said before, Father Baen will only be with us a day or two."

"I canna wait that long to put my hands around her neck and my cock inside her," Gunn grumbled. "We will wed today."

Her frustration mounting, Rose slammed her fist on the table. "I will not wed Gunn."

Rose sensed Gunn's eyes on her but refused to acknowledge him. She had angered and embarrassed him, and his expression told her he could not wait to punish her.

"Yer forgetting, niece, I hold the upper hand. Ye want yer vassals to live, do ye not?" Rose nodded. "Then do as I say, and all will be well. After ye and Gunn are wed, yer vassals can carry my demands to Dragon."

"What demands, Uncle?"

"That he abandon Dragonwyck, of course." He raised his hand. "Say nay more, lass. Yer constant chatter upsets my digestion."

Rose lowered her head and concentrated on her meal, hoping that Dragon would not be too angry with her for leaving Dragonwyck and that his pride would not prevent him from coming to her rescue once he learned where to find her.

At last the meal ended, and Murdoc escorted Rose to her chamber. She began pacing, too keyed up to sleep. Night arrived; all was quiet within the keep. Her nerves on edge, Rose wondered if Robina had successfully freed her vassals. All she could do was wait and fret until Murdoc learned of their absence and all hell broke loose.

Rose was still awake in the small hours before dawn when someone scratched on the door. Though the sound was barely discernible, she nearly jumped out of her skin.

"Rose, are ye awake?"

Rose rushed to the door. "Robina. Why are you still here?"

The key rattled in the lock, and Robina stepped inside. "Yer vassals refused to leave without ye."

"You were successful, then?"

Robina beamed. "Aye, but Piers wouldna leave without ye. He and Vella await us at the postern gate. Hurry, lass."

"You should not have returned for me," Rose said.

"Tell that to yer vassals. Donna tarry, lass."

Rose did not wait for a second invitation but followed Robina out the door and along a rush-lit passageway. Rose's chamber was in a deserted part of the castle so she was not worried about Murdoc hearing them, but there were bound to be guards about. Fear gnawed at Rose as she followed Robina through the darkened hall.

"Where are the guards?" Rose hissed.

Laughter rumbled in Robina's throat. "I put valerian in their barrel of ale. They will likely sleep 'til sunup."

Rose watched in silence as Robina disappeared down a dark passageway leading to the kitchen. When Rose attempted to follow, a large hand clamped down on her shoulder. She darted a glance behind her and saw Gunn, his face contorted with rage. She tried to free herself, but his vise-like grip held her fast. She was caught, but at least Robina had escaped.

"Damnation, woman!" Gunn roared. "Who let ye out?"

"Let me go!"

"I asked ye a question. Who let ye out, and where did ye think ye were going?"

"Home!" Rose blasted. "Nobody let me out. I simply walked through the closed door. Did you not know? I am a witch."

Gunn's expression held a healthy measure of skepticism and a small part of fear. His grip, however, remained firm.

"Donna jest with me, Rose. Yer no more witch than I am a warlock. What ye are is a bitch. My head still aches where ye bashed me with the pitcher."

As he pulled her away from the passage, Rose darted a glance over her shoulder, relieved that Robina had not returned to help her.

"We will see how easily ye can walk through doors with a guard stationed outside yer chamber."

Gunn walked up to a guardsmen slumped against a wall and nudged him with his foot. When he did not awaken, he shook him violently. The man looked up groggily, tried to rise, and fell back against the wall.

"What in the hell is going on here?" Gunn took a good look at the guard and spit out a curse. "He isna sleeping, he has been drugged."

Gunn dragged Rose to the solar and pounded on the door. He continued pounding until a sleepy-eyed Murdoc, still pulling on his hose, opened the door. "God's nightgown, Gunn, how can a man get a decent night's rest with ye knocking down his door? What is it now? Is the enemy at our gates?" Then he saw Rose and came fully awake. "What are ye doing with my niece?"

Connie Mason

"I caught her trying to escape. I donna know how she got out of her chamber and she willna say. Something strange has happened, Murdoc. I couldna awaken the guardsman in the hall. He appears to have been drugged."

"Wait here," Murdoc said harshly. He disappeared into his chamber and returned a moment later with the key to Rose's door. "I still have the key. How did ye free yerself, lass?"

Her chin went up. "I walked through the closed door."

"Ye have a wicked tongue, lass." He handed the key to Gunn. "Take her back to her chamber and lock her in. I will get to the bottom of this, and when I do, heads will roll."

A silent prayer trembled on Rose's lips. *Please, God, do not let Murdoc catch Robina.*

None too gently, Gunn returned Rose to her chamber and locked her inside. Daylight arrived; the sun moved high overhead. Rose's attention sharpened when she heard noises echoing through the halls and a commotion in the courtyard beneath the window. Peering over the sill, she saw a large gathering of armed men. A moment later the door to her chamber crashed open and hit the wall with a loud bang. Rose flattened herself against the window embrasure as her uncle stalked toward her, his face a mask of fury.

"Robina did it! She let ye out of yer chamber, dinna she?"

"Nay, I told you—"

"Donna lie! Robina is missing and so are yer vassals. Gunn stopped ye from joining them, dinna he? They

328

willna get far. I canna believe Robina would betray me. Ye better pray I donna catch her."

He turned and stormed away, slamming the door behind him. Rose stared at the door, her knees quaking beneath her.

Chapter Seventeen

Roses are nature's jewels, with whose wealth
she decks earth's beauty.

—Croly

Rose hated doing nothing while those she cared about were in danger. Unfortunately, there was no way she could stop Uncle Murdoc from intercepting Robina, Piers and Vella before they reached Dragonwyck. Though she had never known Murdoc to be brutal, there was always a first time, and it was all her fault. If they had not agreed to help her, they would not be facing danger now.

Rose heard the door latch rattle and swung around to face the portal. Her pulse racing, she glanced about the room for a weapon with which to defend herself. If she was going to escape, now was the time. The pitcher she'd used on Gunn had been replaced with another, and she grasped the handle, raising the pitcher high as she waited for the door to open.

When a gray-haired woman that Rose recognized as Murdoc's cook pushed the door open and slipped inside, Rose lowered the pitcher and returned it to the washstand.

"Thelma, what are you doing here?"

"I've brought ye something to eat, Rosie, lass. Murdoc gave me the key and told me to see that yer fed. I donna know what Murdoc is about these days," she said, shaking her head. "He shouldna keep ye confined like this. And now he's chased sweet Robina off. Robina is a good woman; Murdoc willna find another like her. I'm thinking Murdoc has lost his senses."

She set the tray she carried down and clucked her tongue. "Murdoc can think of nothing but getting an heir, and Gunn can think of nothing but power. I'm thinking 'tis Murdoc's fault Robina hasna given him an heir. His seed may be plentiful, but it isna potent enough to make a bairn."

"If you don't agree with what my uncle is doing to me, will you help me escape?"

"I donna know, lass." Her expression grew thoughtful, and then she smiled. "Mayhap 'tis possible. Murdoc left men behind to protect the keep, two of them my own sons."

A glimmer of hope lit Rose's features. "Will they help me? Murdoc must be stopped. He has to be mad to believe I will wed Gunn under any circumstances. I am Dragon's wife, and naught can change that." A sudden thought occurred to her. "Is Father Baen still in the castle?"

"Aye, lass, he is on his knees in the chapel."

"Can you bring him to me?"

Understanding lifted Thelma's frown. "Aye, Rose, I'll fetch him for ye." She gestured toward the tray. "Eat something while yer waiting."

After the cook departed, Rose sat down and sampled the food Thelma had brought. She was famished and finished everything on the tray. She seemed to be hungry all the time lately but didn't have the time now to consider the reason for her increased appetite. She had her suspicions but set them aside for the time being.

Thelma returned with Father Baen a short time later. The priest, a tall, thin man, bustled into the chamber behind Thelma and smiled benignly at Rose.

"What can I do for ye, my child? I hope ye can explain Murdoc's hasty departure. He knows I canna stay long. I hoped to wed ye to Gunn today."

"Father, I cannot wed Gunn today or any day. I am already married. Did Murdoc not tell you I have a husband?"

The priest looked at Thelma for confirmation. When Thelma nodded, he scowled. "Murdoc said yer marriage to yer English husband wasna legal, that ye were already promised to Gunn."

"Murdoc lied. I was never promised to Gunn. Neither my father nor uncle signed a betrothal agreement. My father would have told me if such a document existed."

"But the court—"

"*Scottish* court, Father. I am an English subject and beyond the jurisdiction of Scottish laws. Uncle Murdoc brought the petition to invalidate my marriage before the court at Stirling, and I would not put it past him to grease palms to attain a favorable decision."

"Are ye sure of this, lass?"

"Aye. I would not lie to you, Father. I cannot wed Gunn. Furthermore, Murdoc is holding me against my will."

"Do ye want to return to yer English husband?"

Rose smiled wistfully. "Aye, he is my life. I love him and miss him. Can you help me? I want to go home."

Father Baen's face hardened with righteousness. "If what ye say is true, lass, then we will leave the keep together. There is no need for me to remain if there is to be no wedding. And I canna join a man and woman unless both are willing. How soon can ye be ready?"

Elation colored Rose's words. "Immediately. The sooner the better."

"Wait here. I will return for ye after I gather my belongings and say a prayer for our safe passage."

"I can never thank you enough, Father."

"Pray for me, child, 'tis all I ask."

"I'll fix food for the journey," Thelma said, hurrying off after the priest.

True to his word, Father Baen returned for her a short time later. "Are ye ready, my child?"

Rose snatched up her cloak and rushed from the chamber. Thelma stood in the passageway with her two sons.

" 'Tis all right, Rose," Thelma said. "Hugh and Douglas understand and willna stop ye."

Connie Mason

"What about the others?" Rose asked.

"Leave them to me, child," Father Baen soothed. "I am a man of God and ye are under my protection; harming ye could bring eternal damnation."

The priest's words held true. Escorted by Hugh and Douglas, Rose and Father Baen walked down the staircase and through the hall to the front entrance without being challenged. The priest had arranged for their horses to be brought around, and Ladybird and Father Baen's mount were standing in the courtyard. Hugh lifted Rose into the saddle, and Thelma handed her a basket containing food.

"Uncle Murdoc will be angry with you and your sons for helping me," Rose said as she took the basket from Thelma.

"Donna worry about us, lass," Thelma said. "Not even yer uncle would challenge a man of God. Return to yer husband, Rose, and give him many bairns."

Father Baen reined his mount through the gate and Rose followed. She could not believe how easy it had been as they cleared the gate without being challenged. God was surely looking out for her.

Dominic led his knights toward the Scottish border at full tilt. His wound, though nearly healed, caused twinges of pain and he could feel himself tiring, but it would take more than a few small annoyances to stop him. Rose needed him; he felt it deep within his soul, knew it with each breath he took. His expression was grim; there was no trace of softness in his dark, merciless eyes. The moment he rode forth from Dragonwyck, he became the fierce warrior men feared, the

334

brave knight bards immortalized in verse.

Dragon had just crossed into Scotland when he saw three riders approaching from the north. He raised his hand to halt his men and waited for the riders to approach. Sir Eric rode up beside him.

"Is it Lady Rose?"

Dominic squinted against the glare of the sun as he attempted to identify the riders. Disappointment cut deep into his gut when he realized that Rose was not one of the two women accompanying the man.

" 'Tis Piers and Vella," Eric observed when they drew close enough to identify. "And if I'm not mistaken, that's Murdoc's wife with them. I recognize Lady Robina because she often accompanied Murdoc on his visits to Dragonwyck."

Anxious to learn why Rose was not with them, Dominic spurred his mount and rode out to meet the travelers.

"Lord Dragon," Piers said. "Thank God. I feared we would not reach Dragonwyck before MacTavish caught up with us. How did you know to look for us in Scotland?"

" 'Twas a wild guess. Quickly, where is Rose? Why is she not with you?"

"I will try to explain, if I may," Robina said. "I am Robina, Murdoc's wife. Murdoc came upon Piers, Vella and Rose while raiding across the border and brought them by force to our fortress. I dinna like what he did and found a way to speak to Rose in private. She said Murdoc was threatening to harm Piers and Vella if she dinna agree to wed Gunn."

"Murdoc is mad," Dominic snorted. "Rose is already

wed. Does he not know she cannot legally wed another?"

"Murdoc is a stubborn man. He claimed that Rose was promised to Gunn and asked the court at Stirling to declare yer marriage to Rose invalid. The court agreed, but Rose dinna, so Murdoc threatened to harm yer vassals if she dinna wed Gunn. She asked me to free Piers and Vella so they could fetch ye to Scotland."

"Why did Rose not come with you?" Dominic asked harshly.

"I went back for her," Robina explained, "and I thought she was following behind me. When I realized she wasna with me, I turned back to find her, but 'twas too late." She wrung her hands, gulping air before she continued. "I saw Gunn dragging her away. He dinna see me, and I hurried back to tell Piers and Vella. We decided to go on without her and fetch ye. Ye are the only one who can help Rose now."

She paused to catch her breath. "I couldna stay with Murdoc after betraying him. Rose said ye would protect me and see me safely to my father's manor near Stirling."

"Aye, I will protect you," Dominic vowed. "Can you find your way to Dragonwyck, Piers?"

"Aye, my lord."

"Then take Lady Robina with you and ask Lady Emily to see that she is made comfortable."

"Be careful," Robina said. "Murdoc canna be far behind us. With Piers and Vella gone, he has no hold over Rose and canna force her to wed Gunn." A sob left her throat. "He will be verra angry with me."

"You did right, Lady Robina," Dominic advised. "Go with . . ."

His sentence trailed off and he cocked his head as the distant sound of horses' hooves reached his ears. "Hark, do you hear?"

" 'Tis Murdoc!" Robina gasped.

"Into the trees, men! Half on one side of the road and half on the other," Dominic shouted as he urged Piers, Vella and Robina into the woods.

"Stay here," he ordered curtly.

Dominic drew his sword and waited for Murdoc to ride into the trap. The riders appeared several minutes later. Though heavily armed and carrying shields, they wore no armor. Dominic let out a war cry and rode out from the trees. Murdoc looked confused as knights wearing Dragon's coat of arms upon their surcoats quickly surrounded him and his men.

Murdoc hesitated but a moment before he drew his sword and engaged the knight nearest him in battle. The fight was fierce. Men fell, others fought on. The Scotsmen were at a disadvantage without chain mail and began to fall back. Dominic saw Gunn fall and leaped from his destrier. Avoiding clashing swords and fallen bodies, Dominic reached Gunn before the Scotsman gained his feet and pressed the tip of his sword against Gunn's neck.

Seething with rage at the thought of Gunn putting his hands on Rose, Dominic prepared to end Gunn's miserable life when an anguished cry stopped the downward thrust of his arm.

"Nay! Desist! Donna kill him!"

"Instruct your men to lay down their weapons and

mayhap I'll spare your heir," Dominic ordered.

"Lay down yer weapons, lads!" Murdoc shouted. One by one, the Scotsmen placed their weapons on the ground and backed away. Immediately the English knights closed ranks around them.

" 'Tis done," Murdoc growled. "Are ye a man of yer word?"

Dominic stepped away from Gunn and sheathed his sword. Gunn lurched to his feet. "Unlike you," Dominic said disdainfully, "I value my honor."

"I am an honorable man," Murdoc growled.

"Tell that to your wife."

Murdoc went still. "What do ye know about my wife? Have ye seen Robina?"

Dominic indicated the woman emerging from the woods. "Is that not Lady Robina approaching?"

Murdoc's mouth hung agape as he watched Robina ride toward him.

Robina reined in beside Dominic and dismounted. "What are ye going to do with him, Lord Dragon?"

"Escort him to his demesne and fetch my wife home. Do you still wish safe conduct to your father's manor?"

"Nay, she doesna!" Murdoc replied. "Yer coming home with me, Robina."

"Nay, Murduc, ye donna appreciate me. Yer not the same man I married ten years ago."

"Ye will do as I say!" Murdoc thundered.

"You are forgetting one thing, Murdoc," Dominic interjected. "I hold the upper hand here. Lady Robina asked for protection, and I granted it."

"Ye had no right. My wife betrayed me."

"Nay, Murdoc," Robina cried. "I did what was right."

"Donna listen to her, Murdoc," Gunn advised. "Let her go."

"Ock, Gunn, do ye fear I will give Murdoc an heir?" Robina taunted.

Gunn laughed. "I fear naught from a dried-up old hag. Yer barren, Robina, accept it. Murdoc doesna need ye."

"Enough!" Dominic roared. "My men and I will escort you to your demesne, and if I find that either of you have harmed one hair on Rose's head, you both will suffer."

"I wouldna harm my own niece," Murdoc huffed. "I only want what's best for the lass."

"I know what's best for Rose, and believe me, 'tis not Gunn. Mount up, we're riding north."

"I'm sorry, Murdoc," Robina said. "I hope ye can find it in yer heart to forgive me." She reined her horse about. Piers and Vella joined her as she rode south to Dragonwyck.

"Yer a fool," Murdoc bit out.

The large party of English knights and their captives continued north. Murdoc's keep was but a few leagues ahead when Dominic rode down the ranks and advised his men to remain alert. The walls of MacTavish keep had just come into view when Dominic saw two riders clear the gate. One wore black robes, and the other was a woman whose long blond hair streamed behind her like a golden banner. Spurring his destrier, Dominic burst forward, leaving his men in the dust.

He heard Rose shouting. The wind picked up her words and carried them to him. He heard her calling his name, and his heart nearly burst from his chest.

Rose, his feisty Rose, his beautiful Rose, was unharmed.

Dominic pulled back on the reins. His destrier pawed air, then skidded to a halt several feet from where Rose awaited him. He leaped from the saddle and ran to help her dismount. Rose slid into his arms, her face radiant as he held her against him.

"You've come! I knew you would, I just didn't expect you so soon. Robina left shortly before dawn with Piers and Vella. Did you see them? Uncle Murdoc rode out to intercept them."

"One question at a time, love," Dominic said, silencing her with a kiss. He didn't care who was watching. He didn't care if all the world knew how happy he was to see Rose unharmed and have her in his arms again.

Rose's arms remained firmly around Dominic's neck as he framed her face between his hands and kissed her until they were both breathless.

"I love you so much, Dominic," Rose whispered against his mouth.

Dominic stilled. "What did you say?"

Rose laughed; the joyful sound made his heart swell with tenderness. "Did you not know?"

"I . . . nay, but I hoped. Unrequited love is not a happy state of affairs."

Rose stared at him. "Unrequited? You mean you . . . oh . . ."

Her words ended in a gurgle of embarrassment as the main party of knights caught up with them.

"What is it, love?"

Rose stared at the new arrivals over Dominic's shoulder. "Uncle Murdoc and Gunn are with your men. What happened?"

"We encountered Robina, Piers and Vella first. While they were explaining what happened at the keep, we heard Murdoc and his men approaching. We hid in the woods and ambushed them as they rode past. There were several wounded on both sides, but fortunately, no one died in the fray."

"It must have been a fierce fight. Uncle Murdoc does not give up easily."

"He did not give up until I had Gunn beneath my sword. Then Murdoc surrendered rather than see him hurt. I released Gunn, but I would have killed him if Murdoc had harmed you."

"Dinna I tell ye my niece wasna harmed?" Murdoc called out. "Tell him, lass. Tell Dragon I dinna hurt ye."

"The lass is dangerous," Gunn said sullenly. "I have a knot on my head to prove it."

Dominic arched an eyebrow at Rose. "What's that all about?"

Rose gave him a pert grin. "He put his hands on me and I took offense. The water pitchers in MacTavish keep make exceptional weapons."

Laughter bubbled up in Dominic's throat. "I should have known my plucky wife would find a weapon worthy of her skills."

"What are ye going to do with us?" Murdoc asked. "Ye got what ye came for. Ye've also got my wife. Send her home, and we will call a truce."

"Lady Robina is under my protection. Should she wish to return to you, I will not interfere."

"Ye canna steal a man's wife," Murdoc charged.

"Why not? You stole *my* wife. Your Scottish courts have no jurisdiction over English subjects. If you want your wife back, I suggest you make things right with her."

"I thought you cared naught for Robina," Rose said.

"I mispoke," Murdoc mumbled.

"Then I suggest you tell her yourself." She laid a hand on Dominic's arm. "There is no need to punish him, is there? No harm befell me. 'Tis true he confined me to my chamber, but I was denied naught but my freedom. I believe Uncle Murdoc lost more than he realizes when Robina left him."

"You are too tenderhearted, wife."

"Please, Dominic, for me. I believe Uncle Murdoc has learned his lesson. There is no way he can claim Dragonwyck, and his greed may have cost him Mama's regard as well as Robina's."

Dominic glared at Murdoc. "What say you, Mac-Tavish? Do you think you deserve Rose's forgiveness?"

"I love both my nieces," Murdoc mumbled.

"You said you were a man of honor. Prove it. Swear an oath to leave me and mine alone, and you and your kinsmen can return home in peace."

Murdoc's head shot up. "No one has ever questioned the honor of a MacTavish."

"Then prove it."

"Are ye going to let an Englishman browbeat ye, Murdoc?" Gunn asked on a low growl.

" 'Tis over, Gunn," Murdoc replied. "Owning a slice of England was a foolish, impossible dream. I will find ye another heiress to wed. My wife is already lost to me. I donna want to lose my sister and nieces.

"Ye win, Dragon. Ye have naught more to fear from the MacTavishes."

"I will accept your word, MacTavish," Dominic said. "You are free to go after you apologize to Rose for the distress you caused her."

Murdoc had a pinched look about his lips, but Dominic had no sympathy for the Scotsman. It took a while, but Murdoc finally said, "Forgive me, lass. I was overcome with greed and wasna thinking straight. Ye and yers have naught more to fear from me."

"I forgive you, Uncle," Rose replied. "Mayhap one day Dominic will forgive you and you can visit Dragonwyck again."

"Not likely," Dominic muttered beneath his breath. "Return the Scotsmen's weapons and let them go," he ordered his men.

"The hour grows late. Will ye accept my hospitality for the night?" Murdoc asked.

"Nay. I am taking my wife and our wounded home," Dominic said. Trusting MacTavish was asking too much.

MacTavish nodded his understanding and rode off, his kinsmen following in his wake.

"Thank you," Rose said, eyes shining with gratitude. "Uncle Murdoc isn't a bad man, just misguided."

Dominic remained unconvinced. "If you say so, love. Let's be off." He pulled her close and held her a brief moment before helping her into the saddle. "I cannot wait to get home. I missed you, Rose."

Rose leaned over and touched his face. "I love you, Dominic." Then she spurred her mount and took off, sending him a saucy grin over her shoulder.

Rose's smile wrapped itself around Dominic's heart and filled it with love. Laughing for the pure joy of it, he mounted his destrier and took off after her. They did not speak as they rode side by side, but no words were needed to express their feelings.

During Rose's absence, the knowledge that she might be in danger had affected him deeply. Without Rose he had become an empty shell of a man, as if everything gentle, everything vulnerable and caring within him no longer existed. Now that Rose was returned to him, he felt renewed, softer, more inclined to forgive. He frowned. Love had a damned seductive way of making a man feel things he'd never felt before.

Rose was happier than she had ever been in her life. Dragon hadn't actually said he loved her, but everything he'd said and done today expressed his deep regard.

Rose touched her stomach and smiled dreamily. Should her suspicions prove correct, she was carrying Dragon's child. She had missed her monthly cycle, her first indication that she might be increasing. She did not dare tell Dragon for fear he would stop her from traveling to London to change places with Starla.

"What are you plotting, Rose?" Dominic asked, glancing at her smiling face. "I have seen that look on your face before."

Rose gave him an innocent stare. "I'm plotting naught, Dominic. I was merely wondering when we would be traveling to Westminster."

Dominic sent her a disgruntled look. "I should beat you for leaving Dragonwyck without my knowledge or permission. What were you thinking? You not only endangered your own life but those of your vassals."

"I did what I had to do, Dominic. I knew it was wrong to deceive you, but I hoped you would understand."

Dominic's expression softened. "Mayhap a beating is too harsh a punishment. I will think of something more appropriate. Do not try anything so foolish again. We will travel to Westminster together in a day or two."

"Thank you, Dominic."

The skies had darkened to a deep purple by the time the party reached Dragonwyck. As soon as they were seen by the guards on the parapet, the drawbridge was lowered and they clattered across. The portcullis lifted; they rode through both the outer bailey and inner bailey and drew rein in the courtyard.

Rose was elated to be home again, despite the fact that she would leave again very soon. As Dragon lifted her off Ladybird, someone called her name and she looked up. Emily stood at the top of the stairs, squealing Rose's name, then lifted her skirts and raced to the bottom. Rose braced herself for Emily's embrace. Then Blythe appeared, and both women tried to hug her at once.

Robina followed at a more sedate pace but was no less enthusiastic.

Rose was grateful when Dragon intervened, though somewhat embarrassed when he swept her into his arms and carried her up the stairs.

"Rose is exhausted, ladies," he tossed over his shoulder. "We are retiring to our chamber. Do not expect to see us until the sun rises tomorrow."

"You must be starved," Emily said, running to catch up with them. "Do you want something to eat first?"

"I *am* hungry," Rose ventured. "And I would like a bath."

Dominic's sigh held a hint of disappointment. "Very well, a bath first and then food."

"I will see to it immediately," Emily replied, hurrying off to the kitchen.

Rose closed her eyes and relaxed against Dominic.

His voice was low and melodic. "Are you sleeping, love?"

"Nay, just enjoying being in your arms again. For a time I feared I would be forced to commit bigamy to save Piers and Vella. Then Robina came to me and things began to look brighter."

Dominic carried her into the solar and sat her down on a bench before the hearth. "Let me build up the fire before you catch a chill."

"The night is warm, Dominic."

"The chamber is damp."

Rose did not argue. She sat back and admired the play of muscles along Dragon back and buttocks as he bent to the task. She loved him so much. Did he love her? Though he had not said the words, his actions said he did. A woman, however, needed words she could hold to her heart and savor.

Dominic rose and dusted off his knees. "Dominic, do you love me?" Rose blurted out.

"Have you not guessed by now?"

"I was never very good at guessing games. Can you not say the words? You know how I feel; now tell me what I need to hear."

He grasped both her hands in his and pulled her gently into his arms. "I have never said this to another woman, Rose, but I am telling you now because my heart is full to bursting with love for you. You are like no other woman I have ever known, prickly on the outside, soft as down on the inside.

"I cannot look at you without wanting to kiss you endlessly and put myself inside you."

Rose slanted him a provocative smile. "Are you very sure you no longer want Veronica?"

"Veronica who? There is only you, love. I want no other. If you were not in need of a bath and food, I would prove here and now how much I love you, how very much I want you."

His fingers drifted gently over her face and he framed her jaw, holding it steady for his kiss. She sighed into his mouth, matching the intensity of his kiss with a need of her own. The kiss grew more demanding, a fire that required tending. She sank her fingers into his hair as he plundered her mouth. Just as the fires inside them flared out of control, a knock came on the door.

"Go away," Dominic growled.

"Master, 'tis Raj. Henry of Ashford is at the portcullis and wishes to speak with you. He says 'tis urgent."

"At this time of night?"

"Aye, master. He says it cannot wait."

Dominic spit out a curse. "Escort him to the hall, Raj, and tell him I will be down soon."

"Whatever could he want?" Rose asked.

"I have a feeling his business concerns King John and the Articles of the Barons. Have your bath and something to eat, love. I will return as soon as I can. Keep the bed warm for me."

He kissed her again, hard, then strode from the chamber.

Chapter Eighteen

There are many facets of Roses that I love.
                                        —Anonymous

Henry of Ashford was waiting in the hall when Dominic arrived. Dominic ushered the marcher baron to the manor office, where they could enjoy a modicum of privacy, and offered him a goblet of wine. Ashford accepted with alacrity and drank down half the contents before wiping his mouth on his sleeve and clearing his throat.

"I regret having to bother you at this time of night, but my mission is urgent," he began.

"I assume your visit has to do with the Articles of the Barons," Dominic said.

Ashford grimaced. "Aye. The king refused to sign them despite weeks of negotiation. Both sides have appealed to the pope, to no avail. John refuses to believe that his failure to meet our demands will result in a civil war. He is wrong. The barons and their vassals are planning to march on London. We need you, Dragon. Every man counts in this battle against the king's injustices."

"A few months ago I would have hesitated, but things have changed. King John does not deserve my loyalty. He held Rose hostage while I fought his war on the Welsh marches. He accused me of conspiring with the marcher barons against him. I swore I was loyal, but he trusted me not."

"Rose is the king's hostage? 'Tis all the more reason for you to join us. When we march on London, the release of your wife will be included in our demands."

"Starla is the king's hostage, not Rose," Dominic revealed. Then, in a few succinct words, he explained the situation to Ashford, including how Rose and Starla had changed places and why.

"I heard you had been wounded but I did not know how seriously," Ashford mused.

"But for Rose I would be dead," Dominic said with conviction. "Now she is anxious to return to Westminster so Starla can go back to the convent."

"I hope poor Starla has been able to cope with the licentious goings-on at court."

"Her mother is with her, which should help. Nevertheless, Rose wants to return to Westminster as soon as possible, and I am sufficiently recovered from my wound to escort her."

"Hmmm," Ashford said, stroking his chin. "Having you at Westminster working on our behalf could be advantageous. Mayhap you can convince the king to listen to reason. He does not realize how close he is to a civil war. You are one of us now, Dragon. Will you join our cause?"

Dominic answered without hesitation. "Aye. Tell the barons they can count on me. When do you march?"

"It will take a fortnight for us to muster and arm our vassals. We plan to meet at a central place and converge on London together. Mayhap the sight of our combined forces will cause the king to acknowledge our demands and set his seal to the articles."

"I am leaving Dragonwyck in a day or two, but I pledge my knights to your army."

Ashford seemed surprised. "Are you not taking your men to London with you?"

"Nay. I need only Raj. Mayhap by the time the army reaches London, the king will be in a mood to sign the articles."

"That is all I needed to hear, Dragon. Your support means a great deal to us. Can I impose upon your hospitality for the night?"

"Gladly. I will summon my steward."

They left the chamber together, and Dominic went in search of Sir Braden.

"Sir Braden will see that you are made comfortable, Ashford. Now if you will excuse me, Rose awaits me in our chamber."

Dominic took his leave. Ashford was all but forgotten as Dominic bounded up the stairs. He burst into the solar and stopped in his tracks when he saw Rose sitting on the floor before the hearth, wearing nothing but a drying cloth and a tray of food perched on her crossed legs.

"You are just in time," Rose greeted. "I saved something for you to eat."

Dominic glanced at the food, then at Rose. The meager leavings on the tray could not compete with Rose. She looked deliciously disheveled and rosy from her bath. Her pink toes poking out from beneath the drying cloth looked more appealing than anything on the tray.

"My appetite is not for food," Dominic said on a low growl.

Rose waved her spoon toward the tub. "The water is still hot; you may bathe if you wish."

Bathing was the last thing on Dominic's mind, but Rose was not the only one who enjoyed a clean body. He stripped off his mail and the rest of his clothing and stepped into the cooling water.

"Shall I wash your back?" Rose asked, rising. She stationed herself behind Dominic, soaped a cloth and began to scrub. "What did Lord Ashford want?"

"The king still refuses to sign the articles after weeks of negotiations, and the barons are going to march on London. They want me to join them."

The washcloth slipped from Rose's fingers. "Nay, you cannot! Papa died for the cause; I cannot lose you, too. Besides, you promised to take me to London."

"I pledged my knights, but I am not joining the barons' army, Rose. I know how important it is for you to return to the palace, and I will honor my promise to take you there. Raj and I will escort you to Westminster. The details are not complete yet, but Raj swears he can get you inside the palace and Starla out with little difficulty. I will present myself to the king soon afterward and demand your release. I nearly died defending England, and King John has no reason to deny my request.

"Ashford believes I could be useful to the barons inside the palace," Dominic continued. "He urged me to use my powers of persuasion to convince the king to sign the articles. John cannot afford a civil war right now."

Rose picked up the cloth and resumed washing Dominic's back. When she finished with his back, she moved around to the side of the tub and slid the cloth over his chest. Her eyes glinted wickedly as she soaped the cloth and plunged her hand beneath the water to his—

"Rose!" He stayed her hand. "Naughty witch. Touch me there, and I guarantee you will end up in the water with me."

"But I like touching you there, my lusty Dragon. Your cock is—"

"Near to bursting," he finished.

She worked her hand free and caressed him. "What are we going to do about it?"

He surged from the tub. A moment later the wet warmth of his arms surrounded her. "I intend to bury my cock deep inside you and pump until you scream with pleasure."

Her wits scattered as her gaze met his and clung. "I can hardly wait."

Suddenly she was floating toward the bedchamber.

Dragon's arms were all that anchored her to reality as he lowered her onto the bed and came down beside her. His lips brushed hers, than slid along her jaw until he nuzzled her throat. A ripple of excitement shivered down her spine. She felt the weight of his hand settle on her breast and caught her breath. The unleashed power of his body lay heavy upon her, but it was not enough. She wanted all of him.

He raised himself up slightly and caressed her stomach, then buried his fingers in the blond thatch between her legs. His fingers delved into her moist cleft. Rose moaned, clutched his shoulders and arched against him. He caressed her, over and over, until she screamed for him to end it.

"Not yet, love."

He lurched away and turned her onto her stomach. Rose glanced at him over her shoulder, one brow raised.

"Before the first rays of daylight stream through the windows, I intend to make love every way possible for a man to love a woman." He caressed her bottom. "Up on your knees."

Trusting that Dragon knew what he was doing, Rose offered no objection as he assisted her. Placing his hands beneath her thighs, he hoisted her bottom in the air and positioned himself behind her. Rose's breath hitched as he opened her, and a rush of heat surged through her. Never had she felt so open and vulnerable to a man. He leaned over her back, pushed her hair aside and kissed her neck. Her heart pounded in her throat, and a shocking spear of anticipation streaked through her.

His fingers splayed along the curves of her bottom, kneading and massaging. Then his hands seemed to be everywhere at once, sliding around to mold and cup her breasts, gently squeezing her nipples, pressing against her stomach and down into the nest of curls below.

He spread her, and then his fingers dipped inside her. She quivered and made helpless noises deep in her throat. He slid his cock between her legs and pumped his hips, inch by slow inch, stretching her, filling her. Her body felt taut and raw with need as mind-blinding pleasure coursed through her. Never had she felt so brazen, so abandoned. She pushed herself up to meet his downward strokes, taking everything he had to give and wanting more.

Her fingers dug into the mattress as he lifted her higher. A sound escaped her throat, a sigh, a moan, as he rode her harder, faster, higher. Their flesh came together again and again. The pressure built; her heart pumped furiously and a scream clawed at her throat.

She felt his hot breath in her ear, pleading in a strained voice, "Come on, love, come on, come on."

His body was wet, straining; granite hard against her, in her.

The end came on her suddenly, like a shock wave, hot and uncontrollable, pushing her into oblivion as spasms that seemed to go on forever rocked her. She was only dimly aware that Dragon still pumped furiously inside her, his tension building, his breathing erratic. When the climactic end came, he plummeted over the edge, joining her in sweet splendor.

Rose's knees buckled, flattening her against the mattress. His body lowered and he followed her down. His chest heaving, he lay heavily on top of her, whispering love words into her ear.

Finally he rolled onto his back, his breathing harsh and uneven. Rose turned onto her side, a smile stretching her lips. "I never knew."

"There are many things you do not know, love. We have a lifetime to explore the various paths to pleasure."

She caressed his chest. "Must we wait a lifetime?"

Dominic groaned. "Give me a few minutes to recuperate, sweeting."

Rose blushed. "I did not mean . . . now."

He rolled over on his side, his eyes gleaming mischievously as he caressed her breasts. "Mayhap I do not need a few minutes. Shall we test my stamina?"

The challenge to his stamina was met, not once, but twice.

Exhausted but happy, Rose and Dominic entered the hall to break their fast later than usual the following morning. Rose ate heartily, causing Dominic to comment, "For a woman, you have a hearty appetite, love. Could it be due to the excessive amount of exercise we engaged in last night?"

"Mayhap," Rose answered.

She thought of the secret she harbored and smiled, praying that Dragon would be as happy as she was about the babe she carried. She had so few symptoms, she sometimes doubted a child grew beneath her heart. It appeared that she was one of the lucky few to escape the morning sickness so many women suffered. Her health was robust and she felt wonderful. According to her calculations, however, it would soon be two months since she'd last bled. As soon as she returned to the palace, she intended to discuss it with her mother.

"Does that smile mean you are planning something wicked?" Dominic asked.

Rose seriously considered sharing her secret with Dragon, but decided to wait until they reached London. She feared Dragon would stop her from traveling to Westminster, and she had promised Starla she would return to the palace as soon as she was able.

"Do we leave for London soon, Dominic?"

"I thought to begin our journey on the morrow. Can you be ready?"

"Aye. You know how badly I want to reach Starla."

"You worry too much, love. Your mother is with Starla; she will let naught happen to your sister."

Rose sincerely hoped Dragon was right.

They left the following morning, about the same time Dragon's knights left to join the barons' army. The weather was good, and all signs pointed to an uneventful journey.

By the time they reached London, Rose felt battered and bruised from the long days in the saddle, but she knew better than to complain. Raj suggested that they wait until it was dark to smuggle Rose into the palace, and Dragon agreed. Dragon bespoke a room for them at an inn, where Rose could bathe and rest until dark.

"When will you present yourself to the king?" Rose

asked as she lay on the bed resting after bathing and eating.

"Tomorrow," Dominic said. "As soon as the city gates open."

"Starla will be relieved to see me, and I know Mama must be eager to return to the convent. You know how she feels about the man who killed Papa."

"About your mother, love. I believe she should remain at the palace. Her sudden disappearance would raise too many questions. She can leave when we do."

"Though Mama may not like it, I am sure she will agree," Rose said. She arched a brow at him and patted the bed beside her. "Come join me in bed."

Dominic looked torn. After a long pause, he said, "I want to, but I cannot. You look far too drawn and tired. We can wait."

Rose knew Dragon was right, but she could not help feeling a twinge of disappointment. They had not made love during the entire journey south, and she was more than ready. She sighed, closed her eyes and immediately drifted off to sleep.

Dragon awakened her several hours later.

" 'Tis time to leave, love. The gates will be closing soon."

"Are you coming?" Rose asked, stretching and yawning.

"Nay, the fewer of us, the better. Raj will take good care of you."

"I know," Rose said. Dragon helped her dress and gave her a lingering kiss.

"That will have to do until I see you at the palace. Come; Raj waits below with the horses."

Deep shadows were creeping along the streets when Rose and Raj rode through Ludgate. When they arrived at the palace, Raj reined his horse around to the left, away from the front gate, and Rose followed. Moving at a leisurely pace beneath the deep shadows of the wall, they reached the garden gate without being seen by the guards patrolling above them.

Raj signaled for her to dismount. "I will go in first. If the way is clear, I will return for you."

The gate gave a single groan when Raj pried it open. "Weeds have grown over the gate since I last came this way," Raj commented as he slipped through the opening.

Flattening herself against the wall, Rose tethered the horses to a bush and waited for Raj to return. A short time later, the gate opened and a large hand beckoned her inside. She slipped through and breathed deeply of the familiar scent of herbs.

"There seems to be a great deal of activity taking place in the kitchen, but I doubt the servants will question your presence in the garden this late in the evening," Raj said. "Go to your sister. I will wait for her by the garden gate."

Rose wound her way through the garden and paused outside the kitchen. Dragging in a steadying breath, she calmly walked through the door. Raj had been right about the activity. Servants were bustling about their various chores without giving her a moment's notice.

Cook was the only one who paid her any heed. "My lady, I did not know ye were still in the garden. One of the serving maids said she saw ye at the banquet table tonight."

"I needed a breath of air, and the herb garden is so peaceful," Rose explained. "You were too busy to notice me when I came through the kitchen earlier."

Cook nodded sagely. "Aye, I can believe that. There is no end to the work tonight, with all the guests invited to the king's table."

Rose nodded in sympathy, brushed past Cook and headed toward the servants' staircase. She reached her chamber without mishap, opened the door and stepped inside.

Starla hated the excesses of court life. She was thoroughly sick of the gluttony and debauchery she'd witnessed at Westminster. Tonight the courtiers and their ladies had stuffed themselves like pigs, imbibed until they were falling down and pawed one another like animals. These past weeks had opened her eyes to the vices practiced by those close to the king, and she liked them not.

She had done her best to stay out of the king's way, but she had not been altogether successful. John had insisted that she attend his banquets and entertainments, and she had had no reason to refuse. If her mother had not been with her these past weeks, Starla seriously doubted she would have survived with her sanity intact. The strange way in which the king stared at her when she was in his presence was truly frightening.

Did he suspect she was not whom she pretended to be?

Mama had left the hall after the meal tonight, and Starla planned to follow as soon as she could extract herself gracefully. With everyone's attention on the entertainers, she felt certain she could slip away without being missed. She edged toward the door, only to be brought up short when a woman planted herself in front of her.

"Lady Rose, has your giant gone missing?"

Starla suppressed a groan. Lady Veronica was the last person she wanted to see. The lady had been the bane of her existence these past weeks. She wondered what Rose would do in her situation. Would she rudely cut the lady off? Would she attempt politeness she didn't feel? Nay, Starla decided, her feisty twin wouldn't allow Veronica to intimidate her.

"Raj returned to Dragonwyck," Starla said.

"How fares your husband? Has he recovered from his wounds?"

"Aye. I expect to see him at the palace very soon."

A feline smile curved Veronica's lips. "It will be wonderful to see my dear Dragon again. One does not easily forget a virile lover such as Dragon."

Flustered by Veronica's brazen statement, Starla could think of nothing to say. The woman was impossibly bold. Did she have no shame?

"If you see Dragon before I do," Veronica continued, "tell him I miss him. He knows where to find me should he wish to visit me in my home." She slanted Starla a contemptuous look. "Marriage to you must be galling for a lusty man like Dragon."

Starla had heard more than enough. Her temperament might be different from Rose's, but she couldn't let this woman insult her sister without retaliating.

"My husband has no inclination to resume his affair with you, Lady Veronica," Starla replied with a hint of Rose's spunk. For Rose's sake, she hoped she spoke the truth. "Attempt a liaison with Dragon, and I guarantee you will be sorry." She sniffed the air and wrinkled her nose. "Excuse me for rushing off, but I smell something rotten in the vicinity."

Turning on her heel, she made a hasty exit. Starla couldn't believe what she had just said. She was rather proud of herself for flying to the defense of her sister. She could hardly wait to tell Rose about the confrontation.

Rose entered her chamber and paused just inside the door. Starla was nowhere in sight, but her mother was seated before the hearth, embroidering a piece of silk. The soft thud of the door as Rose pushed it shut brought Nelda's gaze up.

Suddenly Nelda's eyes widened and she rose from the chair. "Rose! You have returned."

Rose ran into Nelda's arms. "Aye, Mama. I wondered how long it would take you to recognize me. Thank God no one else guessed." She paused. "No one *has* guessed, have they?"

"Not a soul, daughter. But tell me, how fares Lord Dragon? Is he with you?"

"Dragon is well. He remained in the city tonight. He intends to present himself to the king tomorrow. Oh, Mama, so much has happened since last I saw you. I know not where to begin."

Nelda's attention sharpened. "What is it, Rose?"

"I disobeyed Dragon and set off a series of events that could have had disastrous results."

"That sounds rather ominous. Tell me."

Rose took a deep breath and launched into the story of her flight from Dragonwyck and abduction by Murdoc MacTavish. "Uncle Murdoc lost more than he bargained for when Robina left him," Rose concluded.

"Murdoc was always hotheaded, but I thought he had more sense than to attempt something as contemptible as kidnapping his own niece. Thank God for Robina and Thelma. At least someone in that clan was levelheaded enough to know right from wrong. I hope Murdoc's wits return before 'tis too late to regain Robina's esteem and earn her trust."

"Aye, Robina is a good woman. I believe she loves Murdoc, but he went too far when he tried to force me to wed Gunn, and Robina could not accept it."

" 'Twas good of Lord Dragon to forgive my brother," Nelda said. "I fear we all misjudged your husband."

"Aye, Mama, Dragon is a good man. And"—she smiled shyly—"he loves me and I love him."

"I am so glad things worked out for you. Starla is anxious to return to the convent. Will it be soon?"

"Raj is waiting by the garden gate even as we speak. He will see her safely back to the convent. Dragon thinks it would be unwise for you to disappear and suggested that you accompany us when we leave. It should not be too long. Can I convince you to remain at Dragonwyck instead of returning to the convent? You see," she confided, "I think I am with child, and you did say you would come home when I made you a grandmother." She touched her stomach lightly. "Dragon does not know yet."

Her eyes shining, Nelda clapped her hands in delight. "What wonderful news! Starla will be so pleased for you. Of course I shall return to Dragonwyck if you think I could be useful."

"I need you, Mama."

"Then 'tis settled. Oh, I do wish Starla would hurry."

Nelda had no sooner spoken than the door opened and Starla stormed inside.

"That woman!" Starla raged. "I swear, Mama, that woman is a viper in disguise. How Rose endured her poisonous barbs is beyond me. This time, however, I gave as good as I got. Rose would be proud of me."

"I *am* proud of you," Rose said, stepping out from behind her mother.

"Rose!" Starla squealed, rushing into her sister's embrace. After a quick hug, she stepped back and frowned at Rose in mock anger. " 'Tis about time you returned. Mama and I were worried sick. What kept you?"

" 'Tis a long story, Starla, and I have not the time to tell it right now. Raj is waiting for you at the garden gate. Ask him to tell you as you journey to the convent."

"What about Mama? Is she not leaving with me?"

"Nay, Starla," Nelda said. "Rose has asked me to return to Dragonwyck with her and Lord Dragon, and I have agreed. Rose needs me. She is with child."

Starla was less enthusiastic than Nelda. "Do you want Lord Dragon's babe, Rose?"

"Ease your mind, sister. I'm content with Dragon and

ecstatic about having his babe." Her voice lowered shyly. "You see, we love each other."

Starla's expression softened. "That is all I wanted to hear. I want my twin to be happy, just as I am happy to return to the convent. And 'tis time Mama returned home. She will be of great help to you. We shall visit each other often."

"As often as possible," Rose agreed.

Tears formed in Starla's eyes. "I had best be on my way." She hugged her mother, then Rose. "I love you both."

"Go with God, daughter," Nelda said, dashing away her tears.

The moment Starla slipped out the door, Nelda regarded Rose with raised eyebrows. "What are you not telling me, Rose? There has been more tension at court than usual. 'Tis no secret that King John is worried about something. Are you and Dragon involved?"

"The king should be worried, Mama. He has refused to seal the Articles of the Barons, and there is likely to be a civil war."

"Your father lost his life over those articles, Rose, I cannot bear to lose another loved one. Please tell me you are in no danger."

Rose hastened to allay Nelda's concern. "Dragon believes King John will relent. John does not want and cannot afford a civil war right now. Even as we speak, the barons are preparing to march on London."

"So that is what all the whispering at court is about. Rumor has it that John appealed to the pope. I suspected it had something to do with the articles but wasn't sure."

" 'Tis true, Mama. Negotiations have been going on a long time, since before Papa was executed."

"I am confused," Nelda said. "I thought Dragon was the king's man. What made him cast his lot with the barons?"

"Dragon always recognized John for what he was—cruel, greedy and manipulative—but Dragon is an honorable man and honestly tried to remain loyal to his king. He lost what little faith he had in the king when John questioned Dragon's loyalty and took me hostage."

"That explains a lot of things," Nelda said.

Rose stifled a yawn, and Nelda patted her arm. "You must be exhausted. You should rest as much as possible now that you're with child. Shall I help you prepare for bed?"

"Nay, Mama, I can manage. Go to bed. I will see you in the morning. There are things I wish to ask you about childbearing, but they can wait."

"When did you say Lord Dragon will arrive?"

"Tomorrow morning."

Nelda kissed Rose good night and left. Rose undressed, made a hasty toilette and climbed into bed. She had just closed her eyes when she heard someone scratching on the door. Thinking her mother had returned, Rose climbed out of bed, donned a chamber robe and opened the door. Lady Veronica breezed past Rose like a ship under full sail.

"Forgive me for calling upon you so late, Lady Rose, but you left the hall before our conversation was concluded."

"I thought we said everything that needed to be

said," Rose replied, having no idea what Veronica was talking about. She should have questioned Starla more thoroughly about her encounter with Dragon's former mistress.

"In that case, you can listen while I talk. When Dragon returns to London, I fully expect him to ask me to become his mistress again. I warn you, do not interfere, for it will only earn you Dragon's contempt." She gave Rose a superior smirk. "You can expect me to be a frequent visitor at Dragonwyck."

"Mayhap I will have something to say about that, Veronica."

Both Rose and Veronica swung their heads toward the open door, where Dragon leaned nonchalantly against the jamb. Excitement bubbled up inside Rose.

"Dominic! I did not expect you tonight. I thought . . ."

Dominic sent her a speaking glance. "A cold, empty bed did not appeal to me." He held out his arms.

Veronica pushed Rose aside and rushed into Dominic's outstretched arms. "I missed you, Dragon. Thank God, you recovered from your wound. I know not what I would have done if you had perished."

A mixture of confusion and hurt darkened Rose's brow as Dragon lifted Veronica in his arms and carried her from the chamber. How could Dragon do this to her? Had Dragon suddenly decided he loved Veronica? Rose understood none of what had just happened.

She turned away, her heart breaking. A loud thump and a screech brought her whirling about. Then Dominic appeared in the doorway, dazzling her with his smile. He held out his arms, and she ran into them.

"What did you do with Veronica?"

"Suffice it to say she will not be bothering us again. Should anyone else decide to barge into your chamber, they will find the door locked."

Chapter Nineteen

The only rose without a thorn is love.
—Mlle. de Scuderi

Rose was truly confused. For a moment she'd thought the unthinkable, that Dragon no longer wanted her. But she had been wrong. He was here with her now, and the look on his face told her it was exactly where he wanted to be.

"What are you doing here?" she blurted out. "I thought you weren't coming until tomorrow."

"Your greeting leaves much to be desired, love," Dominic said with a twinkle. "From what I observed, I would say I arrived at a most opportune moment. I cannot believe I actually contemplated marrying Veronica. I will be forever grateful to King John for giving me you."

" 'Tis difficult to be grateful to a man like him," Rose grumbled. "What made you decide to come to the palace tonight?"

"After you departed with Raj, I could not bear the thought of leaving you in the palace without protection, so I left the city shortly after you did. I was the last person to pass through Ludgate before it closed. I did not come directly to you when I arrived because I thought it prudent to greet the king first."

"Did you speak to him about the articles?"

"Nay, but he agreed to meet privately with me tomorrow." His arms tightened around her. "Forget about the king, love. Tonight is ours. Do you realize I have not loved you since we left Dragonwyck? I need you, Rose."

"First tell me what you did with Veronica," Rose persisted.

"I told you to forget her. I merely dumped her out in the passageway and told her to find another man upon whom to lavish her affection. I explained that I am already taken." He kissed the tip of her nose. "Now where were we?"

"Right here," Rose said, rising to her tiptoes and kissing Dominic full on the mouth.

He kissed her back. Rose clung to him, savoring the slow surge of his tongue, the intimate exploring and caressing. Heat seeped through her veins; a hot lick of sensation traveled to her toes and curled them. She could not breathe, she could not think beyond the joy she felt at being in Dragon's arms.

His head angled over hers, and she clung desperately to his lips. He deepened the kiss, thrilling her with its intensity, its promise. How could she doubt he loved her when his lips wrote love letters on her lips? Tongues tangled, breaths mingled, and her thoughts evaporated.

He tasted of pure heat and untamed wildness; he tasted of love. She pulled him closer, inhaling deeply of his scent, wanting to absorb him into her pores.

"Enough of this," he growled as he untied the belt of her chamber robe and pushed it down her arms. "I want you in bed, naked, welcoming me with open arms and open thighs." Then he scooped her up and carried her to the bed.

He eased her down and stared at her for a long, suspenseful moment before tearing off his own clothing and joining her. Then he kissed her, a thoroughly mesmerizing joining of lips and tongues and souls. She rode the spiraling wildness of the kiss as sensation after sensation battered her.

Then his long fingers splayed over her stomach and gently pressed. She sucked in her breath, wondering if he could sense their child beneath the flat surface. But apparently he felt nothing, for his long fingers continued their downward trek and slid between her thighs. She wanted to scream as he cupped her, explored her, fondled and separated her, then dipped inside.

His mouth followed the path of his hands, spreading wet heat between her breasts, down her stomach and into the thatch of springy curls crowning her thighs. Then his tongue found her; that tiny, sensitive bud nestled in a fold of flesh that was so responsive she could not stifle the cry rising in her throat. He continued to lave and nip and suckle her tender cleft, unleashing something savage and untamed inside her.

Heat built, then tightened, then contracted as his talented finger stroked inside her weeping sheath. She cried out, then fractured, pleasure spilling through every vein. Tremors of delight skipped across her skin, through her body, scattering her wits and leaving her breathless.

Rose had barely regained her composure when she felt the slide of Dragon's body over hers. She opened her eyes and found him grinning at her. She tried to speak, but the words caught in her throat as he grasped her hand and placed it on his cock.

Dominic watched Rose's face when she fell apart, certain he had never seen anything to compare with the look of rapture on his wife's lovely countenance. It was a look he never tired of, one he wanted to hold in his heart forever.

He gazed down at Rose's hand, curled around him, and his control flew out the window. "Put me inside you," he said in a voice he hardly recognized as his own. It was all he could do to keep from exploding as Rose placed him at her entrance, raised her hips and took him inside her.

Something feral in him took over; he buried himself to the hilt and began thrusting, hard and deep. He groaned his pleasure as she tightened around him, her muscles squeezing, making him expand and grow harder, longer, thicker.

"Can you come again?" he asked in a strangled voice.

Her sharp intake of breath and arching back provided the answer. Pumping vigorously, he brought them both to a breath-stealing, tumultuous end.

He pulled out and collapsed beside her, sated and ready for sleep. When Rose nudged him, he opened his eyes and found her looking at him, a secretive smile curving her lips. His curiosity piqued, he raised himself up on his elbow, one brow lifting upward. "Do you want to tell me what you are smiling about or must I guess?"

"Guess," she teased.

"I'm too tired for guessing games, love. Can it wait until tomorrow?"

"I suppose."

He thought he heard her sigh, but his eyes were already closing and his mind shutting down. The day had been long and eventful. He was nearly asleep when he felt Rose's breath brush his ear and heard her say—or at least he *thought* he heard her say—"I'm with child."

He reared up, fully awake now. "What did you say?"

"I'm going to have your baby."

He grasped her shoulders. "Are you sure?"

"As sure as I can be at this stage. Our child will make its appearance in about seven months. Does that please you?"

His eyes widened, then narrowed. "How long have you known?"

"I suspected before I left Dragonwyck."

"And you said nothing?"

Rose had the grace to look guilty. "I feared you

would not take me to London if you knew. Are you angry?"

"Damn right I'm angry. 'Tis no wonder you were so tired before. Had I known, you would still be at Dragonwyck, tucked safely away in the solar."

" 'Tis precisely why I did not tell you. It all worked out, Dominic. As you can see, I am well. In fact, I have never felt better."

Dominic looked into her glowing face and believed it. Relief shuddered through him, quickly replaced with elation. Rose was going to have his child, an heir for Dragonwyck and the beginning of a dynasty. He was the luckiest man alive. But that did not let Rose off the hook. When would she learn to obey him? That thought made him smile. There was no rose without a thorn, and his Rose had more than her share of thorns. He sighed. Apparently, avoiding the thorns was going to be a way of life for him.

"Are you still angry?" Rose asked as the silence stretched between them.

"Would it do me any good?"

"Nay, but knowing you are not angry would make me feel better."

"I'm not angry. But I'm still in shock over the thought of becoming a father. Think you I will make a good one?"

"The best. Should I take that to mean you are happy?"

He pulled her into his arms and nuzzled her neck. "I am happy, sweeting. But no more dangerous stunts, is that understood?"

"Aye, my lord," she said pertly. "Now you can go to sleep."

Fitting her into the curve of his body, Dominic drifted off. His dreams began almost immediately. He smiled in his sleep as tiny replicas of Rose romped within the confines of his mind.

Dominic awoke early. Rose was still sleeping, so he dressed quietly and found the garderobe. He returned to the chamber, washed and cleaned his teeth, careful not to awaken Rose. He left the chamber in search of breakfast and bumped into Lillian in the passageway.

She bobbed a curtsy. "Lord Dragon, I did not know you had returned. Everyone was ecstatic when word arrived of your miraculous recovery. No one was more thrilled than Lady Rose. Oh, forgive my rambling, my lord," she said, coloring prettily. "I am Lillian, your lady's maid."

"Good morrow, Lillian. Rose is still sleeping. Come back later."

"Lady Rose is still abed?" Lillian gasped, obviously shocked. "Is she ill? She rarely misses morning Mass."

"She . . . we . . . stayed up late . . . talking," Dominic said lamely.

Lillian's cheeks flamed. She bobbed another curtsy and fled.

Dominic smiled all the way to the hall, where he broke his fast with the other guests of the king. John had promised him an audience at Terce, so he wandered out to the tiltyard and watched a group of young squires at their training. When the church bell announced the hour of Terce, Dominic returned to the

palace, where he cooled his heels in an anteroom before he was admitted into the king's privy chamber.

" 'Tis good to see you looking so well, Dragon," King
John greeted. "I commend you on your recuperative
powers. We were told there was virtually no hope of
your survival, that your wounds were mortal."

"I had a guardian angel looking after me," Dominic
said. It was true. Rose's appearance at his deathbed
had wrought a miracle.

"I suppose you want permission to take your wife
home to Dragonwyck," John said gruffly.

"May I speak freely, sire?"

"You usually do."

"I understand you refused to seal the Articles of the
Barons."

John stiffened. " 'Tis no secret. That damnable charter is an insult to the crown. No king should have to
suffer such restrictions."

"The barons think differently. The threat of civil war
is very real, sire. You would be prudent to take the
charter seriously if you wish to avoid a conflict."

"I have already conferred with the council. They
suggested that I send the archbishop and the Earl of
Pembroke to negotiate with the barons. I do not want
war, but I cannot set my seal upon that self-serving
document unless a compromise more favorable to the
crown can be reached."

Dominic did not want to push the king too far lest
he jeopardize his freedom to take Rose home where
she could be properly looked after until the birth of
their child.

"Forgive me, sire. I would not speak so boldly if it

were not necessary. I am aware, as I am sure you are, that a civil war would divide the country, and you cannot afford that kind of turmoil."

"I alone shall decide what is good for our country," John railed. "You may go."

Dominic took a deep breath and continued, disregarding the king's dismissal despite the danger to himself. "If negotiations fail and the barons' army reaches the city gates, the citizens will flock to their cause. You cannot afford to ignore the charter. Lives will be lost; you stand to lose your life as well as the throne."

John surged from his chair. "Are you threatening me, Dragon?"

Dominic refused to cower beneath John's fierce anger. "Nay, sire, I but hope to prevent a civil war."

"Leave me before I lose my temper and find a place for you in my dungeon."

Realizing he had done everything he possibly could for the barons, Dominic bowed and quit the chamber. Mayhap John would have to see the army at London's gate before he would acquiesce.

Dominic returned to Rose's chamber and found her staring out the window, a wistful look in her eyes. She turned and smiled at him.

"Did you see the king?"

"Aye. He refuses to listen to reason. I know not how to proceed. A civil war could begin very soon. It will tear England apart."

Rose came to him and placed her arms around him. "You have done all you could. I hardly think the barons expected miracles from you. We are talking about King John, are we not, and we all know him to be obstinate, evil and greedy. He will not agree to set his seal to anything that diminishes his power."

"I fear you are right, love."

"We should return to Dragonwyck immediately. I want to go home, Dominic."

"Aye, 'tis exactly what we shall do. I do not want my pregnant wife caught in the middle of a civil war."

Joy suffused Rose's face. "When?"

He paused, his expression determined. "Now. As soon as you and your mother are ready."

"An hour. 'Tis all the time we need."

"Good. I will get the horses while you fetch your mother. Are you able to travel?" he asked worriedly. "Will riding a great distance hurt our babe?"

"Worry not, Dominic. I am not yet at the point where riding will endanger our child."

Dominic gave her a quick kiss and strode to the door. When he opened it, however, he was brought up short by a palace guard standing in the passageway.

"I bear a message from the king, Lord Dragon," the guard said. "His Majesty wishes you to remain at Westminster."

Dominic stared at him. "Did His Majesty say why?"

"If he had a reason, he did not divulge it. He said to tell you he may wish to speak with you again about that matter you discussed with him earlier."

"I understand," Dominic said. The guardsman left. Cursing beneath his breath, Dominic closed the door and waited a moment before confronting Rose, for he felt her disappointment as keenly as he felt his own.

"I do not believe this!" Rose raged. "The king is a monster."

"We all agree on that point, love, but unfortunately, he *is* the king. Look on the bright side."

"There is no bright side."

"Aye, there is. If John is willing to discuss the charter further, we should take that as a good sign. Mayhap he is having second thoughts."

"Mayhap he is trying to decide whether or not to separate your head from your shoulders. We should leave now, before the barons reach London. We can sneak out the garden gate, and no one will be the wiser."

"You know I cannot do that. If there is even a small chance of convincing the king to accept the charter, I must remain and do what I can to help the barons. With his barons aligned against him, John doesn't have the manpower to go to war. He depends on the barons behind the charter to fight his wars. He enjoys being king too much to risk his throne."

"Can the barons succeed should the king remain stubborn?"

"Aye. They have manpower and determination on their side."

Rose sighed. "If you feel so strongly about it, then of course we must stay."

A sennight passed before Dominic heard from the king again. It was a time fraught with tension and anxiety. He tried to conceal his apprehension from Rose, but she could read his feelings as easily as if they were her own, and in the end he was glad for her support. With each passing day he realized how lucky he was to have his wife. Giving him Rose was probably the kindest thing King John had ever done, for John was not a man given to humane acts.

The day Dominic received King John's summons, he knew something momentous was about to take place. Rose was with him when the summons came, and Dominic tried to allay the worry that darkened her lovely blue eyes.

"Try not to worry, love. I truly believe the king is beginning to see that the barons are not going to give up, nor will they disappear."

"I wish we were home," Rose said on a sigh. "Think you he will let us leave after this is resolved?"

"I am sure of it. We are neither prisoners nor hostages. John wants me here to help during negotiations. Kiss me for luck, love."

Dominic hugged her tightly as she kissed him and sweetly clung to him. Her fervent kiss reminded him of the nights they had spent passionately loving one another and falling asleep in each other's arms. He could hardly wait to take Rose to Pendragon to meet his parents and brother.

Though Dominic had left home to make his own way many years before, he was still very fond of his family and had never completely lost touch.

Dominic became aware of the unusual number of people milling about and talking in hushed voices as he strode along the passageways toward the king's chambers. Something of import was afoot, and Dominic's intuition told him that the king was finally ready to accept compromise.

Dominic was ushered immediately into the king's privy chamber. King John was not alone. With him were the archbishop and the powerful William Marshal, the Earl of Pembroke. They seemed to have been arguing but fell silent when Dominic entered the chamber.

"Lord Dragon," the king said, "I do not believe you know Pembroke or our good archbishop." Introductions were made, and Dominic waited for the conversation to resume.

When the king began to pace, Dominic knew an important decision was at hand. What he did not know was where he fit into the scheme of things. Suddenly John stopped before Dominic, staring pugnaciously into his face.

"The barons' army is camped in the meadow at Runnymede, between Windsor and Staines. They threatened to batter down London's gates if I did not negotiate with them. The archbishop and Pembroke have been dealing with the barons on my behalf."

"A wise move, sire."

"To your way of thinking, mayhap," John said sourly.

"There are some extremists among the barons who cling to the original demands and refuse to negotiate," Pembroke interjected. "They want to fight, and the moderate barons cannot change their minds."

"I am prepared to grant the barons' general demands, but the more militant of the barons are not satisfied with my concessions," John groused.

"The negotiations have broken down," Pembroke explained. "Ashford asked for you specifically, Dragon. He thinks you may be of some help in resolving the standoff. The barons respect you, and Ashford believes the militant faction will listen to you."

"Humph!" John snorted. "My champion is now the champion of my enemies."

"The barons are not your enemies, sire," Dominic responded. "They want to be treated fairly, and you have not been fair to them in the past."

"I am the king. I do not have to be fair," John thundered.

"You do if you wish to keep England from civil war," the archbishop reminded him.

"I see I am outnumbered. Very well, return to Runnymede and take Dragon with you. Mayhap he will be of some help with the negotiations."

Dominic had but a short time in which to explain to Rose why he had to leave. He found her sitting on a bench in the herb garden she had become so fond of. Her face held an anxious expression as he joined her.

"What did John want? Did he give us leave to return home?"

"Not yet. He is sending me on a mission with the archbishop and the Earl of Pembroke."

"What kind of mission?"

"The barons' army is encamped at Runnymede, near Windsor. Negotiations have broken down, and Ashford asked that I meet with them and try to convince the more recalcitrant barons to return to the negotiations table."

Rose clutched desperately at his arm. "I do not want you to go."

"I have no choice, Rose. If I can prevent a civil war, my time will be well spent. Then we can go home."

"I want to come with you."

Dominic stared at her. "What? Impossible. You are a woman."

Rose sniffed disdainfully. "I am well aware of my gender, my lord, but that does not make me any less capable than a man." Her eyes brightened as she warmed to the subject. "Raj is gone; you have need of a squire."

Dominic leaped to his feet, an incredulous expression on his face. "You are with child! This conversation is at an end. You will wait here for me, is that understood?"

Rose forced down a stinging reply. Angering Dominic was definitely not the wisest thing to do. Giving him the slightest hint of what she intended would probably result in having him lock her in her chamber and throw away the key.

"Understood," Rose answered. Oh, aye, she understood, but she just did not agree.

Later that day, Dominic left for Runnymede with the archbishop and Pembroke. Their squires followed behind, one of whom was Lord Dragon's new squire, a fresh-faced lad with smooth, beardless cheeks and a pair of legs that would put some women to shame.

Rose felt no qualms about disobeying Dragon. She had given no promise and therefore felt no guilt. She was heartily sick of being held hostage. She missed riding and hawking and hunting, and going where she pleased when she pleased. Rose had told no one but her mother that she intended to follow Dragon to Runnymede, and she had only told Nelda because she knew her mother would worry after she disappeared.

Once she had made up her mind, Rose had asked Lillian to find her the sort of clothing a squire would wear. At first Lillian had been reluctant, but Rose had placated her by saying she intended to surprise Dragon by dressing as his squire and riding with him to Runnymede. Lillian had thought it a great lark and joined in the game. The clothing Lillian had procured for her fit reasonably well, and when Dragon left the palace, she joined the ranks of squires accompanying their lords.

It was not difficult for Rose to remain anonymous in the group of men and youths riding to Runnymede, for in addition to squires, several knights and their pages rode with the group, providing escort as well as protection. Once they reached the meadow where the barons' army was encamped, Rose was just another face among the crowd.

Dominic greeted Ashford, then followed him to a grassy area that was large enough to accommodate those involved in the negotiations. After listening to some of the barons speak, Dominic decided that Pembroke had been right in his assessment of the extremists who clamored for war. None of the concessions the king offered seemed to satisfy them. Time passed. Negotiations were at a standstill when Ashford asked Dragon to address the barons.

Not quite sure of what he could say to change their minds, Dragon surveyed the sea of expectant faces. His gaze traveled beyond the barons to the group of squires and pages gathered nearby. His gaze returned to the barons, then abruptly returned to a group of youths standing off to his right. His brow furrowed and his expression grew incredulous as recognition dawned. He would recognize her face anywhere.

Once again Rose had deliberately defied him and done as she pleased without a thought to the consequences. He imagined a lifetime of dealing with his contrary Rose and wondered if he was up to it. At least he would never be bored.

Looking away from Rose, Dominic returned his attention to the barons. His words were not as eloquent as those of an orator, but they were from the heart. He told them that a civil war would tear the country apart and result in needless deaths. He said the king was willing to compromise and that they should take it as a good sign. He went on to explain that the Articles of the Barons were likely to become the cornerstone of English law.

"The king has sent trusted men to parlay with you. We can reciprocate by finding middle ground upon which to agree." He paused. "Keep my words in mind when you resume your negotiations with Lord Pembroke. Think of all you will have accomplished without bloodshed. Should King John set his seal to this charter, you will gain the satisfaction of knowing you brought the king to his knees."

Rose felt like cheering. Dragon's speech was not only inspiring but thoughtful. And she could tell by the barons' faces that they were giving Dragon's words serious consideration. She wanted to crow with pride. Dragon had been instrumental in preventing a civil war, and she had been present to hear his impassioned plea for cool heads and common sense.

Pembroke and the archbishop took over where Dragon left off, and the negotiations resumed. Rose turned away, deciding to rest beneath a tree while compromises were discussed. She had taken but two steps when someone grabbed her from behind. Without a moment's hesitation, she grasped the hilt of the knife she wore at her waist and prepared to defend herself.

Suddenly the knife was wrested from her hand and strong arms held her immobile against an iron-hard chest.

"Leave off, Rose. I do not want to hurt you."

Rose sagged in relief. "Dominic. How did you know?"

Dominic snorted. "Think you I am blind?" He pulled her behind a tall hedge where they could talk in private. "What am I to do with you? You seem determined to defy me."

Rose's pert chin rose defiantly. "I have a mind of my own, Dominic. I pray you do not expect everything to go your way in this marriage. I cannot be a submissive wife."

"You are carrying my child!"

Rose grinned. "Indeed I am. I was in no danger, Dominic. The distance to Runnymede is not far, and I was among friends, not enemies. Besides, I wanted to be on hand for the momentous occasion. What is decided here today could make history, and I did not want to be left out."

Dominic sighed. "I love you with a passion, Rose,

but 'tis going to be a challenge to keep from beating you upon occasion."

"Challenges are your forte, are they not, my lord Dragon?"

"You are my forte, sweetheart." He grasped her shoulders and planted a hungry kiss on her lips. "We should return to the negotiations before someone comes along and catches me mauling my squire. Stay here," Dominic ordered when they reached the negotiations area. "With any luck, we can soon return to the palace and prepare for our journey home."

Rose sat on the ground and watched the proceedings. Angry voices were raised and questions asked, but it appeared as if the barons were of a mind to accept a compromise. She fell asleep with her back propped against a tree but was awakened by a great roar reverberating through the meadow. She jerked upright and saw Dragon striding toward her.

"What happened? Is there to be war?"

"Nay, the negotiators have agreed upon a compromise. The final draft is to be hammered out in discussions at Runnymede later this month. Are you tired? I know 'tis late, but Westminster is but a short ride."

Dragon grasped her hand and lifted her to her feet. Rose yawned and dashed the sleep from her eyes. "I am not tired at all. I rested while the negotiations were taking place."

"Bring our horses. I want a word with Ashford before we leave."

Rose found their horses and brought them back to the tree to await Dragon. He joined her a short time later.

"Well, love, 'tis over. Ashford says the barons are satisfied with the king's concessions. They believe this fifteenth day of June will go down in history as the day the Articles of the Barons were sealed by the king."

The moon was casting long shadows over the land when they reached the palace. Rose went immediately to their chamber while Dominic, the archbishop and Pembroke reported directly to the king. Fingers of a glorious dawn stretched out across the heavens when Dominic finally joined Rose. She was sleeping soundly, and he tried not to awaken her as he shed his clothing in the dark and climbed into bed beside her.

She stirred and whispered his name.

"Go back to sleep, sweeting. We will talk later."

He brought her into the curve of his body; she turned in his arms. "We will talk now. How soon can we leave? Once I depart this den of vice I never want to hear the king's name again."

"I am still the king's vassal; naught can change that, and he did give me you. That is something to be grateful for."

"Fate brought us together," Rose murmured sleepily. "And fate will keep us together. I love you, my fierce Dragon."

"I love you, my prickly warrior woman. If we have a son, I hope he has your courage, but if our child is a girl, we will name her Lily, or Pansy, or Violet, for they are flowers without thorns."

"A flower without thorns offers no challenge," Rose

countered. "I thought you thrived on challenges."

Dominic sighed heavily. "You have been both the thorniest challenge and the sweetest joy since the day we wed. Good night, my Rose."

Epilogue

More than anything, I must have roses, always,
always.

—Claude Monet

March 1216

On a cool March day ripe with the promise of spring,
the lord and lady of Dragonwyck toasted their toes
before the hearth in the hall, planning the christening
of their eight-week-old babe. Lady Nelda sat beside
them, cradling the newest addition to the family in her
arms and cooing nonsensical words into a tiny pink
ear.

"I believe little Lord William is hungry," Lady Nelda
remarked.

"He is always hungry," Rose said with a long-suffering sigh.

"My son is a growing lad," Dominic said proudly.

"And a greedy one," Rose added. "I fed him but an hour ago."

"I look forward to Will's christening," Nelda said. "Think you all the guests will come?"

"Aye, as long as the weather holds," Dominic answered.

Rose held out her arms. "I will take little Will if you are tired of holding him, Mama."

"I hardly think Will's slight weight will tax me," Nelda replied. "But if you . . ."

Her words fell off when Raj entered the hall and strode toward them. Dominic could tell from Raj's expression that something unusual had occurred.

"What is it, Raj?"

"Murdoc MacTavish and his wife are at the portcullis, master. They beg your leave to enter."

Rose got to her feet. "Uncle Murdoc is here? And Robina is with him? Please Dominic, let them in. I do so want to see Robina. I cannot believe that Uncle won her back."

"Aye, let them in," Nelda urged. "I want to give my brother a piece of my mind for what he did to Rose. 'Twas despicable of him."

"How many men accompany him?" Dominic asked sharply. He had made the mistake of letting Murdoc and his kinsmen inside the keep once and he was not going to make that same mistake again.

"MacTavish is alone but for one man driving the cart carrying MacTavish's wife."

"Very well, open the portcullis," Dominic ordered. When Rose started to follow Raj out the door, Dominic stayed her. "Let them come to us. I swore your uncle would never again set foot inside my keep but I bow to your wishes in this matter. However, I trust him not."

A short time later, Murdoc and Robina strode into the hall. Rose rushed forth to embrace Robina but was more reserved with her uncle.

"What brings you to Dragonwyck, Murdoc?" Nelda asked. "I should think you would be ashamed to show your face here after your detestable act. I never thought my own brother would wish harm to one of his kin."

"I asked Murdoc to bring me," Robina explained.

"I made a promise to Dragon and I mean to keep it," Murdoc vowed. "Robina wanted to come, and I couldna sway her. I knew you wouldna turn her away even if I wasna allowed to pass through the gate."

"I cannot believe you returned to Uncle Murdoc," Rose said, bringing Robina closer to the fire. "You must tell me everything."

"I was wrong, niece," Murdoc said when Robina remained silent. "I dinna realize how much I would miss Robina until she left me. She is the best thing that ever happened to me. I went to Stirling and begged her to return."

"I never expected Murdoc to show up at my father's manor," Robina said, taking up where Murdoc left off, "much less admit he missed and needed me. He refused to leave without me." She sent Murdoc a loving gaze. "He has changed. He doesna blame me for releasing ye and yer vassals, Rose. He realizes his mistake and is sorry for it."

"All that is behind us," Murdoc said gruffly. "I am glad Robina wished to come to Dragonwyck, for it gives me the opportunity to apologize to Nelda. Rose forgave me, sister. Can ye? I was mad with greed for something I could never have. 'Tis the only way I can explain what I did."

"I will consider it," Nelda said coolly.

"Thank ye, sister, for that much." His gaze shifted to the bundle in Nelda's arms. "Is that what I think it is?"

Dominic took a protective stance beside his son. "Aye, 'tis my heir, William."

"Ah, wee Willie, is it? A fine name for a braw laddie." He grinned at his wife. "Do ye want to tell them or shall I, Robina?"

Rose's brow furrowed. "Tell us what?"

Robina smiled shyly and removed her mantle, revealing her swollen stomach. "I bear Murdoc's bairn. I canna believe it! After all these years a bairn is growing inside me."

" 'Tis true," Murdoc said proudly. "Be it lad or lassie, it matters not, the bairn will be my heir."

"What about Gunn?" Dominic asked. "I notice he is not with you."

"I found a Highland heiress for Gunn, and he is content with the lass and her fortune."

"I hope ye are not angry with me for coming to Dragonwyck," Robina said anxiously, "but I wanted ye to know about my bairn, and to tell ye how impending fatherhood has changed Murdoc. I hoped ye and

Nelda would forgive him, Rose. If ye want us to leave, I willna hold it against ye."

Rose looked at Dominic with pleading eyes. "Can they stay? It would be nice to have Robina here for William's christening."

"Robina would like that," Murdoc allowed, "but I willna ask for myself for I donna deserve yer kindness."

Though Dominic was reluctant to offer hospitality to the Scotsman, he could not find it in his heart to deny Rose anything. "Aye, Murdoc and Robina can stay for the christening if they like."

Little Lord William began to fuss, and Rose held out her arms. " 'Tis time for Will's feeding."

"I will carry him for you, mistress," Raj said, carefully lifting the babe from Nelda's arms.

Dominic stifled a smile. Raj never missed an opportunity to hold the infant, and Dominic had not the slightest doubt that the gentle giant would protect Will with his life if there was a need. Dominic's gaze followed Rose from the hall, his groin tightening at the sight of her swaying hips. He had not loved his wife since Will's birth and he was bursting with need.

"Make Murdoc and Robina welcome, Lady Nelda," he called over his shoulder. "Rose and I will see you all at the evening meal." Without waiting for an answer, he hurried up the stairs after Rose.

Raj passed him in the gallery, having just delivered Will into Rose's arms. He knew not what Raj thought about his haste to reach the solar, but he heard Raj chuckling all the way down the stairs. Dominic shook his head. Did everyone in the keep know how besotted he was with his wife?

Dominic entered the solar and stopped in his tracks just inside the door. The sight of Rose nursing their child always moved him. A lump gathered in his throat and he swallowed convulsively.

"Come in and shut the door, Dominic," Rose said.

Dominic closed the door and settled down on a bench beside Rose, watching with avid interest as Will pulled greedily at her nipple.

"Thank you for allowing Robina and Uncle Murdoc to stay with us, my love. You have a generous spirit."

"I would do anything for you, Rose. And I do believe Murdoc is sincerely sorry for abducting you. 'Tis amazing what the love of a good woman can do for a man."

"Love is amazing, is it not?"

"Aye," Dominic agreed. "As soon as our greedy son is through feeding, I will show you just how amazing love can be."

"Our guests . . ."

". . . can fend for themselves. It has been eight weeks since Will's birth, and I am starved for you. Is it safe to love you, Rose?"

Will's rosebud mouth slipped from Rose's nipple. She smiled down at his dark head and placed him in his cradle. Then she walked slowly into Dragon's arms.

AUTHOR'S NOTE

King John sealed the Articles of the Barons, known today as the Magna Carta, on June 15, 1215. The remarkable fact is not that war broke out between John and his barons in the months following the compromise but that the king had ever been brought to agree to such a document at all.

I hope you enjoyed *The Dragon Lord*. My next three books will be set in England in the early 1800s. I'm calling the series *The Rogues of London*. Look for *The Rogue and the Hellion* in June 2002.

For a bookmark and a newsletter, send a long, self-addressed, stamped envelope to me at PO Box 3471, Holiday, FL 34690. Visit my website to learn more about my books at www.conniemason.com or e-mail me at conmason@aol.com.